The Pearl
Button Girl

Annie Murray was born in Berkshire and read English at St John's College, Oxford. Her first Birmingham novel, *Birmingham Rose*, hit the *Sunday Times* bestseller list when it was published in 1995. She has subsequently written many other successful novels, including *War Babies* and *Girls in Tin Hats* and the bestselling novels *Chocolate Girls*, *Sisters of Gold* and *Black Country Orphan*. Annie has four children, all Birmingham-born; she lives near Oxford.

Birmingham Rose
Birmingham Friends
Birmingham Blitz
Orphan of Angel Street
Poppy Day
The Narrowboat Girl
Chocolate Girls
Water Gypsies
Miss Purdy's Class
Family of Women
Where Earth Meets Sky
The Bells of Bournville Green
A Hopscotch Summer
Soldier Girl
All the Days of Our Lives
My Daughter, My Mother
The Women of Lilac Street
Meet Me Under the Clock
War Babies
Now the War is Over
The Doorstep Child
Sisters of Gold
The Silversmith's Daughter
Mother and Child
Girls in Tin Hats
Black Country Orphan
Secrets of the Chocolate Girls
Wartime for the Chocolate Girls
Homecoming for the Chocolate Girls

ANNIE MURRAY

The Pearl Button Girl

PAN BOOKS

First published 2025 by Macmillan

This paperback edition first published 2025 by Pan Books
an imprint of Pan Macmillan
The Smithson, 6 Briset Street, London EC1M 5NR
EU representative: Macmillan Publishers Ireland Ltd, 1st Floor,
The Liffey Trust Centre, 117–126 Sheriff Street Upper,
Dublin 1, D01 YC43
Associated companies throughout the world
www.panmacmillan.com

ISBN 978-1-0350-1998-4

1 3 5 7 9 8 6 4 2

A CIP catalogue record for this book is available from the British Library.

Typeset in Stempel Garamond by Jouve (UK), Milton Keynes
Printed and bound by CPI Group (UK) Ltd, Croydon, CR0 4YY

Visit **www.panmacmillan.com** to read more about all our books
and to buy them. You will also find features, author interviews and
news of any author events, and you can sign up for e-newsletters
so that you're always first to hear about our new releases.

I would like to dedicate this book to every reader who picks it up, starts to read and enjoys getting caught up in this story, which is the beginning of a journey into other stories . . .

'Workshop of the World'
A Birmingham poem

Nails, harnesses, taps, saddles, bridles, army accoutrements, lamps, chandeliers, candelabra, bronze inkstands, engravers, vases, cut glass, china, earthenware, tripods, lamps, ormolu, silver plate, hinges, coffee mills, pullies, castors, latches, Italian irons, man traps, shoe scrapers, garden labels, sad irons, three-legged pots, lath nails, shoe bills, heel and toe tips, wrought-iron hurdles, plain and ornamental gates, pilasters, palisading, park fencing, tree guards, stable racks, mangers, garden chairs, wagon arms, chains, screws, cables, wire, ale, cabinetmakers, musical instruments, printers, silveroid, boots, trivets, hydraulic machinery, spectacles, shoes, case makers, nuts, bolts, screws, bedsteads, umbrellas, false legs, plugs, ceramics, sewing machines, oil lamps, buckles, washers, buttons, paint, varnish, gas fittings, toys, glass, electroplaters, rings, necklaces, decanters, bells, bottle jacks, clasps, parkesine, coach lamps, compasses, lamps, fenders, ecclesiastical ornaments, ships' lamps, mathematical instruments, weighing machines, coffin furniture, saddle furniture, argentite, stair rods, watches, pewter, thimbles, pharmaceuticals, sheet-glass, dioptic apparatus, astragals, tubes, lacquers, Vesta and lucifer boxes, jewellery cases, pins, kirby grips, tinder boxes, spittoons, bells, snuff lasso rings, gasaliers, pen nibs, standard lamp posts, gas railways, carriages, potosi silver, candlesticks, snuffers, trays, weights, brass cocks, door handles, vinegar kettles, knobs, bolts, locks, escutcheons, tin-plate, carriage lamps, lacquers, mother of pearl, enamellers, pokers, weighing scales, coal scuttles, Archimedes drills, rivets, wire rope, hemp and twine rope, bicycles, gears, umbrella ribs, pens, alloys, japanners, spelter, repoussé, badges, spinners, burnishers, chains, anchors, lithographers, sauces, plumbing, casting moulders, finishers, polishers, ships' berths, chasers, window blinds, fire screens, carriage wheel ribs, window sashes, measuring rules, fire screens, chimney pieces, door frames, picture frames, pier glasses, balustrades, cornice poles, lamps, curtain rods, sword handles, gun furniture, packing cases, railway signals, flint-glass, whips, photographic chemicals, electric dynamos, lighting accessories, brackets, doorplates, finger plates, looking glasses, annealers, brushes, glass eyes, ashtrays, butter dishes, beads, pumps, safes, cots, gas meters, stoves, boilers, retorts, varnishes, chocolate, paints, signs, coaches, toys, chemicals, photographic assayers, plates, drop stampers, soap, surgical dressings, gauges, custard engines, chemical appliances, drug grinders, tankards, inkstands, syringes, beer makers, lift die sinkers, pumps, water closets, ale and wine measures, bar fittings, corkscrews, picklers, garden syringes, portable shower baths, pewterers, paper boxes, cards, pasteboards, papier mâché, belts, bricks, balloons, airships, sheep-shearing equipment, guns, boot blacking, flat irons, sugar sifters, mangles, beer kettles, saucepans, sporting trophies, tankards, nutcrackers, metal rollers, walking sticks, parasols, cigarette cases, grates, milk churns, cisterns, buckets, stampers, watering cans, baths, pipes, basins, flock mattresses, salt cellars, coffin furniture, shirt studs, saws, nipples, braces, bits, brooch pins, lockets, files, rasps, clasps, hatchets, matchets, shrouds, horseboxes, doormats, steam whistles, toasting forks, emery paper, metal hothouses, tea services, pumps, watches, tea urns, cotters, straw bonnets, hats, butter knives, pickle forks, boxes, trunks, grinders, soap, washing powder, paperweights, vases, chalices, fish hooks, piano wire, trouser straps, bellows, gates, fencing, caddies, card cases, pistols, blunderbusses, anvils, sugar crushers, pocketbooks, pianos, birdcages . . .

I

One

August 1851

'I don't believe you, Richie.'

Ada pressed her nose against the train window as Mom started up again, her sharp, nagging whispers as she held Mabs, the baby, on her lap, trying to quiet her.

'All your carry-on makes me feel bad, that it does.'

She had been on at Pa like that all week.

The thundering locomotive started to get up speed, hauling the rocking carriages between miles and miles of fields and crouching villages which slid past Ada's gaze. Until just a few days ago she had had no idea how much countryside there was away from home, how big it all was. And now they were travelling north to Birmingham. Home: they had only been away just inside of a week, but now going back felt so exciting!

'Give it a rest, May,' Pa hissed, his lips close to his wife, May Fletcher's, ear. Of course, with the other passengers in the carriage he wasn't going to sock her one the way he might at home. Not often – just if she really kept on. 'Ain't we just had the best week of our lives?'

Then Ada saw him whisper something else, still right up close, and Mom softened, darting a quick, intimate smile at her husband before looking down into her lap, her face hot with blushes.

Ada watched as her father turned his thin, leathery face,

lit with a smile, towards the other gentlemen and ladies sharing the compartment. Compartment! Oh yes, the Fletcher family was travelling in style, not sitting in open trucks under any old weather like the poor passengers. *Women, eh?* Pa's look seemed to say to the other men. *Don't take any notice of my wife.* And with Pa's charm and cheeky expression, the couple sitting beside him even gave an uncertain smile.

Poor Pa, Ada thought, on her father's side, as ever. Why did Mom keep having to go and spoil things? But the smile she saw between her parents warmed her heart. For all she adored her pa, she knew he always did things his way and Mom had to follow along – it wasn't always easy for her.

Mabs, the baby, not quite a year old, started grizzling out of hunger and in protest at the angry rash on her bottom, and all May Fletcher's attention was taken up with pacifying her, as she had had to do the whole time they were away.

'Here, lad –' Pa moved up close to Ada and craned round to see out – 'look at all that. There's a wide world out there! Haven't we had the time of our lives, eh?'

Ada leaned in to him, nodding happily. They had! What a week, when they had seen and heard so many extraordinary things that she felt as if she would be digesting it for the rest of her life. And Pa, her wonderful pa who was like a god to her, had made all of it happen.

She was always Pa's lad. May had produced a run of girls: Ada, then Elsie, tiny and premature. They had been afraid she would die as soon as she was born and Mom always said that Elsie had had a good-luck charm: the dark mole at the corner of her left eye, shaped like a tiny heart. After her came Dora, a lispy, dreamy little girl who now sat silently squeezed in next to Mom.

So Ada had become Pa's lad and at ten years old, that's

what he still called her. She also looked like Pa, both of them small – 'A short-arse, I am,' he'd say, 'but no one's gunna keep me down.' They were both lightly and strongly built with straight, honey-brown hair, brown eyes and faces rippling with liveliness.

For want of an actual son, Richie Fletcher had encouraged his daughter to do things he would have done with a boy. Run fast, climb, fist-fight and tear about, even if Mom insisted she wear a frock. Not to mention manage a hammer and nails and any other skill he might pass on.

Little John, the son Richie had craved, arrived when Ada was six. But so far he had turned out a gentle mummy's boy, soft, plump and blond with his mother's stone-grey eyes. He stood close to May now, four years old, a hand clutching at the skirt of her new lawn frock with pink roses on, as if he was constantly afraid she might disappear.

John was still a baby and as Pa said, a milksop at that, so having a brother had not evicted Ada as firstborn son.

Ada closed her ears to Mab's blarting. Pa had his arm round her back which made her feel happy and like a queen. She could sense the throb of his heart in that energetic, wiry body.

'Look.' He pointed as smuts drifted in through the little open window above them, black grit and weightless grey ash a pale scatter on Ada's brown sleeve. 'There's Birmingham.'

In the distance, dark slabs of the city had begun to appear, solid flanks of buildings rising out of the green Warwickshire countryside. Above them stretched factory chimney stacks and the slender reach of church spires. High above it all loomed a thick pall of grey, a brooding storm belonging entirely to this town crammed full of industry, snorting smoke and cloud up to the heavens.

From here there was nothing to be heard of the sounds that were normal as breathing to all of them – the turmoil of the streets, the screech and spark of metal, thump of presses and hammer clashing on anvil.

But within a short time, they could smell it. The midden stench that hung over the place, ordure mixed with acid, with metal dust and coal smoke from the churn and clang of industry. The stink seeping sharp into Ada's nostrils had surrounded her since her birth, was familiar as her own body. But today it felt like something new. Only now she truly noticed it.

They were nearly home. Already the past week seemed like the strangest and most wonderful dream Ada had ever had. A dream which people were saying had changed everything. The Great Exhibition, a triumph of Great Britain in the world: nothing would ever be quite the same again.

'Never forget, this, will we, eh?' her father murmured close to her ear. 'And on top of it all, you saw the Queen!'

Ada turned, the brim of her straw bonnet scratching his cheek so that Pa jerked back for a moment. They both grinned, skinny faces mirroring each other's.

She wouldn't forget, ever. This week that Pa had given them.

He moved close again to whisper in her ear. 'You'll always be my lad, eh? No matter what. Don't you ever forget that.'

Only later she heard those words echo again in her mind and realized how sad he had sounded, frightened almost. At the time she barely noticed. Only after what happened did they come back to her, and the way he squeezed her hand and pulled her close to him. Thinking about it, her heart would come close to breaking.

Two

Everyone else was going, Pa had said. All right, not *everyone* – as Mom niggled at him – but crowds in their thousands, pouring in and from all over the world! Rich and poor, the humblest Britons scrimped and saved for months. They squirrelled away pennies in special jars or in didlum clubs, paying in a small sum each week to save up for tickets to travel all the way to London, on a *train* – for this biggest and grandest event the world had ever seen. An event in which their lively and inventive city, and all the things pouring out from its factories and workshops, would have prominent place.

The Great Exhibition was to be the first international exhibition in the history of the world, a giant wonderland, boasting the creative genius of this nation and others round the world, all created at the behest of Prince Albert.

'You're off your head, Richie Fletcher,' Mom protested. 'We can't afford that, not for all of us, all the way down there – for a week.'

Pa sat on his chair by the range, hunched forward as if he was about to spring to his feet and rush off somewhere. He looked directly at his wife, a once pretty woman with black hair, a softly rounded face and grey eyes. Child-bearing and rearing had shrunk the flesh tighter over her features. Though only thirty-seven years of age with five living children, she was thin and shrewish-looking and had lost several teeth which now made her smile a rare thing.

'May,' Pa quickly lost patience. 'I've told you – business is booming. And Jem says . . .'

'Jem,' Mom tutted. 'What do I care what Jem Atherton has to say?'

Jem was Pa's pal and workmate, a stocky, jolly man, his hair always having a green tinge from the copper in the foundry. Pa worked in the manufacturing side, not in the foundry, so it didn't happen to him. The two of them were thick as thieves except when their ding-dongs ended in bawling and yelling and knocking lumps off each other. Ada never did understand what they were scrapping about and they always made it up so in the long run, it didn't really matter.

'Stop mithering, May,' Pa went on. 'Everyone wants our stuff the world over. Arkle and Lilley're gunna be in the exhibition!'

Ada, stirring the stew pot over the fire as Mom had instructed, was all ears.

Arkle & Lilley, where Pa and Jem worked, was a brass foundry and manufacturer, where the alloy of copper and zinc for which the city was famous was converted into wondrous articles, shiny and useful. They made frames for pictures and looking glasses, coffin furniture and every handy thing from drawer knobs and keyhole escutcheons to finger plates. Not to mention the ends of cornices for curtains, all stamped with intricate designs like the one holding up the curtains in their front window, with fancy brass and crystal flowers dangling from the ends.

And Pa, her pa, fashioned many of the dies or moulds in which the designs would be stamped into the metal.

He was an expert, Pa was, an artist at his trade like his own father before him. Old Man Seth Fletcher had been a die sinker at Yates, Harper & Co. That was why they had such a stylish, well-made item for holding up the front

8

curtains. And it was how come Pa came bouncing into the house after work one day and said they were going to knock out the front window and put a bow one in instead to make it nice. And it was why he was talking about putting down carpet . . .

So why wasn't Mom content? Ada thought irritably.

In any event, what Richie Fletcher said was law in their house whether May liked it or not, so to the Great Exhibition they would go. And all their travel and accommodation was to be organized by a firm run by a Mr Thomas Cooke.

The Fletcher family, all seven of them, went piling on to a train at Curzon Street station in the middle of Birmingham. All sitting pretty in a proper compartment. And at all the country stations on the way during that thrilling ride, they waved at the throngs of people on the platforms, catching smuts from the passing train in the folds of their clothing, who had come to stare at these adventurers as they passed. How important they felt, waving back at these wondering faces!

Then London, and the exhibition's home in the Crystal Palace – most of it made down the road from where they lived in Birmingham, the glass from Chance & Co. Ltd in Smethwick and the ironwork from Cochrane & Co. in Dudley – 1,851 yards long, a yard for each year. The glass palace was so vast that in some places trees growing in Hyde Park had had to be included inside, making the place look like a magical heavenly garden.

'It's only a shilling each to go in now,' Pa said, the first day. Once the bigwigs had had their turn at a pound a day, a price had been set for everyone else.

And go in they did – three days in a row, gaping at more and more sights. It was exhausting and overwhelming, and their mother kept complaining about how very hot it was in this giant greenhouse of a building. And all that week Ada felt her eyes were not big enough to take it all in, the vast array of *things* from every corner of the world, including theirs, especially theirs.

So many astonishing creations from factories all over the country. The magnificent wooden display case with Arkle & Lilley's brass products shining like gold treasures which Pa proudly showed them. So many things, a seemingly endless display of manufacture and creative brilliance, and they walked, gazing at everything – huge machines and tools, textiles and looms, stained glass and the biggest diamond in the world – until they had blisters and their legs ached.

Best of all, Ada loved the crystal fountain, the centrepiece of the palace, with scented water cascading endlessly from it, catching the light that poured through the overarching glass. And the display from India with a stuffed elephant. The animal towered above them, draped in the finest golden robes, its little glassy eyes seeming to twinkle down at them.

Walking and walking and drinking it all in. Feasting off sandwiches and Bath buns washed down with Schweppes ginger beer in one of the refreshment areas with its trees and statues. Falling into bed each night in the lodging house where they stayed, worn out and drunk with amazement at all they had seen.

And one afternoon, they almost could not believe their eyes. A murmur passed through the crowd. The exhibition was as packed as ever and Ada heard the sudden excited murmur that passed along the huge building, almost like the sound of wind in the trees. 'She's here. Her Majesty – she's come back again!'

They heard later that the Queen visited the exhibition over and over again, so thrilled and fascinated was she by this phenomenon conjured up by her husband.

The crowds were herded back to each side of the walkway down the middle of the long hall and Ada, standing between Pa and Elsie, heard the cheers and clapping break like a wave along the crush of people as their sovereign, Queen Victoria, was ushered into the building.

'I can't see,' Elsie complained, frantically jumping up on to her tiptoes, then falling back down.

The cheers rose around them as the Queen made a gradual progress towards them and Elsie was almost in tears. Ada could not see either.

'Come on you two.' Pa reached down and hoicked them up, one in each arm, staggering a little with the effort. Ada saw her mother gather Dora up with Mabs on her other arm. John was so young he would hardly know what was happening and he clung on to Mom's skirts as usual.

And along she came, the applause and cheers reaching a crescendo as she walked slowly past, giving a sedate wave. Ada saw a small, fresh-faced little woman, looking about her in seeming wonder, a tall, black-haired man in military dress walking at her side. Ada could hear her parents cheering and moments later, it was all over. She had gone. Pa lowered the two of them to the ground.

'Well, there you are. It's not everyone's seen the Queen, is it? And Prince Albert with her.'

'My oh my,' Mom said, sounding quite bowled over and flustered.

It was the happiest moment of the whole week. Because much of the time Mom had been nervy, having to keep Mabs and the others happy, and nagging all the time: 'Richie, don't spend any more . . . We can't manage this . . . How're we ever going to get home . . .?'

Until Ada was disgusted with her and thought how much better it was to be a man and do all the interesting things and be in charge of everything instead of traipsing along moaning the whole time.

Pa was in his element. He had triumphed, bringing them

all here. There was only one moment in the week when he was unsteady and things seemed to go wrong. And this gave Ada a sick, shocked feeling, like when she once sliced her finger with a knife and saw her own flesh gape open and seep.

Her father was full of energy that week, wanting to see everything, drink it all in. London itself, not just the exhibition. Westminster Abbey, the Tower of London. The best day was when Mom said she was too tired for any more traipsing and would stay behind with Mabs and John. Then Dora, who was five, and overwhelmed by all the activity, said she would stay as well.

So it was just Ada and Elsie, who was seven then, a pretty, pink-cheeked, big-eyed child, with the heart-shaped mole at the corner of her eye. And all day long, she carried her beloved rag doll Lucy.

'Promise you won't keep blarting?' Ada hissed to her as they set off with Pa, because Elsie was always emotional. But she promised and kept the promise. And held Ada's hand for most of the way, Lucy clutched in the other. They went to Leicester Square to see a mysterious miracle creation called Cantelo's Hydro-Incubator. Through the glass fronting this long low box in which rows of eggs were kept warm, you could watch chicks hatching one after another – hundreds a day, they claimed.

'Oh, I want to hold one!' Elsie cried, enchanted.

Ada watched, fascinated, as a tiny, damp, yellow head emerged from another shell.

'You could make a fortune with that,' Pa commented.

There was a gigantic globe showing the whole round, blue world, this ball on which they all apparently lived. They stared and stared. They followed Pa round the city like 'troupers', he said. His two piano keys, Ada fair like him, and Elsie raven-haired like Mom and determined to keep walking however tired and hot she was. Because Elsie, though tiny, and a quiet child with a faraway look, had a steely side to her when she was determined.

Ada, even though her feet were stinging with blisters in her old shoes, gazed up at the buildings which seemed bigger even than those at home and would not have stopped walking for anything.

But what happened was one evening when they were all together, on the way back to their lodgings. Amid all the swirling crowds of Londoners and visitors, Pa took them down into the special tunnel which went under the Thames.

Ada carried Mabs for a bit because Mom said her arms were going to drop off.

'Come on, chickie.' She held out her arms and Mabs gave a chuckle. Out of her brother and sisters, Ada loved Mabs the most. At not far off a year old, Mabs had black curly hair and huge brown eyes. She gurgled as Ada rubbed her nose against hers and clenched her chubby knees on Ada's body.

'You're a lump,' Ada said. '*My* arms're going to drop off an' all.'

'Oh, I'm not sure about this, Richie,' Mom said as they entered the tunnel.

It seemed gloomy, and so loud with the echo of voices.

'Is the river over our heads?' Elsie asked, worried.

'It's not the river we need to worry about – it's those thieving cockneys.' Their father bent down, speaking quietly. After all, they might be surrounded by these same thieving cockneys. 'Pickpockets and swindlers the lot of them.' He pressed his hands on his own pockets as if protecting them from an onslaught of marauding Londoners. Elsie tried to grin at him while looking more frightened than before.

'Come on – stop mithering, you lot.' Pa looked around

at the seething, lively crowds. 'Cor, summat smells good down 'ere.'

Mom and Elsie both forgot to be scared when they caught sight of the array of stalls lining the tunnel, lit with flares and selling snacks and trinkets. There was a rich smell of hot meat mixed with roasting, sweetened nuts. Ada was busy with Mabs, the little lights reflecting back in the child's wondering eyes as she took everything in.

Pa went to buy them all some roasted nuts. The woman on the stall, a voluptuous person with black hair piled high on her head and vivid red lips, measured out nuts for all of them into twists of paper. They were all walking away, popping hot nuts into eager mouths – Elsie carried Ada's and fed her – and all seemed rosy until the woman yelled after them.

'Oi, you! Get back over 'ere . . .'

Everyone in the crowd was suddenly staring at Pa as if he had done something wrong. Ada felt a horrible chill inside at the sight of all the hostile faces. Whatever was going on? It was as if everything had suddenly gone bad. They all scuttled back to the stall.

'This is a wrong'un.' The woman handed back one of the coins Dad had handed over. 'You pay up proper or I'll 'ave the Peelers on you!'

Ada thought Pa might lose his temper. But to her surprise he looked suddenly stricken and small, as if he had shrunk into himself in the face of this accusation. After all, he was far from home and there was no one here who could come to his aid.

'Ever so sorry, missus,' he said humbly, as the woman loomed in front of him, hand on one hip, the other holding out the shilling accusingly. Pa was rifling through his pocket, bringing out pennies and tuppenny bits to exchange. 'I can't think how that's happened. Someone must've slipped it me. Here –'

Almost cringing, in a way Ada hated to see, he handed coins into the woman's pudgy palm and took back the offending one. He stared at it, bewildered. 'Sorry, missus – no harm intended.'

Ada felt bad seeing Pa like that, with that big woman glaring at him as if he was some sort of criminal and counting suspiciously through the substitute coins. She tossed her head and walked off, chucking them in the tin behind her counter and subsiding on to her stool again.

'Flaming cockneys,' Pa murmured to Mom who was staring at him, horrified. 'Handing out fakes.'

He was getting his spirit back now things were sorted out and they were not about to clap him in irons which is what Ada had thought, with all those cockneys staring and muttering, ready to jump on him. Show over, they all turned away, and Ada felt as if she could breathe again.

'Let's go home, Richie,' Mom begged, tears in her eyes. 'Please – we don't belong here.'

Three

'I know you're in there. Come on – open up.'

Ada saw her mother freeze and shrink into herself as they heard the woman's fist pounding on their door.

The five of them were at the table in their cramped back-yard home of only a few weeks. This comedown. This new frightening life which had been thrust upon them.

It was a dark, stifling place compared with the cleaner, more spacious brick cottage they had been used to. Here, the walls seemed to sweat and seep all by themselves and the stench from the earth midden, close by at the end of the yard, filled their nostrils day and night.

May, Ada, Elsie, Dora and even little John were working at the table, sorting bristles for the brush factory. There were seemingly endless heaps of them which had to be separated black from white, a slow, delicate operation, made even harder in poor light.

Mabs sat on a mat on the rough brick floor or toddled about, snot trickling endlessly from her nose. Hour after hour they worked, trying to scrape the rent together and make enough to feed them all.

'You'll have to open up, Ada,' May whispered, cowed as

the banging at the door went on. 'She won't take no for an answer.'

Liza Jenks, or Fat Liza as she was referred to with no affection at all, had been known to kick doors in with a blow of her hefty leg while on her rounds.

Ada, her hands shaking, jiggled the bolt back and opened the door as far as she dared.

'About flaming time.'

Liza Jenks was the most terrifying person Ada had ever met. A mound of pasty flesh tightly encased in a long skirt of heavy black cloth. Her wide shoulders and mountainous breasts strained at the seams of her black blouse, across the chest of which there always rested a chinking, rattling necklace of silver medallions. The hem of her skirt was an inch or so too long so that despite her girth, she seemed to move along silently as if on wheels – unless she had to hoick the already filthy hem up out of the mire to expose her fancy black button boots. Over her shoulders she wore an ancient black shawl of shiny stuff with a scalloped edge, crossed over at the front and tucked into her waist, leaving her hands usefully free for carrying her clinking cloth bag and thumping on people's doors. Her curranty eyes peered out from the pillowy flesh of her face and her oily brown hair, parted straight down the middle, was yanked back into two plaited coils pinned above her ears like handles.

''Ere – give this to yer mother.'

Liza brought out a little brown bottle and shoved it at Ada, who shook her head.

'No, thanks. She don't want it.' She managed to get the words out, though her throat was strangled with fear. Because she knew what was coming next.

''Er's on my list,' Liza Jenks said. 'So 'er's 'aving it.'

Ada heard the chair scrape as her mother got up from the table.

'That'll be a tanner,' Liza insisted.

May had already twice handed over sixpence for Liza's bottles of hooch. God alone knew what was in her potions. Ada knew Mom was a fool to have ever started this, but Liza was like a boulder falling on you. You couldn't refuse.

'Goo on, wench – warm yer cockles.' Liza held out her grubby hand, palm up, waiting to grasp the money in exchange for a small bottle that was somehow already in May's hand. 'Give us it back empty and I'll give yer a farthing.'

'I can't afford . . .' May tried hopelessly to hand the bottle back.

'Don't remember you turning me down last time – nor the time before.' Fat Liza's voice had sunk low and dangerous. She stepped closer, with a faint rattle of her medallions and a clicking from her supply of little bottles inside her cloth bag.

Ada shrank from the stink of her, of stale sweat and spirits.

'Yes – because you . . .' The words 'forced it on me' could not seem to get out of May's throat. Liza jabbed her fingers into May's ribs.

'Pay up or my Wally'll be round. He looks out for me, my lad – me a poor widow woman, trying to 'old body and soul together . . .'

Though they had only been living in the yard a few weeks, May already knew about Wally Jenks. The last thing you wanted was him – a male version of his mother, thick as porridge and keenly devoted to violence – turning up to kick in their door and grab anything he could as 'payment'.

It was no good May pointing out that she too was a 'widow' – the story she told, better than deserted wife – or that she had five small children while Liza had three strapping, grown-up sons. She fished down her cleavage and

18

brought sixpence out of a twist of cloth. Liza closed her palm on it like a trap.

'Any road, if you don't want it you can sell it to 'er in there.' She nodded towards next door where their neighbours, the Connell family, lived. As May shut the door, trembling, Fat Liza was stepping next door to start on Sarah Connell, reaching in the bag for another bottle as she did so.

May stood the little bottle on the table and sank back down on to her chair, looking unwell. Ada felt sick and wobbly as well and Elsie, Dora and John all stared in mute terror.

'How did I ever get into this?' May murmured, desperately.

Fat Liza's first approach had been friendly – a gift, a little 'pick-you-up' to a newcomer to the yard. Then the 'list'. The threats.

May stared at the bottle, then pulled out the bung and took a sip. She closed her eyes, shuddered as it went down. It seemed to strengthen her, but Ada hated that now she could smell it on her breath.

'Back to work,' her mother said.

Four

After the Great Adventure, they had arrived back at their house feeling as if they had been away for several years. All the old familiar things seemed to take on a glow.

'At last!' Mom had cried as they walked through the door. She even went round touching things – the sideboard and table, the dangling flowers on the curtain rails.

Ada watched her mother relax back into her familiar surroundings, not being assaulted constantly by newness and being a stranger and traipsing the exhausting streets with a young, restless infant in her arms. Back with her own things and neighbours, something in Ada relaxed as well. She and Elsie were soon out with the other children, swinging on the ragged rope which hung from the street lamp post and bragging about the week they had experienced to the kids who had not been to the exhibition.

Things went back to normal. Ada, Elsie and Dora went back to the schoolroom – Mom and Dad were determined they would have lessons until they were at least eleven or twelve. And nothing seemed amiss.

Then, one night in early October, Pa went out, as he often did. But this time, he never came home.

The last thing Ada ever heard of him when she was half-asleep, was the creaking of the door of the room she and her sisters slept in. She opened her eyes to see a candle raised high, her father looking round at them all. The candle vanished as the door closed and she heard the sound of his boots going down the stairs, the way she did on many other nights.

It was the last time she had seen him.

''E never come into the works all day,' Jem Atherton told them the next evening, his plump face saggy with woe. 'Reckon summat's happened.'

May, who had woken to find her husband had not come home, was merely in a state of bewilderment at first. Ada was not downcast – not then. Pa would be back. He had had one of his bright ideas about something and would come whistling into the house full of excitement and with liquorice or bulls' eyes for them all.

Like the way he would be out late some evenings and return tired but full of cheer. And the time a few months back when he had come home with a grin on his face and his hand pressing on his jacket pocket where there was something wriggling about. He'd sat down with them and brought out a tiny, sniffly puppy the colour of sand. Dora started giggling and said, 'He looks like a piggly!' And the name Piggly stuck.

So far as Ada was concerned, Piggly was one of the best things ever to happen. She spent every minute she could with the little dog who became unofficially hers. She fed him and ran around with him. Let him curl up on her lap and even sleep in bed with them all. The others loved Piggly but Ada was *in* love. She adored his sandy-coloured coat, his wet black nose pushing into her ear in the morning, his antics with any scrap he could find to play with and his warm body curled up beside hers. Piggly was her first and so far only love.

Piggly's name may have stuck but he did not. He ran off after a couple of months, never to be seen again. Ada sobbed at night, missing his warmth and his soft paws. She had a pain in her chest for weeks afterwards.

'I think my heart is broken,' she said seriously to her mother.

May smiled. 'It'll mend, babby,' she said, gently.

Ada was not so sure.

But Pa was not Piggly the pup. He would be back.

Days passed. Mom wept and tried to believe in him. Her Richie. He had gone off to make his fortune. He had met with some accident. She went and asked at the General Hospital but there was no sign of him. Even so, he would be back. But days became weeks and she was at her wits' end.

How was she to make ends meet? Pay the rent? Jem could only do so much to help – he had a wife and four children himself.

To make things even worse, rumours were going round about someone robbing the works Sick Club. Everyone paid in a halfpenny a week as insurance against family illness. And the fund had gone missing – the week before the Fletcher family set off for that jamboree in London. Fingers started to point. And Richie showed no sign of coming home.

And then a bloke from the works called Ebenezer Mullin who Mom had only clapped eyes on once before turned up at the house spluttering with rage and making threats, demanding to know where 'that bastard Richie' had gone.

May was in a constant state.

'Ada and Elsie can't stop at school,' she wept to Jem, who rubbed his hand back and forth over his head of thick stubbly hair as if trying to force an idea out of it. 'I'll have to send them out to work.'

When Pa didn't come home and still didn't come home, Jem found them this back house in one of the courts of dwellings in yards crammed round the back of Summer Row. It was not far away from Arkle & Lilley's where Pa had worked and would save them two bob as the rent was three shillings. Jem hired a cart, enlisted some other blokes and helped May pile on everything they could manage.

May had been convinced she was moving into a den of thieves and begged Jem to screw a bolt on the door. The home they moved out of had a front room and back with a scullery kitchen, two bedrooms upstairs and their own earth privy in a yard outside – even a little patch to plant a few veg. But here in this yard, while house numbers one to three of the five – half-houses in reality – were back to back with others facing the street, theirs was one of two, side by side, thrown up against a high factory wall. They were airless one-room dwellings downstairs with a small scullery, two bedrooms upstairs and a shared brick wash house and earth lavs. The water pump was right out in the street.

And even though May insisted on bringing her beautiful window cornices and thick green curtains, the downstairs window facing the yard was too narrow and who was to screw them to the wall? In the end she made a few bob selling them, and the rag of faded dark blue curtain that was there already stayed and would have to do.

Once their precious possessions were loaded in – Pa's chair took up too much room but what was she to do? – May sank on to it and burst into shrieking tears.

'Look what he's done to me! Alone in the world in this terrible place! Oh, Lord above, what am I going to do?'

While Mom and the men moved their chattels into the house that chilly Sunday afternoon, Ada stayed out in the yard. Elsie and Dora huddled close to her as she held Mabs in her arms. John kept whining after his mother and driving May distracted.

They watched as the blokes hauled Mom's – and what had been Pa's – bed up through the window on a rope.

'Here, you lot – cop 'old of some of these,' Jem said kindly to Elsie and Dora, since their hands were free. He pointed to the pots and pans.

As they helped, making journeys into the mean little room, other children in the yard gathered to watch the entertainment.

That was when Ada first met Nellie, one of the crowd of children spilling out of the house next door to theirs and, it seemed, the only girl. Her feet were bare like most of the rest of the family playing in the yard. Nellie had straggly brown hair with an odd, powdery whiteness to it. She was pale and painfully thin and Ada noticed how strangely dry and chapped her lips were.

At first she seemed rather lifeless and bewildered when she sidled up to Ada, but she had a friendly look to her.

'You moving in?' She gave a little smile, stretching those crusty lips.

Ada nodded. What did it look like?

'How old are you? I'm Nellie Connell. I'm eleven.'

Ada couldn't help liking her, even though she was feeling a bit prickly herself. There was a sweetness to Nellie and once she started talking to you she was livelier than she seemed at first.

'I'm ten,' she said.

'That's nice. Another girl on the yard – there's too many boys.'

Looking at the roiling children who seemed to be Nellie's younger siblings, Ada could see what she meant. Nellie told her she had three older brothers and three younger.

'That your sister?' Nellie tickled the little girl's cheek and Mabs chuckled. Nellie laughed too and suddenly her pale face looked sweet. ''Er's a pretty babby.'

Ada felt gratified. Mabs was a lovely child with her dark curls and huge brown eyes.

'There's five of us – Mabs is the youngest. She's a heavy lump, but if I put her down she'll be into everything.'

'Give 'er me – I'll hold her a bit,' Nellie offered.

Nellie came up close and as she did so, Ada caught a funny smell on her, pungent, like pickled onions. Despite this, to her surprise Mabs went readily to Nellie who swung her round, making her laugh until they were both giggling at the sound of Mabs's loud chuckles. Already there was a feeling that she and Ada would be friends. Nellie filled her in on the yard.

'There's Mr and Mrs Spragg at number one. She's all right. You wanna watch him though, got a temper on him, he has, lamp you one soon as move.' She frowned. 'Says he's got the gout. Number two's Mr and Mrs O'Shea. Well, they say she's not really his missus but that's what they call her. They came over the water from Ireland like my mom and dad. And number three's Florrie and Dorrie. Twins. Dunno their other name. Florrie wears a tortoiseshell comb in her hair so you can tell them apart. They don't say much – except to each other, I s'pose.'

Ada was intrigued by this. She couldn't remember ever seeing twins, let alone ones who looked exactly the same.

Even though her heart was heavy as lead with Pa gone and leaving their nice little house, meeting Nellie made her feel things might not be so bad.

Five

It was Sarah Connell, Nellie's mother, who told May Fletcher where they could get outwork in the area. Sarah – and often two of her young sons, William and Tom, eight and five, who mostly stayed home from school – sat at the table carding for the button factories in the area. They had to sew horn or pearl buttons on to cards for sale in the shops as well as helping mind the pale, sickly shred of a baby, little Peter.

Sarah told May about the brush factory in the next street. May immediately called at the factory asking if she could take on outwork – to be done at home.

Sarah Connell was thin and sickly-looking, but at her best, without the drink inside her, she was gentle and kind. It was only after Liza Jenks's first 'friendly' visit to May with her 'gift' of a bottle of 'tonic' followed by her second, more threatening appearance, that May realized how it had happened that Liza Jenks had managed to get poor, overwhelmed Sarah so helplessly in her thrall.

Seamus Connell, Sarah's husband, was a barrel-shaped bruiser of a man who had come to Birmingham from County Wexford, worked as a railway carter, met Birmingham-born Sarah and settled down.

Ada was frightened of Seamus Connell – he was a gruff, blunt man with weather-beaten, stubbly cheeks. He spoke to his children as if they were a litter of pups to be grunted at and booted out of the way. As she could barely understand a word he said, Ada found it hard to tell whether the words spoken were callous or affectionate. Of an evening, Seamus and skinny runt Ted O'Shea took themselves off to their favourite watering holes and reeled home later. But Seamus could manage his drink. And sometimes a night of boozing brought out Seamus's voice, a rich baritone that would bounce Irish songs that brought a tear to your eye round the walls of the yard.

Sarah's drinking was another matter because she would be knocked out for half the day when Fat Liza had been round. The Fletchers heard many a loud ding-dong through the wall from the Connells' on account of it.

The first Saturday, as the family were still settling into the yard off Summer Row, Nellie knocked on the door in the late afternoon.

'Coming up the Bull Ring?' she asked Ada.

'Yes, you go,' May told her. 'Your legs're younger than mine. Get me a pound of cag-mag from the Shambles – they'll be selling it off.'

'Mom,' Ada reproached her. 'The Shambles was gone before I was even born.'

'All right, Smithfield.' Ada saw her mother smile for a second. 'I know the Shambles is gone but that's what my mother and her mother before her used to call it.' The rickety old stalls round St Martin's Church in the Bull Ring had been replaced by a bigger, more solid building housing the meat market. 'I don't know why they have to keep on changing things all the time . . .'

She handed Ada an old cloth bag and coins wrapped in a twist of rag. 'Give it a good sniff before you hand over the money – and make sure it's not all bone.'

Ada set off with Nellie. She liked going into town and it wasn't far. It felt adventurous going without her mother, like exploring. They set off, chattering and giggling together. Ada liked Nellie's infectious chuckles and she started to enjoy herself. But then as they hurried along New Street, Nellie said, 'Why ain't you got a father then – has he passed away?'

Ada felt her blood pounding. She couldn't bear to say that Pa was dead. He couldn't be dead! But to say he had upped and left was just as bad. He would never have meant to leave them all alone, leave *her*! Something had happened – and one day he would walk right back in again . . .

'No, course not,' she said firmly. 'I dunno what's happened. He's got held up somehow – but he's coming back.' She drew herself up tall. 'I'm the man of the family for now.'

Nellie snorted with laughter. 'You? What're you on about?'

Ada felt a lump come into her throat. *My lad – you're my big strong lad.* But she couldn't speak.

'If you ain't got no father at home you'll need ways and means,' Nellie went on. 'I can teach you a thing or two.'

Ada was about to ask what on earth she was talking about, when Nellie took a little brown medicine bottle out of her pocket, pulled out the bung and swigged from it.

'What's that?' Ada asked, half afraid of the answer. Liza Jenks had already paid them her first visit – surely Nellie was not drinking her hard stuff at her age?

'Brewery vinegar,' Nellie said, holding it out. 'Want some?'

Ada screwed up her face as she caught a whiff of it. No wonder Nellie always smelt the way she did. 'No! What d'you want to drink that for?'

'I like it,' Nellie said, pushing the bottle back into her pocket. 'It's a pick-me-up.'

They passed St Martin's, its sooty spire reaching up to the sky and went along Spiceal Street. The stalls were lit with flares now it was getting dark. Since Pa had left they had not had as much to eat, and all of them had shrunk thinner. Saliva rushed into Ada's mouth when they passed the lady selling hot roast chestnuts, the delicious aroma mingling with cheap cigarette smoke and rotting vegetables, a tang of orange on the mizzling wet air. Everyone was shouting louder and louder, trying to get their wares sold off at the end of the day.

'Go to Jamaica Row and get your cag-mag first,' Nellie instructed.

Ada was startled. Nellie looked a washed-out feeble thing who wouldn't say boo to a goose – but suddenly she had become quite bossy. Ada was the one used to being the boss, but for now she did as she was told.

They headed towards the meat markets. The shouting grew even more insistent and Ada found herself amid a jostling crowd all vying for the best bargains. The air was full of the smell of raw meat. The street lighter was going round as they got there. As he lit each of the nearby lamps, the faces of the shopping crowd appeared, shimmering out of the shadows.

'Come on,' Nellie said. 'We'll be here all day else.' With surprising force she elbowed her way to the front, tugging Ada along with her. A few people said, 'Oi – watch it. Stop yer shoving,' and one tried to hold Ada back by the arm. Nellie ignored them and Ada had to yank herself free, determined to be as daring as Nellie.

The man selling off the meat was standing on the base of a cut-off barrel.

''Ere yer go – nice and fresh – sixpence the lot!'

Ada asked for cag-mag – the mix of meat offcuts and remains – and handed over the money, carefully sniffing the paper-wrapped package.

'Fresh as a daisy, wench!' the bloke grinned at her. 'No need for that.'

She didn't dare unwrap it to see how much meat there

was. Cag-mag was heavy because there was so much bone in it. She tucked it into her bag and was soon jostled out of the way by other impatient Saturday-night shoppers.

'Let's go in the Market Hall,' Nellie said, suddenly very businesslike.

Ada loved the enormous building where she had been with Mom from time to time. It was packed full of hundreds of stalls, and there were the mixed smells of fish and cooked meat, of onions cut open to show their quality, of flowers, and of the smoky, musty clothing of great crowds of people.

She had to work hard to keep up with Nellie's darting figure. Nellie was suddenly full of energy and like a little mouse, able to squeeze her skinny body through any cranny in the crowd.

'What you got to buy?' Ada asked, grabbing Nellie's bony shoulder to stop her after they had pushed their way to a section of the market selling vegetables.

'Buying?' Nellie looked at her as if she was a fool. 'I ain't got any money, so what d'you think? Now – keep your eyes peeled and just keep moving, slow like, all right?'

To Ada's amazement – and panic – she saw Nellie turn into an expert pilferer. Even her face seemed to change, from the pale passive look it wore most of the time, to a shrewd, calculating sharpness. While she was facing forward all the time, her hands were doing something else, as if they belonged to another person altogether. She had her mother's cloth bag hanging on one arm and as they moved round the market Ada saw Nellie watching the stallholders like a hawk. In a trice, a potato from one stall, then from another, an apple, onions, small turnips, carrots all found their way into Nellie's bag without a farthing being exchanged for them.

Ada thought her heart was going to burst out of her

chest. Nellie was a thief, bold as brass! What if they got caught while she was with her? She hadn't stolen anything – she quickly checked her bag to make sure Nellie had not sneaked any of her thievery in there as well. Mom was so upright, had taught them all right from wrong – and taking what wasn't yours was definitely *wrong*. She could see that Nellie was well practised at this game. Ada was shocked to the core and frightened to death someone was going to notice. Torn between wanting to run home and staying with the one person who seemed to want to be her friend, she hovered around, anxiously trying to look as relaxed and normal as possible.

Gradually she let herself trail further behind, trying to pretend she was not with Nellie. She let her eyes skate over the girl as if she was nobody, while at the same time every hair in her body was alert for what Nellie was doing.

Nellie, so close to the stall that her skirt was touching the oranges piled at the front, slipped her hand down and in a blink an orange was in her hand, then popped into the bag. Just as she slid the orange in, the stallholder turned from serving another customer and Ada nearly jumped out of her skin. He must have seen – Nellie was going to get arrested! She'd go to prison, they both would because she was with her! Ada thought she was going to be sick.

But the man's eyes skated over Nellie, pale, blank-looking little Nellie, as if she was invisible. He leaned across and took a hand of bananas and payment for them from another customer and Ada's panic subsided.

Nellie looked back over her shoulder and waited for Ada to catch up. There was nothing in Ada's bag except the meat Mom had asked for and some potatoes she had bought, whereas she could see Nellie's was now hanging heavily.

'Let's go,' Nellie said, in a businesslike manner.

As they left the Market Hall, Ada was still expecting a great shout to rise up, a hue and cry. But they stepped out into the dark and drizzle and everything was as it had been before.

'Nellie,' she exploded as soon as they were away and heading up towards St Martin's again. 'You stole all those things – you're a thief!' It suddenly dawned on her what Nellie had meant by 'ways and means'.

Nellie looked back at her in the gloom of the street lamps. Her face took on that sharp, energetic look, her eyes narrower and sly-looking.

'What if I am? It's there for the taking. And if I don't, how else 're we s'posed to fill our bellies? There's my wages, but it's never enough . . .'

Ada had a horrible realization. Two of Nellie's three older brothers were working. So why did they not have enough? Her own mother slaved for every penny to feed the five of them. *So how much of the household money must Sarah be handing over to Liza Jenks?* Ada asked herself. Seamus Connell didn't stint himself down the boozer either. Were they both spending nearly all their wages on intoxicating drink? Ada was deeply shocked – she wasn't used to this.

'Come on.' Nellie, suddenly more her old self again, dragged Ada over to the hot-chestnut seller. A moment later she was holding out a paper cone containing a tuppenny-worth of hot, delicious-smelling chestnuts. 'Go on – take some.'

Saliva rushed into Ada's mouth and she couldn't resist digging into the paper and chewing on the nuts.

'You said you didn't have any money!'

'This is my bit of my wages,' Nellie said, munching hungrily. 'Tuppence a week. Mom thinks she gets it all, but she don't.'

Ada had to digest this information as well. Not only

was Nellie a thief but she was also lying to her mother. She started to feel, though, that she didn't entirely blame her.

'What if they catch you?' she asked, breathless as she scurried after Nellie. 'Thieving.'

'They won't.' Nellie gave her a scornful glance. 'I know what I'm about.'

'I wouldn't dare,' Ada said. She was still stunned by this new Nellie.

'You've never had to, 'ave yer?' Nellie turned to Ada and grinned and suddenly her face was friendly and full of fun. She elbowed Ada. 'You'll learn.'

'I won't!' Ada protested.

'Suit yerself – if you want to go hungry.'

As they passed the grand King Edward's school building in New Street, she said, 'You could do better than outwork though. They need hands at the button factory. You and Elsie could come, earn yourselves a wage.'

Ada thought about this with a sinking heart. Now Pa was gone, the reality was that she was not going back to school. She might as well go out to work like Nellie and help Mom. She pulled her shoulders back. The man of the family. Pa would be proud of her, wouldn't he? She was going to go out and earn her own wage.

Six

Nellie took Ada and Elsie to Tompkinson's Pearl Button Works where she worked, a two-storey building in a backyard, to see the forewoman, Mrs Rundle, a dark-haired, grim-looking woman of an age Ada could not guess. Could the two sisters be taken on? Mrs Rundle looked them up and down, asked if they could count and add up and nodded. They could do with a couple of extra pairs of hands.

Ada knew Mom didn't want them to go out to work. She was frightened to let them out of her sight. But she gave in when Ada said that she and Elsie might each earn three or four shillings a week. At the moment, if they ever made twelve shillings on the outwork from the brush factory it was a good week but it was almost always less. May was the one who worked fastest on the bristle sorting: she could likely still make not much short of that on her own.

Before Ada and Elsie set off with Nellie on their first day at the button works, they went to find their mother, doing the washing in the brew house. Their neighbour, Mrs Spragg, was a kindly lady in her fifties with velvety-looking cheeks and steel-grey hair in a bun. She had lived in the yard the longest and was reckoned to be the gaffer, safeguarding and sometimes enforcing the rules.

'You can take your turn in the brew 'us of a Thursday,' she told May. 'Thursday morning, first thing.'

The brew house, a low, brick building at the end of

the yard, was where the copper tub was for laundry. The women had to carry pails of water from the street pump and light a fire under the copper to heat it.

Before, in the old house, May had had her own copper in a little brick building out at the back. Now she was having to share.

'And I'm damned if I'm hanging my drawers up in front of every Tom, Dick and Harry,' she vowed. So 'drawers' – which meant underwear of any kind – were dried inside on the range which was almost permanently festooned with washing.

That morning, steam was billowing out of the brew house into the bright, freezing winter air. When the little girls peeped inside, May was pushing clothes hard round in the water with a stout stick. Outside stood the maiding tub and wooden dolly, like a little four-legged stool with a long handle in the top and a crossbar for pushing down on, to swish and pound the filth out of the clothes. Mom was always worn out after a day of maiding and mangling and hanging out.

She straightened up, lifting the edge of her pinner to wipe steam and perspiration from her once beautiful face.

'You got your piece?'

Ada and Elsie nodded. Each of them carried a slice of bread smeared with dripping for their dinner, wrapped in a scrap of newspaper.

'You want to put her in the pocket of your pinafore.' Elsie had her little doll, Lucy, clutched in her hand. May squatted down to look into her little girl's face. 'Don't want to lose her, do you?' She stroked Elsie's hair out of her eyes.

Lucy had a few strands remaining of her black wool hair, a lopsided face embroidered in black cotton and a rag skirt wrapped round her. Elsie adored Lucy and refused ever to be separated from her.

Ada saw her mother's eyes fill with tears. Elsie was so small and almost like the dolly herself, with her mother's dark hair and big grey eyes, which held an intense look, as if her thoughts were like a volcano smouldering inside her. She had been born early and too small.

'She's a little miracle,' Mom would say sometimes, looking at Elsie's doll-like figure. 'She's lucky to be alive.'

She was more protective of Elsie than she ever had been of Ada. But suddenly their mother wrapped her arms tightly round them both, sobbing. Ada could feel the throb of it all through her.

'This would never have happened if your father was still here. Oh, Lord above, what's happened to him?'

Ada felt her throat ache all over again. She wanted to cry as well, but she was determined not to. How could Pa have gone off and left them like this? She was so frightened of what might have happened and she heard Elsie give a sob beside her.

Mom gently pushed the two of them away and stood up, wiping their cheeks with the corner of her shawl. However much it broke her heart to send her two little ones into the factory, they needed the money.

Nellie was coming along the yard.

'Go on with you both.' May turned away, hiding her upset. 'You be good, all right?'

'Come on,' Ada said bossily, to cover up how upset she was. 'Or we'll be late.'

Nellie hurried them along to the Tompkinson's works amid various people all heading the same way: men, but more women and a number of children.

As they arrived at the narrow entry into the yard, a man was unloading bulging jute sacks off a cart in the street, hefting each one on his shoulder. Ada and Elsie followed him along the entry, and Ada noticed something she had been too nervous to take in last time they came – that the ground all along the path was speckled with white. She could feel the crunch of shell fragments under her boots.

They followed the man into the gloomy lower floor of Tompkinson's and saw him twist round to lower the sack to the earthen floor at the end of a row of others stacked along the back wall of this store room. Closer to the door and the available light was a long trestle table.

Nellie, sure of the way, hurried them up the stairs leading to the shop above, their boots clumping noisily on the wooden treads. Elsie had stowed Lucy the doll in her pocket and was now tightly gripping Ada's hand. Ada took in a deep breath which smelt of dust and jute sacking, and tried not to show how nervous she was as well.

Upstairs, she forgot everything else in a moment of wonder at the sight that met her eyes. When they had come to see Mrs Rundle, they had met her in the yard. But now she was standing just inside a work 'shop' along which were crammed lathes turned by treadles and hand cranks. It was full of the bustle of people getting to work, a few men, but mostly women, exchanging a brief greeting before bending over the machines. From one end she could hear the jagged sound of sawing as a man bent over a work table. Machines began to turn, workers bent over them to carry out the series of processes involved in button making that she would soon know well – cutting blanks, facing and turning, and backing and edging – which at the moment were a mystery of the adult work before her new, child's eyes.

But what made the place strange, like a wonderland that the working men and women had wandered into, was that everything was white. Shell dust coated every surface – the floor and sills, tables and shelves, as well as faces and hair – as it would do hers and Elsie's by the end of that day. And even though the window was cloudy with dust, the winter sun pierced through and she saw tiny lights across the room, where the rays caught particles of shell, making them glitter like tiny rainbows.

Nellie had already gone and started work. Mrs Rundle came over to Ada and Elsie as they stood there. She looked stern and Ada felt herself shrink inside.

'Right, you two.' She looked at Elsie. 'You're on sorting. Aggie?' she called to a woman along the room. 'Take this one and show 'er what's what, will yer?'

She pushed her hand in the middle of Ada's back as she anxiously watched Elsie being taken along the room.

'You can cut blanks. Gert here'll learn yer.'

By the end of that first exhausting day, Ada had learned that the man sawing at the end was cutting open the shells into wide, flat sections which he passed to Gert for her to cut out the round button blanks – the process which Ada was to be put to as well, on a spare cutting machine next to Gert.

Gert, who told Ada she was sixteen, was a plump, blonde, plaintive young woman, who had a way of saying 'Oh' or 'Ow' in response to any information, her tone making it sound as if the world had ended. Despite her way of talking she was in fact a cheerful soul. Amid various whispered stories about people she knew in factories who had cut their own fingers off – the blood! – she showed Ada the way to cut the blanks. Her foot working the treadle, she expertly used the cutting tool to make all the little rounds of shell as the basis for the buttons, all close together like a honeycomb.

'You gotta do it close and you gotta do it gentle like,' Gert instructed. She was kind with it and Ada was grateful and liked her. 'Or you burn the shell edge and it don't look nice.'

Ada screwed up every ounce of concentration and by the end of the day she was not doing too badly.

'You'll be all right at this,' Gert assured her.

Ada saw Elsie in the dinner break when they ate their piece with Nellie.

'You all right, Else?' she asked. 'Not too bad, is it?'

Elsie had been put to the table where the buttons were counted and sorted ready for carding. She nodded, looking ahead of her with wide eyes as she bit ravenously into the bread. But she looked tired and utterly miserable and cuddled Lucy close to her all through the break.

That night when they got home, Ada was ready to drop as well. Work started at eight and ended at seven. Although it was only two streets away they hardly had the energy to get home. Later, Elsie sat on Mom's lap and sobbed from sheer exhaustion and Ada saw tears running down her mother's face as well. The little ones, Dora and John, sat quiet, awed by their big sisters going out into the world of work.

Ada sat on the rug next to the fire nursing Mabs. Her back ached from bending over all day and her feet were sore. But her sister's warm body on her lap was a comfort as they sat on the little red and blue hearthrug they had had in the other house. It reminded her of sitting by the fire with Pa in his chair and she felt as if she wanted to sob and sob. But she pushed the feelings away. She was the one who had to be tough, she reminded herself.

The thought made her sit up straighter again and she kissed Mabs and swallowed down her tears. Whatever happened, she was going to be strong and make sure the others were all right – even Mom. That was who she was. Ada Fletcher. The strong one, tough as any man.

Seven

'Here – look at these.'

It was a few days after Ada and Elsie had started at Tompkinson's and they had just gone into the gloomy downstairs entrance to the works. As usual, bulging jute sacks were stacked in rows against the wall and Ada had thought nothing of it. But one had caught Nellie's eye.

'Come over 'ere!' She darted over to a sack that was propped by the sorting table, beckoning to the others. Ada looked round. No one was coming in or out and she and Elsie scurried nervously over.

'Oh,' she breathed, as Nellie pulled back the open edge of the sack. 'Oh – they're so pretty.'

Even in the dim light, she could see the shells, hundreds of them, pointed like little hats and beautifully decorated with patterns, creams and different shades of brown and tan. She picked one up, turned it over and saw the faint pearly gleam just visible at the edge of the inner whorl which twisted away mysteriously into darkness.

'Trochus, that's what these ones are called,' Nellie said. 'Here – take some.'

To Ada's alarm she stuffed a few shells into her pockets and pushed one at Ada. Elsie's eyes were round as saucers.

'No one'll miss a few.'

So far all Ada had ever taken away was the remaining edge of a slice of shell once all the blanks had been cut out, leaving a little filigree shell frame. She was enchanted by the shells, the iridescent, pearly secrets coiled up inside them.

And now she couldn't resist. Surely no one would notice just one? She grabbed it, a shell patterned with cream and a rusty-reddish brown, shoved it into her pocket as if it was burning hot, then ran off, dragging Elsie up the stairs.

It was hard to get used to Nellie's thieving. Mom had always taught them strictly that taking anything that did not belong to you was stealing and a sin. After all, Mom used to go to church when they lived their life before – though these days she never seemed to have time.

But everywhere Nellie went – whether for fruit and veg in the Bull Ring or matches from the huckster's shop on the corner near their yard which sold almost everything you could want – she stole something, as if it was something she just had to do. And she was good at it. Mostly she looked so blank, so pale and vague, that half the time no one noticed her at all, and when they did they never suspected her capable of anything. In reality she was anything but vague. And one day, surely someone would notice? Ada was terrified of being there if Nellie ever got caught.

It felt as if the trochus shell was glowing like a foundry fire in her pocket all day, giving away her crime. Ada was sure everyone could see. But once they got home at night she got out her treasure and gazed at it in the candlelight. It was so beautiful – like a little magic house, mysterious and lovely. She could not bear to leave it anywhere and it became a habit to keep it in the pocket of her skirt so that it went everywhere with her like a lucky charm.

As the weeks passed she collected more shells. She learned that the mother-of-pearl craftspeople making buttons or handles for cutlery or the gleaming lids of little mother-of-pearl jewellery boxes – some of many items produced in the area – used a variety of shells. And these shells arrived in their magical sackloads to be sorted in the basement of Tompkinson's.

By the time Ada saw the shells in the works, they had already been cut open ready for the blanks to be stamped out. She learned the layers of the shell – there was the outer bark which had to be smoothed off on the lathe, then came the inner, hard layer of shell and finally, laid down on it over years by this slow miracle of the sea, the shell's inner, iridescent secret – the gleaming nacre, or mother-of-pearl.

'Where's the sea, from here?' she asked Mom one evening. She had seen rivers, the big Thames in London, a glimpse of the meagre river Rea running under the town and the oily sludge of the cut which snaked through Birmingham carrying the working boats – but not the sea, ever.

'Oh, a long way off,' Mom said, vaguely. She was still working, heaps of bristles round her on the table, sitting up every now and then to flex her aching back. 'I've never seen it.'

The days of work at Tompkinson's were so long and exhausting. And once Ada had mastered the work she found her mind wandering back to their past life. To her beloved pa, to everything that they had lost. And all the bewilderment about his disappearance, the sadness, the betrayal of it, until she ached with grief and wanted to sob over the lathe. She learned quickly to find a thought, any thought, to distract herself out of these memories which felt too much to bear.

The shells brought her comfort, transported her in her imagination to the seas and mighty oceans that she had never seen. She loved them. Loved the tiny whisper of waves when some of the shells were pressed close to your ear. Even in the dusty light of the shop at Tompkinson's and despite her aching back and sore fingers, Ada managed to find a magic in the work. In the pretty gleam of the buttons that emerged at the end, after polishing. Elsie spirited away a few of those too, for games at home as well as for their clothes.

And Ada's collection of shells at home grew as she became bolder. It was not hard to slip a hand into one of the sacks to find these treasures. There were varieties of snail shells, pointed trochus and gorgeous abalone like a shining bowl or a donkey's ear. Shells arrived with magical names and even more magical appearance: the round-edged black Tahiti, like an open hand of mother-of-pearl, fringed with black . . .

Her own collection was sacred to her, so she brought home extra snail shells for Dora and John to play with.

'They're the brightest thing in the house,' Mom said, when Ada lined hers up on the table. And it was on a morning so bright itself that the sun even found its way through the shadowy yard to warm a path through their window and light up the shells. For the first time in as long as Ada could remember, her mother smiled.

'We're managing, aren't we, Mom?' Ada dared to say. Pa would be proud, she thought. His lad out earning a living.

Mom looked down at her, the smile lingering on her gaunt face.

'By the skin of our teeth,' she said. But suddenly she looked past Ada and her eyes filled. 'I just don't know what's going to happen when . . . I can't ask Jem – not now . . .' But she stopped herself and turned away.

Gradually they got to know the yard. And the house – neither the best nor worst of these cramped, leaky places, where you could see the sky through chinks between the roof tiles. The yard was awash when it rained, pooling muck from the heaps of refuse and ash that built up at the far end. In the summer the stenches from the middens and clouds of fat flies were utterly disgusting, the sticky twists

43

of flypaper they dangled inside to trap them hanging black and heavy with them.

On good days, with the wind in the right direction, they caught whiffs of cocoa from the deliveries to Cadbury's at the nearby wharf. But mostly the smells were of smoke and the cocktail of chemicals from the industry all around them.

What made a yard were the neighbours.

Mrs Spragg was kind and sensible despite Mr Spragg, a man who seemed much older than his wife and who was mostly silent and morose and given to savage bursts of temper. The twins, Florrie and Dorrie, were identical as peas and still dressed the same even though they were in their fifties. They had each had a husband at one time and both had died within weeks of each other, which as May remarked, 'makes you wonder'. Though they were friendly in a distant way, they did not seem to need anyone but each other.

Nora O'Shea at number two was a shrill Irish shrew with a miserable runt of a husband. She took herself off to Mass every Sunday, forever seemed to be praying this novena or that saint's day and her greatest pleasure was sourly judging people and nosing into their business.

Sarah Connell, Nellie's mother, knew the O'Sheas of old. 'They moved over here with us when they knocked down the Froggary,' she told May, rolling her eyes. 'I could have done without her and that waster of a husband following us here. But God knows, it was a blessing we found a place to live at all.' This was followed by a sigh. 'This city ain't what it was, that it ain't.'

The old street, the Froggary, rough as rough, lined with damp, rotten little dwellings, had been home to many of the Irish who, like Sarah's husband Seamus, born somewhere amid a succession of fifteen children, had crossed the water looking for work and better fortune. The already dilapidated street had been knocked down to make way for the London and North Western Railway station, making hundreds homeless. So they felt lucky to be here in the yard in Summer Row, even though it was hardly a palace.

Ada always liked Sarah Connell. She was a scrawny, gentle woman, too gentle for a man like Seamus who was tough and blunt as a sledgehammer. He regularly hammered at his wife with his brawny fists and conjugal demands. Ada would hear him on at her through the wall and the bruises would be on her the next day. Unlike Mrs Spragg, who had been known to take a rolling pin to her husband, Sarah was too beaten down to fight back.

'Seamus wasn't always the way he is now,' Ada heard Mrs Spragg say to her mother. 'Handsome lad, he was – devoted to her . . . And he could sing like a dream.' She sighed. 'The mood doesn't seem to take him often now – it's a shame, that it is.'

But now and again Seamus Connell would indeed sing like a dream and laugh, too, so that the whole yard would join in. But being a vassal at work in a country that treated him with contempt, he had turned into a king and despot at home. And at home was a wife worn to a thread by child-bearing and carrying little coffins to the cemetery. A woman who had found consolation in the only way she could.

But the Fletchers had never known the Connells in younger, happier times.

'He's a thug and a bully, that one,' Mom said. 'Better to have no husband than one like that.'

As the weeks passed, Ada also realized just how in thrall Sarah Connell was to Liza Jenks.

Every time Liza came barging into the yard – and those visits became more frequent – Sarah's was the only sale she could guarantee. With a husband who knocked her about, seven tearaway kids and the worst house on the yard, she was ready pickings, even though the pennies which went on drink were fewer pennies to put food in her children's bellies. And Seamus, also a boozer, was pacified so long as he got fed himself.

But Sarah was a kind person, and when Seamus was out of the way, which was most of the time, she would come out on her better days and cant with the other women in the yard. After Liza Jenks had been, you didn't see Sarah for a while. She was a quiet drunk – she stayed swaying indoors and slept it off.

Even though she knew Nellie and the family better by the week, Ada never went into number four. The kids were always chased out to play in the yard or on the street. So she did not know how bad it was. Not until life changed. And she was going to have to get to know the house all too well.

It was a February evening of bitter cold and rain, the sky hanging low over Birmingham's soot-blackened buildings. Cartwheels splashed up filth-laden water from the roads, steam rose from the pelt of hard-worked horses, and their breath, in clouds, unfurled from their nostrils, rising in the sallow lamplight.

As Ada and Elsie hurried home with Nellie from their day's work at Tompkinson's, all around them could be heard the sounds of coughing, of men hawking phlegm into the running gutters. The clash of hooves mingled with the creak and clatter of carts over the road's slippery setts. Every so often into the cold air, warm, ale-laced breaths came gusting out of pubs along the street.

The girls' faces gleamed wan as moons against the dark of their clothing, the shawls wrapped tightly about their heads, skirt hems soaking up the wet and grime. They still had their shoes from the life 'before', though after two months working at Tompkinson's they pinched even more.

'My toes're burning,' Elsie sobbed, tears and rain running down her once rounded little cheeks. Her already large eyes looked even bigger in her hollow face. Inside the boots her poor toes were red and swollen with chilblains and she was hungry and exhausted, as she was every day now, after all the hours standing bent over a table, sorting and counting pearl buttons for carding.

'Never mind – nearly home!' Nellie tried to jolly her along. Nellie's clothes were barely more than rags. Her boots, hand-me-downs from her brothers and much too big, made her slop noisily along. But Nellie was hardened by knowing no other life, more used to all this than Ada and Elsie, and she could still be cheerful. 'Let's sing a song, shall we?'

'Tom, Tom the piper's son,' she began singing. Ada, worn out and heartsick herself, managed feebly to join in. But Elsie carried on blarting all the way along the dark entry and into court twelve.

As they crossed the yard, Ada made out the shape of a figure standing in their doorway, lit from inside by the faint glow of an oil lamp. But it was not her own mother waiting at their door – it was Nellie's, Sarah Connell.

'That you, Ada? Elsie?' Mrs Connell's high voice reached them. 'Nellie – you go in.' She gestured to her own door. 'See to your brothers.'

And Ada knew immediately from the hardness and panic in her voice that there was something wrong.

Sarah Connell pulled Ada and Elsie in through the door out of the rain. The sickly, metallic stink in the air turned Ada's stomach and the room, usually neat, was in disarray. She caught sight of a pail heaped with rags stained a dark colour, the edge of one dripping on to the floor. She knew by the smell and sight of it that it was blood.

In those seconds she also took in that there was a fire

burning in the range, that her brother and two other young sisters were huddled together on the rug: Dora with Mabs on her lap and John, in a stunned huddle, completely silent.

'Where's Mom?' Ada asked, a terrible feeling rising in her. Elsie's sobbing had quietened and she was gripping Ada's hand.

'You two little wenches're going to have to be brave.' Sarah Connell's voice only just held back the tears and she couldn't seem to look them in the eyes. She took Ada by the shoulders, her fingers digging in.

'Your mother's upstairs. She passed on – an hour ago. The baby – it were the finish of her. Of them both.'

Ada looked up at her, starting to feel that she was whirling around, a sick, dizzy feeling. The baby? What baby? Passed on? What did any of this mean? And the stench, the red rags in the pail . . . Lights began to flicker at the sides of her vision and a moment later blackness slammed down on her, shutting all of it out.

II

Eight

1857

'I can smell it on you. Lying to me again is it, you . . .'

As usual Seamus Connell reverted to the Irish language to spit out his worst insults as he stood teetering drunkenly over his wife, saliva spraying from his lips.

Sarah, her mouth already bleeding, cowered in the corner, arms up to try and defend herself as Ada had seen her do so many times. It sickened her with rage and disgust. Many was the time Ada had pulled the youngest boys to the opposite side of the room, her arms around them – especially Tom, her favourite – trying to make them feel safe.

'What kind of wife d'you call yourself? You're wed to that filthy liquor!'

This time, Ada and Nellie with Tom and the two little ones melted out into the yard. The babby, Anthony, another poor unfinished boy with a vacant look and the worst of the lot, had been born since Ada moved in with the Connells and he was three now. There was nothing any of them could do against their father's fists. William, who was fourteen now and out at work, had once, recently, tried to stand up to his father and protect his mother. Seamus knocked him across the room, out cold. His face was a mass of bruising for days.

Sarah's drinking had got worse every year. She'd be begging Liza for it now, even when she'd not got a farthing.

Seamus was a man hardened by life and a hardened boozer himself. A man who these days gave his wife nothing except grief, misery and too many children. And he was full of his right to lay down the law.

As Ada and Nellie went into the yard that Saturday afternoon, Mrs Spragg came out of her house carrying a pail with a cloth over the top. She looked across at them, hearing the carry-on from indoors, pulled her lips down in a grimace of sympathy, then made her way to the lavs, shaking her head.

Nellie's face tightened, seeing this pity towards her family, and a moment later she dashed across the yard.

'Come on, let's play tag – got you, Tom!'

Tom joined them in a frantic way, all of them children again, glad to distract themselves from what was going on indoors, the Connell children sick of being the shameful family of the neighbourhood. Ada took Petey's hand and they ran, giggling, away from Tom, who slowed down, pretending to give them a chance. Little Anthony stood watching, bewildered until Nellie scooped him up into her arms as she ran past.

'Here yer go – you can be on my team, Ant.'

It wasn't even a proper game, they just pelted around, chasing and tagging and all glad to laugh and be distracted. Petey was loving the attention and laughter, and Ada played along, pretending Tom was a monster they had to escape. They all ended up by the entry to the yard, panting and laughing, trying to make the game more than it was – anything except think about what was going on indoors.

Nellie fumbled in her pocket and produced a tuppenny bit.

'Hey, look what I've got – let's get us some rocks?'

The girls and Tom took the little ones along the road to a huckster's shop and they bought sherbet for Anthony and

Petey and a few toffees for the three of them. Ada relished the buttery taste of it as they made their way back to the yard, Tom walking ahead carrying Anthony, Petey beside him, all united for once, in sugary bliss and sunshine and ignoring the grown-ups.

'That was nice of you,' she said to Nellie. It was likely all Nellie had, held back from her wages – and she had shared it with all of them.

Nellie hooked her arm round Ada's shoulders.

'That's all right,' she said easily, through a mouth full of toffee. She gave a bright smile. 'We're sisters, ain't we?'

Despite these happy moments, Ada more often wanted to explode with rage and impatience at the Connells – at Sarah for her trapped passivity and weakness, at Seamus because he was a thug and a bully.

But they had given her a roof over her head for more than five years now and where else was she going to go?

After Mom died, and after Ada was left alone, Jem Atherton had come to the yard looking terrible.

'I'm sorry, Ada, for your trouble. But there's no more I can do – the wife's sick, like . . .'

And by then the Connells had taken Ada in. She never saw Jem after that. Nor her brother or any of her sisters.

She felt utter loathing towards Seamus Connell. Sometimes at night, she lay next to Nellie's scrawny figure, breathing in the vinegar fumes emanating from her. Nellie's dry, chapped lips were from supping on the vinegar that she was as stuck on as her mother was the drink. But Nellie was truly the nearest thing she had to a sister now and despite all her thieving ways, Nellie could laugh and be fun and they looked out for each other. She was not the object of Ada's rage. Ada sometimes dreamt of all the ways she might murder Seamus Connell. But if she hated him, there was one person she loathed more and that was Nora O'Shea.

Nora would even stoop to telling on a wife to her husband: how many times Liza Jenks had been round, Sarah being out of it all day only to drag herself up for when Seamus came home. Nora was a pious leech who fed off other people's misery and her own righteousness. Her spite and nosiness were all wrapped up in a package of religious sanctimony.

'That woman,' Nora would say, folding her arms across her bony chest, her lips puckered up as she jerked her head like a chicken towards the Connells' house. 'A disgrace, so she is. There's that poor husband of hers, him a hard-working man and her nothing more than a godless slattern, so she is.'

And Ada was certain it had been Nora O'Shea who sneaked on them to the parish when she and Elsie and the others were left alone. Because that was exactly the sort of thing Nora O'Shea would do.

That terrible afternoon, a day Ada would never be able to wipe from her memory – 15 February 1852. That dark, wet day, the iron stench, the pail of bloody rags and Mom gone.

Ada and Elsie were allowed to go upstairs and see her. Sarah kept the younger ones downstairs. They had already seen and heard enough that afternoon.

Ada led the way up the splintery curve of the staircase, Elsie a step behind, clasping her hand. Ada would never forget the desperate grip of that little hand. Elsie was silent now, her hunger and her burning toes overtaken by this much greater horror.

Whenever Ada thought back to that afternoon – and she tried not to, ever – that was the one thing she always remembered: the feel of Elsie's nails, digging into her palm.

Mom was on the bed, very still, her face like candle-wax and blank. She didn't even look like their mother any more.

'Mom?' Elsie's voice was a croak.

Still holding hands, the two of them went fearfully to the bed. Mom's arms lay limp and straight. Ada reached out to touch her hand, wanting reassurance, wanting her mother to get up suddenly, to smile and tell them everything was going to be all right. But Mom's hand was cool and stiff. Ada drew back as if she had been stung.

It was the worst moment of her life. Worse even than Pa going. Because now there was no shelter under the heavens. No Pa, no Mom. As what had happened sank in, she became numb with terror.

'What're we going to do?' she asked Sarah.

In those days, Sarah Connell was drinking, but not to the extent she did in later years. She was a sweet person, too sweet Ada thought sometimes. The sort of frightened gentleness that was always expecting violence and trying to avoid it. When Seamus was on at her with insults and fists, these days Ada wanted to take the poker to him, but Sarah never fought back – she always tried to appease him.

'Seamus, don't take on so. Look – here's your bit of dinner, you come and sit down . . . You'll feel better when you've got summat inside you.'

Back then Sarah could still think more clearly and she had a good heart.

'Don't you worry, little Ada,' she said. 'I'll keep an eye on yer – and you and Elsie are working now, you can keep paying the rent while we think what to do.'

But of course this could not last. The neighbours rallied round over their mother's funeral. Mrs Spragg was especially solid, her lined kindly face and threadbare black coat there beside them with Sarah Connell on that freezing morning in the cemetery. Even Jem Atherton and some of Pa's other workmates chipped in to give his wife a half-decent burial, despite the way Richie Fletcher had vanished on them.

Both Elsie and Dora caught a chill out there by the grave. Elsie was coughing and coughing and two days later she was too poorly to go to work, so Ada went by herself.

All that morning, cutting blanks at Tompkinson's, she fretted about her brother and sisters alone at home, with Dora and Elsie both poorly. Sarah had said she would look in, but you never knew with Sarah Connell and she had enough on her plate.

'I'm going home,' she told Nellie when the dinner bell went. 'I need to see how Elsie is.'

Elsie had a fever and had been tossing and turning all night beside her. Ada's own throat was on fire but she was not so sick that she couldn't work.

She knew deep in her veins that it was Nora O'Shea who betrayed her family. A woman who, as Mrs Spragg said, 'wouldn't give a blind man a light'.

As she ran into the yard that dinner time, Sarah Connell was at the door of their house once more, her back to Ada, arguing frantically with someone who was inside. Mrs Spragg was in the yard, as was Nora O'Shea, both staring at the house, their faces grim. Ada could hear a man's voice in the house, raised impatiently over the sound of crying. All of them – Elsie, Dora, John and Mabs – must have been blarting.

The moment Ada appeared in the yard, Mrs Spragg rushed forward and shouted, 'Sarah!' across the yard. She then went to Nora O'Shea and seemed to be ordering her furiously to clear off inside. Ada had never seen Mrs Spragg look so fierce.

Sarah Connell turned. She looked distraught and as soon as she clapped eyes on Ada she came tearing towards her.

'All right, bab, you go in and get your dinner . . .' She was talking very loudly and Ada couldn't make any sense of all this, but the next thing was, Sarah's bony fingers were digging into her shoulder and her lips came up close to Ada's ear.

'*You're one of mine*, all right? If they ask, you're Ada Connell.' She gave Ada a shove. 'Go on – into my house – you're home for your dinner.'

Before Ada had time to reply she saw a flint-faced woman coming out of her own house, dragging a screaming John by one hand and Dora by the other. Sarah pushed Ada in through her own front door.

Ada rushed to the window, a scream rising in her that she had to stifle. The bottom half was broken and boarded up and she couldn't see out. All she could do was swing the door open so she could peer out through the crack, her whole body howling at her to do something.

The woman dragged John and Dora who were both struggling and crying. Behind them a young man appeared, a big beard bushing out below a homburg hat. He carried a howling Mabs with one arm and was dragging Elsie with the other, coughing and so feverish she could barely stand. Dangling from one hand, clasped desperately tight, was her little rag doll, Lucy.

Ada could not bear it any longer. She ran round the door and out into the yard.

'No! Stop that – you can't! Don't take 'em! Where're you going?'

She felt herself grabbed by the waist, Sarah holding her in an iron grip.

The man barely glanced round but Sarah said, 'This is my daughter. They're all friends, you see – she's upset to see them go.'

Ada was so hysterical that afterwards she could barely re-member struggling and screaming. 'Who are they? Where're they going? Don't let them take them!'

'Shut it!' Sarah pulled her back to the house and grabbed her by the shoulders. 'D'you want to go to the workhouse an' all? 'Cause that's where they're taking them. And there's nowt we can do about it.'

Ada stopped struggling, her legs giving way under her. Sarah released her as she sank to the floor. The workhouse! That place of dread that Mom would have worked her fingers to the bone to avoid. The Archway of Tears that no one on this earth wanted to walk through and that Ada believed, at that moment, no one ever came out of. Elsie, sick and feverish, timid little Dora, and John, the mummy's boy. And Mabs, her lovely, big-eyed, chuckling little sister.

'But they can't! Why've they taken them?' Ada became dimly aware that two other sets of eyes were watching her – Sarah's two youngest boys, Tom who was five and sickly Peter who could hardly walk even though he was two, were watching, round-eyed and scared.

'Someone told them your ma died, that you're living on your own,' Sarah said quietly. 'You're orphans now. Too young to fend for yourselves and they won't let you stay on your own – and there's the rent . . .'

'Who told them?' Ada sobbed.

'I don't know,' Sarah said grimly. 'But I can guess.'

This could not be real. Could not. After a moment Ada looked up at Sarah Connell.

'But we'll get them out, won't we? I've *got* to get them back again. All of them!'

Nine

'All right, Gert?' Ada called out as she went to her work-place in the shop at Tompkinson's.

Gert smiled round with her usual sleepy amiability.

'I'm all right, Ada, ta.'

Gert always seemed to be all right whatever life threw at her. Since Ada started at the firm, Gert, who was now twenty-two, had married and birthed two sons, handed them over to her mother and come back to work much the same as ever, placid and never questioning her lot or anything else.

Ada smiled as she got ready to operate her machine. Gert was a relief after the constant carry-on in the Connells' house. And these days she was a relief after Nellie. She pushed down on the treadle to turn her lathe, the smile fading. The way Nellie was going, she was fast becoming someone Ada felt she did not know any more.

In the years Ada had worked at Tompkinson's she had never felt the need to move on anywhere else. If she changed jobs, she could either go to somewhere where she was covered in oil or metal dust all day, with no beautiful shells, or with her skills she could just go and work in another button factory, likely at the same wage, so what would be the point of that? She was used to it here – even liked it most of the time. And being at work was better than her life in the yard. She liked the other girls. And Gert – well, she was just Gert. And she had known her a long time now.

Mr Tompkinson was no better or worse than any other employer. And Mrs Rundle, the forewoman, was a sour-looking old puss but fair enough in her treatment so long as you got on with the job. Which was why Nellie was forever getting it in the neck, turning up in the state she was often in these days.

Ada had long got used to being powdered white with shell dust and washing herself off each time she got home. To having her nose burn inside and bleed, and to having coughs from breathing in the dust. All of them suffered with bad chests. It was part of the job, working in this industry, and it was a lot cleaner than many.

Since she was able and keen, Mrs Rundle had made sure she got a chance to learn the other button-making processes. After the blanks were cut there were lathes to 'back' them: shape them so they had a slight curve on the reverse side which made them easier to fasten. Backing was what Gert was on now.

Ada, standing next to her, was on turning. Her lathe had a 'form' or sharp cutting tool attached with which she could cut patterns into the button – a simple circle ground into the button's face, or several circles – and there was another tool for straight lines or tiny zigzags. Then they moved on to 'edging' – which could mean scallops or little nicks in a pattern round the edge.

After that the buttonholes were drilled and the buttons were polished – Nellie was further along the room on polishing – then sorted and finally sewn on to cards. A lot of the carding was sent to women outworkers doing the job at home.

Ada straightened up for a moment and looked along the dusty-white workshop. The summer light, the familiar people, many of whom she had worked with ever since she started there, the beauty of the shells – all of that was a comfort.

But there were also pangs of anguish if she allowed herself to dwell on things. At the far end, the table where once Elsie had stood counting buttons when she started work, such a tiny thing among the huddle of other young children.

For a moment the pain of loss rose in her, so raw and sharp that even after all this time, she gasped. Elsie. And Dora and John and Mabs. Elsie would be getting on for fourteen by now. Even Mabs would be nearly six. This seemed impossible. Would she even know any of them, if she saw them? It broke her heart to think she might walk past her brother or any of her sisters in the street and never know they were there.

She swallowed as tears flooded her eyes. She felt so powerless to know what to do. I once had a family, she thought. A whole family.

Her very first night in the Connells' house, after that terrible day, Sarah had told her to bed down with Nellie, on the floor close to the range. There were two small rooms upstairs: Seamus and Sarah Connell were in one with little Peter, who at two still seemed far more of a baby than he should have been, and the other was where the other five boys bedded down together.

There was only a bodged rug between the girls and the cold floor. Ada had brought her old eiderdown with her from the house and laid it over both of them. Nellie, whose covers were bits of frayed jute sacking, was thrilled to see this new, cosy item.

Ada lay on the hard floor that night in a bad state. Shocked, distraught. Hating everything about the place, the noise and brawling boys, the seeping smells all through the house: of urine, sweat and alien bodies, of the foul waste pail in the scullery, of the leftover stench of boiled fish.

Everything familiar, everyone she loved, had been snatched from her. It felt as if her life had ended. She lay curled up, cuddling the pale blue eiderdown to her, the last thing she had of home. She cried until her whole body felt emptied out. Nellie curled up next to her, trying to comfort her.

'Never mind, Adie,' she kept murmuring. 'Never mind.' There was nothing she could say.

Pa, Ada prayed in her head. I need you, come back. Please, *please* come back and help me . . .

All these years she had held on to the dream that Pa would just walk back in one day. Pa – the one who made her feel strong and daring. The father who had taken them all the way to London! She didn't feel even half as strong without him here, however hard she tried. And now the others were gone she had nothing and no one of her own. She clung to her prayer – Pa was out there somewhere. One day he was going to come back . . .

'No – my father's not dead,' she would tell people. 'He's gone to work in London.' Or, 'He's gone to Australia to make his fortune.'

She pictured him in a hot dry place, his strong hands lifting a nugget of shining gold, his dusty face creasing in delight, doing a little jig in his boots.

'I'm a rich man! Now I can go home to my family!'

Pa would strike his share of gold and come back rich as a king! Or maybe he had gone to America? She knew that whatever her father had in mind that night when he left, it would be daring and exciting; he would succeed and one day he would come back to her. Her pa, the father she remembered, would never have just left her for no good reason.

She tried not to dwell on all this most of the time. It felt too much to bear. She turned her face towards earning her living to keep a roof over her head and gave Sarah Connell nearly all her wages. She had nowhere else in the world to go.

But sometimes it all welled up.

Elsie and the others had been taken off to the work-house. That's what she was told.

'Where's the workhouse?' she sobbed to Mrs Spragg that day. If it hadn't been for Sarah Connell she knew she would have been taken there as well.

'Lichfield Road, ain't it?' Sarah Connell said.

'Not any more,' Mrs Spragg said, her own voice rough with tears. Ada could hear how upset this kindly woman was – what a terrible thing to see a family ripped apart. 'They put up a new one – out by the prison.'

'Can I go there?' she asked Mrs Spragg. Ada had only known these few streets. She had no idea where the prison was, or Lichfield Street or any of those places.

Olive Spragg leaned down and Ada saw the tired lines of her face close up. She put her arm round Ada's skinny shoulders and it felt nice.

'Even if you did, bab,' she said, 'it wouldn't do you any good, I promise you. It's better to try and put it out of your mind.'

In those years, Ada had progressed round the workroom at Tompkinson's so that she knew almost all the button-making processes except for sawing the shells because they reckoned to get a bloke to do that.

She went to work, came back to the yard and the Con-nells' house and now and then went into town to the Bull Ring with Nellie. That was her life.

But just once, she did go to the workhouse. One Sunday

morning, just two months after the others were taken. She couldn't settle. Elsie's terrible coughing, her feverish face and Dora and John's wracking sobs echoed in her mind. She should have saved them. Should have been able to do something.

Without a word to anyone she set off. She kept asking – is this the way to the workhouse? Pitying looks came back at her.

'What d'you want to go there for, missy?' a kindly man asked her. 'That's no place for you.' But he could see the desperation in her eyes.

'Just follow the Turnpike Road . . .' He pointed, smiling kindly.

Ada walked and walked. There was a chill wind which cut through her clothes but she crossed her arms, keeping her head down and hugging herself tight in her skimpy frock.

At last she saw a forbidding brick building looming in front of her. The place frightened her. Was that the prison, or the workhouse? An archway led through what looked like the main entrance and she could see more buildings behind, as if there was a whole town there all of its own. Distantly she could hear singing, as from a church.

She looked around for someone to ask and a woman was coming along carrying a baby. Ada's heart bucked. The woman wore her dark hair fastened loosely at the back, a grey dress and a shawl and she was a bit like . . . Mom. Ada's heart started banging. But as she drew close of course she wasn't the mother Ada had known. Her features melted into someone else's, a stranger's. Mom was in the cemetery. A lump rose in Ada's throat and her legs felt weak and shaky.

'Is that the workhouse?' she managed to ask.

The woman gave a harsh sort of laugh.

'What else would it be?' She stopped for a moment. 'See that entrance there? There's many go in through the Archway of Tears but not many that come out. You want to keep well away from there if you know what's good for you.'

She walked off, leaving Ada with a sinking feeling of despair. What if she did go in? Was anyone allowed? Would she find Elsie and the others in this huge, forbidding place? Would she ever get out again? The woman had really frightened her.

With no idea what to do she waited in the street, aching with longing. If she stood here long enough maybe she would catch a glimpse of one of them – enough to make her sure where they were. Just to see any of them would be something.

After a while the church noises stopped and she heard other sounds. People moving around, voices in the distance. But however much she peered in through the gate, she could not see anyone.

Finally the porter came out through the gatehouse. He was dressed in black with a little cap and did not look friendly. Ada backed away, afraid he was going to grab hold of her.

'What are you hanging about for?' he asked.

'Nothing!'

She turned and fled back the way she had come.

She went back to her life with the Connells. She helped Sarah Connell in any way she could.

Sarah had given birth to little Anthony while Ada lived with the family. Two more babies arrived without taking a breath, breaking Sarah's poor heart even further. And over the years Ada came to feel as if the boys were her brothers.

Tom, who had been five when Ada came to live with them, was a sweet boy with a head of dark wavy hair. And in a household without enough of anything to go round, Tom latched on to Ada straight away. He would come and sit beside her and lean his head on her shoulder. And sometimes at night he even crept downstairs and slipped in next to her in her bed on the floor, curling up like a puppy. She would wrap her arm round him and find comfort in cuddling him. He reminded her of when Piggly used to curl up beside her and she could fall asleep, warmed by knowing that at least somebody in this world really wanted her.

Ten

'He should have been drowned at birth, the little rat!'

The words frothed from Seamus Connell's lips after he had careered across the room and crashed into the wall by the door. For a moment he looked round in drunken bewilderment as if he did not know what had hit him.

He had tripped over little Anthony, the youngest boy, three now but looking much younger. Anthony's legs did not work as they should and he was still crawling about on the floor.

'Holy Mother, can you not keep that little bastard out of my way?'

'Oh, leave 'im alone,' Sarah murmured from the settle where she was sprawled. 'Poor little mite.'

Without sitting up she reached vaguely about with her hand as if to find her little boy and pat his head, but she was nowhere near and she sank back in defeat.

Ada hurried over to Anthony who sat snivelling after the blow his father's boot had dealt him. He sat looking up with terrified eyes. Ada lifted the urine-soaked little fellow out of the way. He had not learned to control himself yet and was constantly soiled and wet.

Anthony wasn't right, anyone could have seen that looking at him. And if they couldn't, Nora O'Shea would have filled them in.

'Brats of that drunken sot,' she'd say, looking in disgust at the boys when they were out in the yard. 'No wonder they're freaks of nature the way she goes on.'

If Ada had ever spoken to Nora O'Shea she would have had nothing but bile to pour out on her. But she never spoke to her at all. Never even looked at her if she could help it.

Each of Sarah Connell's recent children had come out worse than the last. Peter, the next one up to survive, was now eight, a sad, vacant child. Anthony was the worst, deaf as well, so that his father's rages burst upon him as an event for which he had not heard the warning signs, even though his widely spaced eyes searched constantly for hints of disaster. He was like a tiny lighthouse, forever circling on the alert for shipwrecks.

And Sarah's drinking just got worse by the year. Nellie's elder brothers had all left home the moment they could and hardly ever showed their faces.

'It's a tragedy what's happened to that family,' Mrs Spragg said to Ada one day when they were alone in the brew house. She gave a sad smile. 'Was a time Seamus used to come home singing. And there've been days they hardly had two farthings to rub together but they still got along happily enough then. It was losing her babbies that did it – terrible when they die like that. But 'er's never been as bad as now. I don't know where those boys would be without you, Ada.'

William, the oldest lad left in the house now his elder brothers had got out of there as fast as they could, was fourteen. He was a quiet, cowed boy, very scared of his father. Ada liked him well enough. There was no malice in him.

Apart from Nellie and the fact that she had nowhere else to go, it was the younger three lads who kept Ada with the Connells. Peter and Anthony were helpless but Anthony was sweet. They turned to her more than they did Nellie. She could comfort them and sometimes get comfort in return. They were the nearest thing she had to family. But of all of them she was fondest of Tom. Like a miracle in the middle of the Connell wreckage, he was a lively, amiable boy and he and Ada had supplied each other with missing affection for years now. Tom, at eleven, was at an age when he was active and ripe for adventures.

'Look what I found, Ade!' he had cried a few days ago. It was a Sunday afternoon and he had been playing out in the street. He opened his gently cupped hands and there, pulsating with fear, sat a young blackbird, brown, a female. 'It's hurt itself.'

Peter came up wanting to know what was going on and tried to grab it off him.

'Get off, Petey!' Ada pushed him away. 'It's poorly – don't go frightening the poor thing.'

Peter stared at her. Ada feared for him. What would become of this little boy? He had grown taller, but still nothing much seemed to go on in his head.

She and Tom spent the afternoon in the yard trying to look after the blackbird, which in the end took off by itself, whether recovered or choosing the safer option it was hard to say. But they did their best with drops of water and breadcrumbs, to make the bird feel better.

'I like animals,' Ada told Tom. 'They're better than us.' She told him about Piggly and had to stop herself crying.

Tom always came to her with his treasures or discoveries, a grin on his swarthy face, eyes gleaming with excitement. Who else was there to tell? His father was hardly ever there, let alone there and sober. And as for his mother . . . Ada was the one who would take notice and they became important to each other.

With Nellie, she never knew. Sometimes she was all over Ada. 'We're sisters, ain't we, Ada?' After all, Nellie didn't have any blood sisters – or other friends, very much. As kids they had played a lot together in the yard, in the street, turning hoops of rusty metal, skipping and jackstones. Giggling together.

Nellie could get the giggles and laugh and laugh, the way her father could in his best moments, until everyone around her joined in too.

But then Nellie would turn. Her thieving had got worse and somehow she had never been caught, though it had been a close-run thing a few times.

What happened yesterday had disgusted and horrified Ada. Nellie grew slyer by the year. The sharp-faced, nasty Nellie had come to dominate her personality and Ada often did not like her.

They were walking home together from Tompkinson's, shaking out their hair which was thick with dust as usual. They turned in to the end of the street, close to the wharf from where they could hear the clank of metal and sounds of shovelling as coal was unloaded from the joey boats, the day boats used for transporting cargoes on shorter runs, but with no cabins for living on.

'Ooh,' Ada said, sniffing the air. 'You can smell it today.'

The smells from the Cadbury brothers' factory were sometimes bitter – almost rank – and at other times sweet enough to make your mouth water, and today was one of those days. Ada felt saliva rush into her mouth. But Nellie did not answer. At that end of the street there was a series of narrow yard entries and she was looking about as if searching for something.

'Just ignore me then,' Ada said, trying to make a joke of it.

At that moment a girl of about seven came out of one of the corner huckster's shops further along. She wore a dark green dress, shoes on her feet and a tatty straw bonnet, and she was carrying a frayed little basket. As she drew near, Nellie slowed.

'Hello,' she said to the girl in sugary tones. Ada was startled. Nellie was smiling away as if she was her greatest friend and Ada had never seen the child before. How on earth did Nellie know her? But the girl was staring back bewildered.

Nellie bent down.

'Listen, sweetheart – I've got a job for you, and if you do it for me I'll give you a penny all to yourself, to buy some rocks, all right?'

The girl's eyes widened a moment at the prospect of sweets. Nellie was already straightening up and holding out her hand.

'Come on, deary – it won't take a moment.'

The little girl nodded, seeming pleased at being singled out. As Nellie took her hand and led her into the nearest dark entry, she hissed in Ada's ear, 'You keep lookout, OK?'

Puzzled, Ada waited in the street. A few moments later Nellie came running out of the entry and gave Ada a shove.

'Move! Come on – quick!' Her hands were busy, rolling a bundle. 'Act natural.'

Ada was sure she heard the girl's wails of distress coming from the entry and to her horror, she recognized the green of the little girl's frock: Nellie was wrapping it round what seemed to be her shoes and bonnet, and the contents of the little girl's basket.

'Nell, what' the hell're you doing?' She stopped, appalled, but Nellie, now with the bundle under one arm, grabbed her with the other and hauled her along the street.

'I said act natural!' she snapped.

'What've you gone and done – did you rob those off that girl?'

'What if I did?' Nellie said.

Her face was nasty. Hard and sharp.

'That's horrible, Nell – and cruel of you. And I bet you never gave her a penny neither.'

Nellie laughed nastily. 'No more did I. What d'yer take me for? Now –' she swerved towards a narrow street – 'to the pop shop with these.'

Ada knew the dingy pawnshop she was heading for. And she knew exactly what Nellie was going to do with the money from the little girl's things. Nellie's vinegar habit had turned into an appetite for a stronger brew.

'You're vile, Nellie.' Ada's temper erupted. 'You're nothing but mean and nasty these days. Don't expect me to come with you. You're getting worse than your flaming mother!'

It was a rare thing for Ada ever to criticize Sarah Connell who had, after all, saved her from the workhouse and given her, if not the kind of home you would yearn for, at least a place to lay her head for all these years.

Sarah's state now filled her with pity and disgust. She could hardly walk, dragging a leg as she did so. She was vague, unable to remember things, and her speech was often slurred even when she had not had a drink for hours. It was terrible to see – and all her lads neglected. If it was not for Ada and Nellie slaving to keep the place as best they could when they weren't at work, everything would have gone to wrack and ruin by now.

But Nellie's vinegar habit, which continued when she could not get anything stronger, had progressed to Liza Jenks's hooch.

Liza Jenks had grown even more vast over the years. If you ever saw her in the street she loomed before you in her tent of a black dress, her round face resting on several chins and her hair still yanked back into plaited doorknobs over her ears. But Liza hardly ever did come out now. It was an effort for her to move and she scarcely needed to. Nellie and Sarah and her other desperate hangers-on went to seek her out. Apart from brewing her vile concoction, Liza scarcely had to move a muscle.

And after that horrible thing Nellie had done to the little girl, Ada had already known that she would shortly be home, already inebriated and rolling into the house in a state which meant Ada would have to do all the work. Again.

Ada felt tears of rage and desperation rise in her as she stormed back along Summer Row to the yard. What had become of her? She had lost everything, even including herself. Here she was, the lad, the 'man of the house' – the strong one ripe for adventures, stuck in this filthy hovel of drunkards. And having to take on Nellie's brothers for want of anyone else showing them more than a passing kindness.

But she had nothing – except for the job at Tompkinson's and the loveliness of the shells. All these years she had carried her favourite trochus shell in her pocket, close to her like a charm. Apart from that she had nothing in this world. And nowhere to go.

The one person she had known from their life before, Pa's friend Jem Atherton, had come to check on her a few times after Ada's mother died. But it had been years now since she had seen him.

As she made her way furiously across the yard, she took a vow. One day I'm going to be free. I'm going to do better than them – than all of them. And I'm going to stay free all my life. I'm never being bossed or pushed around by anyone – and I'm never, *ever* going to get married.

Eleven

It was the evening of a stifling summer day. Not a breath of air seemed to enter the house, even though they kept the door open on to the yard and the flies came and went as they pleased. The flypaper was thick with them and the stench of the earth privies was overpowering. But it was too hot to shut the door. Too hot for anything.

The light was dying gradually but the night gave no relief. The younger boys were upstairs but they were noisy, thumping and fighting, too hot to settle.

The only other person downstairs apart from Sarah and Ada was William, the quiet one, who was knotting and untangling a length of tufty string again and again, obsessed with perfecting knots.

Sarah sat bent forward, tense and restless. While Seamus was out, which was most of the time, she had no need to disguise her desperation for the drink she so depended on.

'Where's our Nell?' she kept asking. 'Where's 'er got to?'

Well, it won't be the Ragged School, Ada thought sarcastically. She herself had gone a few times to one of the schools set up to help young children with their reading and writing, evenings and mornings at the weekend. But it was hard to keep it up. She was already dropping with tiredness in the evenings after a day at the works. And there was too much to be done in the house.

'I want her to go down the road for me,' Sarah whined. She swayed in her chair, desperate. 'Oh, where *is* the wench?'

Ada suddenly found Sarah looking intently at her.

Ada looked away, pretending she had not seen. There was a lot she would do even now for Sarah Connell – except go to that evil piece of work Liza Jenks and plead for booze. To avoid any questions she got up and went out to the privy, holding her breath as much as she could in the cobwebby gloom while she was relieving herself.

When she went back, Sarah was gone.

'Will, where is she?' Ada demanded.

William shrugged without even looking up.

'Why didn't you stop her? She's in no state . . .'

There was a thump and a cry from upstairs and Ada started to lose her temper.

'Go and see what they're doing.' She shoved Will's shoulder. Time for him to do something, the dozy sod, she thought. 'Go on! I'll go and see where's she's got to.'

As if she didn't know.

She hurried out into the glow of the sun's dying rays, along the gloom of the entry and into the street. Squinting ahead she could see no sign of Sarah. She would have been able to pick her out in a crowd with her dragging limp. Ada hurried along, looking this way and that, her blouse sticking to her back with sweat.

She knew roughly where Liza Jenks's place was, near to the wharf, in a yard off Edmund Street, though until now she had refused ever to go there. She wasn't going begging to Fat Liza. Not for anything.

She hurried as best she could. Everything was stinking more in the heat. The mud in the gutters was dry and cracked. Loud voices came from watering holes and gaggles of jostling men spilled out of them into the street. She crossed over to avoid an especially rowdy one where a fight was breaking out.

By the time she got to the end of Edmund Street she

caught sight of a familiar movement ahead. Sarah's thin figure was hurrying along with her one leg dragging, supporting herself against the wall of a warehouse as she went along. And despite her difficulties Sarah moved with surprising speed.

She can get along when she wants her booze all right, Ada thought grimly. But she knew really that she was not angry with Sarah. She had followed because she was worried about her. Sarah was so frail and unsteady on her feet. So heartbroken, deep down. Despite everything, Ada loved her and didn't want anything bad to happen to her.

A moment later, Sarah disappeared. Hurrying to where she had last seen her, Ada realized Sarah had slipped along an entry. She followed through the gloom, emerging into a wider yard than the one they lived in, to see Sarah heading to one of the houses on the far side. Now she could hear her sobbing breaths of desperation.

She was too late to stop Sarah knocking on the door, so she waited at the end of the entry. Sarah leaned on the wall, head drooping. Any moment now Liza Jenks's face would appear like the full moon at the door. Ada's stomach turned with disgust, waiting for Liza's booming voice – 'Ooh, look who's back again, can't keep away, can yer?' – taunting her because she knew her power over Sarah and all the desperate women like her who she had pressured into dependency.

Again Sarah knocked, louder this time. She let go of the wall and straightened up, agitated.

'No!' Ada heard her cry. 'You can't be out, you beast. Where are you? Open up!'

She hammered again with both hands. A woman put her head out from the door of another house to see what was going on, but seeing someone at Liza's house she rolled her eyes and went smartly back inside.

When there was still no answer, Sarah leaned against the door as if giving up in despair. She almost toppled into the house when the door swung open and clung on to it to stop herself falling. As she righted herself, Ada heard her say, 'Liza?'

Sarah tiptoed inside and disappeared. A moment later screams came from the house that chilled Ada's blood.

She could never remember getting across to that door. She was standing in Liza Jenks's downstairs room. That was all she ever could recall. Taking in the sight that Sarah had come upon, making her cry out and sob, her hands clasped to her face.

An oil lamp was burning on the floor beside the range. In the dim light, Liza's huge form could be seen sitting in her chair, resting, it would seem, at first glance. Until Ada took in the strange angle of her head, the silent stillness like none ever seen before in Liza Jenks. The long gape along the side of her neck, the dark stain down the front of her. And the metallic familiar stench of spilt blood.

Liza Jenks's eyes stared upwards, her expression still pugnacious, as if frozen in accusing the person who had slashed her throat from end to end.

And in the flurry that happened next, the neighbours, the horrified talk, someone running for a policeman, Ada saw Sarah recover herself enough to sidle across the room. On the sideboard was an array of little medicine bottles which Sarah grabbed with both hands, cramming as many as she could into her pockets.

'Where the hell've you been?'

Nellie came rolling in later after Ada had got Sarah home, pockets clinking, both of them in shock. Both agreed that they would not shed a tear over Liza Jenks, but even so, Ada could not escape the smell of blood, as if her nose and memory had been lined with it. The horror was still fresh on both of them.

'Out,' Nellie replied with a drunkard's amiability. Unlike Sarah, who only drank at home, Nellie was now hooked on the life of the public houses. 'Where d'you think?' She grabbed the edge of the table. 'What's up with you two?'

'It's Liza Jenks,' Sarah managed. She'd had a good go at the bottles she'd taken from Liza's as well.

'Liza Jenks?' Nellie laughed. 'What about her?'

'Found her with her throat slit like a pig,' Ada said brutally. 'And I was here looking after your mother while you were out filling your neck.'

Nellie sobered up a fraction and had the grace to look shocked.

'What d'yer mean?' she gaped. 'Someone's done the old witch in?'

Seeing the answer in Ada's eyes, Nellie started laughing, so much that she had to collapse on the chair and was cackling her head off when Seamus Connell walked in.

'What in God's name's up with you?' he demanded, looking round at the womenfolk of the house.

'Someone's done for Liza Jenks!' Nellie proclaimed, still laughing drunkenly.

Seamus's bleary blue eyes stared at her as he took this in.

'Well, the Lord be praised.' He jerked his head at Nellie to order her off his chair and sank on to it, sticking his legs out for Nellie to pull off his boots. 'Give us a hand, wench.'

A moment after Nellie had hauled off his second boot, nearly falling over backwards doing it, Seamus was fast asleep.

'Never mind, Mom.' Nellie went over to Sarah who was on the settle, pale and haunted-looking. 'I'll bring you your poison from the outdoor.'

Twelve

'Someone must've come creeping up behind her, with a great big sharp knife . . . Ooh – can you imagine?'

Gert shuddered all over – while relishing every detail. In fact Ada had never seen her look so animated. She was full of the murder, wanted every scrap of information. The girls at the button works were avid to know all about it and Ada was quite the centre of attention the next day. Nellie tried to muscle in on it but didn't get far.

'Shurrup, Nell, we want to hear Ada,' Gert said. 'You weren't even there.'

'Where were you then, eh, Nell?' one of the other girls asked, sarcastically.

Nellie's drinking was becoming well known and more and more of the menfolk had reported seeing her about the pubs and not always behaving herself. She was becoming harder, sourer, and it did not make her popular.

Nellie made a 'mind your own business' face and started treadling busily, bent over her lathe.

'So ain't they arrested anyone?' Gert persisted to Ada as they started up their machines.

Mrs Rundle came in then, so they all had to be quiet, but Ada shook her head. 'Not so far.'

'Fancy. All that blood! Mind you, she sounded like a right one.' Gert made a face and the two of them laughed, heads down so as not to provoke Mrs Rundle.

A little later, once their forewoman had gone safely past, Gert turned to Ada.

'Hey, you don't think they'll think it was 'er did it? Ma Connell?'

'No!' Ada stopped treadling, a chill going through her blood. 'Course it weren't us. We went in and there she was, just sitting in the dark . . .' It was her turn to shudder at the memory.

Gert shook her head.

'The neighbours must've seen you though. So maybe they saw who done it?'

Ada stared at Gert. She hadn't seen this side of her before – alert and sharp. It was almost as if she wanted Ada and Sarah arrested just for her amusement.

'Stop your clacking, Gert,' she said crossly. 'Course it weren't us.'

However desperate she might have been, the thought of gentle Sarah Connell murdering anyone was ridiculous. Ada had been right behind her when they went to the house that afternoon anyway.

She spent all morning turning it over in her mind. Had anyone been out in Liza Jenks's yard when they went in? That woman had looked across at them, did she see who they were? Might she have thought . . .?

Ada told herself not to be so stupid. Of course they hadn't done it . . . But the thought shook her up terribly.

They came that evening. Ada was boiling potatoes and frying rashers of bacon over the fire to feed the hungry boys. Nellie, as usual, was not in and Sarah was drowsing off the effects of the remainder of the bottles she had taken from Liza Jenks's house.

They thundered on the door.

'Police – open up!'

'For the love of God, it's not locked.' Seamus levered

himself out of his chair, not seeming to take in who it was stepping into his house.

Two policemen ducked through the door, pulling their helmets off and holding them. They looked enormous to Ada in the cramped little room. One had a black, bushy beard. Ada saw their faces crease in disgust at the smell of the place, little Anthony on the floor staring up at them and the rest of them all crowded in.

'Mrs Sarah Connell?' the beard boomed in a loud baritone. 'You're under arrest.'

This was the moment that, in Ada's memory afterwards, was all eyes. The little boys, staring, bewildered. Seamus, not yet reaching anger, intimidated by these huge men, his face and watery eyes full of bewilderment. Sarah sitting up, cloudy and stunned.

'What in hell's name . . .?' Seamus started to say.

'You're under arrest,' said the other policeman, nondescript but for a rough scar Ada could see worming down his left cheek, 'for the murder of Mrs Liza Jenks.'

The bearded policeman fixed Sarah with an iron look as the other man dragged her to her feet.

'You were seen leaving the house . . .'

'No . . .' Sarah tried to struggle, weak and fuddled by drink. She looked overpowered and terrified.

Ada found herself shouting out before she even knew it.

'No!' she cried. 'We never touched her! I was with her – we went in and found her, covered in blood. It wasn't us – we never – she was already dead! Whoever it was they were there before us . . .'

'Yeah, course they were . . .' The scar-faced one said sarcastically. There was a click as they fastened Sarah's hands into handcuffs behind her back, already dragging her away.

Only then did she seem to come to, struggling, tossing her head about with her long, unkempt hair.

'No! Let me go – you can't take me – I never did it – she was covered in blood – it weren't me . . . My boys, what about my boys . . .!'

They hauled her screeching to the door while Seamus cursed and tried uselessly to stop them. As Sarah disappeared outside, flanked by the dark wall of the two men, all they heard was a terrible, anguished cry which cut right through to Ada's heart: 'Noo-o-o-o-!'

Ada was cuddling Peter and Anthony, two terrified little boys. Neither of them understood what had happened. Tom came and stood close to her, his hand on her arm as if he needed to grasp hold of something sure, while William, never a boy of many words, sat quiet as if someone had punched him. Their father paced up and down, helpless and distraught.

'Where will they take her? My wife – they can't take my wife. My Sarah – the Lord knows she'd not hurt a fly . . .'

On and on he went and eventually, to Ada's astonishment, he flung himself in his chair and burst into distraught weeping.

'This cursed country'll be the death of me, so it will . . . Sarah, my Sarah, come back to me, my girl . . .'

The words spun in Ada's head. This man, who she had scarcely ever seen show the least sign of affection to his wife, now weeping like a baby. And the sight of him made her cry as well, tears rolling silently down her cheeks as she held the sobbing boys.

The door opened again and in came Nellie, very well oiled and with a silly smile on her face until she came upon the scene inside. She stared at her father, bent forward, head in his hands and his shoulders heaving, at Ada, at her distraught brothers.

'What's going on? Where's Mom?'

'They arrested her,' Ada said. 'Two Peelers came – took her for Liza Jenks's murder.'

Her own emotion welled up then, the fear and awfulness at what had happened, and she really burst into tears.

'She never did anything, I know she didn't – but someone must've seen us go in there and thought she was the one.'

Nellie's legs seemed about to give way. She sank down on the floor beside Seamus.

'It'll be all right, Pa. Mom never did anything.'

For a second Ada thought he was going to accept her comfort, but he suddenly erupted to his feet.

'All right, is it you're saying? How can it ever be all right – and you going the same way, sodden as a rat, look at the condition of you.'

Nellie scrambled to her feet, inflamed with rage.

'This is your fault – yours!' she yelled. 'You're the one reduced her to this with your drinking and your bullying. You're the one they should have arrested, you thick navvy . . .'

The next thing was, Seamus raised his fist and knocked Nellie across the room before storming out of the house.

'Yeah – we all know where you're going!' she screamed after him, still sprawled on the floor.

William leapt to his feet, his face tight with emotion.

'I'll go after him,' he said, and hurried out.

Nellie picked herself up slowly, nursing her cheek where he had hit her. She sat on the floor, drew her knees up and sobbed.

Ada cuddled little Anthony and looked round the room, weighed down by total despair.

This family: the four younger boys, two of them hardly capable of wiping their own backsides, Nellie in the state she was in, the parents gone . . . She owed the family a roof over her head all these years, but dear God, what was going to become of them all?

Nellie crawled over and rested her head against Ada's knee and Ada's sense of hopelessness deepened. Nellie really did seem to be turning into her mother.

'Oh, Ada,' Nellie mumbled. Ada could hear she had had an awful lot to drink. 'You're my best friend . . . I don't know what I'd do without you.'

Ada reached down for a moment to stroke Nellie's head and she started sobbing again.

'What're we going to do, Ade? I dunno what to do . . .'

But then she reared up suddenly, her face distorted with terror. 'Lord above – if they say she did it, she'll hang!'

The words cut through Ada and her bones seemed turned to ice.

Nellie got up and started pacing just as her father had done, utterly distraught. 'What'll we do? Whatever can we do?'

'I told them she never did anything,' Ada said. 'I was there – I saw, but they wouldn't listen.'

But she was starting to feel crazed doubts about all of it. Had Sarah had time to finish off Liza Jenks – or had she gone there earlier and then returned to the scene of her crime to make it look as if she was innocent?

Nellie came over and started tugging on her arm,.

'You've gotta tell 'em, Ade. Go now – go to the police station. You've got to save our mom from the hangman!'

Thirteen

'So you were present, with the accused on the evening of the murder?'

Ada stood in the awe-inspiring chamber of the Warwick Assize Court in her grey Sunday dress and hat, trembling so much that her legs would hardly hold her as the red-faced man in the wig fired questions at her.

She could not bear to meet Sarah Connell's pleading gaze. Sarah sat in the dock, bone thin and white as a sheet. She wouldn't have access to her chosen poison in the prison, Ada knew. She looked as if she was suffering in every way and it made Ada want to weep. For all her faults, Sarah was the nearest person she had had to a mother in all these years. As for Seamus, having to sit listening to this, he was a broken man. Nellie, beside him, the only other family member present, clung to his arm, her face white and taut. He had come to Ada that morning, in his musty Sunday best, bashful and nervous.

'Do I look all right, Ada? Respectable enough?'

His blue eyes looked into hers. He had shaved and brushed his hair and for once she saw a smart, handsome man, bashful as a boy. It wrung her heart.

'You do,' she said.

Seamus nodded, gave a little grunt and turned away. 'Ta. Thanks very much.'

Now they were in court, Ada felt as if her chest was going to explode, she was so frightened. But she tried to speak calmly. She was the only person who stood between Sarah and a long spell in prison – or even the rope. No one else had been arrested for Liza Jenks's murder.

'Yes, sir. I was.'

'They'll have put her in the lock-up at Moor Street,' Mrs Spragg told Ada the morning after Sarah was taken away.

They had all wasted the night in lying down since no one except the youngest boys could sleep. Ada's mind was jagged with desperate thoughts and even if she ever got close to sleep, Nellie would suddenly start up, gasping in horror.

'She'll hang for this – I know she will!' she kept saying, hugging her knees and rocking in anguish.

Mrs Spragg laid a hand on Ada's shoulder.

'You've been good to them, the way you look after those boys,' she said. 'It's a terrible thing you all having this trouble – over *her* of all people.' She shuddered. Ada knew she meant Liza Jenks. 'By all accounts it was a savage business. Wicked, that's what it is.'

Ada nodded, the hideous memory of that night and the sights and smells that met them in the gloom of Liza's downstairs room coming back to her and turning her stomach.

Mrs Spragg had loathed Liza Jenks, Ada knew. For a crazed second she wondered if it had been Mrs Spragg who had finished Liza off, before telling herself not to be so ridiculous. This was the trouble – there was an endless number of people who would likely have relished Liza getting her comeuppance.

'Moor Street? Ada said, hurrying away. 'I'll go down there now.'

Mrs Rundle would know soon enough why neither she nor Nellie were at work that morning.

'We know Sarah'd never've done that,' Mrs Spragg called after her. 'Whatever they say.'

She had to explain to the court about Liza and why they had gone to her house, and all of it sounded so bad she could hardly get the words out. Even the truth painted a picture of Sarah as a desperate drunk. And the man in the wig seemed in a great hurry to get everything over and done with.

'So,' he interrupted. 'Mrs Jenks traded in inebriating drink – of her own devising?' The man spoke with distaste. 'To individuals such as Mrs Connell?'

The way he said it made it sound as if Liza was the one who was respectable. Ada began to feel her blood boiling.

'Mrs Jenks –' she struggled for words – 'used to sort of force people. To buy her hooch . . .'

'Force them?' The man almost laughed, disbelieving. 'How so?'

Ada hardly knew how to explain.

'Well, she'd come to the door first with a sample – kindly, like. No charge. Then she'd be back, charging them a time or two and after that they'd be on her list and if they didn't pay up . . .'

How to explain? That it was Liza Jenks herself, just *her*, that bulky, bullying figure in the doorway. And the need it answered to women crushed to the bone by life and child-bearing and poverty.

'She kept coming. She was threatening and people couldn't stand up to her . . .'

He held a hand up. 'Just answer my questions, please. I didn't ask for a speech. Did you imbibe the er, "hooch" that Mrs Jenks was peddling?'

'No. Never.'

'You did not share Mrs Connell's dependency on this trade?'

'No.'

'Or, therefore, her motives for the resentment, loathing even, that was apparently felt towards Mrs Jenks?'

'No, sir.'

'Indeed, Mrs Jenks's neighbours have said they had never seen you before. Unlike Mrs Connell who was a familiar figure to them.'

Ada looked down, her face flushing. It felt as if anything she did – either speak or keep quiet – could make things worse for Sarah.

'And what did you find when you entered Mrs Jenks's house?'

'We found her dead. Covered in blood.'

He stopped for a moment and stared at Ada, at Sarah, then back.

'Both of you hated Mrs Jenks.'

Ada felt as if she had walked into a trap. She hesitated. Then, desperate for him to understand her, she looked directly into the man's eyes.

'There's dozens might've wanted to do her in, sir. She was a bully. And she got people so they couldn't help themselves.'

'That's not what I asked. You, and Mrs Connell, both had reason to hate this woman. So one evening you decided to go and teach her a lesson – a lesson which went too far . . .'

'No.' Ada's voice rose, even though she was trying to stay calm. She felt tears of desperation rising in her. How could she make him believe her? 'That's not what happened. She was dead when we found her.'

Ada could feel Sarah's gaze piercing through her.

'You strongly disliked Mrs Jenks. But it was Mrs Connell who conceived the plan – to go to her house, to rob and murder her . . . And you were seen, both of you, leaving the yard after the event—'

'No!' Seamus, unable to bear any more, leapt to his feet. 'That's a lie! My wife could never harm a living soul!'

'Quiet!' the man in the wig commanded. Seamus sank, shaking, into his seat, cap between his hands.

Ada heard Sarah sobbing softly from across the room.

'We didn't like her,' Ada managed. 'No one did. But that weren't why we went. Mrs Connell went to get some drink – and I followed after because she wasn't well and I was worried about her walking so far.'

Ada could not control herself any longer and she burst into desperate weeping, speaking between her sobs.

'We were there – that's true. We went into her house – but we didn't do anything to her. We could smell her even before we saw . . . Someone else had been there before us . . .'

She stared imploringly into the man's hard eyes.

'There's nothing else I can tell you. That's the truth.'

It was the truth. And yet soon after, they sat like stones as the jury pronounced Sarah guilty. The judge began his summing-up, saying that in his judgement, Sarah Connell had had sufficient motive for the murder of Mrs Liza Jenks. That she had been seen at the scene of the murder and her protestations of innocence were all lies covering a greater and mortal guilt.

Ada felt her legs turn to water as the judge solemnly picked up the black square of cloth which had lain unseen on the bench beside him and rested it on top of his wig. The words swirled round in her mind, impossible to take in.

'. . . find you guilty of the murder . . . shall be taken from here to a place where you will be hanged by the neck until you are dead. And may God have mercy on your soul.'

Seamus leapt up, giving a great howl like an injured animal. He tried to go to his wife who had her head in her hands.

'No! Sarah! You can't . . . She's my wife . . . Sarah!'

Two men dragged him from the court and Nellie ran after him. Sarah was being hauled out as well, since she could scarcely stand.

Ada sat stunned as the judge stood up, pressing the end of his pen on to the bench to break the nib which gave with a snapping sound. Then, briskly, he left the court. Ada had to remind herself to get up, to move her legs, and she walked, dazed, out into the Warwick street to find the others. There was no sign of them, but she knew immediately that they would have gone to find the nearest pub to try to drown their pain.

She could not think straight. Ignoring everyone else who was coming out of the court, she leaned against the wall, head down as the stress and chill horror of what had happened flooded through her. She and Nellie would have to go home and tell the boys that their mother . . . It was too terrible even to imagine.

Rage surged in her. Nothing, nothing in this world was fair or right. Her own family all separated without a moment's mercy. An innocent woman sent to prison. Sarah's family – all those boys . . . There was no one to turn to, to set right the wrong. These men, that judge looking down his nose at her. They were supposed to be the ones who knew things – and they were all wrong. Thinking they had the right to separate people and ruin their lives without a by-your-leave. How could anyone call this justice?

She wanted to shout and rave. I was there – I know what happened! Why won't you believe me?

At that moment she was the one who felt like taking a knife and dragging it across that judge's throat.

Fourteen

Three Sundays and the weeks they spanned between were all they had. Three Sundays had to pass to allow for Sarah to appeal against the sentence and then they would hang her. None of them had any idea what to do. And in the meantime life had to go on, work had to be done . . .

'Where is she? Where's Nellie?'

Ada jumped, suddenly realizing the forewoman was standing over her as she was about to start work at Tompkinson's.

'I don't know, Mrs Rundle,' she admitted, picking up a button and fixing it into the lathe. Her mind raced, trying to find the right thing to say. Nellie had gone out the night before and was still not home when Ada left for the works. Ada could not bring herself to blame her. Everything was terrible at home. Seamus beside himself, the boys weeping, all of them, even though the youngest had no real understanding of what was going on. The thoughts of Sarah in the condemned cell. The horror and terror which kept them all from sleep.

'She went out early – I thought she was coming in,' Ada said. ' But I don't know where she went.'

'I've made allowances for her,' Mrs Rundle said, the expression on her thin face seeming in conflict between sorrow and annoyance. 'It's shocking, what's happened. But all the more reason to keep another wage coming in, I'd've thought. I've warned her. She can't keep going on like this.'

Ada couldn't argue. Mrs Rundle, in her stiff way, had

been kind to both of them after the shock news of the verdict on Sarah. Everyone knew and all the neighbours were canting about their business, ready to believe the worst.

Gert rolled her eyes at Ada as Mrs Rundle walked away.

'It's a shocking do,' she said. 'But they'll let her go if 'er goes on.'

'I know,' Ada shrugged. 'But she takes no notice of me.'

It was a nightmare that never ended.

Seamus and Nellie were allowed to visit Sarah. Deprived of her usual alcoholic diet and sitting alone in the condemned cell, playing over and over the fate that was awaiting her, Sarah was more than half out of her mind. This much Ada heard from Seamus. Nellie could not even talk about it.

Seamus paced up and down in the house, raging and weeping.

'What can I do? The state of her, all alone in there – I don't know what to do.'

Neither Ada nor William or Tom knew what to do either and it was an agony to watch.

Every night Nellie went out and returned very late, weaving drunk, long after Ada had lain down. And Ada herself could not sleep. In the day she was easily kept busy, her job, holding together the household of distressed males and Nellie. But at night her mind played it over and over again. She did not know exactly what happened in a gaol but she had heard about hangings. Imagined herself walking out to a high gibbet, the roar of crowds. She could almost feel the rope about her neck. She would jerk out of a half-slumber, gasping in horror.

Meanwhile, during these days of dread, life somehow had to go on.

Sarah Connell was clueless at domestic life – not like

Ada's mother whose own mother in her turn had taught her well. And Sarah, ground down and overwhelmed, had fallen into bad habits. But she was a kind, loving mother when she was sober enough to pay her children attention. And she was always there, like a stick of furniture that sits in the same place.

Her absence felt worse than if she had died. It was unjust and wrong. It left a gaping hole in the house because she was still the one person who had made it a home. But it also filled all but the youngest of them not just with grief, but with a burning sense of injustice.

Peter and Anthony barely took in what had happened. Especially Anthony who could hardly understand anything. Ada tried to comfort them the best she could, but just looking at them made her despair. What was going to happen to these sad little boys? It would be a miracle if Anthony, with his odd little face and big eyes, would ever be able to do any sort of job. Peter was a bit better but he had started wetting the bed again, just adding to the work and washing and stench in the house.

And their bereft, angry older brothers were not much better – the ones who had already left home, who came round enraged and bitter, trying to make sense of what had happened. William, the oldest at home, had a factory job to which he went, tight-lipped, every morning.

Tom, who Ada loved the most, was now eleven and rode the milkman's cart with the churns, helping with deliveries. He was a dark-haired, handsome boy in a cap, loud and cheeky in the daytime, putting on the swagger, trying to look older than he was. But Ada knew about the little lad who sobbed himself to sleep at night and needed her to put her arms around him.

The night after Sarah was sentenced, she took Tom on her lap and held him tight, his head pressed against her chest while he hid his face and pretended he wasn't crying. In later days she could see he longed to be cuddled again but was too proud to be seen being a baby like that, even if his heart was breaking, like all of them. In the evenings, though, he would often come and stand by her, put a hand on her arm as if he was testing that she was really there.

'What's to eat?' Seamus demanded as he did every night, always taking for granted that there would be food ready to be put on the table.

Ada sometimes thought that if he walked in and there was not a soul in the room he would still ask the same question of thin air. At least Sarah had managed that – there would have been hell to pay if she hadn't.

Ada was frying mutton chops over the fire and he came and looked over her shoulder. He was so close she was wrapped in the heat of him, this rough, powerful man, stinking of sweat and stout. Seamus nodded approval.

'Hope there's bread aplenty to go with it?'

'Yes,' she said, shifting herself to get further from him.

Seamus gave a grunt before moving away again. But he turned, suddenly.

'You're a good wench, Ada.'

She looked back at him again, into those frank blue eyes, something she hardly ever did. And the lost look of need in them startled her, made her realize how a woman might fall for a man like him. A man who had once been young, capable of happiness and could sing like a dream.

She gave a nod and turned back to the pan.

'Herself not here?'

Ada shook her head. Nellie scarcely ever was here. Most of the work fell to her and she was permanently exhausted.

It was taken for granted that she was the one who would cook. With five wages coming into the house, they could afford to eat all right these days. But someone had to find time for buying food, for thinking about it and cooking it – on top of working.

Ada felt she owed the family and Nellie was not going to be any help, that was obvious. Just as she was no help minding Anthony, now his mother was not here. He was too young for the schoolroom and might in any case never be capable for it. Mrs Spragg kindly took the little lad in during the days for the moment, to be with one of her grandchildren.

Ada turned the small chops as they spat in the skillet, a painful wrench of feeling inside her. Our mom used to do this, she thought. She looked at her own hands lifting and turning the meat and they looked like her mother's.

Tears burned in her eyes. It was happening more and more these days. She was full of upset about Sarah Connell, but it also brought back all that she had already lost: Pa, then Mom. The others ripped away from her. She had tried to push it from her mind all these years. But what happened to Sarah, the horror of it, and it being all wrong and cruel, had broken her open.

Turning over the chops in the skillet, she pictured her happy childhood home, the range Mom kept shiny as a pin, the beautiful curtains and rug by the fire, the five of them all there together, Pa coming in, grinning and chucking her under the chin . . .

Her chest grew tight and she forced these thoughts away. 'Tea's ready,' she ordered, harshly. 'Come on, lads – get round the table.'

And if there's none left for you, Nell, she thought bitterly, that's your sodding lookout. Because it was obvious now that she was the one being left here as skivvy and mother to this houseful of men.

By the time Nellie deigned to come home that night, Seamus was sprawled asleep in the chair and all the boys except William were in bed. Ada was tired out and seething with fury.

'Where the hell've been?' she erupted.

Nellie gave her a foolish, superior look. 'Wouldn't you like to know?'

She walked unsteadily across the room and peered into the empty skillet.

'What's to eat?'

'If you want summat to eat get here when it's on the table,' Ada said.

Nellie rummaged in the cupboard and brought out the last heel of bread, took a bite of it and chewed loudly, waving the rest of it in the air.

'You're turning into a mean old . . .'

She brought out the remains of a bottle of vinegar and drank on that, head back, before slamming it down empty, pulling the back of her hand over her chapped lips. She staggered across the room and knocked into Seamus's chair. He woke with a start.

'Holy Mother – what was . . .?'

''S'only me, Da,' Nellie said, managing to deposit herself safely on the other chair.

'Where've you been?' William's face showed his disgust. 'Look at you.'

'For God's sake,' Seamus said blearily. 'The state of you girl – just like your mother.' And then, remembering, his face creased and he bent over his knees, gasping as his griefs all assaulted him again.

'I'm not,' Nellie retorted, far too loudly.

'Don't wake the others,' Ada snapped at her. It had taken a long, weary time to get the younger boys settled down that night and right now it was all she could do not to go over and slap Nellie's silly face, however sorry she felt for her. 'Wake them again and I'll cowing well kill you.'

'Oooh, hark at her making threats!' Nellie mocked. 'P'raps it was you did for old Fatty Liza, after all – blamed it all on our mother.' Her face turned vicious. 'After everything this family's done for you, you ungrateful cow.'

The words took Ada's breath away. So nasty, so untrue – that Nellie could think such a thing – even if she was half out of her head with drink.

Ada stared at her. Never had she felt such contempt for anyone.

'You've still got most of your family, Nell,' she said, bitter emotions pouring out of her. 'I wish I had mine – even just one of my sisters – they were worth ten of you! Our Elsie'd never have turned into a selfish drunken trollop like you. You don't care about anyone but yourself. You never lift a finger – you just leave all the work to me.'

She stormed out of the house across the wet yard, pulling her shawl over her head, hating herself. Here were the Connells facing the worst calamity anyone could imagine and look how she was carrying on! But she was so upset and overwrought herself she could not help it. For want of anywhere else to go she went and spent a penny in the lav. Afterwards, miserable, feeling her way back through the smoky darkness, she bumped into Mrs Spragg.

'Ooh – is that Ada? Lor', you made me jump! Eh –' Mrs Spragg reached out for Ada's arm. 'Nell come in yet?'

Their neighbour was concerned about them all and she always did her best to help. It was no use trying to hide anything from her.

'She's come in, and so mopped she can hardly stand. Oh,

Mrs Spragg, I don't know what to do – Nellie never helps and I'm so tired.'

Ada burst into tears.

'Oh now, bab – you're doing the best you can.' Mrs Spragg sounded upset as well. 'It's a tragedy what's happened to them. But it's the waiting that's the worst. When it's all over, she'll come round, I expect.' She reached out, touched Ada's arm. 'You're a good wench, Ada – and I'll help any way I can.'

'Ta, Mrs Spragg,' Ada sniffed. She had never been more grateful to this kindly woman. She marvelled once again at how nice and patient she was when her husband was such a miserable old sod.

'It's always darkest before the dawn, bab,' Mrs Spragg said, patting her arm. 'Go on with you – get yourself off to bed.'

Fifteen

Three Sundays. The weeks in between. Days of agony. The rising and setting sun of days which could not be halted or slowed to give them extra time.

But now, the date when Sarah Connell was to hang had drawn unstoppably nearer until it was only three days away.

What do we do? Ada asked herself. Everything felt impossible. To stand outside the prison while they put her to her death? No! Yet to leave her alone to her fate seemed wrong as well. Ada started to wish it could all be over, this agony of waiting along with her helplessness in the face of all the grief surrounding her. She tried to comfort Nellie and the rest of them when there was no true comfort to be had.

What she did not see, what none of them saw two days before the hanging date, was a young boy, dragged by his mother from Liza Jenks's yard, scolding him all the way to the police station – 'Why didn't you say so before?' – his mouth spilling words that up until then no one had heard.

Ada and Nellie were not long back from work at Tompkinson's that evening. Ada was cooking and for once Nellie was helping. It was a cool night and everyone was in by the fire when the door opened slowly.

It was Nellie who looked round first. She gasped.

'Mom?'

Ada turned her head to see Sarah Connell, like a ghost by the door.

'Mom!' Nellie was throwing herself on her mother and

the two little boys came clutching at her as the tears ran down her cheeks. 'Why're you here?' Nellie shrieked. 'Are you saved?'

Ada stood agape in the middle of the room, her heart pounding. Sarah, here – something they had never, ever expected to see! And even in this joyous surprise she was shocked by the sight of the woman. She was bone thin, hair bedraggled, the terror and agony which had consumed her days etched on her haunted face.

She sank on to a chair, Nellie kneeling beside her and Sarah with her arms round her two baby sons, kissing and kissing them as she sobbed. It took a while before she managed to sit up and speak, in a thin, reedy voice, and tell them what had happened.

'There was a lad, come in to the police – told his mother he'd seen someone in the yard, a man I think – went into Liza Jenks's house that afternoon. No one else saw him and the boy hadn't thought . . . He was only young, seven or eight. He hadn't remembered until . . . He heard them talking about me, about what was to happen and how no one else had been in the yard . . .'

Ada thought to sit down then, by the table, her legs suddenly shaky at the thought that if the boy had left it two more days . . .

'Oh, thank God,' she murmured, tears spilling from her eyes. 'Thank God . . .'

Within a few moments they heard steps in the yard and the door opened. Ada would never forget the expression on Seamus Connell's face when he caught sight of his wife returned to her house.

'Sarah?' He stood stock-still, shook his head as if his eyes might be playing tricks on him.

'I'm home, Seamus,' she said, weeping. 'They know it wasn't me.'

For all her wariness of the man, in that moment Ada saw in him the young Irishman, full of hope and spirit, who had courted Sarah and married her. He walked behind her chair, and trammelled as she was by children, he wrapped his arms around her from behind and pressed his cheek against hers.

'You're home, my darlin',' he kept saying in a broken voice. 'You're home again.'

Soon after, William and Tom came in and Ada would never forget the look of hunger in Tom's face when he caught sight of his mother. Mrs Spragg called in, smiling and full of kindness, with a pan of soup she had made specially.

'Here you are,' she said. 'You'll not have had time. I put plenty of spud in it.' She came over and gently touched Sarah's shoulder. 'I'm glad to see you back, Sarah. Time for a fresh start, eh?'

Sarah seized Mrs Spragg's hand and looked up at her old neighbour, her eyes shining in her thin face.

'You're an angel, Olive. Yes – everything'll be different now.' She looked round at Seamus, at Ada and all her children, seeming alight with passion at the new life she had been given. 'It will, won't it, my darlings?'

On the way out, Mrs Spragg patted Ada's shoulder.

'Thanks, Mrs Spragg,' Ada said, smiling at her. And for those moments she felt full of a glow of warmth and hope for the future.

Sixteen

'Ah – look who's come waltzing in at last.'

Mrs Rundle stood, arms folded in front of a very groggy-looking Nellie, who had at last put in an appearance.

'Sorry, Mrs Rundle,' Nellie mumbled. 'Only I was feeling poorly yesterday.'

Mrs Rundle's eyes met Ada's for a moment before she fixed her gaze back on her wayward employee. Nellie had already had a stern talking-to from Mrs Spragg that morning, having been dragged into the brew house for the purpose. It was three weeks since that joyful day when Sarah Connell was returned to her family and things had slid quickly downhill.

'I'd've shown you the door already if I didn't know what's been going on at home,' Mrs Rundle said, lowering her voice. 'But you've had enough chances, Nellie. Any more carry-on and you can look for work elsewhere – that clear?'

'Yes, Mrs Rundle. Sorry, Mrs Rundle.'

Nellie was deathly pale and looked as if she was about to be sick. A moment later she ran out to the lav. She came back looking a fraction better and Mrs Rundle watched her, gimlet-eyed. She shook her head as Nellie hurried back in to get started. Ada gave Mrs Rundle a grateful look.

'The old girl's all right really,' Gert murmured. 'Behind that fizzog of hers.'

Ada looked along the workshop, seeing Nellie bent over her lathe. She was so sorry for Nellie, for all that she and the family had been through. But lately all she could feel was frustration with her.

Sarah's pledge to the family that her spell in prison had torn her away from alcohol lasted for two days before she was begging Nellie to bring her 'just a bit of comfort'. Nellie tried to hold out, but soon the two of them were at it together, as bad, if not worse than before.

Sarah's weeks of isolation in the condemned cell, all those hours to picture her own forthcoming death dangling from the rope, had broken her mind. They would hear her at night, screaming with nightmares and Seamus trying to quiet her, at first with tenderness but as it went on, with panic and even brutality. And it seemed that Sarah, her body and mind already hooked on the drink, could find no other remedy for the horrors that tormented her.

The tiny ray of light they had glimpsed had vanished and every day Ada felt more hopeless. And on top of that, she realized that Nellie, her old friend, the girl of jokes and games and the closest thing she had had to a sister in all these years, was becoming even more of a stranger and one she didn't like at all.

Two nights later, Ada slipped out of the house. The little ones were in bed, Seamus was out and Sarah in a stupor on the chair. Ada stood looking over her for a moment before she left. Sarah's face was shrunken and deathly white, dark rings under her eyes. Ada had the creeping feeling that she looked like a corpse. For an awful moment she thought it would have been better if they had hanged Sarah, put her out of the agony that was her life. She had an impulse to shake her awake, make sure she was still alive, but she could hear faint breaths coming from her.

She was relieved to escape. More and more she felt she couldn't breathe in that house. But tonight she had another mission in mind. Nellie had hurried out without even helping to clear the tea away or even mentioning that she was going. Once Ada had finally finished all her chores and washed up, she felt she could slip out herself.

It was dark, and damp underfoot. Ada made her way cautiously along the street, feeling her way between the dim pools of light offered by the street lamps. People passed in the murk, coughing or exchanging a few words. She heard bursts of shouting and singing from the pubs and cramped drinking dens tucked away along the side streets.

A claw-like hand grasped at her arm and Ada jumped violently. A crabbed face appeared, looking up at her in the gloom.

'Spare us a farthing, pretty one?'

It was an ancient-looking lady, her voice deep and rough as a man's. Ada recognized her. Old Alice Beard was a widow and well-known beggar in the area. Ada sometimes saw her tiny figure shuffling along the street, her patched grey cloak hanging limp round her ankles. Ada did not know into what mean crack in the town's teeming hovels she squeezed herself at night, but in the day she roamed about, living on what she could beg off the street. It was a wonder she had managed to avoid the workhouse this long but somehow she slipped around the edges, making shift in whatever way she could.

'I ain't got money on me,' Ada said, truthfully. Her heart was beating hard. There was something about Alice Beard, a threatening force to her, the deranged look in her eyes and the way her fingers dug sharp into Ada's arm. She managed to pull away from the old lady's grip. 'Sorry,' she murmured and hurried on.

'God bless yer, pretty maid!' Alice shrieked after her, sarcastically.

Ada felt shaken up, annoyed. The street did not feel safe. Who knew what cut-purses or lunatics were lurking in the shadows? Rage rose up in her.

'Nellie, where the hell are you?' she muttered. She had worked all evening, cooking, seeing to the boys, dragging in Peter and Anthony's urine-soaked bedding yet again after hanging it on the yard line this morning. Sarah was no good to anyone and where was Nellie? Nowhere to be seen, as usual.

Noise was coming from another pub further along the street and a cluster of four young men burst out of the door, jostling and laughing. Light spilled on to the pavement along with wafts of ale and smoke.

The lads were vying with each other and it sounded as if the brawl could turn nasty any moment. As they jeered and cuffed each other, Ada caught sight of the object of their quarrel at the centre of the knot of men – three of them, not four. The fourth person was Nellie.

Ada melted against the nearest wall in the shadows, heart thumping wildly.

'Hey, boys!' Nellie's voice was shrill and already slurred with drink. 'That's enough of that . . . Oi – gerroff me, will yer? I'm going 'ome now . . .'

She swayed, unsteady on her feet and quite unable to work out in which direction home might be found. The lads played with her like a ball, pushing her from one to the other.

'There you go . . .' They shoved and jostled. 'Oi – over 'ere, that's it, give 'er a shove . . .'

'Pass 'er 'ere – who's gunna 'ave 'er then?'

'Tell yer what, boys –' one of them, thick dark hair under a cap, broke away to fumble in his pocket – 'heads or tails?'

The lad flicked the coin and failed to catch it. There was a metallic clink as it hit the ground and rolled away, and he lurched after it.

'You can't do that,' Nellie was shouting.

'Oh ar, we can!' The dark-haired lad gripped Nellie by the shoulder. 'It's tails – that's me then!'

Ada dashed forward, taking them by surprise, and grabbed Nellie's arm.

'Nell – where've you been?' Trying to stop her voice trembling, she added, 'I'll take her home with me.'

'No, you don't, 'er's coming with us,' the dark-haired lad protested. 'This trollop's had I dunno how many drinks off of us and I won the toss – so I'm 'aving 'er.'

'No, you're cowing well not!' Ada argued with a vigour that surprised her. She had bottled-up anger to spend and here was a place to do it. 'You get your filthy hands off her! Her father'll be here any minute and you don't want to meet Seamus Connell in a rage – he's twice your size and he can punch like a prizefighter.'

'Dad?' Nellie peered along the street. 'That you?'

Ada never knew if Nellie was playing along or if she really believed Seamus would stir himself to come and find her. But it had the desired effect.

'Come on back in,' one of the others said, yanking on his pal's arm. ''Er's not worth it.'

They slid away, throwing choice epithets behind them – 'filthy hooer' being the loudest.

'Ow, Ade – you're hurting me!' Nellie tried to twist away from Ada's grasp.

That's nothing to what I'll do in a minute, Ada thought furiously. She hauled a cursing, struggling Nellie along the street.

'Gerroff me, Ada!' Nellie yanked her arm down, trying to loosen Ada's iron grip, but Ada clung like a limpet.

'Just keep walking, Nell,' she ordered. 'You gotta come home. You can't keep stopping out like this, you don't know what'll happen to you.'

'I don't want to come home!' Nellie stopped dead suddenly, her voice rising to a wail. 'It's when I get home I know everything's bad. When I'm out I can think our mom's home and she's all right, like she used to be, when we were little . . .'

Nellie crumpled then, broken by sobs, falling to her knees there in the road. 'She's never done anything wrong, ever. She's an angel, our mom is – but now . . . I can't hardly stand to look at her.'

Ada's heart melted and she was in tears as well. For all that she wanted to scream at Nellie for her part in making everything worse, for bringing Sarah the liquor she craved, she knew really that it was not Nellie's fault. Sarah would have got it from somewhere in any case. If she had been bad before, hooked on the bottle, now she was a broken woman.

'Come on – get up.' She helped Nellie gently to her feet and put her arms around her, holding her tight. Her friend was now, for once, more like her old self and Ada felt nothing but kindness and pity for her.

'You're . . . 'Nellie stumbled over her words as they went along the entry in Summer Row. 'You're my sister, ain't you, Ada? My one proper sister . . . You're the best, you are . . .' She swayed on her feet. 'I want to lie down.'

'Let's get you in,' Ada said, in the yard.

'I feel bad,' Nellie mumbled. She jerked round and spewed violently. Ada jumped back to avoid the splash of it on her boots. Nellie bent over, moaning, and it was a while before she could stand upright again.

Ada opened the door and shoved Nellie in through it.

'Lie yourself down,' Ada said. 'I'll talk to you when I can get some sense out of you.'

She lay beside Nellie that night, pulling the cover over her nose to try and block out the stink of booze coming off her, feeling utterly desperate. When things were good between her and Nellie she really did love her like a sister. But it seemed to be impossible to knock any sense into her. And as for her family – what was going to become of all of them?

*

Ada got up early the next morning, put on a pan of gruel for the lads, cut hunks of bread and threw a handful of chitterlings into the skillet to fry for Seamus's breakfast. She had heard Sarah crying out in the night, the haunting, unearthly cries of a tormented soul, and there was no sign of her coming down this morning.

Nellie was still motionless on the floor. The boys had tried rousing her but nothing seemed to work.

'For God's sake,' William said, looking at her as he sat down at the table. 'Look at the state of her.'

Ada prodded her with her foot.

'Nell. Get up. NELLIE.'

Nellie whimpered and curled up but Ada was not in the mood to show her any mercy. Her sympathy of the night before was wearing thin in the cold light of morning and all that needed doing. If she went on like this, Nellie was going to get the sack.

'You gotta get up for work. You know what Mrs Rundle said.'

'Saint Monday,' Nellie mumbled, eyes still closed.

'It's Wednesday today – just sodding well get UP!'

Monday was a notorious day for workers not showing up – keeping 'Saint Monday' as a day to recover from a weekend of excess from the Saturday wage packet. Tompkinson's Works had no patience with this – and Ada knew Mrs Rundle had no more spare tolerance for Nellie's carry-on whatever the day of the week.

'What're you gunna do when they give you the sack – stay home and keep house?' Her voice was loud and bitter.

Seamus walked in then, from the lav. He looked down at his daughter with a grimace of disgust.

'Get up now, girl. What're you doing still down there?'

Nellie stirred and managed to lift her head up, looking

queasy, wrinkling her nose at the smell of the chitterlings spitting on the fire.

'The head on ya.' Seamus said, disgusted.

'No worse than you,' she replied with a sneer.

At that, Seamus's blue eyes flashed with anger and he was immediately worked up. Ada heard the breath whistle in and out of his nostrils and the veins stood out on his strong neck. He drew his foot back and delivered a hard kick to the region of Nellie's backside.

'You be getting up now. Do as I say!'

'Ow!' Nellie shrieked. But it got her moving and she struggled to her feet, clutching her hip where he had kicked her. 'That cowing hurt!'

'I've never missed a day's work from the drink,' Seamus roared. 'Not once. Your mother's fit for nothing – now you're going the same way. I've fed and clothed this family and it's Ada here having to do all the . . .' He flapped his hand as if unsure how to sum up all that Ada did every day.

For a moment he turned and once again Ada found herself on the end of his forceful blue gaze. It shook her inside. Pa. He was the only other man who had looked at her like that. Just for a second, that forceful look, full of energy, of regard, warmed her hungry heart and she gave a faint smile.

'You're a good wench,' he said appreciatively.

'You took me in, Mr Connell,' Ada reminded him.

'So I did.' He nodded, calmer suddenly, his breath coming more steadily. He laid a hand on Nellie's shoulder as she sat up. She flinched.

'Get yourself to off work. And if I smell a drop of it on your breath again, you can leave my house and not come back – d'you hear?'

Nellie lowered her head, eyes burning with resentment, but she managed a nod.

Seventeen

Nellie tried to pull herself together. She came into the works and got on with the job. She slipped out most evenings but did not stop out late. Ada could smell the drink on her breath but Nellie came in quite merry so Ada held her tongue and said nothing.

Why should I have to be in charge of any of this anyway? she asked herself. Sarah Connell was an invalid now. There were moments when her head cleared and she came downstairs and sat, quiet and gentle with her children. But when she spoke it was often disjointed, fanciful. She could hardly manage to do anything and Ada did all that she could for her.

She was already doing most of the work and trying to look after Nellie's father and brothers as well. Nellie would have to sort herself out.

But a couple of Saturday nights later, Nellie didn't come home. Seamus had been out all evening. For a moment, as he came in, stunned with drink, Ada saw the glimmer of hope in his eyes. That Sarah would be downstairs. That somehow she would have recovered herself, would be a wife and mother again. But Sarah was already in bed and Seamus threw himself into the chair by the fire.

'Where's herself?'

Ada knew he meant Nellie. She, eyes stinging, was struggling to sew in the poor light of a candle. Tom was almost through the seat of his trousers, all of them had toes poking out of their socks and she had torn the hem of her work dress again.

She shrugged, keeping her eyes on her work.

'Damn her,' Seamus said, furiously.

He hadn't the energy to get worked up and soon he was asleep, snoring loudly in his chair by the dying fire.

Ada kept sewing, waiting. Seamus's chest rose and fell with his loud breaths. These days she had more pity for him as well. Sometimes, at night, she heard his sobs from upstairs. And she knew Nellie did too. For all he was rough, Seamus was a hard-working man who fed his family. Now the wife for whom he had seldom had a kind word had been both returned to him in body and stolen away in spirit. Her being here was crueller than her absence. Seamus's black hair had turned almost white within those few weeks.

It grew late and still there was no sign of Nellie. Ada put her sewing away and was moving the pots on the range. Seamus woke with a jerk at the noise and sat up, looking round bewildered. His eyes focused gradually.

'Where's Nellie? Still not here then?'

He got out of his chair as Ada shook her head. She was by the range, her back to him, when she realized with a jolt that he was standing right behind her. She turned, heart thudding, stomach turning at his pungent smell of drink and sweat.

Seamus looked down blearily at her and he laid his heavy hands on her shoulders. Panic rose in her.

'C'mon now, Ada,' he said in a wheedling voice, as if there was something she knew she ought to be doing. 'You're a good girl, so you are.'

He lurched forward, grabbing her and pulling her towards him, and suddenly his whiskery mouth was pressed on hers, all wet, tasting foul. His hand on her buttocks forced her against him and she could feel a hard lump pressing into her down there at the front.

She managed to get her hands against his chest and shove him with all her strength.

'Stop that – get off me!'

Seamus teetered backwards, steadying himself against the range.

'Lord God Almighty!' he thundered. 'Will you not give a man comfort . . .'

Ada was too frightened to be sure what he wanted. She ran to the door.

'You shouldn't touch me,' she hissed. 'You're old enough to be my father. I'm going to look for Nellie.'

Her legs weak and trembling, she hurried out into the darkness.

I'm not going in there, she thought, standing outside the pub where she knew Nellie often went. A woman's shrill voice rose above the other drunken, male voices and she didn't like the sound of it in there. She had already had a mauling from one man and she wasn't looking for another.

After a few moments, two men came out and lingered, talking, by the door. Ada went up to them. She saw them take her in, the look in their eyes the way a fox might eye a chicken, as if it was their instinct to look at any woman like that.

'Is Nellie in there? Nellie Connell?'

'Who?' one said. He was very tall and lanky.

'Oh, ar – Nell.' The other one laughed. ''Er's in there all right. Where else'd 'er be?'

They seemed about to move away.

'Hold on – could you just . . .' They stopped. 'Can you get her to come out? Tell her Ada's waiting for her.'

'Ha – you'll 'ave a job,' the lanky one said. But he ambled back inside.

'Is Nell a pal of yours then?' the other asked, leaning against the wall.

'Sort of, yes.'

He had narrow eyes which Ada didn't much like the look of and she was glad when the lanky one came back.

''Er won't shift,' he said. 'Can't say I didn't try.'

The two of them went off, laughing. Ada stood in the bitter cold, furious.

I'm not freezing to death out here, she thought. She had her shawl close round her but she was already tight in the chest, and shivering all over. She didn't want to go into the pub.

She was about to go home and leave Nellie to sort herself out when there was a loud crash from inside, then laughter and an outcry of voices. It sounded as if a table had collapsed. Amid the shouting and jeering, the door opened and Nellie appeared with a cut on her cheek, being hauled out by the arm of a man with his fair hair slicked down.

'Go on,' he said, his voice full of contempt. 'Time to go – before you do any more damage.'

Nellie staggered into the road on the force of the shove he gave her and almost fell over.

'Oi!' she raged. 'You can't throw me out . . .'

'Nell!' Ada ran forward to grab her, where she was slipping on the cobbles. 'Come on. What've you done to your face?'

'Ada?' Nellie leaned on her arm and started cackling with laughter. 'I broke the table. I was having a little sing, like, and . . .' She was giggling so hysterically she could barely speak.

'Oh, for heaven's sake,' Ada said, losing any patience. She started shrieking into Nellie's face. 'D'you want to end up like your mother? 'Cause that's the way you're going. And the only person who can stop it is you. Please, Nell . . .' Her voice fell then and she burst into tears. 'Just pull yerself together . . .'

In the face of Ada's tears, Nellie stood swaying, her eyes not even focused.

'Wassup with you, Ade?' was all she managed, in a baffled tone.

Ada's despair turned to back into fury. She grabbed Nellie again and yanked her along.

'Oh, just get home, you noggen. I've had enough – of the whole cowing lot of you.'

Ada kept hoping Nellie would pull herself together, go back to being a friend, an equal at home. With her mother so ill and incapable it felt unbearable to Ada to see her friend sliding down the same path. When Nellie was sober they talked about it and Nellie would be sorry and promise it was the last time. That she'd never be so silly again. Half the time she couldn't remember anything about the night before anyway.

Somehow she got into the works and struggled on. Until the day when she didn't turn up.

'Nellie's poorly,' Ada lied to Mrs Rundle, whose expression was so sceptical she felt her own face burn with blushes. 'I left her lying down – I've never seen her so bad.'

Mrs Rundle folded her arms across the dark grey overall covering her thin chest.

'Doesn't care much for her wage, that one, does she? Pours most of it down her neck by the state of her.'

Ada looked into Mrs Rundle's thin face. They both knew it was true and there was no further lie she could bring herself to tell.

'She'd better be in tomorrow,' Mrs Rundle said, walking off.

Nellie was in the next day. Ada, who had gone on ahead after nagging Nellie not to be late, was already at work, bent over fixing a button into the lathe when a voice was heard singing, even over the rhythmic clatter of the machines . . . 'Jeanie with the Light Brown Hair' floating up the stairs.

For a moment, Ada did not register anything except that the singer had a strong, tuneful voice and her eyes prickled with tears at the sound. Until she realized in panic who was singing.

'*Oh, I long for Jeanie, and my heart bows low –*' Nellie burst through the door, obviously the worse for drink and finishing with a loud flourish as if she was blasting across a music hall – '*Never more to find her where the bright waters flow.*'

Ada dashed across the room, but Mrs Rundle was already on the warpath.

'Good at singing, ain't I, Mrs R?' Nellie asked cheerfully.

'Take her home,' Mrs Rundle instructed. 'She's had her chance.' To Nellie she said slowly and clearly, trying to get through to her, 'You've had your warnings. You're finished here, Nellie Connell. Get out and don't come back. And don't expect me to give you a reference.'

Eighteen

'Tell you what, Ada,' Nellie wheedled, when she had sobered up after this latest episode. 'You're working so I can stay at home and keep house – look after Mom and the boys.'

Ada looked into Nellie's face, which once, long ago, she had thought sweet, and saw the devious creature she had become. The offer was music to her ears all the same. Everything fell to her these days and she was sick of it.

'All right,' she said, though her heart was sinking with doubt that Nellie would be able to keep it up. 'You can start by getting the tea ready.'

With a confused look, Nellie went over to the range.

'What do I have to do?'

'You can make a stew out of that scrag end I bought. Oh, and Mrs Spragg won't need to be minding Anthony no more if you're here, will she? She's done more than enough.'

When Sarah came home it had been assumed she would be able to look after her own children, but this was not to be the case. Sarah could not even look after herself.

She was about to go out and gather in the washing but Nellie grabbed her.

'You'll tell Da that's what we're doing?'

Ada nodded, slowly. 'Get that meat in the pan, Nell,' she said. 'Stick a bit of lard in and fry it to start, all right?'

She went outside, her face grim.

'What's up with you?' Mrs Spragg asked. She was

holding Anthony by the hand, slowly bringing the lad across the yard.

'Nellie wants to stay home and keep house,' Ada said.

Mrs Spragg rolled her eyes. 'I'll believe that when I see it.' She lowered her voice so as not to be overheard by Ma O'Shea or anyone else. 'Any sign of *her* rallying?'

Ada's eyes filled with tears and she shook her head. She had just been upstairs to see Sarah. She lay there, weak and blank, staring at the damp patches on the ceiling.

Christmas was coming. Despite everything, Ada did her best to make it as happy a day as she could manage.

Tompkinson's announced that they were giving their workers Christmas Day off for the first time! Ada could hardly believe it. She asked Seamus for change to buy a little something for the young ones and as soon as work was over on the Friday, she rushed into Birmingham, excited to explore the market stalls, lit by flares in the gathering darkness.

The atmosphere was festive and her mouth watered at the scent of roasting chestnuts drifting from a cart close to the entrance of the Market Hall. The smell competed with the hot-potato stall, the tang of tangerines, and frying onions and sausage. She did not have time to linger in the crowds milling along Spiceal Street. Hurriedly, she picked out a little model railway engine for Anthony and a spinning top for Peter. For Tom she bought a tinny little pocket knife that folded in on itself. There was no more money for presents for the adults, but at the last moment, with her remaining pennies, she bought a bag of mixed nuts for them to shell and a thick bunch of holly with bright red berries. She carried everything home, happy to be doing something nice for everyone.

Seamus arrived home with a goose, freshly plucked,

flung over one shoulder and slammed it down on the table. Nellie took one look at it and burst out laughing.

'That looks rude!' she giggled.

'Well, I'm glad I don't have to pluck it anyway,' Ada said.

'I got the feller to do it, so,' Seamus said. 'He'd do it quicker than anyone. Oh, and Harris'll let us use his oven.'

Harris, the baker along the street, would let people cook a joint of meat in his big bread oven.

'That's good,' Ada said, relieved at not having to cope with this huge bird herself.

'I'll take it down there,' Seamus added as he walked off.

Ada watched him, this strong, sad man. Mixed with her revulsion for him was a crumb of admiration for the way he just kept going, despite it all.

'Cor, look at that!' Tom cried when he found the penknife on his bed on Christmas morning. The boys were so excited on finding their presents that it lifted Ada's heart for the day. Tom spent the whole morning opening and closing the knife, testing the edge on anything he could find.

'Don't you go cutting up the table – you need to find a bit of wood to whittle,' Ada ticked him off, but she kept a twinkle in her eyes. It made her happy to see how thrilled the lad was. And Peter spent the whole morning, while the delicious scent of roasting potatoes wafted from the oven, spinning and spinning his top until Ada thought the sound would drive her mad.

Still, she thought, only got myself to blame.

She had even found a little present on her own bed when she woke: two soft cotton handkerchiefs with lace edging that the older boys had clubbed together to buy for her.

'What's all this?' she asked when they came down.

'You never got me nice hankies,' Nellie sulked. For her they had bought some dried fruit and nuts in a little box.

'That's 'cause Ada does all the work,' William said. 'While you're out filling your neck.' But he said it in a teasing voice and Nellie immediately opened the box and put a Brazil nut in her mouth.

'Ooh – that's nice that is. I'd rather them than a snot rag any day.'

'We wanted you to have summat,' William said. 'You've been good to us, Ada. Happy Christmas.'

Her eyes filled with tears – so they did notice some things she did after all!

'Well, ta very much,' she said, hugging each of them. 'That's nice of you.'

It made her happy the whole day. She was in a good mood with Nellie, who had been a help this morning, peeling spuds and parsnips and seeming to be in good spirits. For the time being they had been friends again.

And eventually, before the dinner was ready, Sarah came downstairs. The children all treated her like a queen, delighted just to see her there with them. They sat her at the table and the boys gave her a pretty lace hanky as well.

'Come on, Mom.' William said. 'You can have a nice dinner with us.'

They were almost desperate to see her put food in her mouth, she was such a little skeleton of a thing.

'All right, my loves,' Sarah said, smiling vaguely. She reached out and stroked Tom's cheek suddenly. 'My beautiful boys.' Ada saw Tom freeze, caught between longing for her love and horror at the way she was.

'Let's all sit down,' Ada said hurriedly, trying to keep the mood up. 'Come on, Nell, get the stool for William – and sort the cabbage out, will you?'

Seamus arrived through the door carrying the tray with

the sizzling goose in it, its skin now dark and oily and smelling delicious. He placed it ceremonially on the table and took his place at the end.

'Will you sit there, Ada?' he said, gesturing to the chair at the other end.

Panic rose in her for a moment. She kept noticing how he spoke to her these days, with a shy respect, and now he was setting her up truly as the woman of the house in a way he had never done before. Ada cursed herself for having seated Sarah at the side of the table. For a moment all she could think of was the feel of him pressing against her that night, his lips forcing on to hers. It felt as if she was being wooed. By this man who was older than Pa. Right in front of his wife.

She looked back at him steadily.

'I think Nellie should sit there,' she said.

Nellie smiled. Her hair was hanging loose down her back except for a few strands from the front caught up and tied with a thin strand of bottle-green ribbon behind her head. Ada was struck for a moment by how much she looked like Sarah, young Sarah with flesh on her bones. Seamus must have seen the same. His face clouded and Tom and the others started to look worried at what might come next if their father kicked off.

'No,' he snapped. 'You're to sit there, Ada. If anyone's the woman of the house these days it's yourself.'

'Go on, Ada,' Sarah said suddenly in her reedy voice. 'You sit there.'

Ada looked at her, confused. Even Sarah was forcing her into this role and it made her feel deeply uneasy. But she did not want to spoil the day when she was working so hard to make it a happy one. She glanced at Nellie and they agreed with their eyes that it was better not to argue.

'All right.' Ada sat at the table and Seamus tackled the goose at the other end.

She did her very best to make it a happy time for the boys. But inside she felt more and more panicked and her skin prickled with revulsion. Because she guessed what Seamus had in mind. He had a sick and failing wife and he wanted Ada to take over as the woman of the house – in every way.

Nineteen

It wasn't long into the new year and cold as it was, Nellie was staying out night after night. Ada didn't wonder where she had been – she knew all too well.

One evening Nellie came rolling in looking mighty pleased with herself and Ada felt her blood boil. Nellie looked pertly at her.

'Well, you've got a face on you like a bag of frogs.'

'And so would you if you was working a job and doing all the rest as well,' Ada erupted.

Seamus and the older lads were there but Ada didn't care. No one else was bothering to tackle the dozy wench or ask how she was managing to pay for her drink – and get it for her mother on the quiet as well. The men didn't care who cooked their tea so long as it was put in front of them regular as clockwork.

Nellie said nothing then, but once they were alone, getting ready for the night, she pulled a drawstring pouch out from her waistband and slammed it on the table. Ada heard the chink of coins.

'There. I earn my keep, I'll have you know.'

'Where d'you get that?' Ada snapped. 'Been stealing off of young girls again, have you?'

Nellie spun round, and her arm lashed out, fast as a snake. The slap stung Ada hard.

'You think you're better than me, don't yer? Miss "Oh, I used to live in a palace and my pa was a prince."' Her tone was mean and mocking. She always got nasty with the drink inside her.

Ada stood up, her voice lowering to a snarl.

'I *am* better than you, Nell. I'm the one trying to look after your family when you don't raise a finger. And we did have a nice house, not like this cesspit. My mother knew how to keep house – and my pa *was* a prince – he was the best . . .'

She stopped, her throat thickening as the grief rose in her that she always tried to keep at bay.

'So where is 'e then, this marvellous prince of yours?' Nellie sneered. 'Went off without a by-your-leave, didn't he? Shows how much he cared about you. At least I've got a father!'

It was Ada's turn to lash out and her hand was slapping against Nellie's cheek before she even knew she was going to do it.

'You're a lazy cow, Nellie. If it weren't for me this family'd live on sop. All you do's pour drink down yer hodge – and you've wrecked your mother!'

'No, I haven't!' Nellie screeched. 'It's the one thing makes her happy . . .'

'You call that happy?' Ada yelled back.

The two of them ended up brawling, tearing at each other's faces. Ada shrieked as Nellie gave her hair a vicious yank and a burning pain jabbed through her scalp. They screamed insults at each other until William came hurtling down the stairs – 'What the hell's going on?' – and at the same time there was a furious banging at the door.

William opened it to find Nora O'Shea outside, a shawl over some long, pale garment and her nose in the air as usual.

'What in the name of God is going on? You're after waking the whole yard with your racket.'

William opened and closed his mouth. Ada and Nellie looked at each other and started sniggering.

'Sorry, Mrs O'Shea,' Nellie called out, with not an ounce of sincerity.

'You're a disgrace – the whole lot of you,' Nora O'Shea kept on, as William managed to get the door shut again in her face.

The girls exploded into giggles.

Nellie took the candle into the scullery to look in the little mirror. 'You've blacked my eye, you cow.'

'And you've scalped me!'

'Oh, just go to sleep,' William snapped, disappearing upstairs again.

Truces never lasted long. A few nights later, when Nellie slipped out, long after dark, Ada followed her.

She managed to keep sight of Nellie along Summer Row as she wove from lamp post to lamp post. Every few moments her shape would appear out of the gloom, her long hair twisted up tight on her head and topped by a jaunty little hat she had 'picked up at the Rag Market' – stolen more likely, Ada thought bitterly, knowing Nellie's light-fingered ways.

At last she stopped. Ada waited, peering out from the entry leading to another yard of houses. How long am I going to have to stand here? Ada thought. The streets were icy and her shawl was not enough to keep out the biting cold. But she wanted to be sure. Nellie might have started with robbing children but now she had bigger fish to fry, Ada was almost certain.

Sure enough, someone else soon came along, a young woman, also in a hat worn at a provocative tilt. In the lamplight Ada could make out a long, pointed feather jutting from the band. She had no idea who the woman was.

The two of them stood talking in low voices. Ada heard the woman laugh – and not a nice laugh – and then they walked off together, turning into one of the pubs further along the street.

A moment later she heard voices. A knot of people were coming out of the pub. Two men peeled off, calling good-byes, and they walked off the other way along the street. But the rest of them started back in Ada's direction – Nellie and the other woman and two men.

Ada shrank back into one of the street's dark entries as they approached, hearing their laughter and chatter.

''Ere . . . Nellie's voice. 'I brought yer summat nice – have a swig of that . . . That's it. Warms your cockles!'

'Give us some,' Ada heard from one of the men.

'Pass 'im it,' the other woman ordered. 'Greedy pig.'

'Cor,' Ada heard in a male voice. 'Hot stuff . . .'

They went on, drinking and laughing.

Slipping out behind, she followed. By now, each of the men had his arm wrapped round Nellie and the other woman's shoulder, both couples lurching along. One of the men let out a grating belch. The other one tried to do the same in competition, but it was a feeble effort and both the women cackled with laughter. Ada wrinkled her face in disgust.

They were heading towards the cut, she realized. Sure enough, quieter now, they all disappeared through the gap that led down to the canal wharf. Sometimes unloading went on very late, but tonight it was quiet. The night was chill, mist was rising over the black line of water, obscuring the stripes of moonlight on its surface. A line of empty joeys, the flat, open cargo boats with no cabins, was tied along the wharf. These day boats would be busy again from early on; their crew lived nearby and were tucked up in their homes. The narrowboats, moored further along, had their families living on board.

Ada heard a faint giggle ahead of her but the four of them moved more quietly now, as they headed along the towpath. She followed, a horror seeping through her in the damp darkness, close to the black water, the scuttle of rats . . . Was this how Nellie earned her money? Going with these men who she barely knew?

Then she heard more noises. A giggle, the low sound of a man's voice. Then horrible, urgent rhythmic sounds, a grunt, a command in a panting voice . . .

Oh Lord, Ada thought. I'm getting out of here.

Spooked now, all the hairs standing up at the back of her neck, she stumbled back to the entrance to the wharf and once she was on easier ground, she fled along the street.

'Holy Mother, what's up with you?' Seamus demanded, jarred awake as she crashed, panting, into the house. He was seized by a fit of coughing which gave Ada time to think. She was so upset she might have blurted it all out, but she managed to button her lip in time.

'I was just looking for Nellie, that's all,' she panted. 'I ran back, 'cause it's freezing out there.'

She realized the boys had gone upstairs and there was no one else at home.

'Well, get yourself by the fire now.' Seamus sat up, all concerned suddenly as she moved towards the range. 'Did you find the wretched girl then?'

Ada had a split second to decide what to say. 'No.'

Once Seamus had gone up, she unrolled the bedding she and Nellie used downstairs and lay down, though she knew she would not sleep.

But it was not long before Nellie came in. Ada kept her eyes closed. Nellie lit a candle. She was panting as if she had been running. She spent an age in the scullery splashing water, before she came to lie down and blew out the candle. Despite all her splashing Ada could smell her, the men on her and the drink, and she shrank from her. Nellie's breathing was still ragged, agitated.

Ada squeezed her eyes closed. How had her life come to this? She let her mind drift back to the past in a way she hardly ever allowed. It hurt too much. To when she was young, Pa's lad, always the one he picked out, full of energy and courage. And now what was she? A drudge in a ghost-woman's house, taking on the woman's lot that she had always vowed she wouldn't.

What shall I do, Pa? she asked, desperately, in her head. *I wish you were here to tell me what to do.*

The tears were still wet on her cheeks as she fell asleep.

Twenty

'Look at this one – it's a whopper.'

Gert held out her hand, displaying a huge snail shell, a tan brown, marked by a delicate black swirl of lines spiralling in towards a darker brown centre.

Ada gazed at the shell and smiled. So many had passed through their hands over the years and yet, when she saw an especially beautiful or big one, she never tired of them.

'It's beautiful, that is.'

It was two days after Nellie's escapade and Ada was glad to be at work. Once she got to Tompkinson's she tried to close her mind to all that was going on at home. It was a happy place, with Gert and the other girls.

'Go on, take it,' Gert murmured. 'I know you like them. Not as if anyone'll miss it.'

Ada looked round and as there was no sign of Mrs Rundle, she slipped the thing into her pocket. It was hard to explain how comforting she found stroking its smooth, ridged shape with her fingers. Her shell collection was like a spark of something beautiful in the world, linking her to her life before. To her mother and to a time when she had a family of her own, in a house with lovely things.

'Ta.' She winked at Gert, dragging herself out of her own troubles. 'You all right, Gert? Kids all right?'

'Jonny's down with the diarrhoea again,' Gert was saying with a sigh. Ada could see she was worried. So many children grew sick, died even, from bad bellies caused by bad water.

'Enough canting – get on with the job!' Mrs Rundle appeared as she sometimes did, seemingly from nowhere. Gert made a face and they both got their heads down.

But then there came a rumpus from the stairs. A man's voice shouting.

'Oi – where d'yer think you're going?'

Feet thundered up the stairs and then the door swung open. Little Petey Connell burst in and stared desperately round the workshop.

'Ada! Ada – you got to come 'ome!'

The bloke following him up the stairs arrived panting and indignant. He grabbed Petey's shoulder as Ada ran over.

'C'm'ere, you! What d'you think you're—'

'It's all right,' Ada said. 'He's my brother – leave 'im.'

'Well, if 'e don't work 'ere he shouldn't be 'ere,' the man grumbled, withdrawing.

Ada squatted down, hands on Petey's skinny shoulders, looking into his terrified blue eyes. She could feel that he was trembling all over. Petey was nearly eight but not fit for school, simple in his mind.

'What's up, Petey? Why're you here?'

'It's our Nellie – they've took 'er away – and our dad ain't there . . .'

'What . . .? Who?' Ada became aware that the room had gone quiet and everyone was earwigging.

Ada stood up. 'I'm coming. Gotta go, Mrs Rundle, sorry . . .'

Before the forewoman could object Ada had hustled Petey down the stairs and out into the busy street, away from all the flapping ears.

'Right – what's going on?'

'Mrs Spragg said to fetch you.' Petey started crying, all his shock and fear pouring out. 'Two big blokes bashed the door in, shouting . . . And they took our Nellie.'

It was Seamus who hurried back into town to the police station at Moor Street, after he got home from work. Ada and the boys waited together, bewildered, stunned. When Ada went upstairs to see if Sarah understood what was happening, she lay gazing blankly, lost in a world of her own. All Ada could do was try to get her to sip some water and leave her be.

When Seamus came back he looked ten years older than he had in the morning, grey and stooped, his face seeming to have crumpled in on itself. He took off his coat, hung it up with shaking hands, and stood in front of them with the watery, bewildered eyes of an old man.

'They say she killed a man.'

They all stared.

'*What?*' Ada managed, eventually. Here it was again, the same sense of horror, of things spiralling away completely out of control.

'They found the feller by the cut yesterday morning, frozen as a plank. They're saying it was her fault.'

Ada's heart started pounding even harder. Nellie had been there all right – at the wharf with two men. But they had been alive when Ada left. Alive and noisy. What in God's name had Nellie done? She knew that none of this should ever pass her lips. None of them knew where she had been, what she had seen and heard . . .

Seamus sank on to a chair in a posture of complete despair. Ada sat down on another chair nearby, pulling the little boys to her. Here was the nightmare they had been in before – all over again.

*

Ada put food in front of all of them, a thin broth and bread. They ate without knowing they were eating. Little Anthony stared round at all his brothers. Petey was quietly crying, Tom trying hard not to and the others were angry and stunned. The air was full of questions and Ada knew the answers to at least some of them but she kept quiet.

'Did you see her?' she asked Seamus.

He shook his head. 'They wouldn't tell me anything – except about the dead man.'

An agonized look passed over his face, then he raised his fist and slammed it on the table. Everyone jumped and Anthony started crying as well.

'What's been going on under my own nose? Why do I have such cursed, damn women!'

That night Ada put the mattress down to sleep, for the first time knowing that Nellie would not be beside her. She lay awake full of a sense of the same horror as when Sarah was in prison. The man's body, stiff as a tree at the wharf, Nellie with a noose about her neck, Nellie hanging, dead . . .

She had been there all right, at the wharf. There was no denying it. But what could have happened to make one of those men lie down on the towpath and never get up again?

Ada knew she was not going to be able to sleep – she felt as if she might never sleep again.

She heard a creak, then another. Bare feet stumbling down the rough wooden stairs. Ada's heart raced. Quickly she got up and struck a match to light the candle, wincing as the cold of the floor penetrated her bare feet.

Seamus had on a vest and ragged drawers, both yellowed with age. His face was stubbly, eyes red and wild. Ada forgot to breathe for a moment. She felt naked. She had taken off her corset and had on only an old petticoat

131

and chemise. She had not even had time to grab hold of her shawl. Her teeth were starting to chatter from cold and fear.

For a moment Seamus seemed lost for words. He stepped forward and Ada retreated towards the range.

'I've come to lie with you,' he announced. 'I can't abide it up there, not the way she is.'

Ada stared dumbly at him, her head starting to shake before her mind had even taken in fully what he meant.

'No,' she managed at last. 'No.' She backed away further and he followed.

'Will you not give a man relief? I've given you a roof over your head . . .'

'No,' she said again. 'Please . . .'

She was still not sure of what he wanted from her. Did he really just want to sleep beside her? But that time before, his lips forcing on hers, the sounds from those men in the dark down by the cut – horrible, animal, sounds.

'I need a woman,' Seamus commanded. 'A woman who'll look me in the eye. God knows, it's been long enough – come on now . . .' His voice started to wheedle. 'Just a little cuddle, colleen, that's all . . . Here now – you're getting cold – come and lie down . . .'

Ada reached out and put the candle and saucer down on the table. She eyed the door. But she was not even wearing shoes and it was icy out there . . .

'Come to me – I need yer . . .'

Seamus came up so that his solid body was suddenly close to hers, with his thick, hairy forearms and his worn, stubbly face, his hands reaching for her.

'Just a little cuddle now . . . Don't make me force you . . .'

'Get away from me.' Her voice was high, plaintive. She tried to get hold of herself, speak more strongly. 'D'you want me to wake the whole yard? Get away . . .'

All she could think of was stopping him. She whirled

round, grabbing the heavy skillet with both hands. Then she raised it high and slammed it down on Seamus's head.

'Aaagh!' He staggered back a little. 'For the love of God, woman . . .'

Ada came at him again, but he stuck out a hand and grabbed the handle, snatching it off her. He hurled it down on the table behind him, his blood up.

Ada grabbed another saucepan from behind her.

'Don't you touch me,' she roared. 'You've got me as your skivvy, but you touch me and I'll never do a thing for you again – ever. You can cook or you can starve for all I care – and all your kids as well. Get away!'

As she waved the pan in his face the words seemed to sink in. Seamus drew back. He sat down suddenly on one of the chairs.

'God now . . .' He put his head in his hands. His shoulders shook and loud sobs tore out of his chest. 'What'm I to do? My wife . . . My daughter . . . What'll become of us . . .?'

Ada put the pan down, feeling the icy cold of the floor again.

'You're a hard woman, Ada . . .'

'I may be hard,' she said, trying to control her chattering teeth. 'But I'm the only one left and I'm not here to be your woman. Not like that. Get back upstairs to your wife – and you keep away from me.'

After a moment, head still down, Seamus got up, weeping, and staggered to the stairs.

It was in the papers. A man had been found on the canal bank, seemingly frozen to death. But another fellow had come forward – he had been there as well. Neither were locals and they had gone to the wharf from the pub in Summer Row with two women who were known to the surrounding pubs as easy wenches and trouble. One was Nellie Connell, the other was named as Clara Thorne. The man swore the girls had fed them what were seemingly knockout doses of laudanum. They had started to 'have their fun' when both of them gradually lost consciousness. The girls had clearly planned to rob the pair of them.

When the witness woke, muzzy and confused, he had managed to stagger away in the darkness of the small hours, dazed and unclear of his exact whereabouts. He had not even seen his companion who he assumed had already gone. But that fellow had not been so lucky. He must have drunk more of the potion Nellie and Clara had meted out and stayed unconscious in the freezing night until death overtook him.

Twenty-One

'Your intent, that January night, when you set out on your ill-fated and criminal quest, was not to kill but to rob.'

Ada waited, beside Seamus, hardly able to breathe. Neither of them had been at the Petty and then Quarter Sessions hearings in Birmingham because it was a foregone conclusion that Nellie's case, serious as it was, would be heard, like her mother's, at the Warwick Assizes.

It was weeks since they had seen Nellie and Ada felt a plunge of dread when her friend appeared in the dock, head down, so beaten-looking she hardly seemed the same Nellie. Ada heard Seamus's intake of breath when he caught sight of her and he gripped his knees with his hands until the veins swelled.

Nellie wept all through the trial, such a poor, shrunken thing, standing there, alone in the dock like a little island in a stormy sea. She was thin, her hair lank and lifeless. Only once did she look across at her father and Ada, then quickly lowered her head as if she could not bear to meet their eyes.

'I never meant it,' she sobbed, on questioning. 'That was never s'posed to happen . . .'

Ada could not help thinking that if the girls had carried out their thieving plan on a summer night instead, things would not have gone nearly so badly for them. But the man, one James Goodwin, a worker from Clay's japanning factory, was now dead and there was no getting around that. She thought of all the times Nellie had got away with her petty crimes, her pilfering and stealing. But she had never meant to do this – not kill someone. It was not in her nature.

'Nevertheless,' the judge went on, 'a man is dead. It is not possible to establish whether the cause of his death was the overpowering dose of laudanum mixed with intoxicating liquor which was meted out to him by you and Miss Thorne, or the freezing temperature of that January night. However, what we can be perfectly sure of is that the one led to the other.'

There was a pause, a stillness in the court except for a sob from Nellie.

'Therefore, Nellie Ann Connell, you stand convicted of the manslaughter of James Elijah Goodwin and I hereby sentence you to ten years' imprisonment.'

A strangled sound came from Seamus's throat and Ada gasped.

'Ten years?' Nellie wailed like a child. 'But I never meant for it to happen . . .! Don't – don't make me . . .'

She was hauled away, sobbing.

Ada and Seamus walked numbly from the court. Seamus leaned one arm against the wall outside to steady himself. Then looked at Ada.

'Herself will be out while she's still young enough to bear a child. We have to thank the Lord he didn't send her to the gallows.'

William brought home a copy of the *Daily Post* to read the details.

Clara Thorne was sentenced to twelve years, since it was she who had bought the laudanum and mixed the drink. The girls had robbed the men of their money – a total of two pounds and three shillings along with a gold watch-chain and ring – and had planned to split the proceeds between them.

Seamus, like someone drawn to a poisoned well, read the news report, in which Nellie was described as a 'pathetic, impressionable young girl', then flung the paper across the room.

'Get it out of my sight.'

Ada grabbed the paper and hid it on the shelf to read later.

They did not feel they could keep the news from Sarah Connell. Seamus relayed what had happened to her. He came downstairs afterwards, looked at Ada and shook his head.

'I don't know if she even heard me,' he said. 'She lies there like a plank.'

After the trial everyone at the works was full of it. And Ada was faced with a household of men and boys whose wife and mother was lost to them in all but body, and now they had lost a daughter and sister as well.

Now all the work of the house fell to Ada – as well as giving Sarah what care and sustenance she would accept, which was very little, and trying to comfort a household of bereft males large and small.

'Where's Nellie?' Anthony kept asking.

'She's had to go away for a bit,' Ada told him, her eyes filling at the sight of his sad little face.

But as ever it was Tom who tore most at her heart. He was now working as a delivery boy for Collins the butcher's, pushing a cart, swaggering about, trying to look like a tough little man when she knew he was soft as butter.

After Nellie was sent down, he sidled up to Ada one night, when his elder brothers were out of the way.

'Can I sleep down here with you, Ada?'

Ada looked into his face, the little child peering out from the twelve-year-old man he was expected to be. Her mind raced. It was a while since, as a little boy, he used to come down and snuggle up to her. It seemed peculiar for him to start sleeping with her again at his age. But, she calculated, having him beside her would surely mean his father could not try anything again?

'All right,' she said. 'You sleep here tonight and we'll see after that.'

The yard neighbours all had their say as well.

'That silly, silly girl. What a thing,' Mrs Spragg said, shaking her head. 'You're going to have your work cut out with all of them.' She walked away slowly, a squat figure in her long skirt. 'You know where to come if you need help.'

'Thanks, Mrs Spragg,' Ada said. Her neighbour had always been kind and it was a great relief to know she could call on her. But all the same, there was only so much she could expect of her.

'I always said they were trouble,' Mrs O'Shea remarked when she and Ada were both pegging out washing in the yard. 'And you a martyr to the lot of them.' She looked Ada up and down. 'I don't know why you stay. You're not one of them are you, after all?'

'Some of us don't mind doing a kindness now and then,' Ada said, looking with loathing into Nora O'Shea's sharp-featured face. It was the first time she had addressed a word to the woman in years. As she walked off she added, 'Not that you'd know about that.'

Much as Ada disliked Nora O'Shea, her words hit home. As the weeks passed she never stopped. All day she was at the works and the rest of the time she was running to the shops, cooking and cleaning and dealing with the washing of the young boys' sodden bedding, spoon-feeding Sarah thin broths and sweet tea, the only intake she would accept.

Having Tom in her bed was a comfort to both of them and so far Seamus had not made any more night-time approaches. But more and more these days he took it for granted that she was to act as his maidservant. Ada was worn out and found herself getting ever angrier.

'What's this muck?' Seamus demanded one night when she put a plate of stew in front of him. He poked at it with a knife. 'Looks like something a dog brought up.'

William and Tom sniggered. It might have been meant as a joke by his tone, but by now Ada was well past any kind of joking. Rage swelled in her. Here she was, collaring for them day and night while the woman of the house lay in a stupor and the lads sat around after work or went out with their girls.

'If you don't like it you can leave it,' Ada snapped. 'But there'll be nothing else unless you want to cook it yourself.'

She stood over Seamus with her hands on her hips.

'Ah, now – don't give out to me like that,' he said. 'I was only kidding yer. You're under my roof – and I'm keeping you, so I am?'

'Are you?' Ada said, eyes blazing. 'I thought I was keeping myself? I earn my own money and I'm doing all the work round here.' She raised the skillet as if to signify what might happen again. 'So don't talk about my food like that.'

The boys all looked at each other. And kept quiet.

Ada stared round at them as she put the skillet back on the range. William and Tom were all right, but the two littlest lads could barely fend for themselves and maybe never would. She was filled with utter hopelessness. She had not long come down from seeing Sarah, who now did not answer when Ada spoke to her. Though Ada and Olive Spragg both tried to coax her to eat, she took in almost nothing now. All her energy had gone. Sarah had turned her face to the wall on her own life – and who knew how long she would linger in that state.

Is this my life now? Ada asked herself. For years and years, never ending? Oh, Pa – is this how I have to live?

The despair of it filled her as she spooned a helping of the scraggy stew on to her own plate. And something stirred in her then.

This isn't the life I want . . . She looked round at all the boys. I can't save them all – I just can't. I've got to get away from here . . .

Later, when she was alone, getting ready for the night, she reached up to the shelf and took down the newspaper that she had parked up there. She read the item about Nellie, her heart sinking even further. Then, leafing through in the light of the candle, she found what she was looking for. The page half-filled with closely printed advertisements:

WANTED

For the household of a gentleman industrialist, near Birmingham, a Kitchen Maid. other work may be required. Pref. Protestant. Must be hard-working, of good, sober character.

III

Twenty-Two

August 1858

The back door of the large house on the hill was painted a dark green. Ada, sweating from her uphill walk, hoicked the bundle containing her pitifully few possessions on to one arm, rapped the door with her knuckles and waited. It felt quiet out here after the bustle of town. She looked round. She had entered from the street through a wooden gate and along a short cinder path. Beside the doorstep, a neglected pink geranium in a pot was wilting in the heat.

Already it felt as if she had entered another world away from the filth of town and the tragic chaos of the Connells.

The door opened to reveal a cheerful-looking young woman with a white apron over her long grey dress and a mob cap with a pale blue ribbon threaded round it. She was chewing furiously on something and had difficulty speaking.

'Oh – 'ello. You the new kitchen maid?' she inquired, indistinctly. 'Sorry,' she giggled, pointing to her lumpy cheek. 'Toffee.'

Ada smiled at this young woman's infectious good humour, immediately feeling better.

'Come on – I'll show yer,' she went on, through the toffee. 'Mrs Simmons – that's our cook – is having a snooze. There'll be hell to pay if we wake her up.' As they walked she gradually freed up her mouth. 'Kitchen, here –'

She flung open a nearby door and Ada saw a wide space, quarry-tiled floor in a warm red, rows of shiny pots along a shelf and the biggest range she had ever seen. In the middle of the room was a long table, the surface scrubbed white, a muddle of onions on it beside a heap of rhubarb piled neatly with the leaves cut off and the remains of a tray of toffee.

'Mrs S made it today – 'ere, have a bit.' As she went to hack off a bit of the toffee from the fast-setting block, the girl looked up, brown eyes smiling. 'I'm Josie, by the way. The parlour maid.' She gave a little mock curtsey. 'On my best behaviour at all times o'course. Here, taste – it's bostin.'

'Ta – I could do with that,' Ada said. 'But can I have a drink of water first? I've come from across town.'

'Hot, ain't it?' Josie said. She pointed at a little cane chair in the corner. 'Go on – sit you down for a bit.'

She fetched a tin mug of water and Ada downed the lot before starting on the toffee, which was delicious. Her spirits were rising by the minute.

'Come on,' Josie said once Ada had had time to recover. 'I'll show you where we sleep. Mrs S'll be up soon and then there'll be no stopping.' She gave Ada a wink and Ada smiled. She was fast warming to Josie.

'What's she like?' Ada dared to ask as she followed the girl's slender form up the back stairs.

'All right,' Josie said. 'As long as 'er daughter's not playing up.'

'Does her daughter work here?' Ada asked.

'No. 'Er's married to one of the blokes in the foundry but there's always summat ailing 'er.'

By now they had climbed two flights of stairs, the second one narrow and with no covering over the bare planks.

'Here – this is us.'

She opened the door into a bare bedroom with three brass bedsteads, three upright wooden chairs and a narrow deal wardrobe down at one end. The windows were so high in the wall that all you could see was sky.

'Oh!' Ada gasped.

The floor was bare boards and the room very plain but there were sheets on each bed and a pale green quilt. To her the place looked like a palace compared to the Connells' house. A bed – an actual, whole bed all to herself!

'That one's yours.' Josie pointed to the far bed, near the wardrobe. 'And if you need to go in the night there's a gaz-under . . . Yes, down there.'

Ada walked round, peered under the bed to see a plain white po' and grinned at Josie.

'Who sleeps there?'

A grey dress and apron lay on the middle bed as if hur-riedly thrown down. They obviously did not belong to anybody very big.

'That's Mary's. Maid of all work – just a young'un. Funny little thing. Any road – that's us up here. And there's Mrs S, and there's Sally Hooper – she looks after the chil-dren, sleeps with them an' all, poor sod . . . And Mrs Lord comes in to do the laundry. There's no housekeeper as such, but *she* –' she jerked her head in a way that Ada took to mean the mistress of the house – 'keeps tabs on everything from her big couch. So, that's us – 'cept for the two blokes who do the garden . . .'

Josie blushed and looked round at Ada. 'One of 'em, Loz – well, Lawrence is his proper name – me and him are walking out together on days off, like. Have to keep it under wraps here though, o'course.' She put her head on one side. 'You got a feller?'

'No,' Ada said decisively.

'All right.' Josie looked taken aback. 'No need to bite my head off.'

'Sorry,' Ada said. She did not want to explain her feelings

about men – first Pa, then Seamus Connell. It was all too painful and complicated. She threw her bundle on the bed and sank down on to the sagging mattress.

'D'you think they'd have a job for a lad? He's twelve. A good lad – hard worker?'

All day her heart had been like lead with unshed tears and now, thinking of Tom, it was all she could do to hold back from crying. She had ripped herself away from the Connell boys. What would become of the younger two was something she could not even bear to think about. She could not save those two little souls – that was beyond her. But it was Tom who hurt the most. The one who felt like her little brother, who had given her affection when no one else had and she was able to give it back. She knew what a sweet lad he was underneath, even though he tried to look like a hard little man.

'Don't go, Ada,' he had sobbed the night before, clinging to her.

'I've got to, Tom,' she murmured. He was the only one who knew in advance that she was leaving. She could not keep it from him. 'But I'll try and fetch you, all right? I'll see if I can get a job so's you can be with me?'

'Your brother?' Josie asked.

Ada hesitated before saying, 'Yeah. I didn't want to leave him but I had to come . . .'

'I don't know that there's a job. You'd have to ask. But I should leave it 'til you've been here for a bit?' Josie went to the door. 'You have a lie-down for a few minutes. Everyone'll be up and about again soon and there'll be plenty to do. Oh –' She turned. 'There's a chemise and dress for you in the cupboard – and a pinner. There's shoes as well – try them for size.'

When Josie had left the room, Ada untied her bundle. Inside was her one spare dress and a pair of bloomers and her chemise which it was too hot to wear today. Wrapped inside was her collection of shells. Before she left she had given Tom one of her favourites, a huge trochus shell, its brown and cream markings smoothed and polished by her loving hands.

She had brought a dozen or so with her – trochus and abalone and a selection of snail shells. Handling each one like an old friend she laid them out on the quilt, eyes filling with tears.

'I'm giving you a good reference, Ada,' Mrs Rundle had said to her gruffly, handing her an envelope 'You're a good worker and I'm sorry to let you go. Heaven alone knows why you'd want to go into service, but I'm sure you've got your reasons.'

Over the years Mrs Rundle had already seen Elsie disappear, then all the troubles with Nellie. She didn't pry. And now Ada was going to have to learn fast in the kitchen with this Mrs Simmons. It wouldn't be the same – pots and pans and endless washing up and cooking instead of the heaven-sent, otherworldly gleam of mother-of-pearl. But for now, this work was going to have to do – and at least she had a roof over her head.

She wrapped the shells back in their cloth and lay on the bed, clutching them to her chest as if they were an injured creature.

A little later she thought she heard stirrings downstairs. Josie did not come back again and Ada got up quickly, feeling she ought to make an appearance.

Opening the cupboard she found a simple grey dress hanging there which she put on and added the white pinafore. There was also a pair of black leather shoes and she slipped her feet in. They were on the big side, but once she had buttoned them up, overall she found to her surprise that they were not a bad fit. They were not new, the leather crinkled by someone else's feet, but she looked down at them in excitement. They were the newest thing she had had in years!

She took another look round the room. Already she had a feeling she was going to like this place. She felt freer – not like all these past years when she had felt so responsible all the time.

As quietly as she could, she crept down the wooden stairs, pausing on the landing below which was carpeted in a dark maroon colour, trying to remember her way to the lower back staircase.

As she moved towards it, a door opened along the corridor ahead of her that led towards the front of the house. A moment later a little figure in black came quickly towards her, carrying a bundle of what looked like clothing. For a second, there seemed something unearthly about her, the pale face turned towards the ground, the girl seeming to glide silently along on the carpet, her feet invisible because the dress she wore was a little too long for her.

For a split-second Ada thought about calling out to her. She must be one of the other maids? Something about her gave Ada the chills. That dress was not a servant's dress. And the girl was so silent, seemed so locked into herself. She did not look up or see Ada, but went to the attic stairs and disappeared up them.

Ada set off down the other stairs, feeling goose pimples on her skin. The back stairs took her straight to the kitchen where Josie was arranging teacups on a tray and a tense-looking woman with a rather manly country face, dark brows and big hands was working on the pile of onions.

'Ah,' she said, wiping her eyes on her forearm. When she spoke she had a country accent as well. 'Just in time. Give us a hand with these, will you?'

Ada pulled her sleeves up. Josie did the introductions and then disappeared carrying the tea tray.

'One of the worst jobs, onions,' Mrs Simmons remarked, streaming. 'You come far, 'ave you, Ada?'

'No,' Ada said. 'Birmingham.'

'Worked in a kitchen before?'

'Only in a house,' Ada admitted. 'But I had to do all the cooking.'

'Well, I'll be very glad of another pair of hands,' Mrs Simmons said. 'Just do what I tell you and no skiving and we'll get on all right.'

When Josie came back she said, 'Mrs Dugdale wants to see you, Ada. She likes to meet all the servants.'

'Wants to know who's living in 'er house,' Mrs Simmons said. 'I s'pose I would, if it was me.'

'Come on – wash your hands and I'll take you,' Josie said.

'She won't bite,' Mrs Simmons said. Then she added mysteriously, 'Woman's got bigger problems than you.'

Ada followed Josie through a green baize door to the front of the house, into a corridor that Ada had seen when she came to be interviewed. Pictures of dogs and horses hung on the wooden panelled walls, and the parquet floor was so shiny that Ada had been almost afraid to walk on it. It looked almost as shiny today.

She touched Josie's arm to stop her a moment.

'I saw a girl upstairs – in a black dress.'

Something about the sight had felt so strange that she was starting to wonder if she had imagined it.

'Oh,' Josie said. 'I s'pect that was Mary.'

She didn't explain further and there was something in the way she rolled her eyes as she said it that seemed not impatient but – some other emotion that Ada could not identify.

'I s'pose it was Mr Dugdale interviewed you?'

Ada nodded. Mr Dugdale, a man she thought must be

in his forties, with a rather bulgy face, prominent grey eyes and receding hair, had stared intently at her, run his eye over Mrs Rundle's reference and asked her if she knew what to do in the kitchen.

'Yes,' Ada replied. She was standing in the parlour they were about to enter and she had been so dazzled by the rich buttery colour of the settee he was sitting on and the opulent gold curtains and thick rug by the fire that she had struggled to concentrate and not gawp about the place. Truthfully, she added, 'Not in such a big house as this though.'

He looked her up and down again and there was such a long pause that he seemed to be thinking about something else altogether. He was not unpleasant – just seemed vague, almost as if he had already forgotten about her. She found it hard to imagine him in charge of a foundry. He was not like Jem Atherton or Pa or any of the other men she had met.

'I'm sure you'll learn fast,' he'd said, getting up. 'Bring your things and start straight away.'

'Come on,' Josie urged now, tapping on the door. 'Mrs Dugdale's waiting.'

Twenty-Three

As they walked into the parlour, a young woman who Ada realized was the nanny, Miss Hooper, a pale, mousey girl of about sixteen, was shepherding three little children out of the room. Ada saw a boy of about six and two younger girls, the little one holding Miss Hooper's hand. They were very sweet-looking children and Ada smiled at Miss Hooper who gave a faint, tense movement of her lips in return.

'Goodnight, my darlings,' their mother said. What a high little voice, Ada thought.

Mrs Dugdale was sitting on the same elegant settee where Mr Dugdale had sat to question her. Beside her on a little table, Ada saw a china bowl full of coloured bonbons. All those sweets for Mrs Dugdale just to reach out her hand and take one whenever she wanted! Ada had to drag her gaze away from them.

The rich, yellow material of the settee looked so smooth and beautiful that once again Ada longed to run her hand over it. But the sight of Mrs Dugdale was even more mesmerizing.

She gave a wide-eyed smile as the two of them came in.

'Come along, Josie – let's see you both.'

Ada had never met anyone who looked so much like a little doll. Mrs Dugdale (Josie had said her Christian name was Jane) was wearing a very pretty summer dress in cream, with sprigs of cherries scattered across it and edged in something Ada knew was called broderie anglaise. On her feet, which did not quite reach the floor, Ada could make out a delicate little pair of crimson shoes decorated with a ribbon rosette. Jane Dugdale had almost white-blonde hair drawn back neatly from a centre parting and covering her ears, a small, heart-shaped face, invisibly pale brows and a lightly freckled complexion. The overall effect was very pretty – but somehow she only looked about Ada's age instead of like a mother of three children.

'So.' She looked Ada up and down. 'This is . . .?'

'Ada, madam,' Josie said. 'The new kitchen maid.'

It was only then that Ada, caught up with an ache of longing, in admiring the pale golden paint on the walls, Mrs Dugdale's clothes and that bowl of sweeties, realized how closely Mrs Dugdale was examining her. Like her husband before her, she seemed to have something on her mind. And the look in her eyes had become hard and suspicious.

'How old are you?' she demanded in her funny little voice.

'Seventeen, ma'am,' Ada said.

'I see,' Mrs Dugdale said. She seemed to relax a fraction. Looking at Josie, she added, 'She's quite tall. Like you.'

'Yes, madam,' Josie said.

It felt from the way she said it as if this was important in some way, though Ada could not see how. It was true though – she was almost as tall as Josie, who was nineteen.

Mrs Dugdale stared at Ada again for a moment, but whatever thoughts had been going through her mind, she seemed satisfied with something. She suddenly became practical, looking Ada up and down.

'Your uniform fits well enough. And your shoes? Good . . . Well – we'll see how you get on with Mrs Simmons.'

'Yes, madam,' Ada said. 'Thank you.'

'You may go,' Mrs Dugdale said. 'Josie, stay – I need you to do a few things in here.'

It was a hot evening, so that they kept the back door wide open while finishing the dinner in the kitchen. Mrs Simmons had already started on the soup and the onions were sizzling in a wide-bottomed pan, giving off a lovely smell. A ham was bubbling in water in another pot.

The gardener, Loz, a blond, handsome lad, appeared at the door and he and Josie laughed and whispered together until Mrs Simmons told him to 'Clear off and get on with something you're *s'posed* to be doing, eh?'

'Finish the soup, will you?' she ordered Ada. 'Nub of bacon first – then them peas – and wash out that jug for me, quick as you like . . .'

Ada spent the next hour scurrying about to keep up with all Mrs Simmons's orders, so much so that she hardly had time to notice anything else. Little Mary the other maid, now in her grey dress and mob cap pulled low over her forehead, trotted in and out – one minute rushing past with a coal scuttle, the next needing a wet cloth to scrub a stain.

'He's gone and knocked a tankard of ale all over the chair,' Ada heard her complain. She sounded annoyed. 'Said to clean it when they go in for dinner.'

'Get the water ready,' Mrs Simmons ordered. 'And put a bit of bicarb in . . . Is Josie laying up?'

'She's nearly finished . . .' Mary came over to the range to fill the huge kettle.

'Hello,' Ada managed . . . 'I'm the new—'

'I know,' Mary said, rushing off again. 'Josie said. See you later, all right?'

Ada, stirring the pea soup, stared after her skinny,

hurrying little figure. Mary had a nice voice, she thought. There was something in it that made Ada warm to her, the funny little thing.

'Go and get a sprig of mint,' Mrs Simmons broke into her thoughts. 'It's down the garden – on the right.'

Ada stepped out into the smell of roses and evening grass. For a moment she felt she was in heaven and she dawdled on her way towards the herb garden, along a lawn edged with beds of sprawling, sweet-scented flowers. She did not know much about herbs but she did know rosemary. She tugged a small sprig from the bush and felt its sharp tang in her nostrils. Then the mint, the unmistakable summer smell of it. Her mother had grown a little patch of it in those days before, when they had had a square of garden.

Now she had a moment to think, life felt good. She'd have to work hard but none of this seemed anything like as tough as having to cook and clean and look after all the Connells with Sarah fading away upstairs and Seamus breathing down her neck. But a pang of grief went through her. She knew Mrs Spragg would care for Sarah in any way she could, for as long as she lasted. But poor little Peter and Anthony. What was to become of them?

And most of all she missed Tom. How could she get Tom out of there, find something for him to do so they could be together again?

She was just straightening up from picking a couple of sprigs of mint when a voice close by said, 'Who're you then? The new maid?'

Ada jumped and turned to find a lad not much older than herself with dark brown hair, rosy cheeks and a strong, well-fed-looking body.

'Who wants to know?' she said tartly.

'Well, I do,' the lad said laughing. 'Who else?'

Ada softened. He looked all right after all.

'I'm Mrs Simmons's kitchen maid,' she said. 'Ada's my name.'

'I'm Harry – I do the garden,' he said. 'Where've you come out here from then?'

'Town,' Ada said. She didn't feel she owed him any other information. 'What about you?'

'Redditch,' he said. 'My father was a gardener and now so am I.'

Ada nodded, not sure what to say. 'Best get back with this.' She held up the mint. 'Be in trouble else.'

Harry laughed. 'You will. Not a bad old stick Mrs S though. You'll be all right with her. See you around, Ada.'

He turned and walked off with a strong, loping stride. Ada watched him. If only Tom could have a job like that, she thought. At the moment she could not think of any way to make that happen.

The three maids were kept busy late into the evening, even after Mrs Simmons had gone home, her work done for the day.

'See you lot all too soon,' she remarked, going out of the back door with a basket over her arm.

Josie rolled her eyes jokingly. 'Can't wait,' she said to the others and Ada heard Mary snigger as she bent over, riddling the fire.

By the time the meal had been cleared and they had had their own supper – ham and potatoes and leftovers of the rhubarb pie, all of which seemed sumptuous to Ada – and everything was washed up and put away by Ada and the rooms tidied and made ready for the next day, by Josie and Mary, the three of them were ready to drop.

'We'll have a cuppa before we turn in,' Josie said. 'Fancy a drop of cocoa?'

'Don't they mind?' Ada said. This seemed a great luxury to her. She was going to be all right here, she thought.

'Nah,' Josie said. 'They don't care what we do. That Mary stuffs her hodge all the time.'

Ada had noticed that Mary put her head down during their meal and ate as if it was a contest.

Josie went to the back door and looked out into the dusk. 'Shall we go outside?'

Ada smiled. She could guess why Josie wanted to go outside – in case Loz was about somewhere.

The three girls took their cups and went out to sit on the grass in the twilight. Following Mary, Ada looked her up and down. She started to have the oddest feeling, something that began in her senses and started to build up in her like a wave coming from a long distance away. The way Mary walked, the shape of her . . .

She sat down beside her, her heart starting to thud, even though she could hardly make sense of why. The cocoa was sweet and delicious and for a few minutes she listened to Mary and Josie moaning and joking about the day together. Then her ears really pricked.

'What was all that about today?' Josie asked, her voice lowered, almost as if Ada should not be hearing it.

'Just the usual,' Mary said. There was something blank in her voice, a deadness.

'But black? He's an odd fish that one and no mistake.'

'I was a widow today. Dunno who's s'posed to have died. And the frock was horrible.' She shuddered. 'All stiff and much too long.' She turned her head suddenly and in a different, strange voice, said, 'I'm never doing it again.'

Something was registering in Ada's mind, something which sent the blood pounding along her veins, so much so that she barely noticed Josie's reply. It was instinct more than any fully formed thought. Her breathing had gone shallow, her heart thumping hard.

Reaching into her pocket Ada took out the trochus shell that she always carried with her like a good-luck charm. It had stayed with her all this time, a comfort like a friend, and so beautiful with its whorls of dark brown over a glossy tan background.

'Look,' she said, her heart still going like a drum. 'Lovely, ain't it?'

The others peered at it. The light was dying and it was hard to see.

'Nice,' Josie said. 'Where d'yer get that?'

But it was Mary who reached out for it, slowly taking it from Ada with a strange, intense look to her.

'It's . . .' she said. 'This is . . .' It was as if her mind was stuttering. 'Those are . . .' She turned it over in her hand. 'You cut them, and then . . . I used to . . .'

'Shut your eyes,' Ada said.

Mary looked at her in the gloom as if she was mad. With those eyes. Big blue-grey eyes.

'Come 'ere.' Ada leaned close to her. 'Shut them. Let me see.'

As the girl closed her eyes, Ada leaned close, peering at her. Even in the poor light she could make out, at the corner of Mary's left eyelid, that dark mark, like a tiny heart. Ada felt her breath suck in, then burst out, 'Elsie!'

The girl's eyes snapped open, staring at Ada in stunned confusion, like someone waking from a long dream.

'I'm . . . No . . . I'm . . . Mary. Mary Lunn.' She was stuttering, shaking her head. Then she looked wildly into Ada's face, as if searching her every feature. 'No! I'm not Mary Lunn.'

Ada could feel Josie watching them.

'You're Elsie. Fletcher. You sorted the buttons. At

Tompkinson's – remember? And we had a pa before, and our mom. And I'm Ada. Your big sister.'

Elsie gazed at Ada and then, in wonder, she reached out to touch Ada's cheek as if unsure that she was really there.

'*Ada?*'

Ada felt as if her chest was ripping open, the tears welling in her eyes.

'Elsie. Oh, Elsie . . .'

And slowly, full of wonder and joy, the two sisters leaned into each other's arms, into the tightest embrace.

'I'm your sister,' Ada kept saying. Tears were pouring down her cheeks as she held Elsie in her arms. 'They took you away – you and Dora and John and Mabs . . .' She gave a sob. 'Why do they call you Mary? That's not your name.'

'I dunno,' Elsie said. 'That's what they called me in the workhouse.'

They released each other and Elsie was still holding the snail shell. She turned it round in her hands, an expression of deep pain flashing across her face.

'Tompkinson's.' She looked up at Ada. 'The buttons . . . And there was Nellie. Nellie . . .?'

'Connell.' Ada nodded. This was no moment to tell Elsie what had become of Nellie, of Sarah and the others.

'Oh, my word,' Josie said, sounding emotional herself. 'When did you two last see each other?'

'Not since February 1852,' Ada managed to say through her tears. The date was engraved on her mind. 'February the fifteenth.'

That night, when they went to bed, the candle blown out, Elsie whispered across the narrow space between the beds.

'Sis?' Ada moved closer. 'What happened to our mother?'

'She died,' Ada said. 'Having a baby.'

There was a silence from the other bed.

'And our pa?'

A lump thrust up in Ada's throat so she could hardly speak.

'He just . . . went, one day. Don't you remember? I always thought he'd come back, but . . . Something must've happened to him. He'd done summat I think, summat he shouldn't of, because there were people looking for him. Those men who came to the house – they were angry with him.' How could Elsie not remember? 'I don't suppose he did anything all that bad,' she said, clinging desperately to her image of her beloved father. 'If it wasn't for that, Pa'd never've just left us and not come back.'

All her own old grief welled up and tears ran down her cheeks in the dark. Finding Elsie again felt like a key to their past, to all of them. It felt like the happiest day of her life.

'Tell me,' she begged Elsie, 'about the others – Dora and John and Mabs. Are they all right? What are they like?'

Elsie whispered that Dora and John were still in the workhouse.

'They call Dora "Annie" there. John kept his name. They're all right.'

'What about Mabs?' Ada asked. Baby Mabs, her favourite.

Elsie seemed vague. 'I dunno. She went – a long time ago. Someone took her away, I think.'

Ada listened, horrified. She had always thought the three of them would at least all be together. Had Mabs been taken away to another family? Would they love her as she had done?

For a moment she was awash with grief. She had to remind herself of now – what had happened today. She had found Elsie and that was a miracle!

'Hold my hand, sis . . .' Ada reached out and found Elsie's little hand in the dark. 'We're back together now and no one's going to part us again. Not ever.'

She managed to lie down again and they fell asleep, their hands still clasped together.

Twenty-Four

Seven months earlier

When Elsie left the workhouse, they provided her with a simple grey dress and a pair of old button boots which she had buffed to a shine. They were not new, but they were the best boots she had ever seen and she could not stop looking at them as she walked out with Mrs Hodges, passing through the Archway of Tears to the horse and trap waiting in the street.

Mrs Hodges was a gaunt, bony woman.

'Mary Lunn,' she announced, pausing at the lodge. 'Leaving for a place in service.'

Elsie, by then, had thought of herself as Mary for years. It seemed strange to her, as she stood holding her little bundle of things, her teeth chattering, that Mrs Hodges spoke to the porter as if she hardly knew him, even though 'Hodge the Lodge' with his drooping moustache was her husband.

'Right you are,' he said. 'It's going to be a cold ride. See you later.'

'Come along, Mary,' Mrs Hodges ordered. 'I've brought you a shawl to wrap up in. Can't have you arriving with a fever. Say thank you then, child.'

'Thanks, Mrs Hodges,' she parroted, then broke into coughing. Her nose was already red raw with a cold.

'Can't think why they want you,' Mrs Hodges remarked.

'No more than a bag of bones but your new master asked for a little'un so that's what they're getting.'

And off they went. Mrs Hodges led her out, walking very straight in her coat and hat, raising a hand to press it tightly on her head as the biting wind buffeted them out to a world crouched under a pall of grey cloud.

They climbed into the trap and Elsie pulled the shawl round her. It stank of Mr Hodges's pipe smoke. She imagined for a second Mr and Mrs Hodges sitting, stiff as statues, either side of a hearth in the evening in their quarters in the workhouse, the air smoky blue all around them.

The carriage driver clicked his tongue and her ears filled with the sound of hooves and wheels on the cobbles. The dark bulk of the building where she had spent all these years slid away behind them and faded out of view, taking with it the only life she could now truly remember and leaving behind her brother and sister. There were too many feelings coming all at once and she forced them to stop by giving her body a little shake. In doing so her elbow knocked into Mrs Hodges's ribs.

'Stop your fidgeting,' Mrs Hodges scolded. 'And that sniffing.'

The Turnpike Road was crowded with commercial traffic, some of it dwarfing their little trap. Elsie kept her mind on the present, breathing in the cold air, laced with horse manure and coal smoke and nasty, acrid smells from more and more factories as they trotted nearer to the heart of Birmingham. Her feet were frozen, the cold air stung her sore nostrils and her nose was running. She wiped it on the scratchy wool of the shawl when Mrs Hodges was looking the other way. And drank in the newness of being out amid the clatter of hooves, handcarts loaded with metal rods and all sorts, dogs weaving in and out of the traffic, barking, and dark-clad figures milling along the pavements.

Because she did not want to think about the unknown house she was going to. Nor about those moments, less than an hour ago, when she had had to part with Dora and John: Annie and John, as she now thought of them. The relieving officer, new to the job and careless, who had come to remove the four squalling orphans from their home, omitted, in the struggle, to make proper record of their names. Since they were deemed to have no relatives in the world, they had all been named after one of the workhouse guardians, a Samuel Lunn. John, only by luck, had ended up with his real name. Over these six years, such a large span of their young lives, they had all but forgotten they were once called other things and lived another life.

Annie and John were twelve and eleven now. Up until then the three of them had stayed together, even though their little sister, Mabs – Martha as she had been called in the workhouse – had been taken away. And now that 'Mary Lunn' was fourteen she was expected to go out and earn her living. Her younger brother and sister clung to her, sobbing, before she left.

'Come and see us – don't forget about us . . .'

The last sight she had of them was their tear-stained faces and she could not bear to keep this image in her mind because there was nothing she could do about any of it and her chest felt ready to crack open. She sat in silence next to Mrs Hodges, trying to push thoughts of their distress from her mind and take in the sights of this city – the city of her birth.

A dray piled high with barrels came lurching towards them, pulled by a massive horse. The driver yelled at them to move over and their driver bawled back. Elsie grinned. It seemed funny to her that they both got so angry.

'I don't know what you're laughing at,' Mrs Hodges said, all aerated. 'We could've been killed.' A moment later she announced, impressively, 'That's the railway station. London, North and Western.'

Elsie saw a cloud of smoke rising from behind the building and heard the whistle and loud, rhythmic 'whooping' of a locomotive, sounding like a huge, snorting animal.

Her heart beat faster. A memory rose up in her mind suddenly like a gush of water, filling her with amazement.

'I been to London – on a train.'

'Don't talk foolish, wench,' Mrs Hodges said. 'Course you haven't.'

A few minutes later, 'Look, that's St Martin's Church – in the Bull Ring.'

The cloud of steam from the horse's nostrils grew bigger as it toiled up the slope of Bradford Street, hemmed in by the dark frontages of factories, men moving in and out of the gates, the clank of metal and shout of male voices, the jewel colours of glass in the windows of public houses.

Ahead of them, further up, a horse panicked and reared between the traces and their driver hauled their own animal to a standstill.

'Don't want 'im getting any ideas,' he said over his shoulder.

I could jump off, Elsie thought, her eyes darting round, knuckles tightening on her bundle. Jump, now, and go off – down that side road, be free . . . The side streets seemed a maze going on and on each side, all packed with factories thumping and clattering. She could do it – run and dodge, get away from them! Her heart was pounding, her blood ready, but now the creature uphill was under control, a man hauling on its bridle. Their own trap jerked into movement and swerved round it, straining on upwards.

As the road flattened out, at the top, the number of buildings dwindled and there was more light and green.

'Here we are,' Mrs Hodges said. 'Highgate.'

Elsie had never seen such a place before, with widely spaced houses and gardens at the front with dripping bushes spilling over the pavement. On the other side of the road there were sheep grazing across the rough grass.

Before long they had stopped outside one of the biggest houses, an imposing, brick dwelling with wide front windows that, whether she liked it or not, was to be her new home.

'So, Mary Lunn,' Mrs Dugdale frowned, looking her up and down. 'You really are very small. Are you sure you're fourteen?'

Mrs Dugdale was very strange, Elsie thought. So small with a tiny voice, like a child herself with her fluffy blonde hair and freckly nose. And the woman seemed angry with her though she could not think of anything she had done wrong.

'Yes, madam,' she mumbled.

As she stood in front of her new mistress in her lovely clothes, a rust-coloured dress and little slipper shoes, the image sliced into her mind again: the inside of a train, all of them squashed in together – John, sisters, somewhere in the background, grown-ups, a father, a mother. A mother who wore lovely colours. A dress sprigged with flowers . . . She kept her eyes down, trying to shut out these thoughts. *My name is not Mary Lunn . . .*

'I want you to understand your place here. You are a maid of all work and you will be guided by Josie Skinner. That is what you are required to do – to take orders first and foremost from me, but in the day-to-day run of things from Josie, not from my husband. Do you understand?'

No, Elsie thought, while her lips murmured, 'Yes,

ma'am.' *But what am I to do if he orders me to do something?* she wanted to say.

Mrs Dugdale's voice twittered on, Elsie catching snatches about laying fires and water and errands . . . But her mind was like a kaleidoscope with sudden glimpses of memory. Another house, somewhere, with a red and green mat by the fire . . . A man, there was a man, a father . . .

It was as if leaving the workhouse, the same walls, year after year, had scrambled her mind, turning it out like the contents of a forgotten old box. And it was too unbearable to think about. She forced the thoughts away again because such loss was worse than never having had anything in the first place.

Josie was called the parlour maid, but she was more like a housekeeper. Elsie liked her straight away. Josie told her all her jobs and Elsie slept in the bed next to hers. It was comforting having her there, like a big sister, because she was funny and kind. There was a kitchen maid there at that time called Dotty and she was all right, but all she could think about was her Albert who she was going to get away and marry as soon as she possibly could.

For years Elsie had been Mary Lunn and that was what everyone called her now. But over those first weeks, as she worked around the house, or lay on the squeaking springs of the bed at night, her mind kept offering her sudden flashes of her past life, odd shapes and images like a puzzle gradually being put together. Other streets, a yard. Pa. She had had a father. Another sister. The burn of chilblains, a bucket with a blood-soaked cloth. A day of fever and being dragged across a yard, her throat on fire. The walls of the workhouse . . .

But now she was Mary Lunn. A maid of all work kept busy from early morning until the last hot water of the day.

And shortly after she arrived in the Dugdale household, she was about her work early one morning laying a fire in the parlour. She had spread out the kindling and was kneeling by the grate rolling spills of newspaper as firelighters, when the door opened.

And she had her first sight of Mr Dugdale.

Twenty-Five

He appeared suddenly at the door, making Elsie almost jump out of her skin, an odd-looking man with a receding hairline of sandy-coloured hair which made his forehead strangely wide, with bulging grey eyes, thin arms and legs and a round tummy which pushed against his weskit. He seemed years older than Mrs Dugdale.

'Ah!' he said, almost as if she had been the very thing he was looking for. 'Well now, who are you?'

She was scrambling to her feet, brushing coal dust off her apron, to give a wobbly curtsey.

'Mary Lunn, sir.'

'Ah. The new maid.'

He came closer; she kept her head down, could see his shiny black boots moving towards her and smell an odd, spicy scent, pomade on his hair, she would learn later.

'Look at me, girl.' His voice was not unkind. She raised her head and looked back into those eyes. He just kept staring, seeming fascinated by her. He even walked all round her and looked at her from every angle. It made her feel hot in her skin. She was not used to men. But she did like the feeling of him paying her attention.

'How old are you?' he asked.

'Fourteen.' Her face was hot with blushes.

'Really?'

'Yes, sir.' So far as she knew, anyway.

'I see,' he said. He seemed to be talking to her while

thinking about something else. 'Mary Lunn. Black hair, blue eyes. Very good.'

'What are you doing, Arthur?' Elsie heard Mrs Dugdale's high voice behind the door. She sounded angry and she pushed her way into the room. Her eyes fastened on Elsie.

'I'm not doing anything, dearest one,' Mr Dugdale said. 'I'm off to the foundry now.' He put his hand on his wife's shoulder and stooped to give her an adoring look. 'Back to you as soon as I can, my sweetest,' he added, before leaving the room.

Mrs Dugdale's blue eyes seemed to glitter as she looked at Elsie, cold as ice chips.

'You get on with your work, Mary,' she said. 'Remember, you are still on trial in this house.'

'Mr Dugdale come in when I was laying the fire,' Elsie said, back in the kitchen.

It felt cosy down there. Mrs Simmons had just arrived for the day and Josie was holding a thick wedge of bread to the fire, the smell making Elsie's mouth water. She had been on the go since well before dawn and her stomach was gurgling with hunger. Josie smiled and cut another wedge for her.

'Did 'e?' Josie was back at the fire again. 'Never mind – 'e won't've minded.'

'What's he like?' Elsie said.

''E's all right,' Josie said. 'For all 'e looks like a frog.'

'I thought he looked like a beetle.'

The two of them burst into giggles.

'What're you two tittering about?' Mrs Simmons asked grumpily. She had to walk a mile to work and Elsie soon learned that she was always grumpy until she had had a hot cup of broth or tea. 'Stoke the fire, Mary.'

'She was asking about Mr Dugdale,' Josie said to Mrs

Simmons, looking round from shovelling coal on to the fire. Elsie saw them exchange looks.

'Oh, 'e's all right,' Mrs Simmons said, sipping from a steaming cup, her temper already recovering. 'Bit eccentric. You'd never take him for a foundryman, would yer?'

'Seems the foreman runs the place most of the time.' Josie blew out the flaming edge of a thick piece of toast and passed it to Elsie. 'He's got all his funny little hobbies. Here you go – get that down you.'

Elsie quickly wiped her hands and took it, hardly able to believe her luck, and spread butter thickly on it, her mouth watering.

'He makes a fool of that wife of his,' Mrs Simmons added.

'Does he?' Josie said, impaling another slice of bread on the toasting fork. 'Or was she one already? "Hello, my little Flopsy-Wopsy,"' she mimicked in a sugary voice. '"How's my ickle Wabbitty-Babbitty today?" She hardly lifts a finger and you'd think she was a baby the way he goes on.'

She and Mrs Simmons both burst out laughing, so much so that Elsie caught it off them.

'You're a bad girl,' Mrs Simmons spluttered to Josie. 'Now – that's enough gossiping. Let's get to work.'

Once Elsie was used to the Dugdales the weeks soon flowed into each other, all much the same. The days much the same too, except for Sunday when the servants accompanied Mr Dugdale to church at St Martin's in the Bull Ring. It was close enough to go on foot and she liked the walk as well, seeing something different for a change. Mrs Dugdale never went to church, though it took Elsie a long time to realize why she never saw her mistress walking far anywhere.

She was kept busy from dawn until dusk, rising before daylight, laying fires, scrubbing and swabbing and dusting.

Up and down stairs with hot water for washing in the mornings and stone hot-water bottles at night to warm the children's beds. Mr and Mrs Dugdale even had a brass warming pan, like a giant frying pan with a lid, that had to be shifted upstairs with hot coals in it, and laid between their sheets to warm them. At first her arms were shaking with the effort every time she had carried it upstairs.

She helped Miss Hooper with food for the little ones which was all right because they were sweet children and she liked to see them, although Sally Hooper did not seem a very happy soul. Every night Elsie fell exhausted on the bed. But even with all the endless tasks, there was a lull in the afternoon when they would sit and chat in the kitchen and sometimes Loz came in to see Josie and they all laughed together. Loz had come into Birmingham from the country, but Harry the other gardener was a workhouse boy as well.

'Better 'ere than in there, ain't it?' Harry said to her. And although Elsie ached with missing the others still left in the workhouse, she could only agree it was. The servants' quarters was a happy place.

'Food's better,' she said. Which it definitely was – it was the best thing about working for the Dugdales.

The Dugdales were comfortably off. The family brass foundry, Edwin Dugdale & Son, set up by Arthur Dugdale's father, was prospering and though wages for their domestic staff were not the highest, they did not stint their employees on food.

'They don't notice what we have, so long as they get theirs,' Mrs Simmons said.

There were leftover cuts of meat and creamy dollops of mashed potato, porridge and toast and the remains of tasty puddings. On the day when Elsie went into the kitchen and saw Mrs Simmons pulling out a huge dish of bread-and-butter pudding from the oven, golden and crisp and speckled with currants, she thought she had died and gone to heaven.

'Oh!' she gasped, sniffing its sweet cinnamon and nutmeg scent. 'Can I have some?'

Mrs Simmons playfully slapped her hand away. 'Once them up there've had their fill. I made plenty.'

Mrs Dugdale did not eat much and there was almost always a lot left over. Elsie made the most of it.

'Hollow legs, that one,' Mrs Simmons remarked soon after she arrived. 'I s'pose they didn't feed yer much in the workhouse.'

'Not like this,' Elsie enthused, cheeks bulging with a mouthful of pie. 'This is bostin.'

'You'll soon catch up on growing if you eat like that, little'un,' Josie said.

Everyone else laughed. But it was true, Elsie was better fed than she could ever remember and despite her hard work, she began to fill out a little. And when there was leftover bread-and-butter pudding she would eat until she was fit to burst.

Knowing little else she decided she might well be content here. There was plenty of food and the other staff were nice enough. Until suddenly things changed.

One spring morning, Elsie was working in the front of the building, the other side of the green baize door separating the main house from the servants' quarters. She was dusting the hall, its picture frames, the small table and chair, and as she was wiping down the coat stand, there was a ring at the door. The household tradesmen usually called at the back. Elsie stood, duster in hand, wondering what to do. Josie came hurrying through, smoothing her apron.

'Who's that, coming to the front?' she said, flustered.

She took delivery of a large box addressed to Mr Dugdale

and not knowing what else to do with it, left it to one side of the hall.

Elsie took no notice, other than having to sweep and mop around it. She had no idea then what part the contents of that box were going to play in casting a shadow over her own life.

There was no warning, except that on a few occasions while she was in the main part of the house, mopping the stairs early in the morning or carrying a pail of water up to the nursery, Mr Dugdale kept appearing.

Josie had told her that in the first place she had worked, all the servants had to turn and stand facing the wall if one of their employers passed them, to try to make themselves as invisible as possible. The Dugdales did not ask that, but of course Elsie would stand out of the way to let the master pass. But instead of going on up as if she did not exist the way she expected him to do, Mr Dugdale paused a few steps above her.

'Carry on,' he ordered. Elsie, kneeling on a step halfway up, looked round uncertainly. 'Yes, that's it – just go on with what you're doing.'

Kneeling on the stairs swabbing the treads each side of the runner of carpet, Elsie felt his eyes on her. He stood watching her for an agonizingly long time as she made her way down. Him staring made her feel prickly all over. Was he inspecting her work?

She got up and picked up the pail.

'Sorry for getting in the way, sir,' she said.

'Not at all.' He came hurrying down at last and looked her over again before walking off.

Every so often there he would be, staring as she worked until her flesh came up in goose pimples every time she set eyes on him. She did not know what she felt. His fascination with her was flattering and peculiar and nerve-wracking at the same time.

One afternoon Josie came down to the kitchen for their afternoon cup of tea. The days were warming up and they had the back door open to let in a breeze.

'Not long now and we'll be able to sit out,' Mrs Simmons observed. 'Still a bit of a nip now though.'

'Mr Dugdale's home,' Josie announced. 'Wants to see you, Mary – up in his office. You ain't broken anything, have you? They'll dock your wages if you have.'

'No. Don't think so.' Elsie's heart started thudding. What had she done? She wracked her brains. Dusting Mr Dugdale's office was something she did regularly, but she could not remember anything different except that the big box that had arrived a few days ago was now up there by his desk. 'What – I've got to go now?'

'Yeah, right away.'

'He keeps staring at me,' Elsie said. She hoped Mrs Simmons or Josie might be able to explain.

'P'raps he likes yer,' Josie joked, pouring herself a cup of tea. She looked at Mrs Simmons. 'He was a bit funny with Dotty, wasn't he?'

'What d'you mean, funny?' Elsie said.

Josie shrugged. 'I dunno. She never really said but she got fed up with him. She was a bit like you – small, dainty.'

Elsie was even more baffled but Josie did not seem to know anything else. 'Go on – you'd best skedaddle.'

Elsie pulled her cap straight and set off upstairs, nerves aflutter at having this sprung on her. She was used to a life of orders and routines, not surprises. And Mr Dugdale was so strange.

Going along to his office on the first floor, she knocked softly and heard him call to come in.

The room was familiar to her from sweeping and dusting

it: the desk and chair, two armchairs by the fireplace, shelves to one side with a few ledgers piled on them. A bare, functional room. But now there was something different. As she walked in she saw a strange-looking box thing standing high off the ground on a tripod. Elsie stood at the door.

'Ah.' Mr Dugdale turned and his eyes drank her in. 'Mary Lunn.'

There was a pause.

'Did you want something, sir?' she said eventually.

'Mary Lunn,' he said again. His voice was kindly. 'Come in. Shut the door.'

Elsie did as she was told and stood with her back against the door.

'Do you know what this is, my dear?' He pointed at the contraption.

She shook her head. It seemed astonishing that he was taking the time to speak to her so nicely.

'Come – look.'

It was long, rectangular and made of brown wood and leather with a little round window at the front.

'Looks rather like a squeezebox, doesn't it?' he said.

Elsie said nothing. She did not know what a squeezebox was.

'This is a very special thing called a camera.' His voice took on a storytelling tone. 'You see, if I go under here –' he lifted a black cloth that was hanging from the back end – 'I can take a picture. Of you. And you will be able to see it afterwards. Now, you go and stand over there.'

'What?' she said. What on earth was he on about?

'I am going to take your portrait. Stand . . . Here, I'll show you.'

He came and seized her by the shoulders, walking her to the spot where he wanted her to pose. He arranged her like a dummy, hands here, clasped at the front, yes, head a little tilted . . . He touched her gently, but she felt strange, like a little child being got ready for bed.

'There . . .' He stood back to look at her.

'But I've got my pinner on . . .'

'Good – yes, that's exactly right . . . Look at the camera – into the little window.'

He disappeared under the hood at the back.

'I want you to stand absolutely still. Don't move until I say so . . .'

Elsie, hands clasped in front of her over her apron, stood trying desperately not to move. The moment she was told not to, her whole body twitched, determined to defy her.

'I said don't move!' Mr Dugdale shrieked at her. 'You've ruined it. No, stay there – we'll see what comes out. DON'T MOVE.'

Elsie fought to stand still, her face burning, fighting her tears. She found she wanted to please him and she was afraid she had done it all wrong.

The next day, he called her into his office to show her the picture.

'It's called a Daguerreotype,' he said. 'It's not bad, all things considered.'

There, in black and white, was an image just like the face she saw if she looked in a mirror, but magically set on a sheet of paper.

Elsie gasped on seeing it.

'Oh, that's me!' She burst into giggles. 'Is that me?'

'It is.' Mr Dugdale sounded amused at her astonishment.

She knew it was she who had stood there. That was her cap, her dress and pinafore. And there was a slight blur to the picture because she had moved. But she saw her own face afresh as if it belonged to someone else: her cheek-bones, her wide eyes and her fierce, closed expression, like a cat. A girl she could almost be afraid of. It startled her.

'What a face. So sweet, so innocent.' Mr Dugdale came close to her. Elsie was not sure if he was talking to her or to himself. 'Here –'

He slipped his hand in his pocket, examined the handful of change he had brought out and put a coin into her palm. He gazed into her eyes so intently that she quickly looked down. 'Come back here tomorrow, my little dear. Oh – and don't tell anyone about what we are doing in this room. It's a private little undertaking of mine and I wish to keep it secret for now.'

Too late, Elsie thought. The others had been all agog to know why he had wanted her upstairs. When she went back down and told them about the funny camera machine, Josie and Mrs Simmons looked at each other.

'What, you mean a picture – on paper?' Josie said, frowning. 'What's he want that for?'

'Pictures of you?' Mrs Simmons said, baffled. 'He's a queer fish, that one.'

Elsie had left the room with a halfpenny squeezed in her hand and, though she could not fathom why, a strange unease which made the hairs at the back of her neck stand on end.

Twenty-Six

As the spring warmed towards summer, Mr Dugdale called 'Mary Lunn' up to his room regularly, on a Tuesday and sometimes also a Thursday afternoon, when it seemed he felt he could be away from the foundry.

'What's he want with you all the time, Mary?' Josie asked. 'More pictures?'

Elsie could hear a tone in her voice that said something she did not understand. Except that as the weeks went by, the strangeness of what she was having to do became a wrongness that she could not fully understand either. But no one dared question the master of the house.

Every time she went up there and posed, she came away with a coin in her hand – a farthing, a penny – once even a threepenny bit. She kept the coins in a twist of rag pushed through a little hole in the ticking covering of her mattress. She had already earned sixpence from Mr Dugdale's strange enthusiasms.

Elsie's pay was six pounds a year and she received her quarterly pay at the end of March, one pound ten shillings all at once – plus, by then, eightpence farthing from Mr Dugdale (not that anyone else knew about that).

'I know you've got no family to send your wages home to, Mary,' Josie said to her when they were due to be paid. Josie's face was unusually stern and she suddenly felt to Elsie like a bossy big sister. 'And when you get your wages it seems a lot all at once. It can go to your head. So you be careful. You need to start saving for your bottom drawer – you know, for when you get married. No, I'm not joking,' Josie scolded when she saw the corners of Elsie's mouth start to turn up. 'You gotta save. I've seen it where I worked before – a couple of spendthrifts who wanted to get married and so far as I know they're still waiting. You'll never get out of here if you don't save up strict like – and who wants to stay in service all their life, eh?'

'All right,' Elsie said obediently, even though up until now she had never given any of this a thought. 'Only I was going to go into town . . .'

'Tell you what,' Josie said. 'Let me keep some of it for you? Stop you going mad with it. Say you save a pound every quarter, or twenty-five shillings even? That's a good amount and you don't need it for anything else, do you? I'll be your bank and then it'll be safe. And you can get whatever bits and pieces you need with the rest.'

When the wages were paid, Elsie happily handed over a sovereign and a crown to Josie. She had a special tin which she kept in the cupboard and she put Elsie's money separately, folded into a scrap of paper. It never crossed Elsie's mind not to trust Josie. Josie was good and kind. And so far as Elsie was concerned, five shillings, plus her eightpence farthing, was still a fortune for spending money!

She set out to walk into Birmingham on her Wednesday afternoon off, clutching more riches in a little rag tucked into her belt than she had ever had in her life before.

'It's got to last you,' Mrs Simmons warned.

It was true that Elsie had little reason to spend money. She was fed and mostly clothed by the Dugdales. She could do with a comb for her hair, new soles for her boots, maybe a pair of bloomers. But mainly she set out to enjoy herself in town, to wander among the milling crowds in the Bull Ring.

She looked around her as she set off along the road and breathed in a deep, wondering breath. Freedom! This was the first time, since she had been taken to the workhouse, that she had been able to walk freely on her own. True, she would have to go back, but for now, she could walk wherever she pleased!

As she walked down Bradford Street, the entries to the backyards nearer the bottom of the street reminded her of where she had lived before. Summer Row. For a second she had an impulse to go there, as if she might still find her mother and Ada and the others, before the truth slammed up against her. Everyone was gone, scattered or in heaven. And she had no idea where Summer Row was.

Soon she was down in the Bull Ring. Every few moments she touched the place where her money was kept to make sure she had not dropped it and no one had stolen it. And though she had not intended to spend much money – wasn't it wicked, to be extravagant? – the temptation was too much and she was having too good a time. She had never had money to spend before.

She found herself buying more ribbons and lace and even a little pair of slippers fashioned out of a silky stuff with beautiful embroidered peacocks on them until she was only left with a few coppers. Then, on a market stall, she caught sight of a little rag doll with a smiling face drawn on and yellow woolly hair. Elsie stopped. Lucy! The doll she had clung to as she was hauled away to the workhouse had disappeared years ago – she never did know where. But seeing this little smiling face – and she was only tuppence – she bought the doll and slipped her into her pocket, warmed by the thought of her nestling in there all the way home.

Josie, obsessed with saving as she was, was scandalized at all this frittering, even of the small ration of her wages she was left with.

'Well, I suppose it's your first wage,' she said. 'But you

want to take yourself in hand. What d'you want in life, Mary? D'you want a home and family of your own? I'm putting every penny away for my bottom drawer, so Loz and I'll be well set up.'

Elsie did think about this. It filled her with yearning – a husband, home, children! This seemed something so wonderful and far off that she hardly dared even wish for it. Nor did she have a Loz in her life, so that the need for a bottom drawer was even more remote. She knew Josie was right really. She ought to save every penny for a better future. But she had had such a lovely, exciting time and the slippers were the prettiest things she had ever possessed! And now she had her little Lucy for company as well. She kept her under her pillow and fell asleep with her cuddled up to her chest every night.

So, on going back into town in June, she was all excitement for a week beforehand at the thought of going shopping. She took five shillings again, just in case.

The place was bustling all around the stalls, the flower sellers – lavender, fresh lavender! – and newspaper vendors hawking their wares – latest from the mutiny in India – rebels enter Gwalior! – stink of Thames in London getting worse . . .!

In the crowded Market Hall she bought a yard of pretty green ribbon, a little plaster dog three inches high sitting up on its hind legs, a bag of bulls' eyes and another of butterscotch. She was going to make a pig of herself – and to share some of the sweets with the others. It felt exciting to be able to choose things for the first time in her life. Even to be able to be generous. She stroked the little dog, grinning into his black and white face with its little pink painted tongue.

'Your name's gunna be . . . Jack.'

She knew the little dog was going to be her friend as well as Lucy.

The Bull Ring was always full of the warm, mouth-watering aromas of cooking meat, of fruit and cakes, and even though she was well fed at the Dugdales', she was always on the go and also forever hungry. After years of workhouse food she could not resist. She bought a pork sandwich with crackling, a raisin bun and a punnet of fresh strawberries and went over to sit by the statue of Nelson. With the voices of the stallholders and the flower girls in her ears, she gobbled the lot down, relishing every mouthful.

Heading home with a happy tummy and with all her new things, she felt very content. If working as a skivvy at the Dugdales' meant she could enjoy her shopping sprees every so often, then it was not so bad, was it? She walked up Bradford Street humming to herself.

Twenty-Seven

At first, Mr Dugdale asked her to take up various poses in her working clothes so that he could practise making his Daguerreotype images.

'Now – let's try and keep still, shall we?'

His voice was kind and Elsie managed not to twitch even though she was constantly worried that she might. She posed with a pail, then holding a besom, another time a brass coal scuttle.

She thought Mr Dugdale very strange and it was annoying missing her afternoon rest time, chatting and nibbling with the others in the back kitchen. But she liked the coppers he handed out.

After a few weeks though, things began to change. There was a great to-do in the house for most of a day while Mrs Dugdale got ready to take the children, and woebegone Sally Hooper the nanny, away for a visit.

'We're going to her mother's again,' Sally told them, gloomily, on one of her rare visits to the kitchen. Mrs Dugdale's mother lived in a village outside Warwick and they would be travelling most of the way by train. 'I just hope James isn't sick, like last time.'

The family taking its leave was like a high gusting wind and then suddenly the house went quiet.

Mr Dugdale got her to take her cap and apron off and loose her hair down her back. He even brushed it for her and she stood in front of him feeling like a doll herself.

Then one afternoon, he said, 'I want to see your shoulders.'

He came right up to her and started to unbutton her dress. Elsie stiffened, feeling her whole being resist. Surely this wasn't right?

'Now there's nothing to worry about, my little dear,' Mr Dugdale wheedled. 'I shall look after you.'

He smiled down at her so nicely that Elsie felt a warm feeling go through her. The way she had felt when . . . A flash appeared in her memory: a man with a smiling face, lined by hard work and mischief. A man who she once knew as her pa . . .

She was filled with longing so acute that she had to look down so that he could not see the tears in her eyes. And she watched Mr Dugdale's fingers working the buttons of her frock, confused, unable to stop him. Only when she had swallowed her tears could she look up, cheeks hot with blushes. His face was full of a strange look of adoration and he smiled at her. Very gently, he pulled the dress down over her shoulders, revealing her little chemise underneath, too small and tight, and her corset. He tilted his head and made a little sound of appreciation.

'Such meek womanhood! That's it, my dear. Stand just like that –' He rushed over to the camera. 'So perfect . . .'

Why? she wanted to ask. *What are you doing this for?* But she did not dare. And with her bare shoulders she felt naked and wrong.

Each time she went back, there was something different. He had brought a folding screen into the room and produced dresses for her to change into behind it. A bright yellow silk, a pink, sprigged summer dress with a hooped crinoline to put on under the skirt and a matching bonnet, tied with a pink bow under her chin. The clothes were only a little too big for her and smelt of cologne and she soon realized they belonged to Mrs Dugdale. She felt very grand when fastened into a pink costume with a hooped crinoline skirt – she had never worn one before and all this dressing up was rather diverting. He laughed at her smiles.

'Look –' A cheval mirror had also appeared in the room so that she could see herself from head to foot. 'See how lovely you are.'

The dress was too long for her, but now that she had filled out it almost fitted. It was so pretty. She stared at her reflection, the respectable young lady who suddenly seemed so much older than she felt, with large, striking eyes and Cupid's bow lips, her cheeks pink with embarrassment.

Mr Dugdale's reflection appeared behind her own. He stooped until his face was right beside hers and she could feel his breath on her cheek.

'There – you see?'

He looked excited, as if he was in another world, separate from her. For a moment, standing close behind her, his eyes rolled upwards in a strange way and she didn't like it.

'Now – stay like that. Just turn and face the camera.'

The next time, he wanted her to take off her chemise, her corset. He didn't ask – just started to unlace her.

'No.' She put her hands up to prevent him.

'My dear – it's all right. I'm making something beautiful.' It was gentle, the way he pushed her hands away, but push he did. 'You must not mind.'

How much? she wanted to say. *What will you pay for this thing I don't want to do?* But she did not dare. And did not like herself for thinking it.

He made her raise her arms to lift her loosened corset over her head. Elsie quickly grabbed at the waist of her dress to stop it tumbling round her ankles.

'Chemise,' he ordered. His voice was sharper now. She managed to pull it off, one arm at a time so that she was naked from the waist up, her breasts like small buds on her slender body. She could feel the tickle of her hair down her back and burned with shame, but at the same time she could not help staring, fascinated. She had scarcely ever looked at her own body and never like this. Her skin was ivory white, her hair very dark against it. She held one arm over her chest, trying to hide herself, still clinging to her dress with the other.

'Put your arm down.'

Mr Dugdale gazed at her as she obeyed. All this attention, like none she had ever known – but wrong.

'I'm . . .' She swallowed. 'I'm . . .' She did not know what word to use. Naked, exposed, frightened. 'I'm cold,' was all she managed.

'You're perfect. Such innocence. Just stay as you are.'

Mr Dugdale hurried behind the camera and delved into it like a rabbit in a burrow.

'Stand quite still now.'

And it was done.

'No!' he cried, as she immediately grabbed her chemise to put it back on. 'Wait.'

He came over to her, his eyes feasting on her. His hand reached out and stroked her cheek, her hair. Finally, he pulled away her arms which she had crossed over her body. He was trembling. With the tips of his fingers, he caressed her nipples, one by one. A shock went through her at each touch, the sensation thrumming through her, and she stepped back, horrified. Mr Dugdale looked strange, breathing hard like a horse, and she knew he wanted something horribly much, even though she was not certain what it was.

'I want to get dressed now,' she said.

'All right.' He turned away abruptly. Then back again. 'But before you do –'

He stepped close again and held his arms out, gathering

her in so that she was pressed against him. His clothes smelt of metal, of the foundry, of sweat.

'You are so pure,' he murmured above her head. 'So young and pure.'

He drew in a long, deep breath, as if struggling to control himself, and at last let her go. Elsie pulled her clothes on as fast as she could; it was like putting herself back together. Because she felt dirty, and as if her feelings had been damaged.

As she went to the door she heard him rattle coins in his pocket. Something rebelled in her. She saw herself marching through the Bull Ring, along New Street even, buying nice things.

'Threepence.'

Mr Dugdale's face changed, as if he was seeing her in a new way.

'Bargaining with me, are we?' His voice was not nice now, it was sarcastic. 'I don't think I like that.'

Elsie held her ground by the door as he sorted his change. He selected a coin, came up to her, laid his hand on her cheek. Then suddenly he pinched it, hard, a nasty expression in his eyes. She did not want him to know it had hurt. She looked up at him and held out her hand. He dropped the coin on to her palm. A tuppenny bit. She closed her fingers over it and left the room, vowing to herself that she was never going back.

Twenty-Eight

Elsie allowed herself to go into town once a month and she went the next day, even though, with Josie guarding her earnings against her own desire to buy everything in sight, she only had a fistful of coppers. After browsing round the Bull Ring she decided to walk up to New Street. The shops were grand up there, with tall glass windows and awnings, and they seemed so impressive that she did not know if she would ever dare to step inside a single one.

She walked along one side of the street, then crossed the busy road to dawdle her way back. Wandering along in the shade of the awnings, she suddenly had a strange feeling that someone was watching her. And when she realized who it was, she let out a long, 'Ohhh.'

From behind the huge glass of a shop window, two vivid blue eyes were gazing at her. The eyes were set in the porcelain face of the biggest, most beautiful doll she had ever seen. Elsie was quite certain at that moment that those eyes were looking straight at her and had been waiting for her. The doll, which was seated stiffly on a table, had tresses of wavy bronze-coloured hair tumbling out from under a beautiful straw bonnet decorated with dried flowers and coloured feathers. Her frock was all in white layers and flounces, with lace all around the neck and hem and covering her feet.

Elsie stared and stared. She already knew that the name of the doll was Alicia Victoria. And she knew that she was hers. The doll was beseeching her, '*Take me with you – I'm supposed to be with you . . .*'

The street was busy and people were milling in and out of the shop but Elsie did not dare go inside. Leaning close to the glass she narrowed her eyes to read the ticket hanging from the doll's wrist: '10/6d'. Her excitement shrivelled. Ten shillings and sixpence. It was so much money, more than a month's pay!

And suddenly she was furious with herself. She had frittered away nearly all her wages – she had half a crown left – when she could have been saving it all the time to claim this, her very own, beautiful doll. Lucy the little rag doll suddenly seemed as nothing – a cheapjack piece of rubbish.

She gazed at the doll in all her finery, then turned away, feeling as if Alicia Victoria's eyes were now accusing her of being a silly, naughty girl. Sadly, she turned towards home, the extravagance of the day turned to dust and ashes. Nothing she had ever bought before, none of her little fancies and sweets, was a patch on Princess Alicia Victoria.

Walking up the hill to Highgate and the Dugdales' house, a piece of butterscotch tucked inside her cheek, she thought, She's mine. She looked at me. I've got the money. I'll ask Josie to give me my savings back. It's all mine, after all. Then I can come and get her.

'So what d'you want it for?' Josie asked. They had this conversation that evening up in their attic, sitting side by side on Elsie's bed. Josie was not being unkind, Elsie knew, because that was not Josie, whom she trusted completely. But Josie was being all grown up and sensible and Elsie seethed with resentment. It's my money – I'll do what I like with it!

She looked away, not wanting to say. That the tin containing the money was in the cupboard just close by was knowledge that burned through her. She could just grab it, and . . .

'Come on, out with it,' Josie laughed, putting her arm round Elsie for a moment. 'I know you and your shopping sprees. I'm just trying to save you from squandering it all. I know it's yours, of course, Mary.'

'I saw a doll,' she muttered. 'And she's . . .' She could not put into words the sheer splendour of Alicia Victoria, how her heart filled with longing every time she thought about her.

'A doll?' Josie said scathingly. 'And how much does this doll cost?'

Elsie stared at her shoes and spoke in a whisper.

'Ten and six!' Josie shrieked. 'Have you lost your wits?' She looked seriously at Elsie. 'I know you think I'm being mean and bossing you, Mary, but I'm saving you from yourself, I truly am.'

But she wants me to save her, Elsie thought, though she kept this to herself.

'Tell you what,' Josie said. 'I'll keep the wages of yours I've got for you so far. If you want to buy a nice doll you can save up – you still have five bob left over every payday so it won't take long, will it?'

Elsie was busy calculating. She still had the half-crown. And there was her secret money from him . . . It would mean she could not buy Alicia Victoria straight away – not this week or next. But soon, she might well be able to. And if she put up with Mr Dugdale and his dirty ways for just a bit longer . . .

She nodded humbly. The desire to sneak upstairs and take back her savings was almost overwhelming, but she would have to face Josie and account for it if she did. 'All right then.'

*

The next times she was called to his room, Mr Dugdale did not make her pose naked – or half-naked – again. She posed in an array of dresses and he allowed her to undress behind the screen.

But he never paid her even tuppence again either. As if a scale of rates had been set he gave her a penny, or a half-penny, looking hard into her eyes each time as if to say, *Don't think you can ask for more. Know your place.*

By the time Mrs Dugdale was due home, Elsie thought she must have been dressed up in every single one of her frocks because how could any woman have so many?

But the day before his wife and children were to come home again, Mr Dugdale was waiting. As Elsie entered the room, she saw hanging from the back of the screen a set of mourning weeds. She looked questioningly at him.

'Put them on.'

His tone had changed over the weeks from kindly wonder to a clipped voice which made her feel as if he despised her. And her own feelings had shifted. Gone was that sense of being special, cared for even. He did not care for her. She would see his face behind her, reflected in the glass, and he was all wrapped up in himself. She wanted to escape from this. She despised him. But she could not disobey, did not know how to. So at least bit by bit, she was going to get money off him.

Added to her wages she would soon be able to buy Alicia Victoria. Changing into the crackling bombazine, laying the crêpe veil over her head, she glanced over at Mr Dugdale who was fiddling with the camera, and was filled with loathing.

I hate you, she thought. Hate the stink of you. Hair oil and sweat and the foundry. It was such a warm day and the dress made her feel hot and oppressed.

'Lie down there,' he ordered when she came out from

behind the screen. He was not kind any more. He treated her like nothing.

Elsie lay down on the rug. Mr Dugdale arranged her, straightening the skirt which was so long it went down over her feet, and laying straight the veil. Was she supposed to be dead? But dead people were not the ones who wore widows' weeds. She could not make sense of it. She just wanted him to get on with it – it was boring doing this when she could be in the garden, laughing and joking with Josie and the others or eating leftover puddings.

'What's 'e doing up there with you every time?' Josie asked her. 'Still making pictures?'

'He makes me dress up,' Elsie said. She couldn't bear to mention the way he had touched her.

Josie looked at her and shook her head. They all thought Mr Dugdale was a bit mad.

She waited for him to go to the camera and take his picture, but that was not what happened.

He came over and knelt down beside her. Elsie's heart started to thud. This was not what he had been doing for the last times.

'Now,' he said. 'Move your legs a little further apart.' In a strange, caressing voice suddenly, he said, 'Sweet, innocent child.'

She imagined he was going to do more things to her to make her look right, arrange her as if she was a doll. Elsie thought about her savings, stuffed into the mattress. Alicia Victoria would soon be hers! She lay there imagining walking into that grand shop and saying, *That doll in the window please.*

He lifted the hem, then her petticoat, and she felt his hand moving up over her bloomers. Elsie stiffened. *What're you doing?* she wanted to ask. She stared at him, loathing the way his face had gone all funny again, rolling his eyes, though she did not dare speak.

But his head turned suddenly and he saw her watching him. It seemed to throw him.

'Close your eyes,' he ordered.

Elsie pretended to obey, peering out between her lashes. His hands fumbled over her undergarments, fast and urgently, feeling the shape of her across her hips. She could smell him and it was disgusting.

Defying him, she opened her eyes again. Mr Dugdale was intent, his hands moving over her, when he suddenly looked up and caught her watching, her gaze blazing into him. It seemed to shock him and he drew back, getting slowly to his feet.

'Damn – damn you . . .' He backed away, turning from her and adjusting his clothing.

Elsie got to her feet and ran behind the screen to grab her own clothes. She was about to rush from the room, but she stopped at the door and held out her hand.

Mr Dugdale came over to her and without even once looking at her, dropped a penny and two halfpennies into her hand.

Head down, her lips moving silently – nasty, dirty pig – she hurried to the back stairs, her mind feeling as if it was boiling with hatred, about to explode. She felt as if his grubby, poking touch was still all over her. For the first time she felt truly grateful to Josie – she was right. They did have to get away from here as soon as they could. And she was never, ever, going back into that room.

She was so caught up in herself that she did not see the new kitchen maid watching her from the far end of the landing as she hurried towards the attic stairs.

Twenty-Nine

The other servants were surprised and overjoyed for the two girls as, clutching each other's hands and beaming all over their faces, they explained that they were sisters and had at last found each other.

'Oh, my word,' Mrs Simmons said, her saggy face creasing into smiles at the sight of them. 'So – not Mary Lunn then? You going to tell them, upstairs? I've heard in some houses they call all the maidservants Mary in any case. Too idle to learn their names.'

Ada and Elsie looked at each other. Elsie shrugged. 'I don't care what they call me,' she said. 'I've been Mary Lunn for years.'

'Ain't that nice, finding you got a sister under the same roof?' Josie said. 'I ain't seen my sister for years.'

'Sister or no sister you'd best get the hot water upstairs for her,' Mrs Simmons said, rolling her eyes upwards. Elsie scuttled over to the range to collect the water.

Ada watched Elsie leave the room, drinking in the sight of her and still hardly able to believe that she was really here – that at last the two of them were together again.

'Nice to see her looking chirpy,' Mrs Simmons said, sawing into a loaf. 'I've never seen her so happy. Bit moody, that one, up 'til now. I thought she was a bit touched, to be truthful. But I put it down to her age. And the workhouse, of course. That's no way to grow up, is it?'

'Never mind – she'll be all right now she's got you,' Josie said.

Ada smiled. She knew Mrs Simmons was right – Elsie had seemed a bit peculiar to her too and her sister was in many ways still a stranger to her. But now they had a chance to be together again and Ada was going to look after Elsie whatever it took. After all, they had no one else.

Elsie climbed the back stairs lugging a heavy pail almost full of Mrs Dugdale's washing water. She too was in a daze of happiness. Ada! Ada was here! And memories of the past which had sunk deep somewhere in her mind were starting to ease themselves out, filling her mind. Mom, Pa . . . The house where they had lived when she was little . . .

Mr Dugdale appeared out of his bedroom when she reached the landing and the smile playing round Elsie's lips vanished abruptly. The blood started to pound round her body as she turned to face the wall, every hair on her body alert to him passing her.

Mr Dugdale stopped. She could hear him breathing as he stood right behind her and she thought her heart was going to burst. She clenched her hands, the pail weighing down her right arm.

Finally he leaned down and she felt his breath on the back of her neck.

'I shall expect you upstairs this afternoon. Make sure you are on time. I'll be waiting.'

She listened to his footsteps moving away along the upstairs landing.

You can wait all you like, you dirty beast, Elsie thought, heaving the bucket towards Mrs Dugdale's door. I shan't be coming whatever you say! Then she paused. But if she could get tuppence out of him this time – or maybe even more? . . . She knocked and heard the little voice from inside: 'Come.'

Bowing her head she went into the room, trying not

to wrinkle up her nose at the sweaty stuffiness of a room where two bodies had slept the night, overlaid with rose water and the rank smell of the egg which Mrs Dugdale had eaten in bed for her breakfast.

'Your washing water, ma'am,' she said.

'About time,' Mrs Dugdale replied petulantly.

Whatever Elsie did was never right. She knew that Mrs Dugdale felt a loathing and resentment for her that she did not direct at either Ada or Josie, taller, more mature-looking girls, who had been chosen for their fitness to carry out strenuous housework. Elsie, with her petite, doll-like size, had been chosen, just as Mrs Dugdale had once been chosen for other reasons. She was a rival. Mrs Dugdale knew it and Elsie knew it. And there was nothing either of them could do about Mr Dugdale's peculiar tastes and habits.

She went to pour the water into the wash jug, a pretty pink thing with roses on the side, with a matching china basin on the wash stand. On a rack nearby were folded Turkish-style linen towels. Mrs Dugdale was in bed still, and Elsie could feel her watching her movements, waiting to criticize.

'I hope you haven't splashed any this time,' she said.

'No, ma'am,' Elsie said.

'Any more mistakes and I'll make sure he dismisses you.'

'Yes, ma'am.' Elsie spoke quietly, keeping her head down.

She never splashed. She did not make mistakes – she was good at her work. But both of them kept up the pretence that Mrs Dugdale had the power to have her sent away.

'Is there soap?'

'Yes. There is.'

Elsie glanced up to see Mrs Dugdale swing her legs over the side of the bed, in a long white nightdress and little frilled nightcap. As she moved, her nightdress rode up right to her thighs. In that second before she yanked the hem of the garment down, Elsie saw with a shock the state of Mrs Dugdale's legs, the deformed, skinny calves bowed outwards. Her mistress had to slide forward so that her feet could touch the floor, feeling her way into her pink silk slippers.

For a moment their eyes met.

Rickets, Elsie thought. Wasn't it only poor children who had rickets? Not people like Mrs Dugdale in fancy clothes and living in big houses! No wonder she never liked to be seen walking anywhere in public.

'Get out,' Mrs Dugdale said. There was so much rage in her voice that Elsie felt she had been whipped from the room. She had seen what she should not have seen.

She closed the door and stood for a moment on the landing, her heart thudding with shock. Mrs Dugdale was so small, the sight of her legs truly pitiful. Elsie realized she had hardly ever seen Jane Dugdale walk any distance. Her own role was to enter rooms and wait on her mistress when she was already sitting down.

Her mind spinning, she went down the back stairs. Did that mean Mrs Dugdale had once been very poor? And how did she come to be married to Mr Dugdale? Had he lured her in too, this man who liked women to be tiny, like helpless little dolls?

She suddenly had a new feeling of sympathy for this woman whose life must have been very different from how Elsie had imagined.

During the afternoon lull when they had washed up the dinner things but were not yet preparing the evening meal, Ada went out into the garden to stretch her legs. She would have asked Elsie to come with her but she had disappeared somewhere.

Ada went up the three steps from the back of the house to the lawn which stretched between beds of rose and lavender bushes. It was refreshing to be out after the heat and steam of the kitchen. She wandered down towards the herb garden smelling the scents of rosemary and marjoram, and looking down at the vegetable gardens at the far end. Loz and Harry were both down there, Loz working away with a hoe and Harry digging over the patch from where the last potatoes had been harvested.

She saw Harry look over and spot her. He immediately went and stood the hoe against the back fence and strode over to her. Ada felt as if her body was all prickles suddenly. She had only just arrived and while she liked Harry well enough, it felt as if he had instantly got some idea about her that she was not keen on at all. He was a likeable enough lad but the main reason she wanted to talk to him was in the hope that the gardeners might find a need for another pair of hands and that she could ask if they would employ Tom. Even though in truth she could see that there was only enough work in the Dugdale garden for two men.

'How do, Ada,' Harry said, striding up to her in his soil-caked boots. His hands were all grime as well and his cheeks smeared with dirt. He looked the picture of health and Ada could not help smiling.

'I'm all right – just having a breather,' she said, fiddling with the edge of her apron as she did not know what else to do with her hands. Harry had a very direct look and it felt as if he was eating her up. And he stood a bit too close to her so that she had to keep edging away. They'd only just met, for goodness' sakes! She felt herself closing in on herself under his gaze.

'D'you, er . . .' He faltered for the first time. 'When you get your afternoon off – d'you fancy coming out for a walk?'

Ada felt panic rise in her. She had barely thought about what she would do with any free time, but she knew she did not want to give over those precious hours to spend them with him. She looked up into his healthy, handsome face, this lad with his strong muscles and ready smile, and wondered why she was not like Josie who would have jumped at any chance to go out with Loz. Why she immediately felt as if she could never trust him.

'Dunno,' she said. 'I expect I'll go into town with . . .' She had been about to say, 'with Elsie', then realized Harry would not know who that was and she did not feel like explaining. 'With Mary.'

'Oh.' Harry sounded peeved. 'Suit yourself then.'

He strode off down the garden again, pulling his shoulders back. Ada knew she had offended him. But, she thought grumpily, why should I say yes if I mean no? What does he expect?

Men were an alien thing to her. She didn't know what to do with them, and from the little she had experienced of them so far, she didn't want to find out.

In the gloom of the house she climbed the back stairs and went on up to the attic. She found Elsie squatting on the floor, bent over something. When she heard Ada come in, she shoved whatever it was urgently under her skirt and looked up, eyes burning with some powerful emotion.

'What're you doing?'

The way Elsie looked back at her made Ada concerned. Finding her sister was the greatest joy she could imagine, but she did see something odd in Elsie. Something locked in but which seemed fierce and wild. Cautiously she went and sat on the edge of the bed.

'It's all right, Elsie,' she said gently. 'It's only me.'

Last night, even this morning, her sister had seemed so happy, so eager to know about their family and Ada and all that had happened.

But now, Elsie had shut off from her. As if she had turned a key and locked herself away inside and become cool and strange. And now, kneeling on the floor, sheltering something secret under her skirts, she looked almost hostile, like a little animal caught in a trap. Ada also took in that her sister was lovely to look at, her cheeks more rounded than Ada ever remembered, her dark, glossy hair and those huge eyes, glinting with emotion. It made you want to keep looking at her, but at the same time, her fierceness made Ada feel uneasy.

With a pang, Ada found herself missing Tom, who still felt like more of a brother than her real sister sitting there in front of her.

'Else – it's me. You don't have to hide anything from me.'

Keeping her eyes still on Ada, Elsie tugged a piece of cloth from under her skirt, and opened it to show the meagre remains of her savings, a shilling, sixpence and some coppers. Ada leaned down and counted it.

'Two and sevenpence halfpenny,' she said. 'Is that the remains of your wages? They ain't paid me yet but I've got a bit from before.'

Elsie was listening intently. Then her plans came spilling out.

'I won't get paid 'til the end of September and then Josie will keep some of my wages but I'll have five bob so that'll be seven and sevenpence halfpenny, only that's not enough . . .' She looked desperate. 'I'll have to . . .'

She looked away across the room and an expression of horror crossed her face. 'I'll *have* to,' she whispered. For a second she looked as if she desperately wanted to speak, to confide something, but she remained silent, as if she just could not find the words.

'Have to what?' Ada asked.

Elsie turned on her suddenly.

'How much've you got?'

'Me?' Ada said, startled. 'A few bob I brought with me. What d'you need it for?'

Elsie's face lit up with hope. 'Josie's keeping most of my earnings for me and I don't want her to be cross with me – but I need two and tenpence halfpenny after I get my next wages . . .'

'What d'you need all that money for?' Ada laughed. 'That's nearly . . . That's . . .'

'Ten and six,' Elsie said, her eyes burning into Ada's with such emotion that Ada felt almost frightened. 'That's how much I need.'

Thirty

The week passed and Elsie could not bring herself to go up to Mr Dugdale's office. Ada would help her with the money, wouldn't she? She clung to this belief. So she could keep away from him. The appointed afternoon came and went and she stayed away. She did everything she could to avoid him, knowing he would never stoop to marching down to the servants' quarters to order her upstairs.

Whenever he was in the house she made sure that she only went upstairs with Josie, especially on Tuesday and Thursday afternoons when Mr Dugdale was likely to be at home.

'What's got into you?' Josie said. 'Clinging to me like my little shadow.'

But for a few days it worked. Mr Dugdale had to spend most of his working day at the foundry and then she knew she was safe. Then, late one afternoon he returned to the house in a temper. Josie was in the hall and she came down to the kitchen with a face on her, carrying Mrs Dugdale's tea tray.

'Well, she's proper mardy today,' she said, the cups clattering as she set it down. 'Snapped my head right off. Here – more washing-up for you, Ada.'

Ada was scrubbing pots in the scullery.

Josie brought the crockery through. 'Change the water – you can't wash these in all that grease.'

'I know,' Elsie heard Ada say indignantly as she came into the kitchen. 'I have done washing-up before, you know. I've looked after a whole flaming family – and they weren't even mine.'

Elsie was taking this in until her mind snapped to attention seeing Mrs Simmons at the table, arranging slices of bread into the bottom of a wide dish.

'Oh!' Elsie gasped. 'You making bread-and-butter pudding, Mrs S?'

Mrs Simmons looked up and gave one of her rare smiles.

'I'll make sure there's plenty,' she said. 'Knowing you as I do.'

Elsie hugged herself in anticipation of her very favourite pudding. Mrs Simmons always let her scrape out the dish until she nearly took the shine off it. But the smile was soon wiped from her face.

'*He* wants to see you, Mary – I mean Elsie,' Josie said. 'Looks like a thundercloud. What the hell've you done?'

'Nothing.' She shook her head, her heart thudding with dread. 'What – now?'

'Yeah – go on, hurry up. He's upstairs.'

Elsie watched her feet as she climbed the back stairs, one-two, one-two, feeling strange. Those feet seemed to belong to someone else. As if none of this was real. She went into somewhere inside her that was numb, where she could not feel anything. She felt like a rag doll. Not like the queen of dolls, Alicia Victoria. She saw the beautiful doll in her mind's eye and suddenly her will was made of iron again. She *had* to have her. Nothing else mattered – just her.

She watched her knuckles lift and knock at Mr Dugdale's door.

'Come!'

Elsie opened the door and stood, half in the room, still clutching the brass doorknob.

'Where have you been?' he said, his face tight and angry. 'I told you to come up on Tuesday.'

Elsie just stood there. No – she couldn't do this, just couldn't. Him touching her, the horrible look on his face. Her stomach was already lurching as if she might be sick. She would beg Ada for the money, insist Josie give her back her savings, anything – but not this.

'Well, come in – close the door.'

'No.'

He was across the room as fast as a snake but she stepped back and ran off along the landing.

'Get in here – now.' He caught her in a couple of strides, seizing her arm.

'I'll holler,' she said, grabbing hold of the banister rail.

'Who's going to come if you do?' he sneered.

'I want paying,' she said, loudly. 'I'm not coming in 'til you give me two and tenpence halfpenny.'

Mr Dugdale stared for a moment, then burst out into horrible laughter.

'You do, do you? Two and tenpence halfpenny?' he mocked, his fingers digging deep into her arm. 'A very particular sum – what d'you want with that, eh? Think you can bargain with me, do you, little guttersnipe?'

He was trying to wrestle her away from the banister. Elsie was clinging on with all her strength but she knew she could not win – not against him.

Just as her fingers were losing their grip she heard footsteps. She looked up into Mr Dugdale's face and felt him loosen his hold on her. A moment later, Josie appeared up the back stairs and Mr Dugdale strode away again and into his office.

Thirty-One

'What's going on, Elsie?' Josie demanded sternly as Mr Dugdale slammed the door behind him. She grabbed Elsie and hauled her off down the back stairs, gripping her arm as if she thought she might run away. Josie couldn't seem to decide if she was worried for Elsie or furious with her.

'Why had he got you by the arm? He's a queer fish that one, you don't want to mess with him – you'll get the sack and the rest of us too if you ain't careful.'

'I'm not the one messing with him,' Elsie retorted indignantly as they reached the kitchen. She was shaking and for a moment she felt as if her legs would give way under her. She had stood up to him!

Mrs Simmons, who was having a few minutes' sit-down, did not look pleased by this noisy invasion. Ada came out from the scullery.

'What's going on?''

'Nothing,' Elsie said sullenly.

'You need to tell us, Mary,' Josie ordered. No one seemed able to remember that was not her name. 'All this dressing-up and carry-on . . .'

Elsie's head was drooping, her cheeks burning. She looked utterly wretched and shamed. 'I can't.' It was barely more than a whisper.

'Loose her,' Ada ordered Josie. 'Come on, we're going outside.'

She put an arm round Elsie's shoulders and steered her

out into the garden. She saw Harry, who was weeding the flower bed further down, look hopefully over at her and was glad Elsie was with her so he would not come and pester her again.

'Come and sit here.' Ada sat down and patted the grass beside her. Elsie obeyed, still not looking at her. Ada leaned down, trying to see into her face.

'I want to be a sister to you, now I've found you, Else.'

Elsie sat mute, staring ahead of her as if locked in her own world. Ada felt a moment of panic. This was her sister, one of her lost family that she had craved for so long. But she was so hard to understand. If only Elsie would talk to her. For a moment she wanted to shout at her, force her to talk but she made herself speak gently. 'You gunna tell me what's going on with Mr Dugdale?'

Josie had told Ada Mr Dugdale had a machine for making Daguerreotypes, that he took pictures of Elsie, made her dress up. It all seemed very strange but if that was all . . .? But Ada knew what men could be like. Every time she thought of Seamus Connell, it was with a shudder of revulsion.

She reached out and tried to stroke her little sister's back. 'Did he tell you not to say?' There was a silence. 'Does he . . . touch you? You can tell me, sis.'

But Elsie sat up straighter as if shying away and Ada withdrew, hurt. There was a long silence and then Elsie turned to Ada and for a moment she had such a wild look in her eyes that Ada felt alarmed again. She spoke with passionate force.

'Josie said I ought to save up my money so I can get away from here and that's why I haven't got enough. But I'm gunna get my money off of her and I'm gunna buy that doll. I've got to have her. She's mine!'

*

The next week, on their afternoon off, Ada and Elsie walked together down Bradford Street, amid the clang and screech of metal from the works housed in tall, dark buildings on either side, across Rea Street and into the smoky bowl of land that held the town of Birmingham.

'We'll go and get her,' Ada had said to Elsie. 'You can show me.'

Ada was still a bit afraid of Elsie. Sometimes she seemed like a happy young girl, sitting in the garden or the two of them playing 'tag' with Josie on the lawn. But she was so moody and at times looked almost crazed. And this doll, in some grand shop window on New Street – the idea of it seemed to have taken over her whole mind.

But, she told herself, if this doll was the one thing that mattered to her – even if it cost a fortune. Ada could hardly believe any doll could cost that much.

She only had a few shillings but she said she would give Elsie two of them and she would have to get the rest from Josie. She asked Josie to give Elsie back just enough of her money to buy something she wanted. She spoke so fiercely that Josie was quite offended.

'It's your money,' she said huffily to Elsie. She looked at Ada. 'I was only keeping it for her so she didn't spend it on fripperies and be sorry later.'

As they walked up Spiceal Street, Ada could sense Elsie getting more and more excited. She was walking faster and faster, chatting nineteen to the dozen, the money burning in her pocket.

'She's the most beautiful thing you've ever seen, Ada. I've called her Alicia Victoria and she's got big eyes and lots of lovely hair – and you should see her clothes, like a princess!'

Ada smiled. It was good to see Elsie happy and excited as a child for once. Her heart bled for her little sister. For a moment she thought of the last moment she had seen her, coughing and half-delirious, clutching her little rag doll while being dragged away by the Union officers, never to see their mom again . . .

'What happened to your little dolly – Lucy, wasn't it?'

Elsie gave a shrug. 'Dunno. She got lost.' Her face took on that closed expression it often did when they talked about anything relating to the workhouse.

They hurried along New Street to the toy shop, its window shaded from the afternoon glare by a wide awning. Elsie rushed up to the window and pushed her forehead right against it. Ada joined her, eyes adjusting to the shade and trying to make sense of what she could see.

As her eyes adjusted, what she saw was a beautiful rocking horse painted dappled grey with a white mane and so large it dominated the window. Around it were an array of games and boxes of tin soldiers and, hanging at various points in the window, little metal cages containing colourful wooden birds. But there were no dolls to be seen.

Elsie seemed stuck to the glass, staring in disbelief.

'I s'pose they change what's in the window,' Ada said, her own heart sinking. 'You know, to sell different things. They must've put the dolls somewhere else.'

'Can you go in and find out where she is?' Elsie said, her big eyes full of desperation.

'Someone might have bought her, Elsie,' Ada warned. She felt bad herself, disappointed for Elsie. But Elsie did not seem to take this in, as if such a thing had never entered into her calculations.

Ada looked nervously at the entrance to this grand shop. And suddenly, again, memories flashed in her mind. The little carved scrolls each side of the doorway, the pale stone edged by black paint, the step leading up into the shop . . .

'We went in here with Pa . . . One Christmas time! D'you remember?'

Even though Elsie would have been very young, two, perhaps, Ada desperately wanted her to be able to recall it, for them to stitch together their early memories so they could share them. But Elsie looked blankly at her.

'I . . . No.' She looked sadly up at the shop sign, then at the shining plate of glass. 'Please, Ada.'

Were they allowed to go inside a shop like that? Ada wondered, nervously. They were not children with Pa – both of them were obviously maidservants in their plain grey dresses. But she could not refuse Elsie now.

'You come with me,' she said, her voice trembling.

As they passed through the wide doorway, hand in hand, Ada almost expected someone to shout at them to stop, to ask them what they thought they were doing. But nothing happened. They stared about them. Ada tried to recall being here before but she only had the faintest memory of the place, the dark wooden shelving round the walls. How was it she had not remembered that the shop was full of toys? It was like a palace of toys!

'Oh, look –' Ada pointed towards the back in relief. 'There are some dolls.'

Elsie's eyes fixed on the dolls, which were arranged sitting on a small table, almost as if they were getting ready for a picnic. She hurried up to them, an awed expression on her face which made Ada smile. Elsie stared and stared, then looked at Ada in bewilderment.

'She ain't here.'

'What, your doll?' Ada did not see how this mattered. 'Never mind – look at all these other lovely dolls!' She picked up a price ticket. Seven and six for one. Nine shillings for another. 'And these don't cost as much, Elsie . . .'

'No . . .' Elsie's eyes were stretched wide, as if watching something horrific happening in front of her.

'Can I help you, young ladies?'

A man was standing over them, his face mostly covered by whiskers and in a waistcoat too tight for his ample tummy. He sounded cross and suspicious. Ada felt annoyed. Did he think they were going to steal something?

'My sister was interested in a doll which you had in your window. It cost ten shillings and sixpence.'

'Ah,' he said. 'Yes, I'm sure she was *interested*,' he said mockingly, eyeing their humble attire. 'Sold – to a family in Edgbaston. Rather beyond your range but if you'd like a rag doll there are some inexpensive ones over there . . . Now, no loitering, please . . .'

He shooed them out towards the front of the shop. Ada felt fury rising in her. Who did he think they were – thieves and nobodies?

'Come on.' She took Elsie's hand. 'Snooty so-and-so. Let's get out of here. We'll go and get a treat – I'll buy you a bun and a cuppa tea, some sweets . . .'

Ada thought Elsie had accepted this disappointment. After all, it had taken her some time to save up and of course it was inevitable that someone might buy the doll in the meantime. She did not seem to want to spend her money on any of the other dolls.

Elsie moved beside her like a sleepwalker as they walked back down to the Bull Ring. But amid the bustle and commotion of the markets, she stopped, abruptly. A stooped, elderly lady with a wrinkled face swooped down on them, holding a tray of lavender.

'Sweet lavender, lovely young ladies – ha'penny a packet – only a ha'penny . . .'

Ada shook her head, distracted by realizing that Elsie was going to pieces beside her. The girl was shaking, whimpering, making sounds of such distress that Ada grabbed her by the elbow, pushed past the insistent lavender seller and got her to a spot near the front of the Market Hall.

'Elsie?' She bent down as her sister gulped and sobbed, her whole body seeming to be overtaken by her trouble. 'What ails you?'

'I wanted her,' Elsie managed to say. 'She was mine, I know she was. I wanted her and she . . . She never waited . . . She went away and left me . . .'

Elsie's crying was inconsolable. As she sobbed and howled, Ada watched, helplessly, a pain in her chest as if it was breaking open and her own tears starting to flow. She understood those awful, bereft feelings. *I wanted them and they all went away . . .*

She drew her little sister into her arms and felt Elsie cling to her, her body shaking and sobbing. Gently she removed Elsie's hat and let her sister rest her head against her chest as amid the indifferent crowds, the two of them stood together and wept and wept.

Thirty-Two

'She can't have gone – she was supposed to wait for me!' Elsie wept so loudly and hysterically that afternoon that people were turning to look.

'Elsie –' Once they had both had a cry, Ada tried desperately to get through to her sister. 'For heaven's sake, *listen*. Are you sure you don't want to go back – buy one of the other dollies?'

'It was *her* I wanted. Not another one.' Ada could feel the girl's whole body shaking. It was as if the world had ended. 'She was *mine*, and now she's gone.'

Ada's mind was in turmoil. All this emotion. She knew it was not just over the doll but even so, Elsie really worried her. Her mind seemed to fix on things in a way that was not good for her.

It took a long time to calm her down.

'We've got to get back,' Ada told her, tugging her arm to make her start walking.

She gripped her sister's hand and Elsie never said a word, all the way back to Highgate. Ada kept sneaking little glances at her. How could Elsie not have understood that someone else might buy the doll? It was as if she had thought this beautiful thing was already hers, that it would just stay there, sitting in exactly the same place until Elsie came back after saving all her money. It was another thing that made Ada wonder about her sister's mental state.

It's this house, she thought, her mind rushing round. *Him* and his peculiar ways. She could not get Elsie to say exactly what Mr Dugdale had been doing up in his office room. But she knew enough from Seamus Connell's approaches to her to guess it was surely Arthur Dugdale who was sending her sister into this state. Poor little Mary Lunn, his captive doll. And he was king in his own house. She thought about Jane Dugdale. She had thought the woman was just silly and spoilt. But after what Elsie had told her, what she saw in Mrs Dugdale's bedchamber, her bowed, crippled legs, it seemed she was also a wife who could hardly walk, like a doll kept on a table to be looked at. The thought made her shudder.

Ada had only been at the Dugdales' establishment for a couple of weeks. She liked Josie, didn't mind slaving for Mrs Simmons and it was quite easy to keep out of Harry's way as he was worked hard in the garden. It was all so much better than living with the Connells. But now she longed to get Elsie out of there, for them to be able to live in such a way that they were not beholden to anyone.

Once they got back to the house, she poured two cups of milk, cool from the jug on the slate-topped table in the larder, and she took Elsie out into the garden.

'Sit down.'

Elsie was like a doll herself. Ada almost had to bend her knees for her to make her sink to the ground. They sat on the grass drinking the milk in the scent of hot lavender and the slow, end-of-summer hum of the bees.

Ada stared at the house. Its bulky brick shape and dark-eyed windows coldly returned her gaze. When she had first arrived it had felt like a refuge after the Connells'. They got fed at least, had a roof over their heads. But if they stayed here they would be prisoners for ever. Prisoners in a house with this man, whatever his twisted obsessions were, corrupting her sister, just as Seamus Connell tried to use her. Ada was starting to feel she had escaped one cage only to find herself in another.

Over the next couple of days, Ada formed a plan. She whispered to Elsie at night when they were up in their attic.

'We'll stay here 'til we get our wages, end of September. Hang on to every last penny, all right? Don't go out anywhere, frittering it. And you're not going in that room with him ever again, however much he orders you. When he's in the house, those afternoons, we'll keep you out of his way. If he calls on you, either Josie'll go or I will.'

Elsie listened carefully. Now that she knew someone was helping – they had told Josie and Mrs Simmons what had been going on – she was calmer.

Ada did not tell the others the rest of her plans. She wanted to make sure she had her and Elsie's wages in her hands, as well as the remains of Elsie's savings.

The weeks seemed to crawl by but Ada and Josie between them did a good job of keeping Elsie out of the clutches of Mr Dugdale.

He did send for her one afternoon and Josie went up instead. She came back looking satisfied. Ada, who had been scraping the bottom of a cooking pot with wire wool, went to the scullery door, hands still black with burnt stew and soap, to hear what had happened.

'When he saw it was me come up, he gave me a right mardy look,' Josie said. '"Where's the other one? Mary Lunn?" he said. "I asked for her, not you." So I said – I laid it on . . .' Then Josie put on such a sugary, subservient tone that they all laughed: '"Oh, I'm ever so sorry but I'm afraid Mary's not at all well. 'Er's been sick as anything all morning and hardly fit to stand. You don't want 'er coming up 'ere in that state, do you, sir?" He looked ever so annoyed but 'e couldn't argue with that, could 'e, filthy old sod?'

Ada laughed along with the others. She liked Josie and appreciated the way she was standing up for them so wholeheartedly.

'I don't know as this can carry on though,' Mrs Simmons said. ''E's the master here. There's no one can touch him and sooner or later . . .'

'Thing is.' Ada wiped her forehead with the back of one hand. 'We've decided to go – Else and me.'

'Go?' Mrs Simmons said.

'We're gunna start up on our own,' Elsie grinned.

'Don't go and leave us,' Josie said. 'We're all just settling in nicely! And anyway – you'll have to give notice, or they won't give you a reference.'

'Oh, you'll soon be off with your Loz,' Ada said. 'Anyway – we don't need a reference. Not where we're going. And not from her, any road.'

Something else happened during that time of waiting that made Ada even more sure they should move on. One afternoon of dying summer she went out into the garden again, sitting in a little spot which was secluded from the house by a laurel bush. In the distance she could hear the sound of hoeing and she had gone off into a daydream, full of her plans for her future and Elsie's. She didn't even hear him coming and the next thing was a voice in her ear.

'Come on, Ada.' Harry's voice was low, teasing. 'How about a kiss, eh?'

Ada nearly jumped out of her skin. He had arrived on the grass behind her like a silent, stalking animal and she had had no idea he was there.

She turned abruptly, trying to speak but before she could get to her feet, Harry dropped to his knees and his hands were on her shoulders, then his arms wrapping round her, lips pressing against hers. She felt the jab of stubble on his top lip, smelt the salty, sweaty odour of this young male.

'Oi!' She resisted with a huge shove. 'What the hell're you *doing*? How dare you creep up on me like that?'

Harry sat back on his heels. 'Ooh, sorry, Miss Prim,' he was still teasing, as if sure he could talk her round. 'Thought you wanted it.'

'Well, I don't,' Ada snapped, getting up quickly. 'What's the matter with you? I've never once said I wanted anything from you.'

'What do you want then, you cold old stick?' he jeered after her.

'Not you, that's for sure,' she retorted, wiping her mouth.

Harry's angry gaze seemed to burn through her back as she hurried away into the house. Ada went fuming into the kitchen. As if she had given him any sign, she thought, furiously putting away the pans she had washed earlier. As if he had even been in her thoughts at all! All she was concerned about was herself and Elsie – and getting them out of here.

Thirty-Three

'Remember the names?'

Ada sat on the edge of the bed in the candlelight. Now it was the end of September the nights were drawing in. She had her piece of cloth with her shell collection all laid out at the bottom of the bed.

She and Elsie had played with the collection many times since they had been together again and Ada still felt the same lift of happiness whenever she looked at them. But now, she had another motive. This was business.

'Tell me an' all.' Josie came and sat by them. 'They're beautiful, they are. So, what're you gunna do, Ada?'

Ada had told Josie that she and Elsie had worked in the pearl button trade before, as children.

'We're gunna set up on our own,' Ada said. 'It doesn't take much to start up small. We'll have the money to get a few tools. I know the trade. And you'll soon learn, Elsie. If we go to one of the bigger firms we can do the blank cutting for them to start and build up from there. There's work aplenty for button makers in Birmingham.'

'Well, give her up there a bit of warning before you go or us lot'll cop all the work,' Josie said.

'A week – once we've got our wages,' Ada said. 'And then we're off. I've got a reference from Tompkinson's already, if I ever do need one. From Mrs Rundle – d'you remember her?'

She looked hopefully at Elsie in the candlelight, but her

sister's face showed no recognition. She was staring at the pale glow of a wide, flat shell.

'Is that – macassar?' Elsie looked up at Ada, suddenly like a happy child, in wonder that this was something she could remember.

'Yes!' Ada said.

'Macassar,' Josie echoed, picking it up and gazing at it. 'My, my. It's lovely, that is.'

'From the East Indies,' Ada said. 'And this?'

Josie gasped. 'Oh – let me look.' She held it close to the candlelight and they could see its mauve and green glint in the light.

'Abalone,' Ada said, proud of her knowledge. 'New Zealand.'

Josie smiled, handing it back. 'I almost wish I was coming with yer.'

'No, you don't,' Ada said. 'You can get married to Loz and get out of here.'

Josie looked at her, slowly handing back the shell.

'You could get married too, Ada.'

'No,' Ada said adamantly. 'I'm never doing that.'

'I've come to tell you Elsie and me'll be leaving come next week.'

Ada didn't tug her forelock or say 'madam' or 'Mrs Dugdale'. She wasn't having that, not any more. She stood in front of her mistress in the pretty parlour with the little bowls of bonbons and potpourri arranged on small tables. This poor trapped woman. Ada felt sorry for her now. But she also felt powerful.

She and Elsie each had their two pound ten tucked safely away with their other bits of money saved and they knew it was enough to make a start.

Mrs Dugdale's expression seemed to be a tussle between bewilderment and fury.

'Elsie?' she said finally, in a disdainful tone. 'Who is Elsie?'

'The maid you call Mary Lunn,' Ada said. 'Her name's not Mary Lunn, she's Elsie Fletcher and she's my sister. We're leaving you a week's notice so you can start looking for someone else.'

'Oh no, you don't.' Mrs Dugdale's eyes were cold as ice. The idea of a servant saying what was to be what completely enraged her. 'You'll work a month if you want any sort of a reference – and you'll be lucky to get anything after this.' Her little face puckered with anger.

'We don't need references from you, thank you, madam – they wouldn't make any difference to anything,' Ada replied very politely, relishing the woman's indignation. 'But we'll work the week as we have worked before.'

'You don't come in here telling me when you will and will not work!' Mrs Dugdale's nostrils flared with anger and her eyes narrowed. 'I'm not having this. You're lucky I don't turn you out on the street now. You will work out the month, or . . .'

Ada waited. Or what?

'We are just offering to work this week so as not to let the other maids down,' Ada said, suddenly feeling more of an adult than her mistress who was pink and vapouring with rage. 'So you can find someone.'

You'd best start looking straight away, she wanted to add. *Or not much'll get done round here, will it?*

'I'm disgusted,' Mrs Dugdale fired at her helplessly. There was nothing she could do.

'Sorry, madam. Thank you, madam.'

Ada left the room, a grin spreading across her face. I'm

not sorry. And I'm not having the likes of you ruling my life, she thought. Not ever again.

A week later, she and Elsie said goodbye to the other staff. Josie came over all teary and hugged the two of them tight. She had solemnly handed Elsie the money she had kept for her in the tin – a few shillings short of four pounds.

'There,' Josie said. 'I know I was hard on you over it, but I bet you're glad you didn't just go and spend it all now, aren't you?'

'Thanks, Josie,' Elsie smiled. 'I s'pose you're right.'

'That's going to help us no end,' Ada said, beaming at her. 'You've been a real friend to Elsie. Now, you and Loz get enough saved up and then you'll be married and out of here as well. Come and see us, eh? I dunno where we'll be yet – but we'll be called Fletchers', all right?'

Josie nodded, but both of them knew really that this was goodbye. Their lives were taking very different directions.

'Good luck to you both,' Mrs Simmons said. She patted Elsie's head, smiling. 'Goodbye, bab – we'll miss you.'

A new kitchen maid had already been hurriedly found so at least Mrs Simmons would have help.

As the two of them went out through the Dugdales' front gate for the last time, Elsie turned and looked back at the house for a long moment.

'Bye-bye, Mary Lunn,' she said. She turned to Ada and smiled and Ada's spirits lifted even further. Elsie looked like a young girl, unburdened and happy at the thought of the future.

And the two of them set off down the hill into Birmingham, carrying their small bundles of possessions.

Thirty-Four

'This will do nicely,' Ada said, looking round the small first-floor room with its peeling distemper and splintered floorboards. The place was no palace but the two of them were as delighted as if it had been. 'We can work in here as well as live here – save money.'

Elsie walked round, heels loud on the boards, stroking the walls as if they were already beloved friends. A powder of greyish white trickled from them at her touch.

'We can make it homely. It's ours – really ours to live in and no one else's!' Her eyes were shining and her whole face lit up. Ada smiled seeing her excitement at the very idea of having their own home, however humble, that they could furnish and arrange however they pleased.

Elsie rushed over to Ada and grabbed her hands, pulling her round and round so that the two of them were spinning in a wild jig, laughing their heads off, their boots clattering on the floor.

'There's work aplenty round here,' Ada said, panting as they finally stopped jumping about. All round the area were workers in mother-of-pearl – some in small, one-room shops producing blanks and part-made buttons to be finished by other larger works who turned out buttons by the thousand, as well as handles for cutlery and shell boxes and all sorts of creations of delicate shell inlay and marquetry. 'And there's a place along the road where we can get the tools . . . Come on – let's get started. We'll get set up all we can today and tomorrow we'll go and find a works that'll give us outwork.'

The girls hurried out to the streets to buy the items they needed to set up home. Even the simplest items seemed exciting – their own choice for their own home. Ada could see the hunger in Elsie's face, the way she relished every little thing, and they found themselves exclaiming and laughing over plates and pots and pans with the sheer joy of it.

They bought a chaff palliasse and a worn but serviceable quilt off the Rag Market, along with a few household items – a pot to heat water and a pan, plates and irons for eating, two pails, one to bring coal up from the cellar and another to fetch water from the street pump – and a few provisions. Their first meal was a pan of porridge heated on their own fire and as yet having no furniture, they ate it sitting on the palliasse, giggling like children let loose to play.

'There's a fried-fish shop along the road – did you smell it?' Ada said, scraping up the last of her porridge. 'When we get some work, we'll treat ourselves.'

Elsie beamed. 'I don't care if we have to live on slop. We can earn our own money and make our own minds up – that's the main thing.'

Ada's first investment was in a blank cutter. Then she and Elsie went round the larger button factories. The sight of the ground around these premises made her smile, the dirt and grime aglint with tiny fragments of shell, like stars in the sky.

It did not take them long to find work. Arthur Beardsmore, Buttons in Pearl, Bone and Wood was a large works situated at the far end of Galton Passage, a narrow slit between Livery Street and Snow Hill, the high buildings on either side crammed full of a mixed variety of smaller works.

Beardsmore's was an imposing, red-brick building. Ada went in nervously, up a well-worn staircase opening into a long, wide room full of lathes and the whirr and bang and clatter of the trade. Wooden boxes were piled around the room full of shell in its various stages of transformation from undersea creature to useful garment fastener. At the near end Ada saw boxes full of hundreds of lustrous white buttons.

She looked round the room. This is what we're going to do, she thought. A works like this – we'll do all of it.

A stocky, busy-looking man with a pencil stub behind one ear came over to them.

'What're you after, ladies?'

'We've come about outwork – blank cutting,' Ada said with a confidence which managed to mask the fact that Elsie had never yet cut a blank in her life.

'You want Cyril – in the office over there . . .'

The man pointed to a little room at the end.

Cyril, a dark-haired fellow with a big nose who was snorting in snuff when they appeared, sniffed hard, then sneezed as loudly as an explosion which made Elsie jump, before looking at them, unimpressed.

'Blanks? All right. We can always do with them. Go and see Fred, he'll sort you out.' He pointed vaguely along the shop.

'Was that Fred who sent us in there in the first place?' Elsie wondered as they hurried along the way they had come. 'We'll be back and to all day at this rate.'

But no. Fred was young and on the ball, and the pair of them were soon furnished with two large boxes of sawn shell sections ready for blank cutting. They lugged them down to the street and burst into giggles. They didn't even know why they were laughing, except that everything felt good and happy.

After that they were never short of work. Ada taught Elsie how to cut blanks since she had been too young to learn before, when she was at Tompkinson's.

'You'll scorch a few,' Ada told her. 'But you'll soon pick it up.'

There were a few tears at first, but Elsie was soon proficient and faster than Ada could have imagined. She seemed on fire with enthusiasm. The two of them worked and worked, taking turns on the cutter at first – thirteen hours six days of the week, on Sunday a rest for church, if they felt like it, or a walk in the gardens of St Philip's Church if the day was too nice to be spent inside.

They had been working their blank cutters like fury all morning and now, these days after saving their pennies, were gradually bringing little comforts into the room – a table and chairs, more coal for the fire now winter was coming, an extra cover for them to sleep under.

'We're free, Ade,' Elsie said one day, when they had just been paid. She was at the window looking down into the street. 'Really free.' It was like an announcement, as if it had fully sunk in.

The sounds of cartwheels and metal-bashing and voices came from outside, as did all the smells of refuse and factory smoke and fumes. But Elsie had a look on her face as if she was staring at the most beautiful landscape ever.

'I'll work 'til I drop – but I ain't never going back again. Not to anywhere where they tell you your life all the time.'

Ada looked at her little sister, straining, even now she was fourteen, to be tall enough to look over the sill, and she felt a rush of love for her. Back. To the workhouse. To service. At everyone else's beck and call. No – never.

'We're going to do it, Else, you and me,' she said, lifting their kettle on to the fire. 'We'll build this business. And as soon as we can afford another wage we'll fetch our Dora and John. And there's someone else I want to come and work for us – Nellie's brother Tom.'

When the two of them had left service at the Dugdales' that morning and walked back down Bradford Street to the heart of Birmingham, Ada had steered their direction away from Summer Row and the yard where the Connells lived. In the weeks she had been in service she had not managed to find employment for Tom and she was disappointed with herself. But there would be time for that – once they could stand on their own feet.

Already now she felt she could be her own person. She was going to build this business until it could rival Arthur Beardsmore's – and she and Elsie would never be in service to anyone, ever again.

IV

Thirty-Five

1861

'Over here.'

Ada gestured to the side of the room where she wanted the lathe positioned. The two men had come puffing up the stairs after hefting the thing from the street. They could not get the cart any closer and had to unload it in Livery Street. Then they manhandled the heavy machine along the cobbles of the narrow gulch of Galton Passage.

The two young men, grunting and cursing, manoeuvred their burden along the entry to the backyard, through the dark store room on the ground floor and up the stairs to the workshop where Ada was waiting.

'That's it – by the windows, next to that one,' she instructed. Ada stood tall, hands on hips, surveying her new premises with pride.

One of the carriers, a dark-haired lad, had his back to her and she saw he was much stronger than the other, puny lad who leaned on the machine wheezing and coughing the second he was able to put it down. The tougher one turned round once the lathe was in place, pushed his cap further back to reveal more of his thick hair and flashed a grin at her. Ada saw a swarthy, handsome face and what seemed a humorous nature but to her, the smile had a sting of arrogance in it and she felt herself bristle.

'Good place you got here,' he said, grimacing. ''Cept for the pong.'

One of the yards abutting theirs at the back belonged to a bone and horn button works. The heaps of bones and sawn-off horns arrived with raw meat and gristle cleaving to them and had to be laid out to dry. The stench of rotting meat was abominable and in the attic where the girls were to live they would have to keep the windows shut. It was the main drawback of the place.

Ada shrugged. 'Nothing I can do about it, is there?'

'Want the other one 'ere then?' The dark-haired lad pointed to the space beside the lathe they had just delivered. It was a wide room and so far there were just two machines placed on the side closest to the windows. Two more were on their way. 'Not short of space, are you?' he added in a sarcastic tone.

Ada nodded. 'There'll be room for when we expand.'

'Oh – you got big ideas then. Working for your old man, are yer?'

'No,' Ada said coldly. 'It's my business – me and my sister.'

'Women in charge eh?' he said, scathingly, as if he did not really believe her. He pushed his cap back and scratched at his scalp again and Ada looked daggers at him. She felt her shoulders pull back, her spine grow taller, proud. She wasn't having this idiot talking down to her.

'It's my business – I started it,' she said, looking directly into his eyes. His were brown and large, like a puppy's. A charmer, she thought. Well, you won't be charming me.

She still didn't have much cotter with men. Not in that way anyhow. She had more important things to do like get her business on a secure footing so that she and Elsie could feel truly safe and not need anyone else. But she noticed that men took an interest in her. She wasn't pretty like Elsie.

She was taller and thinner, kept her honey-brown hair fastened back simply in an austere kind of way. But she knew she gave off a kind of energy, a confidence. She had her own purpose and it intrigued them. And maybe even her indifference to men was a challenge they liked to take up. As for this one, he was smiling but mocking her at the same time. He got under her skin like a splinter. And now he was holding out his hand.

'Sam Bligh. Work for Whitty's hauliers.'

Well, obviously, Ada wanted to retort, since that was the firm she had taken on to transport the lathes. They had brought the two they already owned from the much smaller workshop where they had first set up. These others, she had managed to get hold of second-hand.

Ada felt she could not ignore this palm that was thrust towards her and she let her own be taken in his. It was so big that her hand disappeared into it.

'Well – good luck to yer,' he said, looking round. 'Look as if you might know what you're about, which is more'n I can say for some.'

Elsie came up the stairs then and looked round, excited.

'Who's this?' Sam asked.

'My sister and partner, Elsie Fletcher.'

Ada felt a shimmer of pride inside as she said this. Sister – and beautiful at that, with her big eyes and neat little figure. And she could say she had family – at least the one little part of it she had left.

Elsie had her hand shaken as well. She looked up at Sam Bligh and Ada saw her eyes light on him with a glow that she found immediately troubling.

'How old're you then?' Sam asked jovially.

'Seventeen,' Elsie said.

'Seventeen?' He was genuinely astonished. 'I'd've put you at twelve!'

Elsie's face fell as he turned away, dismissing her as a child.

'Right, well, I expect you're going to be off?' Ada interrupted curtly. 'Can't be standing about all day.'

'All right, boss lady.' Sam gave her a mocking little bow. The other lad had just about recovered so the two of them prepared to take their leave.

'Thanks,' Ada said coolly.

'Goodbye, Sam,' Elsie said, at her elbow. She was gazing dreamily up at Sam, much to Ada's irritation.

'Good luck,' he said. He winked at Elsie. 'See yer.'

'Ta-ra,' the other lad gasped.

Sam tilted his cap and gave the sisters a grin as he turned to go.

'I like him,' Elsie said as they disappeared down the stairs.

'No, you don't,' Ada snapped.

'You don't have to be so short,' Elsie complained. There was a blush on her face.

'And you don't have to look at the bloke as if he just stepped off a cloud,' Ada snapped.

'I never did,' Elsie said, though she added dreamily, 'but he's nice-looking, ain't he?'

'Huh,' Ada retorted. 'Don't waste your time. Come on – we need to get sorted out. Where's Tom got to?'

'Gone to buy bread,' Elsie said. She looked round happily. 'It's a good place. We'll do all right here.'

'We're going to do more than all right,' Ada said, pulling her shoulders back. 'We'll see to it that we do.'

In the sudden quiet, Ada took in the length of the workshop they were renting, up a flight of stairs, light slanting in from windows facing the yard at the rear side and a much more meagre illumination through the windows facing the narrow gulley that was Galton Passage.

She looked along her newly rented workshop, doing rapid sums in her head about the shell stock they would need and how soon they could get up and running.

Our shop. Fletchers' Pearl Button Works. She would get a sign painted. They had built this, she and Elsie, by more than two years' non-stop work and struggle. Her business – already there were a few of them working there and she was going to make sure it got bigger until they could do every process involved in button making and sell their stock straight into the market. Not for nothing had she toiled all those years at Tompkinson's.

Ada felt powerful and strong these days, the way she had felt as a girl. Pa's lad. A terrible pang filled her for a moment. How certain things had felt back then. Her pa, who could work magic with anything. Now, she had to provide for herself, find her own strength and will to succeed. But she had both those things – in plenty.

She peered out of the window which faced Galton Passage, taking in their new position. Across from them worked a family of lapidaries by the name of Drake. They seemed nice enough. So far, from what she had seen, it was a good neighbourhood. They were on their way. She turned back to Elsie, suddenly lit up.

'Fletchers' is gunna be the best. And we'll make sure we employ no one but the best!'

Thirty-Six

Two years earlier – March 1859

'The Archway of Tears. Oh, Ada, I dunno as I can go back in there.'

Ada and Elsie stood looking up at the workhouse that Sunday morning. It was six months since they had left the Dugdales and both of them had slogged every hour, living frugally as mice, to build their little business and keep their heads above water. There was so much demand, so many businesses making pearl buttons that they were doing all right, even just supplying blanks. Bit by bit they were building and Ada was talking about taking on more workers and getting lathes for backing and turning as well.

And now, it felt as if they could begin looking to the other people in their lives.

Ada had watched Elsie grow into a happier, more stable person. But here, gazing up at this place where she had spent so much of her childhood, she seemed frail and fearful again.

'Stay out here, if you want,' Ada said gently, understanding why Elsie had shrunk into herself again. The sight of the place made her own innards twist with dread. 'I'll go and ask.'

'No.' Elsie pulled her shawl round her. 'I'm coming. They'll've come out of chapel by now.'

They announced themselves to the porter – still Mr

Hodges and his moustache. He showed no sign of recognizing Elsie and directed them inside.

'Knock at the Board Office and wait.'

As they passed through into the dark entrance, Ada saw Elsie shrink even more, hugging her arms around herself.

'That smell,' she whispered. And Ada became aware suddenly of the demoralizing waft of singed porridge and boiled onions, of the unaired emanations of bodies, of sadness and despair. These walls which gave shelter to the city's lost – the desperate families, the old and sick, the destitute, the orphaned children. Sadness seemed to breathe out through every sullen brick.

'Was it always bad?' Ada whispered back, dreading even to imagine all the years her siblings had spent in here.

They had found the right door and stood working themselves up to knock.

'We did play sometimes,' Elsie said. 'Did some lessons. But . . .' She was close to weeping suddenly. 'We never knew anything – where we were even, really. And what had happened to Mom and Pa – and you. And when we would ever get out . . .'

As she spoke, a tiny wisp of a woman, bent over like a hairpin, shuffled past along the nearby corridor towards a door. She wore a limp, shapeless dress and lopsided mob cap.

'That's the room where they put the tramps – when they first come in,' Elsie whispered.

The woman was coughing terribly. She pushed the door open and disappeared.

Ada steeled herself and knocked, hearing a woman's voice call, 'Come in!'

'That's Mrs Hodges,' Elsie said. 'She ain't too bad.'

Catching sight of the Matron's round face above her black bombazine dress and apron, her lower half concealed under the table where she was sitting, Ada thought she

233

looked quite frightening enough. If she was not too bad what were some of the others like? But she was determined not to be cowed.

'Yes?' Mrs Hodges said, shuffling the papers that lay in front of her. 'What is it you want?'

'We've come to ask for our brother and sister.' Ada spoke up, determined not to be cowed. 'Their names are John and Dora Fletcher. They were John and Annie Lunn here. We want them to come home with us.'

Mrs Hodges raised her head then and looked closely at the two of them. Her eyes fastened on Elsie.

'Mary Lunn?' she said uncertainly. 'Is that you?'

There was a second while Elsie looked cowed. But then Ada was proud to feel her sister straighten up beside her. 'My real name is Elsie Fletcher.'

'I see.' Mrs Hodges frowned in consternation as if she did not in fact see at all and something most irregular must have happened. It dawned on Ada that someone had made a bad error when admitting her brother and sisters to the workhouse. But she was not going to admit this. 'Well, I suppose I can have a look.'

She got up from the desk and their eyes followed her to a table at the side of the room where a row of ledgers was stacked, tilted against both each other and the wall. She selected one, blew dust off it and opened it on the desk. Ada and Elsie dared to move closer, watching her run a finger down the rows of names written in slanting copperplate. Mrs Hodges made little whistling sounds with her lips before her finger halted on a name.

'Ah, yes. Lunn. Annie . . . I thought so. She went from here just over a year ago . . .'

'A year ago!' Elsie burst out, unable to hold back. 'But she was only twelve! That was only just after me – you took me to the Dugdales'. She was going to wait for me . . .'

Elsie was silenced as the woman looked up at her sharply.

'Mary Lunn. That's enough. There are some families who look for charity cases and . . .' She glanced down at the ledger again.

Elsie was silenced, hanging her head. Ada had a sudden impulse to grab her and run out of the door. She could not bear to see her sister reduced again like this.

'Annie Lunn went into service in . . .' She ran a stubby finger further along the line of blue copperplate. 'Birmingham is all it says. John Lunn – has gone to a position with a firm in Smethwick.'

She slammed the book shut suddenly, as if she felt she had given them quite enough of her time, and stood up.

'Can you tell us where we can find them?' Ada ventured to ask. 'Or our other sister, Mabs – Mabel Fletcher?'

'Martha Lunn,' Elsie said. 'She was sent away near the start – never saw her again.'

With reluctance, Mrs Hodges picked out another ledger, then another and finally located a name in it.

'Martha Lunn . . . Yes. She went to a family. As a baby.' She slammed the book shut. 'That's all that's been put down. I can't tell you any more than we've got here.'

The way Mrs Hodges was pressing her hand on the cover of the ledger as if afraid they might snatch it from her made Ada feel sure she was lying but it did not seem possible to argue.

'So,' Mrs Hodges said, slipping the ledger back between the others. 'There we are.'

The girls fled from the building, gulping in air as if they had been held underwater for all the time they had been in there. Ada felt that she wanted to run and keep running as far as she could. Elsie was crying and she soon had to stop, sobbing and gasping.

'How could they just give them away like that?' she said, trying to catch her breath. 'They were s'posed to wait for me . . .'

'They couldn't help it,' Ada said. 'Dora and John, I mean. No one would have asked them, would they?' She put her arm round her sister's shoulders. 'It sounds as if our John's got work all right – and Dora. We'll have to wait 'til we're on our feet. I don't know how we're ever going to find her. It was only by a miracle I found you, wasn't it?'

Elsie's tear-stained face turned up to her. 'It was, Ade. I can still hardly believe it even now.'

Elsie was calming down now they were further from the dreaded sight of the workhouse.

'Look – let's get us summat to eat. I'll treat you.'

Ada led Elsie to a bakery and they came away with two big currant buns for a halfpenny and walked along, devouring them. They were warm and spicy and delicious. Soon they both felt a lot better. They started giggling together in relief, buoyed up by the food.

'I don't know as I can face all this carry-on again today,' Ada said, exhausted. 'Let's leave it 'til next week, then we'll go and get Tom.'

The following week it was Ada who was the more nervous of the two of them. She felt shaky and her hands were clammy as she led Elsie along the entry in Summer Row and into the yard. All that she had left behind, all she had tried not to think about, came back to her with force and with the feeling of guilt she could never shake off. The Connell boys, Sarah lying mad and in despair. Now, fresh from the workhouse a few days ago, she thought, I wonder if they took Sarah to the asylum, whether she's locked up all over again . . . Sarah and Nellie both.

'D'you remember it?' she asked Elsie quietly, once they were in the yard.

Elsie looked round in amazement, memory dawning. She nodded, wide-eyed.

'Our house was over there?'

Ada nodded. 'After they took you all and Mrs Connell hid me, I lived with them, there, next door.' She pointed. 'Where Nellie lived, remember?'

Her heart was hammering. She did not want to face Seamus Connell, face any of it – her own desertion of the boys. She was afraid to find out what had happened to them.

She was just about to move forward when a familiar figure emerged from the brew house at the end of the yard. Ada saw that Mrs Spragg had aged a little but she did not look very different, her uneven walk on her bad hip still the same. She narrowed her eyes and peered short-sightedly at them.

'D'yer want summat?' she asked, firm, a bit hostile. But as she moved closer recognition came to her. 'Oh, my word – is that Ada?'

'Yeah, it's me, Mrs Spragg,' Ada said. 'And this is Elsie.'

Olive Spragg stopped and peered into their faces in wonder. 'Well, I never. I didn't expect to see you again – either of you.' She limped to her door. 'Come in, wenches.'

Mrs Spragg's downstairs room had not changed at all either, so far as Ada could recall, the spotless range and old horsehair settee, the much-mended net curtain over the window. Without even asking she put the kettle on the range.

'Sit yourselves down – I s'pose you want to know how things are with them?' She jerked her head towards the Connells' house.

'And everyone – yourself too,' Ada said, politely.

237

'I'm as you can see,' Mrs Spragg said. 'But I lost my old man last winter.'

Ada glanced at Elsie, but realized she did not remember miserable old Clarence Spragg.

'Sorry,' Ada said as Mrs Spragg clattered cups.

'Ah, well,' Mrs Spragg said. 'It's the way of the world. He always had a weak chest.' She came over and perched on a chair while waiting for the water to boil. Her face turned sorrowful. 'Poor Sarah didn't last long after you went. I did my best but she was fading, you'll remember?'

Ada nodded, her heart like a stone in her chest. Her eyes filled with tears.

'There's nothing you could have done,' Mrs Spragg said. 'It was all of it – and thinking she was going to be hanged on top of all that. Turned her mind. She was a soul in torment – best out of it in the end, that she was. Anyway, before long Connell'd spruced up and got himself another wife – Colleen, her name is. Young Irish slattern not long off the boat. 'Er's got more idea about keeping pigs than a house – but 'er's all right in her way.'

'What about the boys?' Ada said.

Mrs Spragg looked away towards the wall behind Ada's head a moment, as if gathering herself.

''E sent the young'uns away soon after you went,' she said, her voice sorrowful.

'Peter and Anthony?' Ada could feel her chest tightening with further grief. She was the only one who could have saved them and she knew she could not do it. Not stay there, just for them. 'Where?'

Mrs Spragg shrugged. 'Some home or other. Or one of the workhouses, poor little mites. The older lads've all gone. William stayed until she turned up.' She nodded towards the Connells' house again. 'No one's seen him.'

'What about Tom?'

'That lad's the only one left and they're keener on his wages than ever they are on him,' Mrs Spragg said. 'Connell's still working by some miracle, he's not a well man . . .' She stopped to attend to the kettle which was billowing out steam, poured water into the teapot and set a cloth over it to keep it warm. Sitting down again she looked at the two of them and suddenly smiled, revealing two remaining teeth in her upper gum.

'You look well, Ada. And little Elsie. You're a picture, ain't yer? I'm glad to see the two of you together again.'

Ada was warmed by this. Mrs Spragg had always been kind and it was good to see her familiar face. She did not want to bring up dark shadows from the past, but now she was here, the need rose in her to ask.

'Any news of Nellie, Mrs Spragg?'

Her old neighbour's face fell. 'Not as I know of. 'Er'll be in there a good while yet.'

Ada's stomach turned with dread at the thought, and she fought to push thoughts of Nellie away. Nellie had gone to the bad and there was nothing she could do for her.

'Now,' she said more cheerfully, 'we just need Tom.'

'You should catch him soon enough,' Mrs Spragg said. 'He'll be off running about somewhere later with some other lads – but he'll be back for his tea first.'

Ada was startled at the thought of Tom off and away like that – but of course he was thirteen now; he wouldn't want to be sitting in with his father and this new stepmother of his.

'Drink your tea,' Mrs Spragg said, handing them each a cup. 'I'm glad of the company. And as I say, he should be back soon.'

The sight of the young man who swaggered into the yard about half an hour later startled Ada. They saw him pass the door – 'There 'e goes!' Mrs Spragg said – a strong boy with a muscular stride and a head of wavy, treacle-brown hair, his cap on at a jaunty angle. Mrs Spragg got up and went to the door before Ada had any time to prepare herself.

'Tom, come 'ere a moment, lad? Someone to see yer.'

Tom turned, looking neither interested nor put out by this news, as if nothing could ever be expected. Ada felt an ache of deep fondness at the sight of him. He was not especially tall, but his build was broad and strong. And he was handsome. He had lost the little-boy roundness of his cheeks, which now stood out at interesting, chiselled angles. But there was a hardness to him, a defence round him like a wall that she could see, of someone who has suffered and become bitter at the world.

'Yeah?' he came to the door.

'Look who's come to see yer.' Mrs Spragg stood back to let him in. 'It's our Ada – and little Elsie, remember?'

Tom pulled his cap off, seemingly automatically, as he stepped inside, eyes adjusting to the gloom after the yard. He stared at the two of them, hard-faced, almost defiant, as if expecting trouble. A moment later his features softened, and Ada saw a glimpse of the boy she had thought of as a brother. A faint, wondering smile appeared on his lips.

'Ada?'

She got up. 'Told you I'd be back, didn't I?'

As she walked to embrace him, Tom had to turn his head while he wiped sudden tears from his eyes.

Thirty-Seven

August 1861

It was the height of summer and after a day of pouring rain it had become oppressively hot. The sky was heavy with cloud. Moist air curled languidly through the open workshop windows, thickening further the stinking cocktail of chemicals and metal dust from the workshops crammed in around them, of smoke and of the middens stewing at the back end of every yard with their dark clouds of flies. On top of that was laid the rancid stink from the boneyard. But on such a day they had resorted to opening the windows or it was unbearable working in there.

Everyone was bent over their benches and lathes.

Once Ada and Elsie had acquired a third lathe, Ada had gone and lingered outside Tompkinson's and waited until she saw Gert come out. Gert, creamy and contented-looking as ever, screeched at the sight of her.

'Ada Fletcher – what're you doing 'ere? I thought you were a ghost!'

'I'm no ghost,' Ada laughed. 'I've come to ask you to come and work for me.'

'Eh?' Gert said. 'Work for you? What're you on about?'

'I can only offer you what Tompkinson's pay you – or barely a halfpenny more. But I'm building my own firm – we're over off Livery Street, so if you still live over that way it'd be nearer home for you. You're a good worker, Gert, and we're making a good business.'

Gert took a bit of persuading that someone she still regarded as a child could now be offering her employment.

'Tompkinson's ain't what it was and that's a fact,' she said. Ada could see she was coming round. 'Not since old Ma Rundle got sick. I know she was tough but she was fair and knew what was what. The bloke they've got as foreman now's a jumped-up fool. And look at you, eh, little Ada!' She stood back in the street and looked Ada up and down. 'Starting out on your own – good for you!'

It was Gert who recommended Jess, who had worked a short spell at Tompkinson's and moved on, but the two of them had kept in touch.

'She'll do you proud, Jess will,' Gert said. 'She's a real good worker.'

And so Ada built up her staff.

Tom was sawing shells into flat sections ready for blank cutting, Elsie cutting blanks, Jess, a sturdy nineteen-year-old with buck teeth and an infectious giggle, was already an old hand of ten years and was on the facing lathe, holding the blanks against a rotating wheel to level them flat. And Gert worked on backing them, her lathe removing the remaining traces of the shells' rough exterior and leaving the button with a lightly curved back.

Ada concentrated on sorting the shells downstairs, supervising upstairs when needed and making up for anyone who was sick – as well as running the business in general.

Beardsmore's, at the far end of Galton Passage, now took their thousands of blanks, made ready for the turning and edging, the drilling and polishing processes which would make them into finished buttons. They had a regular arrangement with them. Ada's next purchase was going to be a turning lathe. Before too long, she vowed, they were going to be able to do all of it.

The midday bustle was starting to echo along the alley again, everyone spilling outside, desperate for a breath of air beyond the cramped, stuffy workshops. Amid the sounds of the echo of chatter from the narrow passage, the thump of presses and shouts from the next-door shop, rose the sound of a sonorous voice.

'Repent, for the kingdom of heaven is at hand – the voice of one crying in the wilderness, "Prepare ye the way of the Lord!"'

'Oh, off 'e goes,' Ada said as she came up into the workshop. 'Dinner time – he beat me to it.'

The voice of Mr Jonas Parry, or the Scholar as he was known in Galton Passage, sounded through the windows at regular intervals. More often than not it was scripture, but sometimes poetry rang from his lips. Jonas was a man in his mid-fifties but with a white beard that made him look old as Methuselah. He worked at Evans's, the paper-box makers across the passage, and was a gentle soul who spent a good deal of time gazing at the sky as if he was having a vision. You could set the clock by him at dinner time as he came out to declaim whatever passage of scripture was burning in his mind.

'Come on,' Ada said as the others downed tools, wiping sweaty hands on their overalls. 'It's hot today – shall us go to St Philip's?'

With their chunks of bread and onion slices wrapped in cloths they all clattered down the stairs and out into the grime and noise of the alley.

In the weeks they had been there, Ada and the others were getting to know the businesses all crammed together along Galton Passage. Besides Mrs Turner's huckster's shop situated on the corner with Livery Street, and Mrs Clarke's coffee shop on the other, there were, among others, the coal merchants at the far end, Evans's box makers, Jones's bedsteads, a gas-fitting makers, press tool makers, japanners and at the far end, Beardsmore's, Buttons in Pearl, Bone & Wood. Almost opposite, next to Evans's, lived and worked the Drake family.

George, one of the brothers who worked there for his father, came out as they reached the alley, already chewing on a bite of bread. George was an amiable lad of about nineteen.

'All right?' he said to them, indistinctly, as he hurried past.

'Hello, George,' Ada smiled. She was rather hoping Tom would get along with George who seemed a solid sort of lad. He could do with someone to lead the way for him.

George was friendly and told them useful things such as that his father Edwin would help them if they needed anything mended in the house and that the baker's round on Livery Street would let them use their oven of a Sunday if they ever wanted to roast a joint.

'Ooh,' Elsie said immediately, eyes gleaming. At present they could only pan-cook their food over the fire. 'That means we can do a bread-and-butter!'

Ada tutted, grinning. 'You and your puds, Elsie.'

That day, Jonas was outside, as ever, leaning up against the door jamb of Evans's, his voice ringing along the alley:

'*A man who looks on glass, on it may stay his eye, but if he pleaseth, through it pass and then the heaven espy.*'

All of them nodded respectfully. He was a tall, bony man with a kindly look to him. They never saw him eat anything, even though it was dinner time.

'George Drake told me the old boy lives all on his own,' Elsie said, when they had passed Jonas, who nodded vaguely at them. 'That's sad, isn't it? D'you think he talks to himself all evening?'

'Well, at least he talks,' Gert remarked, 'which is more than you can say of my old man.'

Gert was always very disparaging about Joe, her 'old man', who she made sound like a mute halfwit while being obviously completely devoted to him and their family.

Ada shrugged. Husbands, what a bother, thank the Lord I haven't got one, was all she could think. Men were trouble, that was how it seemed to her. All of them, one way or another. The only man in her life who had been any good, who she could look up to, was her pa. No one could hold a candle to him. The ache of losing him passed through her again.

She wondered if Pa would have been proud of her now, a woman who had started her own business, determined to make a success of it, even if the worry of it often left her tossing and turning at night. Could they turn round enough work to keep everyone on? How long would it take to save for the next new lathe – where could she get a used one? She was always tired. And now she was looking forward to this dinner-time break, a sit-down with all the other pale factory workers who came out to turn their faces to the sunlight in the burial ground of St Philip's Church, the only green space for miles around.

But just as they set off along Livery Street, a wagon pulled up at the end of Galton Passage.

'Oi – what about your delivery?'

Ada looked round to see Sam Bligh leaping down from the driver's seat. The sweating horse tossed flies from its head and lifted its tail to deposit a helping of dung.

'Oh, flipping hell,' Ada groaned, dragging her feet back towards him. 'Why does he have to come now?'

Elsie, on the other hand, hurried back, beaming at the sight of Sam.

'You go on,' Ada said to the others. Gert and Jess nodded and kept walking.

'No – I'll help,' Tom said, turning back.

'No, Tom – you go. He doesn't need you,' Ada argued.

'Don't boss me, Ada,' Tom retorted, his face darkening as he strode ahead of her.

Tom had taken to the work well and was soon a skilled cutter. But he was a young lad and his temper, his bottled-up years of loss and resentment, had begun to seem more and more out of control. To Ada's irritation and against her orders he immediately came back with her, even though she wanted to keep Tom away from Sam Bligh. Tom, as well as Elsie, had taken a shine to the bloke. Ada did not want Sam influencing Tom – she had enough trouble with him these days as it was. She had tried working him until he dropped, stopping him going out in case he fell in with all the wrong crowd.

At first Tom had been biddable, just pleased to be with Ada and touched and grateful that she had cared enough to come back for him. But over the months he had grown more rebellious. He was barely a man with stubble on his chin but he wanted to be away, doing as he liked, and it was becoming harder to stop him.

'You're not my mother,' he yelled sometimes. 'You can't tell me what to do with my wages. I'll go out when I want!'

The trouble was, Ada felt more and more as if she *was* his mother. She was terrified Sam would lead Tom down the wrong paths and that she wouldn't be able to stop him. Because she already sensed that Sam Bligh was trouble.

He had already unloaded the first sack of shells and swung it over his shoulder to take along the entry to their store room.

'I'll give yer a hand,' Tom said eagerly, jumping up on the cart.

'Good lad,' Sam said. Doffing his hat, he added mockingly, 'All right, ladies?'

'All right, Sam?' Elsie lit up at the sight of him, not seeming to notice his tone of voice.

Ada glowered at him. Sam Bligh, she had worked out, must be about the same age as she was, twenty – possibly a year or two older. Tom, at fifteen, was hungry for a man to look up to and Sam offered friendliness and a kind of glamour. Like Tom, he was strong and good-looking. But what was needed was a good man, steady and sensible, not one who would lead Tom into trouble. And so far as Ada was concerned, good men around the place were not exactly ten a penny.

'Well, you look pleased to see me,' Sam teased her.

'We were just going out for our dinner,' Ada snapped. 'So make it quick.'

'Always in a hurry you, ain't yer?' Sam came up and stood close to her, looking down at her, forcing his eyes on hers as if trying to peg her to the ground and dominate her. Just for a second Ada understood Sam's attractive power. He was handsome, strong and capable. There was a magnetism to him. How might it be to be wanted by a man? To be loved and cared for and to be able to love in return, safely and without holding back?

But this was not that man, Ada told herself forcefully. This one was arrogant, full of himself, and she did not trust him. She held his gaze, blazing back at him. She knew what male lust looked like, that selfish, forcing look – she had seen it in Seamus Connell. Here it was again, trying to press itself on her. And she wasn't having it. She took a step backwards.

'I can help as well, Sam,' Elsie said, eager to break through the look that was crackling between him and her sister. She all but came and stood between them. 'Me and Ada can carry one together.'

'All right then, little'un.' Sam broke away from Ada and petted Elsie's hair as if she was a child. She jerked her head away crossly.

They all worked swiftly to get the supplies of shells stashed in their place, Ada keen to get rid of Sam Bligh as quickly as possible. Once they had shifted all the sacks, Sam laid an arm round Tom's shoulders.

'Good work, lad,' he said. To Ada's fury she saw Tom glow at this approval. 'Fancy joining us at the Crown later? Me and the lads?'

'No!' Ada said. 'You're too young.'

'Ooh –' Sam mocked. 'Mother says no,' he said, looking into Tom's eyes. They both laughed and Ada's blood rose even further.

'Leave him alone,' she said, stepping up close to Sam. 'He doesn't need your sort leading him astray.'

'Oh? What sort am I then?' Sam said, with a swagger.

'Oh, Ada – don't be like that,' Elsie said, with a smile at Sam that made Ada want to puke. 'He's only being friendly.'

Tight-lipped, Ada paid Sam what they owed him. 'Right,' she ordered. 'Get you gone.'

'Yes, ma'am.' He bowed and made such a silly meal of it that both Tom and Elsie laughed.

'I'll go with him if I want,' Tom said sulkily, as Sam climbed up into his seat and took hold of the reins. 'You can't say where I can go – bossing me about like that.'

Ada stared after the wagon as it went off along the street. 'I'll get a different haulier,' she said.

'For heaven's sake, what ails you?' Elsie snapped. 'He's nice. And we don't know another haulier anyway.'

'Oh,' Ada turned away, her mind made up, 'I'll soon find one.'

The three of them lived in the attic above the shop, where there were two bedrooms and a third room where they cooked and ate.

Tom hurried over to Jamaica Row at the heart of Birmingham late that afternoon as the cheap meat was being sold off. He came back with a shin of beef, a pound of liver and half a dozen eggs. Ada set to cooking, stewing the beef for the next day and frying the liver with onions. They mopped up the gravy with hunks of bread.

'I met George from opposite as I came in,' Tom said, his strong jaw working on the bread. 'Said for us to come over tomorrow afternoon – have a cup of tea with them.'

'That's nice,' Ada said, scraping up the last of her food with her knife. 'I met Mrs Drake and she seems like a friendly sort. We could all go, couldn't we, Else?'

'Eh?' Elsie was in a world of her own, staring across the room.

'Tea with the Drakes,' Tom repeated. 'Tomorrow afternoon.'

'Oh,' she said, not seeming interested. 'All right.'

Tom looked at Ada and rolled his eyes. But Ada's eyes were on Elsie. She had seemed more balanced since they left service, happier in herself while they were working up the business, more like a normal young girl. The relentless work had kept her on the straight and narrow. But Elsie could get easily knocked off kilter, her mind spinning into obsessions. Ada was frightened to see the signs of it in her again – and she had more than a suspicion that Elsie's mind was becoming fixed far too stubbornly on Sam Bligh.

Thirty-Eight

Bells rang out all over the city the next morning and the girls went to church at St Philip's. Tom was supposedly a Catholic but his idea of a good Sunday morning was to spend it asleep.

Ada had liked going to St Martin's, the big church in the Bull Ring, when she was in service with the Dugdales. She enjoyed being able to sit there in the gloom with the light filtering through coloured stained glass, and for a little while to think her own thoughts, about things more than just the everyday. And she liked singing the hymns. She and Elsie had neglected any churchgoing over the last two years – it had all been work, work, work, every day of the week. They were still slogging hard these days, but at least they felt they could have a breather on a Sunday morning.

St Philip's was a wide, grand church. Ada felt down at heel in her old brown Sunday-best dress and hat, but she and Elsie sat quietly near the back, Ada trying to soak in the calm atmosphere. To think about her life. Not the past – she avoided that as it was too painful. But the future. How she might live it better, build the business – give herself, Elsie and Tom, and her workers, the best life she could.

But Elsie, beside her, was anything but calm. Though her sister sat quite still, Ada could sense vibrations of emotion from her. That strangeness that she had seen in her when she first found her again seemed to be resurfacing. She was glassy-eyed, seeming almost hypnotized, and when she was like this, Ada found her worrying. She had to elbow her to remind her to stand up and sing the hymn.

'*Just as I am, without one plea, but that thy blood was shed for me . . .*'

Ada wanted to sink into the music but she kept eyeing Elsie. She knew – or at least guessed – that Elsie had a crush on Sam Bligh, a man Ada wanted to avoid like the plague. And she knew that Elsie's overheated emotions might easily get her into trouble.

Tomorrow, Ada thought, I'll look for someone else to deliver to us. I've got to keep her away from Sam Bligh.

When they went down to Galton Passage that afternoon, George Drake was waiting and he came out to meet them. It was clear that George took his responsibility as their host for tea very seriously.

'Ada?' He shook their hands in turn, his pale, lightly freckled face creasing into a shy smile. 'Elsie? Tom? Come on up – everyone's there.' He beckoned them in through the door which had a small brass plate beside it:

Edwin Drake & Sons
Coloured gem cutters and polishers

They followed him up to the first floor as he talked over his shoulder.

'We've got the top floors – Mr and Mrs Phillips live down here . . .' Ada realized she had seen the elderly couple coming and going from the ground-floor rooms.

They reached the first floor and passed the half-open door of the Drakes' workshop.

'Can we have a look?' Ada asked, intrigued.

'Oh – yeah, course.' George seemed surprised that

anyone should want to see what to him was an everyday sight, but he pushed the door open.

Inside, there were three work tables into which were set various tools, some of which – a grindstone – Ada could easily identify and others that she could not. In the corner was a safe. The three of them stared.

'Look –' George unlocked the safe and brought out a small tray. In the soft light through the window they saw the rich gleam of stones: emeralds, rubies, the deep-sea blue of sapphires.

Elsie gasped. 'Ooh, aren't they beautiful!'

Ada saw George's eyes light on Elsie and linger there.

Ada leaned in to admire the gems as well. 'I can see why you need to keep them locked away,' she said, smiling at George. He seemed a likeable lad.

'We've got semi-precious as well,' George said, nodding. 'But yes – we don't do diamonds but these are worth a king's ransom in any case.'

Carefully he locked them away again and turned the key in the door as they left the room. They followed him and the sound of voices up the next flight of stairs to where the Drake family lived.

As they walked in, Ada felt herself immediately enveloped in warmth. It was hot and airless in there with the fire in the range blazing, but it was more than that. She saw a cosy room with a great deal of furniture and a goodly number of people all gathered in one space: a horsehair sofa, store cupboard, sideboard and table, and round the table were gathered the rest of the Drake family.

'Ah – here they are!' Mrs Drake sang out happily.

She was a stout, very rounded woman, her cheeks pink from the fire, hair in two plaited coils over her ears, and a country face which made it clear from whom George had inherited his freckles. Her voice was booming and sounded warm-hearted.

'Come on in, all of you, and sit down. The kettle's just on the boil. Go on, shift, Ernie, Lizzie. Let our guests come and sit at the table.'

She waved her two youngest children away as if batting flies and they scurried over to sit on the cracked brown leather sofa, leaving someone who Ada assumed was an older daughter, smiling and very pretty, at the table. As they took their places, their mother went on, 'Now, I'm Matty – Matilda really but I can't be doing with being called that, so Matty will do. That's it – sit you down.'

Ada took a seat, with an anxious glance at Elsie who still seemed locked in her own world. At least she had shown some life when George showed her the gemstones.

Tom was sitting looking chiefly enchanted by the heaps of bread and butter on two plates on the table and the fruit cake, as well as the convivial scene around him. Ada felt a pang at the sight of his happy face. It was a long time since any of the three of them had been part of a proper family.

'Now, before I make the tea,' Matty Drake said, 'let's set out who we all are. You're Ada – and . . .?' She looked at Elsie.

'Elsie.' Suddenly she smiled and her face lit up to show its true prettiness. George Drake was gazing at her in wonder.

'Well, as I say, I'm Matty,' their hostess said. 'This is my husband, Edwin.' Mr Drake, a thin man in his mid-forties with a drooping moustache, smiled at them from the head of the table. She turned to the young woman. 'This is Nancy, our daughter – her husband, Walt's, gone fishing or he'd be here though it means there's more room to sit down . . .'

'Nancy's just of age so we've washed our hands of her,' Edwin Drake joked, showing clearly and affectionately that they had done no such thing.

'Oh, Dad,' she protested fondly. Nancy, with thick blonde hair and big blue eyes, was also, clearly, expecting a baby – which must be her first, Ada thought. She seemed very nice and Ada smiled shyly at her.

'Pleased to meet you all,' Nancy said. 'Walt loves his fishing – so I come over 'ere of a Sunday.'

'And these two –' Matty pointed at the lad and girl on the sofa who were making a show of being on their best behaviour – 'are Ernie – he's fourteen and works in the business – and Lizzie – she's eleven.'

'I'm working in the business too,' Lizzie said, indignantly. She had her father's slender frame and brown hair.

'I'm training her up,' her father said, proudly. 'Come on Matty – that pot's crying out to be filled.'

As Matty Drake poured water into an enormous crock teapot, Nancy offered round the plate of bread and butter.

'Here you are – tuck in.'

'Cor, thanks,' Tom said, enthusiastically, doing just that.

'Ta.' Ada smiled at Nancy. 'D'you live far?'

'Ooh, no. Walt wanted us to get our own place but I said I wanted to be as near as we could – we've got rooms round in Edmund Street. He works for one of the foundries. Here –' she aimed the plate at Elsie, bending to look into her face. 'Ooh, aren't you pretty? Come on, don't be shy. You must be about the same age as our Ernie, ain't yer?'

'I'm seventeen,' Elsie said.

'You're never?' Nancy said. Ada saw George, who was sitting opposite Elsie, take this in quietly.

'She's always been little,' Ada said.

'Small and delicate,' Matty said, lugging the teapot over to the table.

'The little pots hold the best treasure,' Edwin Drake announced.

Matty paused, the teapot suspended in mid-air. 'D'you just make that up?'

Edwin's brow creased. 'I think I might've done,' he said.

'You mean, good things come in small packages, Dad,' Nancy laughed.

'Oh, yes – p'r'aps I do.'

'Not me then,' Ernie said, pretending to be gloomy. He was blond, friendly-looking and rather solid like his mother.

'Don't take any notice,' Matty said, handing round cups of tea. 'Now.' She sat down and beamed round at them all. 'Here we are then. Eat plenty, all of you. Can't have anyone leaving here hungry.'

They passed a jolly time with the Drakes, who wanted to know all about them.

'You got family close by, have you?' Matty asked, sitting back with her brimming cup of tea.

'Not really – we don't have much family,' Ada said. There was only a certain amount she was prepared to tell them, or anyone. Matty stuffed them with food – which Tom took good advantage of – and Ada wondered how they were ever going to return the compliment. But the Drakes were all so friendly that it did not seem to matter too much.

The room grew warmer and warmer as they all sat there and Matty, round cheeks burning, threw open the window as far as it would go – 'stinks out there but we need some air' – and kept boiling the kettle for more tea, adding to the pot until the brew was 'maid's water' as she said, but, 'Would anyone like one anyhow?'

They learned that while Edwin was Birmingham born, Matty had grown up with family who ran a pub in a village near Oxford and moved to Birmingham with her elder brother when he came to take on a pub in the city. This was where Edwin had met her.

'He fell for the barmaid, didn't you, love?' she chuckled. 'Came along and swept me off my feet. 'Ave a job now, wouldn't you?' she added, looking down at her considerable girth.

Edwin Drake seemed to decide there was no tactful answer to this.

'Anyhow, I always liked it up 'ere,' Matty said. 'More going on. The country's all cows and mud and that. Bit quiet for me.'

'Nice to visit though,' Lizzie said. 'There's a pond with ducks and our nan sends us to collect the milk and eggs . . .'

'You'd best marry a farmer if you want to stop down there,' her mother advised.

'When's your baby due?' Ada asked Nancy quietly. It couldn't be long, she thought.

'Less than a month to go now.' Nancy beamed. 'I dunno if I'm excited or scared out of my wits.' She eyed Ada. 'You must be my age. You got anyone?'

Ada saw Elsie's eyes swivel towards her.

'No,' Ada said firmly.

'Never mind,' Nancy said, touching her arm. 'You got time yet.'

Not me, never, Ada wanted to retort, but she kept quiet, not wanting to be rude.

When the feast was over and they were leaving, full of both tea and thanks, George took them down again. He said goodbye to Ada and Tom. As Elsie was going out, he said, 'You're quiet. I hope you had a nice time?'

Ada turned to see a blush rising in his cheeks as he looked at Elsie, and it deepened as she turned her striking eyes up to him. She's so pretty, Ada thought. I just wish she wasn't so odd. She could see George had taken a shine to her sister.

'Oh – yes, thanks very much,' Elsie said. But it was with a faraway look, as if in some way she was not really there.

She turned away and George's eyes followed her. He did not look hurt so much as puzzled as Elsie crossed the alley and disappeared inside, obviously not caring if he was watching her or not.

'Elsie, that was a bit rude,' Ada said as they went upstairs.

'What? Why?' she said. 'I said thank you, didn't I?'

'They're nice people.'

'Very nice,' Tom agreed, mellow after a bellyful of bread and jam and cake.

'Didn't say they weren't,' Elsie said. And she slipped away into her dreamworld again.

Thirty-Nine

Ada leaned against the closed door of the cubicle, shut her eyes and breathed in the steam rising from the bath which was filling beside her. She sighed out a long breath and opened her eyes again to watch the luxurious sight of the warm water and the misted tiles which covered the walls and floor.

It was Saturday afternoon and she and Elsie had walked over to Kent Street Baths. The enormous municipal building felt like a palace to both of them, such a grand building with tall chimneys and arches along the front and fancy windows. They had only been once before because it was hard to find the time. And some things on offer in the huge building were of no use to them – swimming pools when they did not know how to swim.

But there was a wash house where they could do their laundry, and these miraculous baths . . . Normally they washed their clothes in the brew house on the yard, taking their turn to light a fire under the copper to heat up the water. To have a proper wash themselves, they stripped off for a dip in the tin bath they dragged upstairs from the backyard to fill by the fire, keeping it topped up with boiling pans of water. It had been the same at the Dugdales', the weekly bath by the kitchen fire, each taking a go at having the room to themselves for a crumb of privacy, drying themselves on scraps of rag.

But this! A whole bath to herself, in a room especially for bathing!

They had walked over after dinner, each carrying a bundle of laundry to scrub and bash on the washboards in one of the wash stalls with its deep, rectangular bin for soaking the clothes. It was always busy, women constantly coming and going with bundles from the houses nearby. By the time they had finished all the work, the bending over and wringing out, they were both soaked and sweating. They hung out the laundry on the huge clothes horses so that they could at least start to dry.

'Let's go and have a bath then,' Ada said.

Any other week, she might have received a more enthusiastic reply from Elsie, who grunted at her and strode on ahead towards the bathrooms. Ada rolled her eyes.

'As you like,' she muttered.

Elsie had been in a sulk all week and Ada had had more than enough of it. It was because she had employed another haulier to transport their stock of shells over from the wharf and had got rid of Sam Bligh.

Up until then she had been in a reasonable mood after their tea with the Drakes on Sunday.

'Aren't they a nice family?' she said once they were home again.

'Very nice,' Ada agreed. 'We're lucky to have such good neighbours.' She had felt truly warmed by being there, so welcome and part of things.

'Good grub an' all,' Tom remarked and Ada elbowed him fondly.

'D'you ever think of anything but your belly?'

Tom pretended to think. 'Er – not much, no!'

'George is a nice lad – don't you think, Else?' Ada said. George was a year or two older than Elsie. And a good bloke – maybe the two of them would get along well – or more than well . . .?

'He's all right,' Elsie said.

'He's more than all right,' Ada retorted crossly. 'They all are – we're lucky to know them.' She had especially taken to Nancy, such a friendly girl and so excited over her first baby.

Though she might have guessed, she did not realize then quite how much Elsie was thinking about Sam Bligh, until the wagon from the other firm arrived on the Tuesday. A voice called up the stairs.

'Fletchers'? Miss A. Fletcher? Got your load 'ere!'

Elsie snapped to attention as Ada headed for the stairs to go and show the new bloke what was what.

'What've you done, Ada? Where's Sam?'

Tom looked up. 'What – you gone and got rid of him?'

The pair of them had both been furious with her. Elsie came and peered at the new bloke unloading the sacks. When Ada got back up she went for her like a wildcat.

'That's you all over, Ada. You're so selfish! You've ruined the one thing I really wanted . . .'

Elsie burst into tears and sobbed heartbrokenly and in such a hysterical way that Tom forgot he was cross for a moment and looked worriedly at Ada. They were just outside the workshop and Ada was sure all the staff could hear.

'What the hell's ailing you, Elsie?' Ada snapped. In her worry about Elsie's unbalanced reaction she spoke more sharply than she meant. All this nonsense over a stupid man who did not deserve it. 'Pull yourself together, for heaven's sake. It's not as if he was interested in you, was it? And the bloke's a wrong'un, take it from me.'

Elsie pulled her hands down from her face and stared at Ada with brimming eyes.

'You don't understand anything,' she wailed. 'You're just mean and selfish and I hate you.'

Ada turned away abruptly so as not to hand out the slap

that was tingling at the end of her arm. *You ungrateful little cow!* The words rang in her head. *Didn't I find you, rescue you, work myself to the bone to set us up so we could have a life . . .?* She had to clamp her teeth down on her lips to keep the words from bursting out of her.

Elsie had been in a sulk ever since. Ada wished she had come to the baths on her own for a bit of peace. She unbuttoned her dress and lifted it over her head, then removed her slip and bloomers. It was a strange feeling, standing naked and feeling the air on her skin, as she hardly ever removed all her clothes at once. There was never time, not for anything. For so long she had worked and worked, with hardly a moment's thought for anything else.

Blushing, she looked down at her chest, the gentle curve of her breasts. For a moment she imagined someone cupping them with their hand, how that might feel . . . Overcome with embarrassment at her own thoughts, she hurriedly tested the temperature and slipped one foot into the warm water. Her thin, white thigh almost seemed to belong to someone else. Lifting the other foot in, she wiggled her toes, smiling with delight at the feel of it. Finally, she slipped right in and the water folded over her like a blanket.

The bath was so big! Lying back, she closed her eyes, trying to let all the worries of the week float away: Elsie's endless sulking, the fact that Beardsmore's, who took the bulk of their work, kept trying to lower the rate they would receive, that Tom was forever pushing to be off and away every spare moment he had. She worried about where he went and who with . . .

There was a knock at the door. 'Five more minutes!'

Ada sat up with a jerk. They only got ten minutes – the queue was always building outside. Hurriedly she soaped herself, working at the grime under the nails of her fingers and toes. Finally, she soaped her hair and lay back in the water so that it splayed and floated round her head and she felt like a mermaid in a fairy story.

Even Elsie seemed in a better frame of mind after her bath, her wet hair combed and loose on her shoulders. Once they had dressed and bundled up their damp laundry to carry home and hang out in the yard, Ada was in a better humour as well.

'D'you want to come into town later?' she asked Elsie cautiously as they turned home into Livery Street. She hoped shopping might bring Elsie out of herself more. 'Go to the Market Hall?' She risked adding, 'D'you remember going with Mom – to see the pets?'

She hardly ever let herself remember, let alone mention that life of before. They each kept silent, the pain of all that had happened and their brief, happy past kept walled up behind them. Just as Ada tried never to think about Sarah and Nellie Connell. Past was past – she had to keep looking forward.

But now, the memory unfolded, walking into the Market Hall with Mom and Elsie and Dora, seeing the rabbits, the chicks and chattering budgerigars in cages, even kittens. A sick feeling rose in her as she let it flower in her mind.

Elsie's brow wrinkled as she shook her head. 'No. Can't remember.' Not sounding as if she cared one way or the other she added, 'I'll come. If you want.'

Ada choked back her impatience. 'It'd be a help. Tom's going off somewhere with his pals.'

But Elsie was not listening. By the entrance to Galton Passage someone was leaning against the wall, one leg bent to rest his foot against it, and nonchalantly smoking a clay pipe. Ada immediately recognized the jaunty angle of his cap, the dark hair. Annoyance surged in her. Elsie was already hurrying on ahead.

'Hello, Sam!' Her little face took on a glow of joy.

'All right?' Sam brushed her off while his gaze was directed back along the street, seeking out Ada.

'What're you doing here?' Ada snapped as she drew level with him.

'He's come to see us, haven't you, Sam?' Elsie said. 'Why don't you come up and have a cup of tea with us and . . .' She seemed to want to keep talking, gabbling at him to make him pay her attention.

'We ain't got any tea – not till we get out to the shops,' Ada said. This was not quite true, though there was little left in the tin but dust.

Sam straightened up, took his pipe from his mouth and tapped it on the wall. He did it so hard that it broke and the bowl fell to the ground.

'Oh, dear.' Ada laughed and Sam scowled.

'Here.' Elsie swooped to pick it up and handed it to him, as if expecting thanks and praise.

'It's no good to me now,' Sam said. He dropped the remains of the pipe and kicked the bits furiously into the gutter. 'I wanted a word – with you, Ada.'

They all looked at each other.

'I mean, us alone,' he said to Elsie.

Her face darkened and she seemed about to say something. Ada jerked her head – go on – and Elsie stormed away into the alley. As she did so, a voice rose from the shadows further along:

'*I will lift up mine eyes unto the hills, from whence cometh my help . . . My help is in the Lord . . .*'

'Who the 'ell's that?' Sam asked.

'Old feller – we call him the Scholar,' Ada said. 'What d'you want?'

Sam stood up straight, as if about to make an important announcement, to put her right, somehow. 'Seems as if we got off on the wrong foot, you and me.'

Ada put her head on one side. She felt clean and sleek after the bath, her hair brushed smooth, and she felt suddenly acutely aware of being a woman, the feel of her body under her shift, her dress soft around her. And the way Sam Bligh was looking at her, it was as if he was looking right through her garments as well. A blush spread through her. And she was angry with herself for her feelings and his effect on her.

'I want you to walk out with me,' Sam burst out. He took a step towards her. 'Can't get you off of my mind, Ada. You're my kind of woman, you are – there's a force to yer that won't let me be.' His face was burning with emotion. 'I had to come and tell yer. I'm your man – I need you to be mine.'

Ada took a step backwards, the force of his desire and certainty washing over her. He seemed so sure that because he had said it, this was what must be true and he must have what he wanted.

'What?' she said. 'Yours? I'm not yours! What the hell're you on about, talking like that? I don't want a man – and I certainly don't want you.'

He stared at her as if her words were not making sense to him. '*The sun shall not smite thee by day, nor the moon by night. The Lord shall preserve thee from all evil . . .*' drifted from the alley in the Scholar's slow, booming tones.

Sam's face darkened, nasty now, bullying. 'You turning me down, wench?'

'I'm not your wench – nor anyone's,' Ada retorted. 'Bye, Sam.'

She walked away from him, into Galton Passage. Jonas Parry was leaning against the wall of Evans's Box Makers, his beard like a white bib across his chest, lips moving. As Ada drew near, Jonas nodded his head in a polite way and Ada returned the gesture. Mr Parry seemed a gentle soul.

'*The Lord shall preserve thy going out and thy coming in from this time forth, and even for evermore . . .*' As she passed him, Jonas raised his eyes towards the thin strip of sky visible above this alley at the heart of Birmingham as if he could see things that no one else could.

'Mardy bitch! Think you're better than me, do yer?' she heard, as she went into the entry. Then very loudly, 'I ain't finished with you, Ada Fletcher!'

'You blokes always think you can get your own way, don't you?' Ada murmured to herself as she went upstairs. 'Well, not with me you won't.'

Reaching her hand into her pocket, she felt for the shell that she always kept in there. Her mind slipped inside, along its secret, sea-washed passage, the curve of its walls shimmering with heavenly, iridescent mother-of-pearl.

Elsie jumped to her feet as Ada came in. 'What'd he want?'

'Oh, he was just on about our deliveries,' she told Elsie, turning away from her piercing gaze. 'Wants us to take him on again. I said I'd think about it.'

Forty

'You're not going,' Ada said. 'Take that off – you're staying here.'

Elsie whirled round, still fastening her straw bonnet under her chin.

'Who d'you think you are, Ada, bossing me all the time? You're not my gaoler!'

'Let her come,' Tom said. 'What's the harm? You could try going out yourself now and then – get a bit of life.'

Elsie carried on tying the faded blue ribbon of her bonnet, staring back defiantly at Ada.

'You're such an old biddy these days, Ada,' she said. 'There's no harm in going out for a bit of fun. And you might . . .'

Elsie had been about to say, 'might find yourself some-one to walk out with.' Until she remembered that the very reason she was going out was because the man she was obsessed with seemed to be far keener on her older sister than he ever was on her. Even though Ada had lied to her about what Sam Bligh wanted, she had seen his face, the way he was looking at Ada. It wasn't as if Ada even wanted him! Elsie was quite sure she could soon change Sam's mind.

'Where're you going?' Ada demanded, as the two of them headed to the door, ignoring her orders.

'Just into town,' Tom said. 'Have a drink, a sing-song – that's all.'

As she marched out with Tom, Elsie felt Ada's eyes boring into her back. She didn't turn round. She knew that face, the lips pulled down, Ada's frown. Well, too bad – she was going to find Sam Bligh, and Tom had a pretty good idea where he would be.

'Where're we going?' Elsie asked Tom as he strode off along the street in the warm evening.

'Horse Fair,' Tom said.

Elsie pictured the street on fair days, full of bustle and the hot smell of horses being bought and sold. She dragged her mind back as Tom said, 'Come on – we don't want to miss the start.'

Start of what? Elsie wondered. Was there going to be a sing-song? She hoped so. She had a nice singing voice when she got the chance.

Even though Tom was two years younger than her he was more than a head taller and Elsie was having to trot along to keep up. She was already perspiring and the summer stink of the city rose from every quarter like the sweat of an animal.

Elsie did not really care where they were going. All she cared about was that Sam Bligh was going to be there. Sam, who she thought about day and night, this man with his dark, curling hair and dancing eyes, who filled her mind and her desires. Sam might be keen on Ada but Ada didn't want him. And Elsie knew that if she and Sam could spend a bit of time together, he would be hers. Because she knew they were destined to be together. She could charm him, make him laugh and he would put those strong, muscular arms of his round her, sweep her off her feet and kiss her. He would look into her eyes and say, 'Don't you worry, little Elsie. You're the most beautiful thing I've ever seen and I'm going to look after you now – you're mine, for ever.'

'Watch it!' Tom flung an arm in front of her as Elsie, lost in her dreams, was about to launch herself into the street just as a towering horse-drawn wagon came clashing along on the cobbles. 'For God' sake, Else, look where yer going – you'll get yourself killed!'

Elsie jumped back.

'Sorry.' She managed to smile up at him. Tom was giving her funny looks, as if he was regretting bringing her with him. He's only a kid, she thought. He's no idea what it is to be in love, like me.

'Come on.' They crossed over, Tom grasping her arm just in case. 'Along 'ere, look.' He pointed out the Crown pub further along. A crowd of men were spilling out of the door on to the street with tankards in their hands. Elsie felt herself shrink. There would be some other women, surely?

As she followed Tom when he pushed in through the doorway and the crowd of beery men she felt their eyes on her, heard lewd comments directed at her, and her body went prickly all over. It shook her. This was not why she had come – for these men to scrape their eyes over her as if they were trying to see under her clothes. It was Sam she wanted, only Sam, with his loving eyes fixed on her alone.

'Sam 'ere already?' she heard Tom say to one of the men.

'Somewhere about.' He jerked his head. 'He's gone down, I think.'

As they went inside, Elsie's heart started to race at the thought that Sam was there and she was going to see him. Tom led her through the crowded tavern where there were a few women – though Elsie couldn't say she liked the look of any of them – but mostly crowds of men, towards the stairs to the basement.

Ah, Elsie thought, this is where we'll do the singing. She imagined rows of benches, a dais perhaps and a piano, someone leading them in her favourite romantic songs . . . And as she went to the stairs, a sweet song echoed in her head:

'Gentle slumbers o'er thee glide,

Dreams of beauty round thee bide,
While I linger by thy side, sweet Ellen Bayne . . .'

Maybe one day she would lie in a lovely grassy field with Sam at her side, singing to her . . .

But the steps to the basement were filthy with ash and dirt and the sounds coming from below were those of raucous male voices. She clutched at Tom's arm as they reached the bottom and a sight met her which was so far from what she had been hoping for that she could not make any sense of it at first.

Crowds of men were lined up on four sides of a pen, hemmed in by wooden barricades. Everyone seemed to be shouting and excited about something. Tom led her round the side and suddenly she saw Sam, talking heatedly to another man.

'What's this?' Elsie tried to ask Tom, but he was too busy getting Sam's attention amid the racket.

'Hey –' Sam turned to them both. Seeing Elsie his face broke into a smile – not so much of pleasure but of curious surprise, like a man who gets up in the morning to put his clothes on and finds a duck sitting on them. 'Tom,' he nodded. And then to Elsie, 'What're you doing here?'

'I brung 'er,' Tom said. ''Er wanted to come. You got my bet in for me?'

Sam nodded, then leaned down towards Elsie and her heart pounded at finding his face close to hers.

'Ada not with yer then?'

'No,' Elsie practically had to shout. 'She likes to stay in.'

Sam straightened up, still looking into her face. Elsie was dazzled. He was looking at her, seeing her at last, now Ada was out of the way!

At that moment a shout went up and Sam's attention snapped away from her to the centre of the room.

''Ere we go!'

Elsie's heart pounded even harder then, not with excitement, but with dread. The air in the room, already thick with the smells of sweat and stale beer, was now filling with the sound of vicious snarling. A man in the corner, who she had not been aware of, was holding a squat, muscular, wide-headed dog on a tight leash. Another bloke appeared down the stairs with a similar creature, also tightly restrained on a leash. But the moment the curs spotted each other their gums were drawn back, hideous growls gargling from their throats.

Seconds later, the men released the dogs into the pen. The sight of them setting about each other was so horrible that Elsie put her hands over her face, squeezing her eyes shut as all these men around her yelled and cheered whichever creature they were supporting. But she could not block out the sounds of their snarls and yelps as they sank their teeth into each other.

It seemed to go on and on. Tom was shouting beside her in support of one of the dogs. Elsie went somewhere else in her head to escape it, floating in the air above, like a magic white witch who could raise herself above such awful things and take her to a different, calm place outside this world.

It was over. The cheers and shouts gradually came back to her as she took her hands away from her face and looked round her. Tom turned to her and laughed.

'Didn't you like it? Thought you'd think it was exciting.'

Elsie shook her head, numbly. This was not why she had come, for men doing such filthy, nasty things. She had come for singing, for pleasure. She had come for Sam. Wildly, she looked round in the crowd of dark, musty clothing.

'Where is he?' She grabbed Tom's arm. 'Where's Sam?'

Tom looked around him. 'Dunno. Gone upstairs for a bit, I s'pose. There's another 'un in a minute . . .'

'No,' Elsie pleaded. 'I don't want to see it – it's vile. I want to go home.'

'Well, you'll have to wait for me,' Tom said crossly. 'I ain't going yet – I've got money on this next one an' all.' He turned away, fed up with her.

Elsie fought her way up the stairs against the tide of men coming down again, tankards refilled, for the next bout. She didn't see Sam among them. Nor could she see him upstairs. She went outside, looking round for him, but everyone was inside now, eager for the dogfight. Where was Sam? Where had he gone?

She only had the haziest idea of the way home, not having paid attention while Tom led her there because she had been so caught up in her daydreams about Sam. The sun was going down now and the streets looked shadowy and alarming. She would have to wait for Tom.

Seething with frustration and longing she leaned against the wall. Maybe Sam would come back from wherever he had gone and find her there.

Forty-One

As the sun lowered in the sky late that afternoon, Ada hauled their one comfortable chair close to the open window. It was an ancient thing upholstered in frayed, faded green material with a worn circle in the back where countless heads had rested. But she had picked it up for a song and it felt luxurious being able to sit there with no demands on her, trying to catch any hint of a breeze in the sultry evening.

She unbuttoned the front of her dress and pulled it off over her head. No one was around and it felt blissful to sit dressed only in her shift, her bare feet resting on the stool, and have a bit of peace.

There was little to see from the window, which looked over the yard at the back. Just the yard walls abutting those on each side, the one belonging to the press-tools firm one side and Clarke's coffee shop the other. Clarke's had no real need of a yard so they let other firms use it for storage. There was a pile of wooden crates stacked out there. And beyond, the boneyard giving off its rancid stench. Even so, this evening she needed the window open.

In the railway station a train was getting up steam, huffing and whistling and throwing up clouds of smoke. Ada sighed. There was something thrilling about these enormous locos but they made it a devil of a job drying washing in the yard. Everything got covered in smuts, so they hung most of it inside now, even in summer – the wooden clothes horse behind her was draped in bits of garments and a bed sheet – but even then the filth floated in through the window.

This is nice, Ada thought, lolling back in the chair. Sounds intruded from outside: a metallic clang from the railway, men's voices in a yard two doors away, the distant sound of hooves in the street.

Normally her mind was full of the business. This week the edging lathe was coming – and not brought by that flaming Sam Bligh either! Soon, as soon as possible, Fletchers' was going to be able to work all the processes for making pearl buttons from start to finish. They would take on more staff, expand into bigger premises. She could train Tom up to take on more of the running of the business. For now, as well as sawing the shells he did all the other heavy labour, shifting sacks and transporting the boxes of work to be done or returning the completed work, squeezing their big basket carriage along the alley to Beardsmore's. But Tom was a bright lad – she could teach him things about supplies and accounts that she had had to work out for herself by trial and error and hard graft.

Ada smiled to herself. All her hard work was paying off and she could see a path to a bigger, more successful business . . .

But now, for once sitting still, she allowed herself to think about other things.

This room. She looked round at the homely scene. Our place. Their few pots by the grate, the table and a chair each, a Turkey rug in front of the fire that Elsie had picked up in the Rag Market. It was frayed and old but added a glow of rich colour. It may not be much, but it belongs to us, me and my sister and Tom – who she counted as a brother. Her little family.

With a pang, she thought of the others – of Dora, John and little Mabs. All her vows to unite her family had so far failed. At least she had Elsie, but life was so busy trying to make sure they had this secure living and she didn't even know how to begin trying to find the others. Would the young ones even remember her now? Mabs certainly wouldn't. And if she did find them, would they ever forgive her?

Where are you? she whispered, her eyes filling as she remembered holding baby Mabs, her huge brown eyes turned to her, laughing at the least thing she did. But now, she would be a girl of ten. And she could be anywhere.

She let out a deep sigh. One day, she thought, I'm going to find you, bring you home. I will, I promise. I just have so much to do now . . .

Her thoughts shifted to Elsie and Tom. What might those two be getting up to out there tonight? Tom could be wild and there was Elsie's ridiculous crush on Sam Bligh of all people. Ada rolled her eyes. Elsie was so extreme, so odd sometimes. But she's grown up now, Ada told herself. She's a woman – I shouldn't have to keep on fretting about her.

She tried to put them out of her mind. Elsie and Tom were her family, the most precious thing on earth, but just for a while she wanted a rest from being the big sister, in charge of everyone.

The engine whistle shrieked and she heard the train ease into movement, getting up speed and lumbering out of the station. It was a good while before the sound of it died away.

'Ah.' Ada stretched her legs out and rested them on a stool. And closed her eyes in the sudden quiet.

Someone hammered on the yard door, down at the back.

'Oh, damn and blast it!'

No one usually called at this time. Ada was tempted to ignore it but, worried there might be something wrong, she grabbed her dress and pulled it on as she ran downstairs.

'George!' she exclaimed, finding him standing all bashful on the doorstep, hands behind his back. 'Everything all right?'

'Yeah, it's . . . I just wondered . . .' George Drake brought from behind him a bunch of pink carnations. 'I thought Elsie might like to, you know – come for a bit of a walk. With me, I mean,' he added as if this were not obvious. His face was all blushes and she could see he had really had to steel himself to come and ask.

Ada smiled. From the moment George had met Elsie it had been obvious he was sweet on her. But he was such a shy lad it had taken him ages to pluck up the courage and actually ask her.

'I'm sure she'd like that, George, but she's not here at the moment.' Seeing how his face collapsed into disappointed lines she said quickly, 'She's just popped out somewhere with Tom and I don't suppose she'll be long . . . But maybe ask her tomorrow, eh?'

'All right.' He seemed reassured. Awkward, he held out the flowers. 'D'you wanna give her these?'

'Oh – they'll keep 'til tomorrow in a jar of water,' Ada said. 'You can give them her yourself, when you see her?'

'All right. Yeah.' He touched his cap cheerfully. 'Thanks, Ada.'

'Oh, George?' she said, as he headed across the alley again. 'Any sign of Nancy's baby?'

He turned, beaming. 'Any day now, they reckon. You could go and see 'er if you like? Our dad's told her to stay put now 'er's so close and she's fed up stuck at home with Walt out all day. She'd like a chat if you have time?'

'Yes.' Ada felt a glow of pleasure, even while straining to think of when she might find some free moments in her busy week. 'I'd like that too.'

She closed the door and turned, still smiling, to go

upstairs. She had really warmed to Nancy – and it made her happy that Nancy seemed to want to be friends.

She was almost at the top, already unbuttoning her dress again, when there was another knock at the door. She went back, thinking George had decided to press the flowers on her after all.

She had only partly opened the door when it was knocked out of her hand and she was forced backwards as someone pushed his way inside. Before Ada could even speak, the door was slammed shut and in the gloom she could make out Sam Bligh, blocking the way.

'What the hell're you doing?' she demanded, furious. 'Barging your way in like that?'

But she was scared. He was a big man and she had no way of getting away from him other than running upstairs. And why the hell should she be running scared in her own home? She stood her ground.

'I want to see you,' he said. 'And you won't let me so this's what I've had to do.'

He stepped away from the door and there was something menacing about the way he moved towards her. Ada resorted to trying to make things more normal.

'Well, if you want to see me you don't have to break in,' she tried, joking. 'Anyway, I thought Tom was coming out with you?'

'He's at the Crown – with that sister of yours.' Sam came right up close to her. Ada shrank into the wall. She could smell him, sweat, manure on his boots. 'So I come 'ere.'

The penny dropped. He had known she was on her own.

'What d'you want, Sam?' She was frightened now. She desperately didn't want to show him he was mastering her, but she could not help shrinking back into the wall as he leaned towards her.

He gave a curt nod. 'Get upstairs.'

276

'No. I don't want you here. Get out of my house.'

He grabbed her, yanking her close to him, and clamping his arms so tightly round her that she could scarcely move.

'You know what I want, you teasing bitch. If you won't give it me I'll have to take it. All hoity-toity, ain't yer? You're enough to run a man out of his mind . . .'

She thought about shouting. But who was there to hear? No one.

And Sam clamped his mouth down on hers, a hot mix of saliva and tobacco ash, forcing himself up against her.

Ada yanked her mouth away, horrified by feeling him thrusting against her. 'Get off . . .' He was so much stronger, was already fumbling with his hand up under her dress. And all she had under it was her shift.

'Oho!' Sam cried, feeling her nakedness. 'Expecting me, were you?'

'Stop it!' Ada struggled frantically, scratching his face, trying to get her knee up to kick at him. 'Stop it, you vile pig . . .'

She sucked her cheeks in, gathering saliva in her mouth which she spat out into his face. It landed right in one of his eyes and Sam recoiled.

'You bitch . . . You mardy little cow . . .'

As he raised a hand to strike her, the door opened and Sam stepped back as Elsie appeared in the doorway. The three of them stood staring at each other, nobody knowing what to say first.

'Sam?' Elsie said. He had lowered his arm, struggling to control himself, and Elsie frowned, puzzled.

'What're you doing here? You were in the pub.'

'Yeah. I er . . . Couldn't see yer – so I come round 'ere . . .'

'To see me?' Elsie's face lit up.

Ada swallowed down the words bursting to escape her

lips which would have told Elsie the real truth. She couldn't stand the thought of being on the end of Elsie's jealousy, of her knowing Sam had come here to see her, precisely when he knew no one else would be here.

'Where's Tom?' she asked.

'He stayed. I'd had enough so I come home.'

Sam was edging towards the door. 'So long as you're all right,' he said. He opened the door.

'You're not going, are you, Sam?' Elsie appealed.

'I'll go back and make sure Tom's all right,' Sam said, hurrying away.

Ada closed the door firmly behind him. She was shaking, fighting not to let Elsie see the state she was in. Part of her wanted to tell Elsie, to pour out what had happened. *That's the kind of man he is – face up to it!* But she didn't know what Elsie's reaction would be – she could be so emotional and at this moment Ada could not face dealing with that as well.

'See,' Elsie was saying as Ada headed for the stairs. 'He's all right – he's just a bit of a lad. I don't know why you're always so hard on him.'

'Why'd you come back without Tom?' Ada said dully. 'I don't like you out by yourself.'

'It was dogfights,' Elsie said, shuddering. 'In the basement. Horrible – I hated it. And I couldn't see Sam so I left Tom to it. And then . . .' She added in wonder, 'He came here, specially – to see I got home all right!'

Ada looked up at Elsie's dainty little figure as she waltzed happily upstairs. She really could not tell if Elsie was deliberately deluding herself. Could she not sense the atmosphere between herself and Sam?

'By the way,' she called after her, managing to control her temper. 'George came round. Wanted to know if you'd walk out with him.'

'George?' Elsie turned, frowning as she reached the top of the stairs.

'Don't be dense, Elsie – George Drake. He's a nice lad.'

'Oh,' Elsie said indifferently, turning away again. 'Him. He's just . . . He's not a real man, like Sam.'

Ada gripped the rough banister and gritted her teeth even harder. We've got to get rid of that piece of work, she thought. One way or another.

Forty-Two

'Oh – just tell him I'm feeling poorly,' Elsie said impatiently when George came back the next day to ask for her. It was a Saturday, they'd closed the workshop an hour earlier and Elsie could easily have found time to go out with George.

Ada, clenching her teeth, stood looking down at Elsie as she sat by the window, stitching up the hem of her dress. Stupid girl, she raged inwardly, a nice lad has taken a shine to you and all you can think of is that pig Sam Bligh! But that was not the way to tackle Elsie so she managed to hold her tongue and go back downstairs.

George's face fell when Ada gave him the message, against her better judgement. She felt bad for the lad. He held out the little bunch of flowers, his face almost as pink as they were. He blushed easily and this made Ada warm to him.

'Here – give 'er these. I hope 'er feels better soon.'

Ada handed them over to Elsie, seeing the indifferent look on her face. 'You're a fool, you are – George is a nice lad and from a good family.'

'That's as maybe,' Elsie retorted. 'But he's not a patch on Sam.'

Ada swallowed the reply, *That's what you think*. It frightened her the way Elsie got so worked up and she did anything she could to avoid quarrelling with her.

Late that afternoon, Ada went round to Edmund Street to see Nancy Drake. She and Walt had a front house opening straight on to the street, having to walk round to their lavs and wash house along the entry, in the yard behind.

Ada knocked on the door, a bit nervous, even though George had said Nancy would be glad to see her. She was not used to ordinary friendships, hardly knew how to conduct herself.

When Nancy opened up, the first obvious thing was how heavily pregnant she was. Her pretty face beamed when she saw who it was. She looked down at herself and laughed.

'I know – look at the state of me! Am I glad to see you! I feel ever so restless today and it's getting so's I'm talking to the walls. Walt won't be back for a bit yet – you coming in for a cuppa?' She grimaced as she turned round. 'I can hardly fit through the door these days. I just want it over now.' Nancy was struck by Ada's beaming face. 'What?'

'Oh . . .' Ada smiled, glowing with pleasure. 'It's just – well, it's nice, that's all. Coming round to see you like this.'

She could hardly say what it meant to her. How new and lovely it felt to be making a friend. She had been so fixed on family these last years, and before that so caught up with the Connells. The last person she had called any sort of friend was Nellie and look what had happened to her. It like felt a miracle to be invited into someone's house in the normal way of friendship, to sit and drink tea.

Nancy seemed to understand. She smiled, throwing a shovelful of slack on to the fire and settling the kettle to boil.

'It's nice for me too. When I'm at work it's all blokes, Dad and my brothers . . . And then Walt, of course.' She glanced down at her swollen belly. 'He wants a boy but I'll be just as happy if it's a girl. That's it, come and sit at the table.' She lowered herself carefully down on the chair opposite Ada, her eyes full of warmth. 'Let's hear all about you then – and Elsie.'

'Oh,' Ada laughed, while thinking just how many things she definitely did not want to talk about. 'Where do I start?'

Nancy made tea and offered Ada a slice of cake dotted with bits of apple – 'Our mom made it, not me, so you're safe to eat it!' – and the girls sat and chatted. Ada found Nancy very sympathetic. She was so pretty with her blonde wavy hair and blue eyes, it was a pleasure to look at her and there were no sides to her. She looked you straight in the eye and was genuinely friendly.

Ada found herself spilling out more about their past than she had intended, long after the cake was reduced to a few crumbs left on the plate. She saw Nancy's expression move into horror and sorrow at all she was hearing.

'They just took them away – all your brothers and sisters? Oh, my word . . . I mean, I've heard of things like that, but . . . To the workhouse?' Ada saw tears rise in her eyes at the thought. 'I dunno what I'd do without my family. And then you found Elsie – what a thing!'

She sat up straighter, rubbing her back and wincing.

'You all right?' Ada asked, suddenly feeling she had gone on far too much about herself, even though it was a relief to talk to someone. She had skated right over her time with the Connells – she was not going to talk about that.

'I'm all right,' Nancy said. 'Just all aches and pains these days.' She grinned. 'So – you don't know where the others are?'

Ada shook her head sadly. 'I dunno where to start. And I'm so busy what with the business and everything . . .'

She kept talking but as time passed she felt that Nancy's attention was starting to drift elsewhere. She kept fidgeting and shifting in her seat. Ada stood up.

'Sorry, Nancy – I've been rattling on far too long and I s'pose Walt'll be back soon. I'd best get home.'

'No . . . Don't go . . .' Nancy slowly got to her feet. 'I'd like it if you . . . I've been feeling a bit . . . Oh!'

She bent over suddenly, gasping in pain and clutching the edge of the table.

'Oh, Nance – is it starting?' Ada cried.

Nancy looked up at her with frightened eyes.

'I think it might be. Oh, Ada . . .' She groaned as the pain surged through her and only a moment later could she stand up again, still gasping.

'Shall I run for your mother?' Ada asked, feeling panic rising in her. She had no idea what else to do.

Nancy nodded, lowering herself on to the chair again. She looked pale and frightened. 'Yeah – can you hurry?'

Ada belted back round to Galton Passage as fast as she could, almost falling over as she tripped on a rough edge in the road. She hardly heard the man who shouted, 'Mind 'ow yer go, wench!' Panic had seized her. Terrible images filled her mind – the ones she always tried to forget. That day with Elsie, crossing the yard in the pouring rain, Sarah Connell's face, the pail, the bloody cloths . . . Her only experience of childbirth.

Finding the Drakes' door open she tore up to the workshop, her legs so shaky she could hardly manage the two flights of stairs. She burst into the Drakes' rooms.

'It's Nancy,' she gasped. 'Needs her mother. It's started.'

There was a second as they all took this in. Nancy's father and younger brother goggled at her in amazement at this female situation while George jumped up. Afterwards Ada would smile at the thought of his frantic, excited shrieking.

'Mom – Mom! You gotta get to Nance's – the baby's coming!'

'I'm not deaf,' Matty Drake retorted, pink and flustered and already gathering herself. 'What's going on, Ada?'

'She's having pains,' Ada said. 'Asked me to get you.'

'Good gal. Do me another thing, will you?' Matty was already panting herself. 'I've birthed a few sheep in my time but I ain't up to this on my own. Run round to Bread Street and send Mrs Mills over . . . Good woman, that 'un, not like some dirty old sots . . .'

'I can go,' George said.

'It's all right . . .' Ada was hurtling down the stairs again while Matty Drake hurried away to her daughter as fast as her plump little legs would go.

Ada sped off to the yard in Bread Street and found Mrs Mills, a dark-eyed, serious-looking woman in her fifties, Ada guessed. One of those women who for years had assisted birthing women and laid out the dead.

'Right you are,' she said calmly, picking up a battered leather reticule as Ada hurriedly gave her the address. Without another word she was gone.

Ada, left standing in Bread Street, found her legs so jellied she could hardly keep upright. She leaned with both hands against the smut-clogged wall of the nearest house, resting her head on the backs of her hands and fighting the images which were flooding her mind. Mom . . . The blood . . . And now Nancy had to do that dreaded thing of bringing another being into life.

'God, you must help her,' Ada prayed. 'Don't let Nance die – please, please, don't let her die.'

A few hours later, after Ada had gone home and struggled to continue with her evening as normal, and while everyone waited and wondered, there came a thunderous banging on the door.

Ada rushed downstairs, Elsie close behind. They all liked

Nancy and even Elsie had managed to put aside her own obsessions enough to wait nervously for news of the baby. Though they did not talk about it, Ada wondered if Elsie could remember the same things as she could about their mother.

George was outside, talking to Jonas Parry.

''Er's had it – it's a boy!' he was saying.

'A great blessing.' Jonas took off his cap and held it to his chest for a moment, his face soft with emotion. He smiled, showing a set of snaggly teeth. 'May God be praised.'

'Thanks, Mr Parry!' George called after Jonas as the elderly man replaced his hat and walked away. Then he turned to the girls, looking ready to burst with excitement.

'A boy – oh, George, that's wonderful.' Ada felt a great wave of relief pass through her. She had not realized she'd been tensed in every muscle hoping Nancy would come through all right. She leaned weakly against the door frame, laughing in relief. 'What about Nancy – is she all right?'

'Think so, yeah,' George said. 'Our mom said it was quite quick for a first. 'E's a big lad. Good size, like.'

From laughing, all of a sudden Ada found tears running down her cheeks. 'Goodness,' she said, embarrassed, quickly wiping her eyes. 'What's got into me?'

'I blubbed as well, I can tell you!' George admitted.

'So you're an uncle,' Elsie said, smiling at the sight of his lit-up face.

George beamed at her as if this was another revelation.

'Yeah – I s'pose I am! Mom says he's a right bonny baby – I'm going round to see him in a bit, when Nance's had a while to recover.'

'Uncle George,' Ada said.

'Makes me sound ever so old, doesn't it?' George laughed. 'I'll be able to play football with him!'

'You might have to wait a bit for that, George,' Ada teased him.

'She got a name for him?' Elsie asked. Ada was happy to see her being friendly.

'Dunno yet,' George said. He looked at them, still seeming stunned. 'Our Nancy – a baby boy. Fancy that! Any road – thought you'd like to know. And Mom said thanks for your help.'

'Oh, I didn't do anything much,' Ada said. 'Thanks for coming to tell us, George.'

She and Elsie watched him skip across the passage to the Drakes' place, both smiling.

'He's a daftie, that one,' Elsie said.

'No, he's not,' Ada said. 'He's a good lad. And you want to remember that.'

'You coming too?' Ada said the next evening. She was going round to see the new baby.

Elsie's eye wandered in a way which made Ada immediately suspicious.

'No – I think I'll stay here,' she said.

Ada looked at Tom who was on his way out, but he shrugged.

'You're not going chasing after Sam Bligh again, are you?' Ada said severely. Elsie had been out a few times lately, setting out with Tom, but Tom told Ada he could not always look after her and she was forever running off – in search of Sam.

'Stop bossing me, Ada,' Elsie said, eyes narrowing.

'He's a bad lot.' Ada felt herself growing more explosive. 'And you can't go wandering about on your own – God knows what goes on in some of them streets after dark.' She stopped, knowing she had already said too much when the clouds began to gather in Elsie's face.

'I've told you – I'm staying here!' Elsie stormed at her. 'And any road, I'll do as I please – stop bossing me, Ada. Go and see Nancy and leave me alone!'

Ada bit back a furious response and went out. She was not at all sure Elsie was telling her the truth but what else was she supposed to do? And she soon forgot about Elsie because when she reached Nancy and Walt's house, George let her in, still beaming all over his face. She found all the Drakes ensconced in the downstairs room with a jug of ale and a feast of bread and cheese, all making merry. Over the warm odours of ale and coal dust and the swirls of smoke from Edwin's pipe, rose the sharp, vinegary smell of pickled onions, reminding her for a painful moment of Nellie.

'Ada!' Matty Drake greeted her while paused in the act of inserting a wedge of bread daubed with cream cheese into her mouth. 'Nance's been asking for you. 'Er's taken little'un upstairs for a feed but you can go up and see them if you like.'

'He looks like me,' Lizzie said. Ada winked at her and Lizzie gave one of her cheeky smiles.

'Don't talk soft,' Ernie contradicted. ''E don't look like anyone – 'e's a babby.'

'Go on,' George urged. 'Nance'd love to see you.'

Ada went upstairs and found Nancy propped up in bed with her little boy at the breast, a cup of tea in her spare hand and a plate of bread and cheese resting on her lap. Ada burst out laughing at the sight of her, which after all her dread thoughts made her feel a lot better.

'Well, you look as if you know what you're doing!'

'Ada!' Nancy beamed, putting the cup down in order to show off the baby better. 'I'm glad you've come – look, this is our Billy. Whoops – mustn't get his head in the pickles!'

'Don't disturb him,' Ada said, leaning over to see the

little baby who was a stocky-looking fellow and eager to suck.

'I don't think 'e'd let me,' Nancy laughed. 'Knows what he wants all right, this one.'

Ada looked at the pair of them, this young madonna with her baby, both seemingly healthy and strong. A shoot of pain sprouted in her. I shall never do this, she thought. The idea of marrying a man, being tied and subject to him and the physical side of things, all of it, repelled her. She knew Walt was a good man, as were the Drake men – it was possible to find such a creature. But even so, no – never. It came to her so clearly in that moment. She might be unnatural, a woman who wanted to be more like a man. But she could never do this – not what Nancy had just done.

She sat down gently on the bed, feeling great affection for Nancy as well as a certain awe of her. She had just done this frightening, miraculous thing.

'So – Billy?'

'William Edwin – after the granddads,' Nancy said, stroking his cheek with her finger. 'Our little Billy. He's beautiful, ain't he?'

'Yes,' Ada said. Because he was. She could feel all the love radiating out of Nancy for her son. And she was glad for her, and so happy that they were friends, even if her own heart was so very different.

Forty-Three

'Damn you, Ada, thinking you always know best.'

Elsie carried on raging to herself for some time after Ada left the house. She was getting ready to go out herself, whatever the hell Ada thought about it!

Standing in front of the looking glass on the wall in a heavy wood frame, she brushed her thick hair and pinned it back prettily from her face – and her face *was* pretty, she assured herself. She inclined her neck and examined her features, the rounded cheeks and big, lustrous eyes. She had on her one good dress in a cornflower-blue poplin, her waist pulled in tightly by her corset. She knew she looked a picture.

'Of course, Sam,' she mouthed. 'You know I love you – and I know you love me, even though it's hard for a man to say it. I've loved you from the very first time I saw you . . .'

Her eyes glowed. 'Don't worry – I know. I know what's in your heart. And I'm coming to find you, my dear . . .'

Tom had already gone out with some of his pals, refusing to wait for her. But he did tell her that Sam had said he had some business at the Country Girl in Navigation Street. Elsie's innards turned over at the thought. It was quite a step away from home and it wasn't a good place. You heard stories about what went on in Navigation Street – a place of roughs and gangs, of women who stood on street corners . . . Even the Peelers walked in twos down Navigation Street once darkness had fallen . . . Her mind stalled, shutting out all these thoughts.

All she was going to do was slip along and get herself to the Country Girl. And anyway, it wasn't dark yet.

She pinched her cheeks to bring up the colour in them, pinned her straw bonnet on with its pretty sprig of flowers tucked into the ribbon at one side and as she set out, blew herself a kiss in the looking glass.

By the time she had hurried across town, already half-afraid of being out on her own, the sun had sunk low and the light in the streets was dim, everyone seeming to walk through a veil of uncertain gloom. There was the evening busyness, people coming and going, dogs scavenging and horses clopping slowly home for the night. The place was full of the smells of the late-summer city, of smoke and filth and dung, of food being cooked on fires in dwellings all around. As Elsie turned into Navigation Street she was assailed by the aromas of hot fat and tang of vinegar over the mouthwatering smell of the fish from the fried-fish business nearby.

There were pubs all along the street and the place was alive with the tang of ale and clusters of people spilling out into the still, warm evening, the sudden high cackle of a woman's laughter, men's loud voices.

Elsie walked tall, trying to look as if she knew where she was going. But as she hesitated for a moment, attempting to find the Country Girl among the pubs and gin dens and cider houses, a hefty young woman came up beside her and elbowed her.

'Oi – clear off. This is my patch.'

Elsie turned to find herself faced with an expanse of white flesh and cleavage above the neckline frill of a very low-cut dress. She didn't even look up to see the woman's face but hurried on quickly until she found the right pub.

There was a knot of blokes outside and she quailed

for a moment. But the drive to find Sam overcame all her misgivings.

'Coming in 'ere, wench?' One of them waved her forward, giving a mocking half-bow at the waist.

His pals began to cheer, joining in drunkenly. And Elsie found herself surrounded by a group of men, of grinning faces and the stench of sweat and decaying teeth.

'You looking for someone, are yer?'

'I'm with Sam Bligh,' Elsie said, trying to sound as if this was the most certain thing in the world.

'Well, you ain't, though, am yer?' one of them joked. ''Cause 'e's in there and you're out 'ere!'

'Let the lady through,' one of the others ordered. 'Come on – stand back, lads!'

He extended his arms out as if holding back the floods and Elsie found herself ushered through into the pub.

The place was crowded and full of smoke, the lamps had been lit and dots of light glinted on the bottles behind the bar and on the dull pewter of the tankards.

To her relief and joy, she caught sight of Sam almost as soon as she got inside. There he was, quite close to her, talking to a man with a bushy black beard. Elsie went boldly up to him, standing at his elbow. It only took him a second to notice her.

'Elsie!' She could see he was surprised, but he seemed pleased to see her, his lovely face breaking into a smile. 'What're you doing here – Tom not with yer?'

'No,' she said, having to shout once again. 'I'm not sure where he's gone tonight.' She was overjoyed, her heart racing like an excited pony. Here he was. Almost as if he had been waiting for her. She had been afraid, though it was hard to admit to herself. Sam was never short of a girl – he was so handsome. But he was not with anyone. And he was hers – she knew this with a deep certainty. Even if he found it hard to admit his tender feelings to her.

'Want a drink?' he asked her amiably. Elsie nodded, smiling. 'You go over there,' he said, jerking his head towards the edge of the room. 'I'll be over.'

Most people were standing, but there were tables round the walls and she could see a couple of empty chairs. One each! she thought, heading over there. Her whole body was electric with excitement. She sat down, her eyes never leaving Sam, who went and waited for the man behind the bar to serve him. She drank him in, every line of him, his dark, curling hair, the strong shoulders.

And in a minute he'll be over here, sitting with me . . . She jealously guarded the other chair. Him and me, talking here together . . . And then maybe he would walk her home. The thought of the privacy of the dark streets made her heart beat even harder. Maybe Sam would even hold her hand . . . Make her promises, even declare his love?

As she watched, a woman came through a door at the side of the room. She wore a dress of a deep cherry-coloured stuff and her dark hair was piled on her head above a pouting, sultry face. She had a rose the colour of blood pinned in her hair. Elsie watched her idly, thinking she looked like a handful. Someone with a hot temper.

And then she did fully take notice. She stiffened, sitting up straighter, on full alert as her heart started pounding again. The woman headed straight for Sam, went right up close and took hold of his arm as if she owned him!

A man came and stood behind Sam, blocking her view, and Elsie had to crane her head to look. The red-rose woman's head was very close to Sam's and they were laughing. Sam said something to her and glanced over in Elsie's direction a moment. He turned and Elsie saw he was carrying a drink over to her.

Ah, she thought, now he'll get shot of that woman and come and sit down. But the woman followed him, weaving through the bodies in the crowded room, as Sam came over.

'Here y'are,' he said, putting the small tankard of ale on the table. 'Get that down yer.'

'Ain't yer going to introduce me then?' The woman came up, and loomed over Elsie, a hand on her waist, one hip pushed out in a way Elsie found intimidating and provocative. It wasn't nice, the way she was standing.

'Oh – this is Elsie,' Sam said.

The woman pouted, her eyes flashing dangerously. Close up Elsie realized she was younger than she had guessed. Only a couple of years older than herself.

'This is Hetty,' Sam said. Elsie looked at her, unsmiling. Why did she need to know who this woman was?

'Hinton,' the girl added, looking down scornfully at Elsie. 'I'm Sam's intended. Ain't I, Sammy, eh?' She linked her arm through his, smiling into his face as if to force him to agree.

'Er . . . Summat like that,' Sam said in a low voice.

'Everyone says we make a handsome couple,' Hetty went on, smugly. Her eyes met Elsie's and they were full of warning, of spite.

Elsie was so furious, she was momentarily lost for words. Who was this strumpet who had got her claws into Sam and was obviously forcing him to do her bidding, even when he didn't want to?

'Is that so?' Elsie said coolly, getting to her feet. She looked at Sam as she spoke. *I'll rescue you*, was her message. *I am the one who really knows you.* 'Well, I've known Sam for a good while and he's never said anything about any "intended".' She lifted the tankard and drank a few mouthfuls, taking her time.

'I'd best be getting home,' she said to Sam, not looking at

Hetty Hinton, as if she wasn't there. 'Thanks for the drink, Sam. See you around.'

'All right, ta-ra, Elsie,' he said, not knowing what to say, Elsie thought. And what else could he say of their private feelings in front of this coarse woman?

Elsie pushed past Hetty, making contact for a second with her fleshy arm, and left the Country Girl without looking back.

The perils of Navigation Street held no fear for her now as her mind was bursting with other thoughts. Instead of fulfilling her dream of walking the dark streets with Sam at her side, her hand in his, here she was, racing home full of rage and desperation.

That Hetty woman, how dare she act as if she owned Sam? "*Intended*"! The smug, stupid cow, Elsie ranted in her mind. She could only have known him five minutes and there she was, forcing him into something he didn't want. It was so obvious – he had not mentioned her when Elsie arrived – he had wanted her to see the trap this woman had forced him into. She could see it in his eyes!

Damn you, Hetty Hinton, with your sluttish flower in your hair and all your carry-on, she raged, striding furiously all the way back to Livery Street. He doesn't want you – he's mine, Sam is, and he knows it. And you're soon going to find that out for yourself!

As she approached Galton Passage she slowed, trying to calm her breathing, to seem as if nothing was going on. She didn't want Ada going on at her again. In fact, she didn't want Ada knowing anything at all about what she felt and what was going on.

Forty-Four

The year waned and darkness drew in early. The air bit cold and yellowish, stinking fogs creeping along the streets, so dense that to venture out was almost to walk blind. It curled into the narrow passages and through the cracks around the windows mixed with the acrid smoke from countless chimneys all over town. Days of heavy rain left the streets awash with mud and filth.

Ada made sure the stove was lit in the shop as they all worked and worked. Even in the afternoons she had to have the oil lamp lit to sort shells down in the store room. Laying them out on the sorting table she checked them for size and quality, discarding those with the worst damage – broken or with too many holes bored through them by other sea creatures. She sorted them into boxes containing each kind of shell to go upstairs and for Tom to start work on them. And in the time remaining, she supervised him and the women in her employ.

She had little space in her mind to wonder what Elsie was getting up to. So far as she was concerned, Elsie was getting on with her work and seemed to be spending time with some new pal. This was a mercy because Tom was no good at keeping an eye on her. Ada didn't mind what she got up to as long as it was nothing to do with Sam Bligh. And she had other things to think about.

Her ruling obsession was growing Fletchers' Pearl Button Works. It occupied her mind day and night. But the one thing she did make sure of doing, a joyful thing in her day, was to pop in and see Nancy. Sometimes she would run round and say hello during the dinner hour. If Nancy was over visiting at the Drakes' she would sometimes drop in to Fletchers' as well, holding little Billy in her arms. The women in the works loved to make a fuss of them both. Nancy's pretty face and Billy's round, astonished-looking blue eyes were a tonic for everyone.

And above all, Ada felt that for the first time in a very long time she was making a real friend.

'You'll come round Sunday afternoon, won't you, Ada?' Nancy would say. 'Walt'll be out fishing and I can't spend all my time round with our mom and dad.'

So a Sunday afternoon started to become a regular arrangement for Ada to find herself one way or another with the Drakes. Sometimes they all met across the passage above the Drakes' business. Or Ada went to sit in Nancy's room by the fire, Nancy sometimes with Billy at the breast or with him asleep in a little wooden cradle close by. They would drink tea and chew over the events of the week, letting off steam about anything that was on their minds. Ada loved having somewhere to go to get out of the house and the two of them had become firm friends.

Every so often Ada took a shell as a present for Nancy, an especially pretty one that she had found among their new supplies.

'Ooh, that's lovely, that is,' Nancy cried, when Ada popped in one dinner time, bringing her a beautiful snail shell. 'Got time for a cuppa, Ada?' she said, adding the brown and white whorl to her collection in pride of place on the mantel.

'Wish I could,' Ada laughed. 'But I'd best get back – no rest for the wicked.'

'Well, at least sit down for a minute.' Ada sank thankfully onto a chair. 'That's a nice thing about your work,' Nancy said, still gazing at the shell. 'We can't just make off with a few rubies or sapphires. We're all worried to death every time Ernie takes them over to the jewellery quarter in case someone duffs him up and steals them all!'

Ada had not thought of this. It seemed astonishing the number of precious cargoes being wheeled in basket carriages by young lads around the town.

'Someone did beat George up once when he used to do it,' Nancy said. She smiled fondly. 'Poor little lad – he was always too soft. Ernie's more of a bruiser.' She looked across at Ada. 'You do know George's soft as an egg over your Elsie, don't you?'

'I know . . .' Ada felt awkward discussing it. Elsie paid scant attention to George for all his bringing flowers, which he had done three times now, and he was so sweet to her. Ada was embarrassed and she realized Nancy could see that because she changed the subject.

'How's that new girl of yours getting on?' she asked. It was one of the things Ada loved about Nancy – if you told her something she would remember it.

'Biddy, you mean?' Ada had taken on a new little girl to train up, only nine years old, from an Irish family. 'She's not doing badly. I know they're glad of her wage and she's an eager little thing. And the other one's doing a good job as well.'

She had bought the next new lathe for edging buttons and taken on a skilled woman called Margaret, a small, neat person in her forties who worked with an expert touch.

'She knows the job all right,' Ada said, while Nancy picked up Billy and sat down opposite her, putting him to her breast. 'Look at him,' she laughed at the little boy as he fed eagerly. 'Nothing wrong with his appetite, is there?'

Nancy beamed down, besotted, into her little son's face. 'He's a proper greedy-guts.' She cuddled him up close to kiss him. 'My beautiful little feller!'

*

Ada went happily back to work, full of the warmth of the welcome Nancy gave her every time she visited. Everyone was hard at work. It was a gloomy day and once again they had had to light the lamps to see what they were doing. She walked past Tom, Elsie, Gert and the others, all bent over, the machines whirring. Jess, who had proved a very good worker, was humming to herself and all their boxes were filling with pearly blanks after each process, ready to go on to the next. Ada swelled with satisfaction seeing it all happen. Margaret was working carefully as she came up close.

'Going all right then?' She nodded towards the lathe.

'Yes, ta,' Margaret agreed. She didn't say anything else, seemed a woman of few words.

Edging the buttons involved adding designs. Ada watched Margaret work tiny scallops at intervals round a button, making a neat pattern. As the button emerged, pretty like a little flower, she felt a burn of pride. Margaret was good and a fast worker. Edging could provide a whole variety of patterns with nicks and V-shapes, scallops of different intervals and sizes . . . Next she was going to get a drill and polishing lathe and . . . She dragged herself back to the present.

'Good,' she said to Margaret. 'Nice job.'

Margaret nodded politely. She knew her job. Ada wondered if she minded working for a woman half her age, but then she had applied for the work, so there it was. If Margaret had anything to say in the long run, then Ada supposed she would say it.

Ada walked to the end of the shop. There was already a row of full wooden boxes waiting for Tom to wheel them along to Beardsmore's. Even now she could hardly believe she had built this. Was still building . . . All those buttons pouring out by the thousand, to fasten people's clothing all over the world.

She stood tall, stroking the trochus shell in her pocket,

her good-luck charm. Pa would surely have been proud, she thought. A lump rose in her throat and she had to swallow it down. If only he was here to see. Or Mom, of course, but it was really her father she had always longed to impress.

As she walked back along the shop again, her pride in the place also weighed heavy. It was lovely getting to know Nancy, but she often longed to have someone older to look to in the business, someone she could rely on. She was still only twenty years old and in everything she did, she had to take charge, lead all the others. It was her father she longed for most. Pa, whose luck seemed to turn everything to gold, who could have advised her and given her strength.

She sighed. She had to accept that this was how things were: she, standing alone, having to be the one the others looked to. What choice did she have?

'Get on with it, Tom,' she snapped as she approached his cutting table and found him slacking. Tom gave her a mutinous look and bent his head over the work. He muttered something as she walked past and Ada did not want to know what it was.

Tom was starting to run wild and Ada wanted to blame Sam Bligh for this, though she wasn't sure precisely what he was getting up to.

One night Tom had come home stinking of ale. He lurched in, flinging his cap on the table from where his dinner had already been cleared away.

Ada, who was sitting at the table going over the books for the business, jerked her head up, startled. She was already in a bad mood: here she was, stuck in working away as usual while the other two were off heaven knew where . . .

'The peg's the place for that,' she snapped as the cap landed by her elbow.

Tom stood in front of her, arms akimbo in a swaggering way which provoked her even more.

'I should be getting more wages than I am,' he announced.

'Oh?' Ada sat up, bristling. 'Who says?'

'You're paying me a woman's wage. I should get double what you're paying – more than.'

Ada sat back in the rickety chair. She drummed her fingers on the table, trying to control her fury.

'Men's wages is higher – you know that. You've got me on a woman's wage and I ain't having it.'

'How much d'you think I pay myself every week?' She managed to keep her voice under control even though she was seething. 'Ten bob. Same as you. Same as all the others 'cept for Biddy. So let's see why you deserve more, Tom. Do you run the business? Is it you doing all the worrying? Do I see you sorting out the accounts, the deliveries, the supplies, and the staff? Do I?'

'That ain't the point – men's wages are—'

'I'm trying to grow this business, Tom. And there're firms where the women earn less than I pay. But I can't pay more, not now – so if you don't like it—'

'You only take women on so you can pay them less,' Tom jeered.

'I take women on 'cause they get on with the job and they know when they're well off!' Ada shouted. ''Stead of keeping on about deserving more. You'd have plenty if you didn't go out getting kaylied every night. I've given you a roof over your head and a job into the bargain. If you don't like it, you can shift yerself and go and find summat else – all right?'

Ada picked up the candlestick and slammed into the bedroom before she could pour out bitter insults about what she had had to do for the Connell family and how he was lucky to have found someone to support him who wasn't

300

always drunk or in prison like his feckless flaming parents and sister!

She sank down on the side of her bed, all her responsibilities weighing on her. She sat for what felt like a long time. It went very quiet in the other room. But sometime later there was a tap on her door. Tom slowly pushed it open, looking crestfallen.

'Sorry, Ada.'

He seemed to mean it. She patted the bed. 'Come 'ere.'

He came and sat on the faded old quilt beside her.

'One day things will be better,' she said. She felt suddenly exhausted. 'If we work hard.'

'Yeah.' He nodded, still seeming a bit resentful. 'Only, Sam said—'

'Did he?' Ada said drily. 'Well, if you want to go and earn more somewhere else that's up to you, Tom. You're like a brother to me, but I don't own you.'

He was quiet for a moment, then his better nature took over and he shook his head.

'Nah. Best if we all stick together.' With difficulty, he added, 'You've been good to me, Ada. I don't want to let you down.'

They sat side by side in silence for a few moments in the candlelight, each calming down from their heated feelings. Ada was just opening her mouth to ask whether Tom knew where Elsie had got to when they heard a faint scuffling from below in Galton Passage. This was followed by sudden blood-curdling screams.

Ada leapt up. 'Is that Elsie?'

Their eyes met for a horrified second before they both went charging down the stairs.

As they dashed along the entry, the screaming had turned to hysterical sobbing.

The first thing Ada made out was the thin question-mark figure of Jonas Parry, the plains of his gaunt face picked out by the oil lamp in his hand. Though it was hard to see, Ada knew it was Elsie who he was tending, trying gently to cajole her towards the entry to their yard.

'What's going on?' George Drake's voice came from their doorway opposite. 'We heard terrible screaming.'

'Mr Parry?' Ada cried. 'Is that my sister – what's happened?'

Elsie, bent over, was wailing and keening like an animal.

'A terrible thing,' Jonas Parry said, sounding distraught. 'A wicked, wicked deed . . .'

'I'll take her,' Ada said. 'Thank you, sir – thank you . . .'

'It's vitriol – it will need cooling . . . And honey . . . Put honey on it . . .' His hoarse words followed them along the entry.

Elsie was so hysterical that Ada could get nothing from her as they led her inside and upstairs, the pungent acid burning agonizingly through her skin.

'What's happened?' she repeated as they got inside. 'Stand up, Else – let me look.'

'No!' Elsie screamed. She cowered, half-covering her face. 'Help me – my eye . . .' But as if knowing it was inevitable she lowered her hands and stood up straighter, still mewling in agony.

Ada raised the candle up to Elsie's face. She heard Tom gasp beside her. Her own horror was silent, hardly believing what was in front of her eyes.

The right side of Elsie's face no longer looked like hers. It was meat, puckered and burnt raw, her eye closed. Her left eye gazed out with an expression of animal pain and anguish.

'My face,' she whispered, full of horror. 'She's taken my face.'

Forty-Five

Elsie did not sleep all that night, never for a moment escaping the agony gripping her inside and out. Through those dark hours, Ada applied icy water, tried desperately to cool the burn of her sister's skin and her right eye. As well as the acid catching the right side of Elsie's face, drops of it had fallen on her right shoulder and breast, burning through her frock to her skin.

Ada toiled to try and help her, tears running down her own cheeks for much of the time. It was an absolute torment watching Elsie's frail form writhing on the bed, hearing the wails of pain which emanated as much from the agony of her mind as her body.

'Who was it?' Ada kept asking her. 'Who did this to you?'

At first Elsie did not seem able to speak at all, so lost was she in her pain. Ada knew Tom was not sleeping either, could hear him moving about in the next room. Every so often he appeared at the door, his face pale and stretched with worry and sorrow.

And it was when Tom was in the room that Elsie finally parted her lips. She was lying curled on her left side, the lower portion of her body under the covers but her arms bare even in the cold, not tucked into the sleeves of her shift as she could not bear anything touching her skin. Tom eyed the red, corrosive burns on her shoulder and arm.

'I'll go to the druggist, soon as it's light . . .' Ada said, desperate for the next morning to dawn.

'The old feller, didn't he say use honey?'

'I'll get that as well,' Ada said, beside herself. 'Anything . . .'

'Who was it?' Tom said. 'Who'd do such a thing?'

'Hetty.' Elsie's voice came from the bed. Ada jumped, had thought they were speaking too quietly for her to hear. Ada moved closer.

'Who?'

'Hetty. Hinton.' Elsie winced as she spoke. 'She said she and Sam're getting wed.' There was a pause. 'She said –' it clearly pained her terribly to speak – ' "You keep away from him, you dirty trollop." '

Ada looked, baffled, at Tom. But he nodded, tutting.

'Hetty,' he confirmed. 'Oh, I know her. Sam ain't gunna marry her – nor anyone. He ain't the kind – and 'er's a proper hooer that one . . .'

Another sound came from the bed: Elsie, curled up even tighter, utterly wretched, was sobbing her heart out.

Ada unlocked the workshop first thing so that the others could all get to work, then hurried out on her various errands. The druggist sold her a jar of some greasy liquid – a mixture containing linseed oil, he told her.

'You've done the right thing, keeping on with cold water,' he said. 'Best thing you could've done.'

She bought a jar of honey and rushed back to Elsie to apply these potions. To her surprise, as soon as she had gently applied the oil to Elsie's skin – she was saving the honey for later – Elsie gradually fell asleep. Rather wishing she could do the same, Ada rushed out again.

Gert and the others were all coming into work and Gert took one look at Ada's face.

'What's up?' she said. 'You look as if you've seen a ghost.'

Ada, overwrought and exhausted, could hardly hold back from bursting into tears. She did not normally confide her worries in her workforce but today it was such a relief to have someone to spill out her woes to.

'Lord above.' Margaret was the first to speak as they all gathered round. 'What a wicked, wicked thing. I'm sorry for your trouble, Miss Fletcher.'

Ada looked at her in surprise. This was the most she had ever heard Margaret say.

'Thank you,' she replied.

'What a bitch,' Jess remarked. 'That's wicked, that is.'

'Poor little Elsie.' Gert was tearful as well. She had known both the girls since they were so young. 'I do hope 'er'll get better soon.'

'You should go to the Peelers,' Margaret said. 'I hope she gets transported.'

'I don't think they do that any more,' Ada pointed out.

'Well – whatever. Needs locking up. Come on –' Margaret suddenly took charge of Gert, Biddy and the others who were coming in – 'get cracking all of you. Miss Fletcher's got enough on her mind. Let's get going.'

Ada hurried across town to Moor Street in the winter-sharp, smoky morning light. She reported what had happened the previous night to a sleepy-looking constable before hurrying back to work.

She spent the day making up for Elsie's absence at her lathe and rushing up and down the stairs to tend to her sister.

Word of the terrible events had spread. Matty Drake came steaming across the passage full of concern and offering remedies which Margaret sniffed at, calling them 'old wives' tales'.

'She means well,' Ada said. 'But where am I supposed to get marigolds from, this time of year?'

George came across, looking anguished at the news.

'I don't s'pose she'd let me pop in and see her?'

'No.' Elsie was adamant. Not the women from the works, nor the Drakes or Nancy or anyone. But especially not George. She didn't want to see anyone looking like this.

Except, as it turned out, for one person.

At dinner time, Ada was down at the back in the storage area overseeing a delivery of shells. The carrier had just brought the last sacks in and taken his leave when the doorway was darkened again. Ada looked round to see the figure of Jonas Parry – imposing despite his thinness – in the doorway in his faded black overcoat. He held a spray of greenery flecked with orange berries.

'I've brought these for missy,' he said in his quaint way. 'Terrible, what happened. I saw that woman – she must've followed her. She meant it all right – that were no accident. A wicked thing. Wicked. How is she faring?'

Touched, Ada moved towards him.

'She's in pain. As you'd expect. And her face . . .' She stopped. Why did she feel as if she wanted to pour out everything to this man? He seemed so patently good and kind. But she did not want to say much about Elsie – it would be like showing her poor, injured face to the world when she least wanted them to see. 'I've been to the police station.'

Jonas shook his head sorrowfully and held out the little bunch of greenery. 'It's not much, but . . .'

'That's very nice of you,' Ada said.

She felt shy of Jonas. Close up, she could see that he had a frailness to him, more than was apparent when he stood in the street, his voice ringing out to the rooftops. His skin looked almost papery. And he was gentle, had helped Elsie so kindly.

Jonas hesitated after Ada took the spray of greenery from him.

'If missy would like me to read to her, I'd be pleased to,' he said.

Ada was startled to find tears welling in her eyes at this. 'I'll ask her,' she said. 'Thank you.'

When he had gone she carried the spray of orange firethorn upstairs and put it in a little blue clay jar. Elsie was so adamant that she did not want visitors that Ada didn't expect her to agree to anyone coming in or to see the livid wounds on her cheek, the sagging outer side of her eye which constantly wept. Ada had spent the day turning people away.

'My life is over,' she had said to Ada, stony-faced, that morning. 'No one is ever going to want to see me like this – let alone marry me.'

Ada had not known what to say, she was so upset herself at the change in her sister's looks. Now, with a heavy sense of dread inside her, she carried the little jar of leaves and berries up to the attic.

Elsie was sitting cross-legged on the bed, her back to the door, staring up at the sky through the window.

'The Scholar came,' Ada said. 'Mr Parry. He brought you these.'

She put the jar on the chest of drawers beside Elsie, who looked round. Only able to see the damaged part of her face, Ada felt a plunge of horror all over again. It was as if Elsie was two people now, depending on which side you looked at her.

'And he said . . .' Ada hesitated. 'If you'd like him to come and read to you, he'd be glad to.'

There was a silence as Ada had expected: Elsie was not going to accept anyone apart from her – and occasionally Tom – coming anywhere near her. Ada turned to go.

'Yes, all right,' Elsie said softly.

'What – you mean, you'd have him come up here?' Ada said, startled.

'Yes. He can come. Tomorrow.'

Elsie accepted some broth that night, and managed to eat a little with bread soaked in it to a pap. Ada kept applying the soothing balms to her face and she said they helped a little.

Tom, who had been silent and brooding all day, had gone out and was not back by the time Ada had prepared the evening meal. Ada sighed over her own portion, eaten at the table on her own. Where could Tom have gone tonight? She hoped he was not going to stay out very late – she needed all the help she could get in the shop this week.

Only another hour passed before she heard boots stomping up the stairs and Tom burst into the room. Ada leapt to her feet.

'For heaven's sakes – what've you done?'

Tom was dishevelled, his face swollen, one eye closed, obviously from heavy blows about the head, and there was blood seeping from a cut on his left cheekbone.

'Don't you worry about me!' he boomed. 'I gave that bastard worse than he gave me!'

Ada stared at him in dread.

'What've you done, Tom? You mean Sam Bligh? You haven't . . .?'

'What, killed the varmint? No – though I wish I had!' He slumped on a chair and started pushing his boots off his feet. He was so overwrought that she could hear he was strung between laughing and crying.

'I went and found him – told him what'd happened, what that bitch done to our Elsie. And d'you know what he done?' His voice rose. 'He laughed – right in my face!'

Ada gasped.

'He was kaylied as usual and he just laughed, "Ha ha ha" – like that. "That Hetty – what a card . . ." and all sorts like that. As if he didn't understand anything – and he didn't give a fig! So I knocked him to the floor and he got up and started on me . . .'

Tom kicked off his second boot and it landed with a thump, revealing the white potatoes of his heels poking through his tattered socks. 'So I thumped him again and I said, "That precious Hetty of yours is in a cell now and I hope they hang her!" That made him look, I can tell yer. "'Er ain't no Hetty of mine," he says. "She said you was promised," I said to 'im. "And either way, it serves you right." And he punched me and I punched him, and—'

'All right – I get the picture,' Ada said wearily. She wondered if Elsie could hear all this. Probably. It would cause her pain, but she needed to hear – to burst the bubble of dreams she had woven around that bounder Sam Bligh for so long.

There was a sound at the door and Ada realized Elsie was standing in the frame in her white shift, a shawl loose about her shoulders. It jolted Ada all over again, seeing her poor face, the awful, sagging eye.

'They've arrested Hetty then?' About Sam she said nothing.

'They picked 'er up at work this morning,' Tom told her. 'She'll stand trial by the end of the week.'

Elsie remained silent for a moment. Then she just said, 'Good.' And went out again.

Forty-Six

For the next few days, Elsie stayed upstairs in the attic almost all the time. The day after the attack, Matty Drake crossed the alley and came to find Ada, carrying a little posy of flowers and a generous helping of bread-and-butter pudding.

''Ere – George said this is 'er favourite.' She handed Ada the bowl of pudding in one hand, flowers in the other. 'These are for her an' all, lovey. George bought them – went all the way into the Bull Ring. He's too shy to bring them himself but he says he hopes they might make her feel a bit better.'

Ada thanked Matty tearfully and took the flowers up to Elsie.

'These are from George,' she said, and delivered the rest of the message.

Elsie shrugged, barely even looking at them. Though she did, later, take more interest in the crisp pudding with plump raisins embedded in it.

The passage was quieter than usual at dinner time during those days, because instead of standing reciting poems or the Word of God, Jonas Parry arrived with a book held in his strong hands, with a delicacy that gave it the air of a holy relic, and went upstairs to read to Elsie.

'My sister can read herself,' Ada assured him after a few days of hearing his deep voice intoning steadily when she crept up to listen at the door. She did not want Jonas to think their family had given them nothing at all. 'At least a little bit.'

'I s'pose none of us got a lot of schooling,' Jonas observed, standing at the foot of the stairs.

'How did you learn to read so well?' she asked. She was warming to this unusual man. He was so gentle and kind.

'I went to one of the Ragged Schools,' he said. 'Evenings, Sundays – any day I could. My mother let me pay out of my wages – not that they were much. But she could see what it meant to me.'

He smiled suddenly, the austere lines of his face shifting so that the joy glowed out of him. 'There's the whole world to be found in books.'

Ada smiled back and Jonas nodded and went off up the stairs. She longed to ask him questions – Have you never married? Are you as alone as you seem to be? – but it would have seemed rude.

Elsie told them that Jonas read to her from the Psalms, and then he brought along a book that he thought might appeal to a 'young lady'.

To Ada's astonishment Elsie even chuckled when she told her that.

'Me, a young lady!'

The book was called *Pride and Prejudice*.

'It's all about a poor father trying to marry off his daughters,' Elsie said. 'Five of them. And they're a handful, and as for the men . . .' The smile faded on her face. 'Honest to God, Ada, I want no more to do with them.' She did not even sound bitter, just sad. And Ada could hear the unspoken thought behind her words. None of them will ever want me now, anyway.

On some days, Jonas came round in the evening when he had finished work instead of at dinner time. One day, when he had been up reading to Elsie for half an hour and came quietly down the stairs, Ada went to greet him.

'Will you come and eat with us, Mr Parry? I've a dish of faggots.'

He hesitated, *Pride and Prejudice* cradled against the dark, fusty coat that she had never seen him without.

'It's no trouble – there's enough to go round. And I'd like to thank you for being so good to Elsie.'

'You're very kind.' He nodded, giving a little bow. 'Thank you. I'd be pleased to.'

Elsie came in to eat with them. The honey and the potion from the druggist had soothed the agonizing burns and the wounds were starting to heal, though they all knew that the one side of her face would never recover – she would be scarred for ever more.

As they were sitting at the table, Tom came in. Seeing Jonas he started and looked at Ada in amazement. She made a face – 'Behave yourself' – behind Jonas's back and Tom slid into the fourth place at the table and said, 'Evenin', Mr Parry.'

Ada was sitting beside Jonas and she felt closely aware of him, this tall, spare figure, his strong fingers as he picked up his spoon, the retiring character of the man. Though he would stand in the street and quote from his beloved books in his strong, resonant voice, in person he was not someone who approached you forcefully. He did not dominate.

'How does it come that you three are left together?' he asked after a while. And to Ada, 'You're a young thing to be running your own business.'

Ada glanced round at the others. Usually she avoided talking about their past, but there was something about Jonas that made her feel safe.

'We lost our mother and father when we were quite small,' she said.

'Just the three of you?'

'Oh – no!' Ada suddenly realized that most people

assumed Tom was their brother. She explained, briefly. That their parents had died, that she had gone to live with Tom's family. She did not explain what had happened to Sarah and Nellie Connell. But she did tell him they were once a family of five children – about Dora and John and Mabs.

'One day, somehow, I want to find them. But it's a puzzle to know how to begin, and my days are so busy.'

'I see.' Jonas had listened carefully to her. 'It's a hard thing to make your way in the world. I did not have that misfortune, though my mother and father had very little between them. I knew my maternal grandmother as well – she came to Brummagem from Llangedwyn as a girl. But alas, they are all gone now.'

'Did you have brothers and sisters?' Elsie asked.

'Two brothers, was all,' he replied. 'They left this world too young – one died of the diphtheria, the other in a fall.'

The image flashed through Ada's mind of the last day she had seen her mother, the rain, the shine on the wet cobbles, the bloody cloth in the bucket . . . The cruel shadow of death passing through. Before she shut the thought out.

'Are you all alone then?' Elsie asked.

Jonas gave a slight smile. 'I never married. So, yes, I live alone.'

There was a silence at this sad thought.

'Well, you're welcome here,' Ada said.

Jonas nodded his thanks.

'Shall I see you tomorrow?' Jonas asked Elsie later, after he had got up from the table and thanked Ada for the food.

Elsie looked up at him and tried to smile. Ada winced. The smile contorted Elsie's face on one side and it hurt her.

'Yes, please,' she said.

Over those early weeks after Hetty's horrific attack on Elsie, George Drake went to the Bull Ring every Friday and brought back a bunch of flowers which he delivered, in person, for Elsie. He did not ask or demand anything in response. He just brought flowers, week after week.

'That's kind of you, George,' Ada always said, feeling for him. He would come in the early afternoon when she was busy in the workshop and could scarcely spare time to be running up and down to Elsie, but she took them up. Elsie would nod but not take too much notice.

'It's very nice of him,' Ada insisted, rather crossly, when George had gone specially to buy flowers yet again: a cluster of small pink roses. 'You could at least say thank you.'

'Tell him thank you then, from me,' Elsie said.

Ada was frightened for her sister's state of mind, especially at the beginning.

'She's suffered a lot,' she confided in Nancy when she had gone round to see her and little Billy. It was such a comfort to have Nancy to talk to. 'I'm scared this will . . .'

She did not like to finish the sentence. Nancy looked up at her from rearranging Billy at her breast.

'Oh, Ada – you mean . . . turn her mind?'

Ada nodded, a lump coming up in her throat.

'I expect she'll come round,' Nancy said, trying to be comforting. 'I do wish she'd swallow her pride and let us see her,' she went on. 'It can't be good for her just sitting there on her own. I could pop in. And George . . .' She stopped as if she had said too much.

'What?' Ada said.

'He'd do anything for your Elsie, you must know that.'

Ada gave a smile. Of course George was sweet on Elsie in a way that was more than friendship. It stood out a mile. But to her shame she had not, until then, given it any proper thought. I'm always too busy, she thought. Her head was forever full of orders of shells and invoices for buttons and accounts . . .

'You did know?' Nancy gave her wholehearted laugh. 'I'd say it was written all over his face – but then I know him better than you.'

'Yes – course I did,' Ada said quickly. 'He's a lovely lad, your George.' But she couldn't help thinking, he hasn't seen the state she's in since it happened, let alone heard what she had said about men.

'I'll see if I can get her to have more visitors,' she said. 'The only person she wants to see is Jonas Parry.'

Nancy shook her head as if this was the oddest thing she had ever heard.

'Well, she ain't going to marry him, is she?' She looked seriously at Ada. 'She needs time to get over it. But I know George. He's not the sort to do anything lightly – and he won't give up on her.'

It was a month since Hetty Hinton's horrific attack. There was no doubt of her guilt and Jonas Parry had been called as a witness. Hetty had been sentenced to seven years' penal servitude, which they all felt was no more than she deserved. And ever since that time and his fight with Sam Bligh, Tom had been much easier to handle. Ada could see that Tom knew he had been a fool over Sam, even if he was too proud to admit it.

Ada had gone very easy on Elsie and kept her off work. Though Elsie's face had healed, she was badly disfigured and it was not going to get any better. But it was her mind Ada was most worried about. She hardly said a word, except when Jonas Parry was around, when she was more like her old self.

Otherwise, Ada was not sure what was going on. She would look at her sister, sitting there in the attic staring out of the window, and it felt like watching an egg that was about to hatch out and not knowing what would emerge.

She ought to start going out, getting back to work, Ada thought. She was afraid to tackle the subject, knowing how fragile Elsie could be. But finally she felt she had to say something. She went upstairs one Friday evening once the workshop was closed.

On the chest of drawers was George's latest offering – more roses, in a deep crimson. Ada smelt them, drinking in the sweet scent.

'These are lovely,' she remarked. 'Isn't that kind of him?'

There was no reply.

'Elsie – don't you think it's time you got out more?' Ada said, perching nervously on the edge of the bed. 'If you're worried about being seen, you could wear a veil . . .'

Elsie suddenly twisted round and glared at Ada with her good eye.

'A veil?' she snapped. 'I'm not wearing a sodding veil. Why should I?'

She got up and paced the narrow space available.

'Why should I cover myself, in shame? It wasn't me did this to my face, was it?' Her voice rose, vibrating with rage. 'All this time I've thought it was all my fault. Pa disappearing, and—'

'How could that be your fault?' Ada interrupted sharply, though in her heart she had shared that feeling.

'And *him*. Dugdale – that filthy varmint with his hands all over me. And Sam. I heard what Tom said – he laughed. *Laughed.* When he heard what she'd done to me. Men are all *vile* and horrible and I'm never letting any of them near me again!'

'What about Jonas?'

'He's different. And he's old.'

Ada felt almost blown over by the force of Elsie's emotion. The egg had hatched all right and emerged in a whirlwind of fury.

'And what does *he* want?' Elsie pointed furiously at George's flowers. 'They always want something and they never give anything back. Well, they're not having it off me. Nothing – ever!'

'Elsie,' Ada pointed out. 'George means well. I don't think it's fair to say—'

'And tomorrow, I'm going back to work,' Elsie cut in. 'And everyone can stare all they want – but none of this is my fault so sod the lot of them!'

Forty-Seven

Ada watched nervously as everyone came into work the next morning. Elsie got up early and had come into the shop before anyone else, working away furiously at her lathe. Ada was relieved because she had been having to make up Elsie's work and she was run ragged.

From where she was standing Ada could only see the unscarred side of her sister's face, her smooth skin, the old Elsie. Under her clothes there were scars on her right shoulder and breast and her right cheek was terribly marked and discoloured, her weeping eye dragged down so that she almost looked like someone else from the other side.

Tom came in early and got to work as well – Ada knew he was full of the feeling of needing to make amends.

Gert appeared in the doorway and Ada tried to meet her eyes, almost as if she needed to warn her. She was afraid Elsie would be snapping everyone's head off. But Gert was not even looking at Ada.

'Elsie – you're back!' She hurried across and as Elsie turned, startled, she took her in her arms. 'Oh, it is nice to see you, Else. What a time you've had of it.'

The women had all kept sending love and good wishes to Elsie who had seemed to pay very little attention to this, and no one had seen her up until now.

Elsie stood unflinching in Gert's arms as Gert stared at her face.

'You poor girl – what a wicked, wicked thing.' She

318

pulled Elsie in tighter and hugged her. 'But you're still our Elsie, eh?'

As she drew back Ada saw tears in Elsie's eyes.

'Thanks, Gert,' she muttered, giving her distorted smile.

As the other women came in they all greeted her fondly.

'Glad to see you back,' Margaret said and Jess hugged her as well.

Biddy went up to her shyly and said, 'Nice to see you, Miss Fletcher. Sorry for your trouble.'

'Thanks, Biddy,' Elsie smiled at the child. She was a sweet little thing.

Ada went across to Elsie. 'You going to be all right – standing all day?'

'Course,' Elsie said, head down, pumping her foot so that the lathe spun whirring round.

'All right – I'll get down to the sorting table,' Ada said.

She was working away distributing shells into various boxes on the long table when Nancy appeared with Billy in her arms.

'All right, Ada?'

Ada looked up, smiling. 'Hello, Nance – what brings you here?'

'Popped in to see our mom. I'll be back at work soon and she's going to have Billy while I'm in the shop. She can't wait to get her hands on him!' Nancy gave her happy laugh. 'Only he's all mithered at the moment, got a bit of a cough, so I said I'd start next week instead.'

Ada went over and on closer inspection saw that Billy was looking pale and a bit snotty.

'Oh dear – you got a cold, young sir?' She tickled his cheek but Billy, who was usually smiley, stared numbly back at her. 'He doesn't look himself, does he?'

Nancy adjusted Billy in her arms. 'No, poor lamb. Anyway, he's a lump – I need to go and put him down. I gather she's back at work?' Nancy raised her eyes to the workshop.

'Blimey, news travels around here,' Ada said.

'I know – only George saw Tom and asked after her . . . Any road, what I came to say was, Mom says will you and Elsie come for tea Sunday? And Tom if he wants?'

Ada wondered if George was behind this invitation. Heaven help him, she thought.

'We'd love to,' Ada said. 'Tell your mother thanks – and go and get that baby in the warm!'

Now that she was out and about Elsie seemed to be determined to face every challenge at once. By Sunday she had already walked into town and brought back meat from Smithfield for Sunday dinner and been out all round the neighbourhood.

'Let them stare,' she said defiantly. 'I didn't do this to myself, did I?'

Ada noticed a different mood come over her when she said at Sunday dinner time that they had been invited over to the Drakes'. Elsie suddenly went quiet.

'So you'll come, won't you?' Ada said.

Tom had already said he was off out – along the monkey run chasing the girls no doubt, Ada thought.

'I dunno,' Elsie mumbled. 'I might just stay here.'

'They invited us specially,' Ada said. She could feel this turning into an argument.

'But I don't want to,' Elsie said. 'George'll keep staring at me – I'd rather just stay home . . .'

'It'll hurt Matty's feelings if you don't come,' Ada said firmly. 'They're kind neighbours – the best we could ask for.' As Elsie glowered at her she said, 'You need to come – and don't be rude to George. He's been ever so good to you.'

*

By the time Ada and Elsie knocked at the door of the Drakes' that afternoon, the family had something else entirely to worry about.

George let them in, not looking his usual cheerful self.

'Come in – Mom'll be glad to have something to take her mind off things.'

'What's wrong?' Ada asked as they followed him up the stairs.

'It's Billy,' George said. 'I don't think our Nance's coming today because he's poorly and, well, Mom's worried. You know how it is.'

'Hello, girls – nice to see you. Elsie, come on in!'

Matty Drake was her usual pink, welcoming self, and the table was generously laid for tea, but she did seem distracted.

'Maybe we shouldn't be visiting you today,' Ada apologized. 'You've got enough on your plate and if Nancy needs you . . .?'

'No, you're to stay, ain't they, Eddie?' she consulted her quiet husband who had little choice but to agree amiably that of course they must. 'The best thing is for Nance to keep the lad warm and quiet and let him sleep. So come on, you girls – I've baked a loaf and a sponge and you're to help eat them!'

A floury white loaf was sitting on the table with a pat of butter and some jam and beside it, a Victoria sandwich cake with a seam of jam. Even though they had had a good dinner, Ada was quite happy to oblige.

'Looks lovely, doesn't it, Else?'

Elsie nodded, smiling. One of her favourite things was cake but the two of them seldom found time to make them, even though they had a proper range with an oven now. Over her shoulder Ada could see George with his eyes fixed on Elsie, as predicted.

'Nancy said she was coming back to work,' Ada said as they all sat at the scrubbed table and Matty handed round cups of tea.

'Ar – soon as she can,' Edwin Drake said. 'Hey, Lizzie – go easy on the jam,' he admonished as the younger Drake children tucked in heartily. Ernie's jaws were working energetically on a slice of bread. 'Anyone'd think you hadn't eaten for weeks.'

'I'm a growing girl,' Lizzie grinned, jammily, and passed the dish to Elsie, trying to look as if she was not staring at her wounded face.

'Nice to see you back, wench,' Mr Drake said quietly to her.

'It certainly is,' Matty Drake agreed. 'That woman wants stringing up, that she does.'

'Thanks,' Elsie said shyly. Ada could see her coming out of herself. Who could resist the Drakes?

'I see the Scholar has been coming over to see you?' Mr Drake said.

'Mr Parry,' George added, in case they could not think who he meant.

'He's been ever so kind,' Ada said. 'Hasn't he, Elsie?'

'He's been coming to read to me,' Elsie said.

'He's getting to be one of the family,' Ada added. Jonas came and shared a meal with them now once a week, always bringing something to share, or at least add to their store: biscuits or a box of eggs.

'Well, he's got no one in the world so far as we know,' Matty said, leaning back in her chair with her cup of tea. 'Never had a wife. Seems to be married to his books. Lovely voice though. Like hearing the clock strike, him out there all regular, with his Psalms and that.'

'When I was a lad . . .' George began.

'Listen to you,' Matty laughed. 'You sound like an old man.'

Lizzie sniggered and George elbowed her.

'But I *was* a lad – I was only about six. He set me to learn the twenty-third Psalm off by heart.'

'And me,' Ernie said.

'He never made me,' Lizzie pointed out, indignantly.

'"*The Lord is my shepherd, I shall not want . . .*"' George and Ernie started reciting together, grinning. '"*He maketh me to lie down in green pastures, he leadeth me beside the still waters . . .*"'

'All right, all right, we know what the twenty-third Psalm is,' Mr Drake said.

'Well, I'm glad,' George said. 'I'll never forget it now.'

'Might come in handy on your deathbed,' Lizzie observed.

'Elizabeth Drake!' her mother exclaimed.

'Oi!' George cuffed her, fondly. 'What a thing to say.'

They all laughed, and Ada was happy to see Elsie laughing too. Her eyes met George's for a moment and he beamed back at her before she quickly looked away.

But Ada could see the hurt mixed in with the deep fondness in George's eyes – he could not work Elsie out and was not sure how to approach her.

The assault on the loaf and sponge as well as the teapot seemed to have satisfied Matty Drake. There were only a few scattered crumbs remaining on the plates and the room was a fug of heat from the fire and the smells of bodies and tea time mingled together.

'Lizzie – clear away, will you?' she asked.

'Why can't Ernie do it?' Lizzie said getting up. 'He's a lazy bag of bones, he is.'

'Ernie – help her,' Matty added.

As Lizzie started stacking the little flower-edged plates they heard feet hurrying up the stairs and Nancy burst in, Billy in her arms.

'Oh, Mom, he's so poorly!' She burst into tears. 'I don't know what to do for the best. Look at him – he's burning up!'

She held out an inert Billy in her arms, his cheeks flaming and eyes closed.

Matty, who had been looking relaxed, leapt into action.

'Oh, the poor little soul,' she cried. 'Take him up to our bed – he looks as if he needs a sponge-down. Lizzie – go and get some cold water . . .'

'I'll go,' Ada said. Matty thrust a basin into her hands and she ran down to the pump and brought back the chill water.

Matty immediately took the water and hurried into her bedroom.

Everyone else sat quiet, worried, listening. Ada thought it was time they took themselves off and she looked at Elsie.

She saw that her sister was watching George, seated on a chair across the room, his eyes fixed on nothing, a tender look on his face, obviously terribly worried about his little nephew. Elsie was watching him now that, for once, he was not looking at her.

'Tell Mrs Drake, thank you,' Ada said to Mr Drake. 'Elsie and I'll leave you in peace.'

Mr Drake nodded absently. 'Right you are – cheerio for now.'

As the two of them crossed Galton Passage to their own entry, Ada said, 'Lovely family, aren't they?'

'Umm?' Elsie said. 'Oh – yes. Very nice.'

'I hope to God Billy's going to be all right,' Ada said. 'Poor Nancy looked worried to death.'

Forty-Eight

'How is he?'

Ada hurried across to the Drakes' the next morning. Mr Drake, who looked as if he had not slept, said that Matty was round with Nancy and 'the babby' and that they were all very worried.

'They go downhill so fast, little'uns like him,' George said. He also looked terrible – pale, with dark rings under his eyes. Billy was the light of everyone's life.

All the workers at Fletchers' were soon caught up in the drama of Billy Drake. Everyone loved Nancy and her smiley little lad and they felt for her.

'You have to wait for the fever to break,' Gert said. 'I remember when my Emmy got the scarlet fever . . .'

Other stories followed. Even the usually quiet Margaret chipped in. 'Goose fat on his chest, that's what he needs,' she commented.

Ada stored this away in her mind just in case. Before the workshop had even finished for the day she rushed round to see Nancy. The night was bitter cold, the darkness full of people coughing in the acrid air, and it caught in Ada's throat.

Nancy opened the door, wild-eyed.

'Oh, Ada, it's you. I thought . . . Walt's run to find a doctor . . . Mom was here all day, but she's gone to do Dad's tea . . .' She burst into tears. 'He's so poorly, Ada . . .'

She pulled Ada inside and hurried back to kneel over little Billy who was laid on a blanket on the rug which

Nancy had pulled away from the fire. The child was so still Ada felt a rush of panic as she sank down beside her.

'Billy . . .' Nancy stroked his hair, laying a hand on his forehead. 'Billy, can you look at Mama? Oh, Ada – he can't even open his eyes.'

Ada could feel her friend's utter desperation pulsing through her. She put her arm round Nancy's shoulders. The young woman already felt thinner than her usual fleshy self, as if her own life was being drained away. Nancy turned and clung to her.

'I can't stand it, Ada. I keep praying God will spare him . . . I love him so much . . . And I don't know what to do for him.'

Ada helplessly rubbed her back. 'He's a strong little lad,' she said softly, praying that this was so. 'He'll come through the fever, once it breaks . . .'

They both jumped as the door flew open and Walt, Nancy's husband, burst in, his usually good-looking face distorted with worry. He yanked his cap off leaving his dark hair standing on end.

'He's just coming – the doctor. I had a hell of a job getting him to come out . . . How is he?'

Walt had accompanied the man to the street but couldn't hold back from running on ahead. He flung himself down beside his little boy and Ada shrank back out of the way.

'Where is he?' Nancy said wildly, just as a voice at the door cried loudly, 'Who wanted a doctor?'

A portly older man with grey mutton chops and the florid face of a habitual drunk, came reeling in. The stink of strong drink rose off him like sweat.

'Where's the patient?' he demanded in a slurred voice.

Nancy looked at Walt, appalled, but she got up. 'Here . . .'

The man, who was carrying an ancient Gladstone bag, stared down at Billy.

'Pick him up then,' he ordered. 'On the table with him.'

Nancy scooped Billy up with the blanket and laid him on the table. The doctor's loud, wheezy breathing was the only sound in the room as he poked a finger down into Billy's neck and waited, feeling his pulse, then felt his forehead and gave a grunt as he straightened up unsteadily.

Opening the neck of his bag, he said, 'Here – spoonful three times a day. And get some water down him if you can. Should remedy the problem.'

He handed Nancy a slender bottle corked at the top and full of a dark, treacle-coloured liquid.

'Thank you,' she whispered.

Ada could see that Nancy was so desperate she would have fed Billy water from the cut if the doctor had advised her to.

'Should be right as rain in a few days . . .' He turned to Walt. 'That'll be a half-crown all told.'

'Right. Yeah . . .' Walt dug in his pockets and drew out enough coppers and joeys to make up the sum. The doctor closed his hand greedily over the money and made his way unsteadily out again.

'Here you are, Billy . . .' Nancy had already uncorked the bottle and found a spoon. She supported Billy's head and managed to get most of the liquid into his mouth. The little boy swallowed, coughed.

Please – let it help, Ada found herself praying as she watched the distraught parents. Make him better, *please* . . .

For the next two days everyone seemed to hold their breath. Jonas Parry came for his weekly evening meal and on hearing the news his face became grave and filled with human sympathy. He lowered his head and began to recite:

'*Out of the depths I cry to thee, o Lord . . . Let thine ears be attentive to the voice of my supplications . . . I wait for the Lord, my soul waits, and in his word I hope . . .'*

By the time he had finished both Ada and Elsie were in tears and even Tom was looking moist round the eyes.

Ada went to see Nancy as often as she could, usually finding her there with her mother, sometimes with George and always, all of them watching and waiting as Billy lay so still, eyes closed, his skin now waxy and pale.

Elsie sometimes went with Ada and she had wept the last time they came away together.

'It's so terrible watching them all,' she said. 'That poor little boy – and all the family. I've never seen them like that . . .'

The usually happy Drake family were all hollow-eyed and desperate over Billy.

Early on the third morning they heard a knock at the door. Ada was already up and dressed and she ran down and opened the door on to the yard.

'George!' For a moment she could not think why he would be at her door at this time. As realization dawned, Elsie came down the stairs behind her. 'What is it . . .? Is he . . .? Oh, please tell us he's better?'

But his face already told a different story. Dear, cheerful George seemed unable to speak. He just stood shaking his head, on and on as if he could not stop. Ada gasped, a hand going to her mouth.

'Oh no,' she heard Elsie breathe beside her. 'Please God, no.'

'He went –'bout four in the morning,' George managed to say finally. 'Our Nancy said he never opened his eyes again. She gave him the cordial, like the doctor said – but it didn't make any difference. And then he just . . .'

He broke down then, his shoulders shaking, weeping like a child himself there on the doorstep.

'Oh, George,' Ada said, feeling as if her chest was about to break open. 'Poor Nancy – and poor Walt . . .' She was about to go to him, to try and offer comfort in some way, but George backed away. For a moment his eyes fastened on Elsie and Ada looked too, to see her sister's face streaming with tears.

'Just thought you'd want to know,' George said, so choked he could hardly speak, before striding away along the entry.

Elsie quickly turned away as well and hurried back upstairs. Ada found her on the bed, letting out such deep sobs that they were shaking her whole body. She sat down beside her and let her cry herself out, stroking her shoulder. Eventually, Elsie sat up, eyes red and looking dazed.

'It's so sad for them,' she said slowly. 'But I don't know why it set me off like that. It feels like . . .' She was quiet for a moment. 'Like all the sad things that've ever happened all wrapped up together.'

Ada, her own heart aching, slipped her arm around her sister's shoulder and they sat for a moment, heads together, Ada's cheek pressed against the rough scarring of her sister's face.

Little Billy was given the best funeral the family could possibly afford. Ada, Elsie and Tom all went to see him when he was laid out in the house in a little white coffin, a blond angel surrounded by flowers. The room was full of the sound of weeping.

'Why has God taken him?' Nancy sobbed. 'My love, my darling little boy . . .'

Matty Drake's face was swollen with crying and Lizzie and Ernie stood beside her sobbing their hearts out. George looked desperate, trying and failing to hold back his own tears.

Ada and Elsie went to the funeral at the church and by then everyone was quieter, as if stunned. And Ada, feeling desperately for her friend and for all her terrible loss, was almost as affected by the change she saw in her sister.

For all her rage of the previous weeks, it was as if the death of this little boy had broken Elsie open. It had begun to let a softer, kinder person emerge than Ada could remember her being since they were both very small, in that long-ago life of before.

Forty-Nine

Winter set in hard and frosts bit into the ground. The cold air sliced into the nostrils and every possible cover had to be found to pile on the beds at night. They kept the stove burning in the workshop and were all glad of the vigorous movements of treadling lathes and shaping the buttons just to keep warm.

It was a time of shared sadness. Everyone along Galton Passage who knew the Drakes and their gem business – and that was most people – felt for them and for Nancy. For the time being, the Drakes turned in on themselves and Ada and the others did not see much of any of them. George's cheerful whistling was not heard echoing between the walls nor was Lizzie playing out with any of her pals. It was as if the cold of winter and pain of loss had enveloped them round like a chrysalis from which they could only wait to be reborn.

Jonas's voice, ringing out along the passage during the dinner break, seemed to take on an extra depth and meaning for a while. He was not just an eccentric with his mind fixed on verses of scripture; his voice also brought a deep comfort, if only partly through its familiarity.

Ada tried to be as good a friend to Nancy as she could. Nancy could not bear the emptiness of home. However much Walt and the family tried to persuade her that she would soon have another child and must not despair, she could not stand to see signs of Billy in the house: his little cradle, his clothes and blanket. Not knowing what else to do with herself she decided to come back to work as planned.

After a few days she came across the passage at dinner time to see the button girls at Fletchers'. It was Elsie who spotted her looking in through the workshop door.

'Look who's here,' she said gently.

Ada turned from where she had been bent over Jess's lathe, which was playing up.

'Nancy!'

She hurried over as Gert, Margaret and the others all called out greetings to her.

Nancy stayed half-outside, seeming awkward and self-conscious. 'Just thought I'd pop over . . .'

'Come on in,' Gert called out. There was a little table in the room now, near the stove, where they would sit during the break if it was cold. 'You had your dinner?'

'Not yet,' Nancy said.

'Come and sit down,' Gert said in her motherly way. She was a matronly-looking figure these days, her blonde hair faded, and there was something comforting and always the same about her. 'We're just brewing up for the dinner break!' She pointed to the big brown kettle perched on top of the stove. 'Plenty to go round.'

Nancy, looking very thin and drawn in the face, gave a faint smile and came to sit down. Ada and the others joined her and they shared out their bits of bread and cheese and cold meat. Margaret got up and made tea and they passed around the assortment of cups and jars they had to drink from.

'How're you bearing up?' Jess asked Nancy, kindly. She was not that different in age from Nancy but as yet she had no family.

'Oh, well . . .' Nancy shrugged. 'You know. Got to keep going.'

'I lost my first two,' Margaret piped up suddenly, startling Ada who still scarcely knew the first thing about her. She could see Margaret had Nancy's instant attention. Margaret sat holding her cup, which had tiny forget-me-nots painted on the rim, and stared across the room, her face clouded. 'Terrible, when they start dying like that.' She looked at Nancy. 'You'll go on to have more – you'll be all right.'

Ada knew Nancy hated people talking about how she would have more children, as if it was replacing Billy, but after what Margaret had said she gave a grateful nod. She seemed warmed by the fact that they would talk to her about it.

'Well – we'll see,' she said.

'He were a lovely babby,' Gert added. 'Beautiful.'

Nancy looked down, eyes filling with tears. To her surprise Ada saw little Biddy, who was perched on a small stool close to Nancy, reach up and pat Nancy's shoulder.

'Me mam lost four of us,' she said. 'Said it were the worst thing ever happened to her.'

Nancy turned and looked at the pale waif of a child beside her. A waif who often seemed much older than her years.

'What's your name, dear?' she said.

'Biddy Ryan,' she said. 'My baptized name's Bridget Mary Ryan. We're all Mary, even the boys.'

Nancy wiped her eyes. 'How many brothers and sisters have you got, Biddy?'

'I've six living, miss.'

Nancy stared at her almost as if understanding something for the first time. 'Your poor mother.' She turned back to the other women. 'My mother never lost any of hers. She says it's 'cause she's a country girl, not brought up breathing in the stink of Brum.'

Gert laughed. 'She might be right there. It don't always hold though – I ain't lost any. And I've lived 'ere all my life.'

Ada, though loath to break things up, indicated that they should all get back to work and Nancy stood up. She smiled round at them.

'Thanks, ladies. You've made me feel a bit better.'

'Come any time,' Ada said.

'We're always ready for a natter,' Gert called, heading back to work.

The most cheerful person in the house at that time was Tom, who having finally seen the light regarding Sam Bligh was keeping well away from him and the company he kept. On top of that, Tom was now walking out with a girl called Dinah. The two of them were only fifteen but Dinah seemed a person with her head properly screwed on and Ada liked her. She was a strong, healthy-looking girl with a head of thick, dark brown hair and brown eyes which looked directly at you. Her family had not long since moved to the city.

Elsie did not go out and about a lot. Despite her defiance about her face to start with, she hated strangers staring at her and she mainly stayed close to home. Bent over her lathe in the workshop there was not much difference to see in her, but Ada still had a shock whenever her sister turned round and the scarred side of her face came into view. She wondered if she would ever get used to it but she tried not to show the wince she felt still, every time. Elsie seemed calmer in herself, as if there were things about her life she had just had to accept.

Week by week, month by month, the business was building. They all worked hard, all were skilled and quick, and Ada had dreams of the day when they would not have to supply grumpy Mr Beardsmore and could work every stage themselves, develop new designs – something Elsie was very good at – and sell directly into the market. But that time still lay in the future.

One evening, after the others had packed away, swept up and gone home, Ada stayed on in the workshop. It was Elsie's turn to make their tea and she had gone ahead upstairs.

Icy darkness pressed against the dusty windows as Ada worked on in the dim light. The fire was a dying glow in the stove now they had finished for the night, the room fast growing colder. All day everyone had been working away as usual, the air speckled white, the boxes of buttons filling to overflowing as the day went by, for Tom to load into the basket carriage tomorrow morning. Tomorrow they would give the place its weekly clean, keep the dust down as much as they could.

Ada stood, pulling her black shawl close round her, looking at the rows of silent lathes.

'We built this.' Her lips moved in a whisper. '*I* built this business.' When she thought back to the yard off Summer Row and her life with the Connells and then her period in service with the Dugdales, it felt like a miracle that she had ever managed to get out of all that and start again.

It was one of the rare moments when she gave herself permission to stop and think. But her satisfaction was tinged with pain. She had worked so hard, which had meant there were so many other things she had not let herself have time to do, or even think about. Her days were made up of work. For so much of her life she had been working and looking after the family. She never went out to entertainments or frivolities as she chose to think of them, to the fairs or shows or musical concerts in the town. Her social life was tea with the Drakes. And as for men, or marriage . . . Here she was, a woman of twenty who had never once been kissed by a man . . . That forced kiss by Sam Bligh did not count in her mind.

She thought about Tom's young girl, Dinah, a girl who looked made for kissing, and smiled wistfully. But Dinah was a hired hand in a corset factory while she, Ada, had a business of her own. A business she was growing, that she was in charge of. And while she could feel a pang of envy for Dinah's happiness and freedom, she would not have swapped places with her for anything.

And surely, the one man in her life who she had loved above all other, her pa, would be proud of all she had achieved?

'You don't get everything in this world,' she told herself as she turned the gas lamps off and locked the door for the night. 'And this isn't half bad.'

Before going upstairs for the night, Ada went down to the store room to check on their remaining stocks. There was enough to keep the work going first thing and she was expecting another delivery in the morning.

An oil lamp, already lit, was hung from a hook, lighting up the freezing-cold room with its door to the backyard and wooden stairs up to the workshop. At least the cold had damped down the stink from that charnel yard outside, she thought, though she was starting to shiver.

Quickly she moved the two remaining sacks of shells, dragging them over to lean them against the back wall so that there was a clear space for the fresh delivery. She did not want to linger – it was so cold down there.

She had just taken the lamp off its hook to light her way back upstairs when she heard a tap at the door. She waited a moment, then it came again, more boldly.

Wondering whether it was one of the Drakes, she lifted the lamp high and opened the door. The chill wind blew in with a lacing of sleet and in the darkness she saw a burly figure, a cap pulled low over his face and with a thick beard. Her heart began to beat harder with alarm.

'Who're you?' she said.

'I'm looking for Fletchers' – Ada Fletcher . . .' He sounded uncertain and not dangerous. And there was something about his voice that seemed familiar.

'I'm Ada Fletcher,' she said, wondering whether this was about business; and if so it was an odd time to call.

'Are you really?' His voice sounded almost tender. 'My, my – a real young lady now, ain't yer? I've had a time finding you – d'you remember me?'

He took his cap off and still her mind was struggling to recognize the voice, the fact that she knew she had seen him before.

'Jem,' he said. 'Jem Atherton. I was at Arkle and Lilley – worked with your father.'

'Jem!' Ada gasped. 'Of course I remember you. Come in . . .'

She stood back to admit him but he held up a hand in refusal. While he was polite, there was bitterness in his tone.

'I've come with a message, that's all, Ada.' His voice softened a little, as if he told himself none of this was her fault. 'A feller come to see me – tracked me down. Rough-looking cove an' all. Told me he had a message from a certain Richie Fletcher and I was to pass it on to you.'

Ada felt as if the ground was heaving about under her feet and she had to grasp hold of the door frame.

'What – my pa – Richie Fletcher?'

'Yeah.' Jem sounded almost apologetic. 'I know you must've decided years ago that he was no longer of this world. I certainly did, Ada, with him disappearing the way he did, not a word to his pals. And by the look of it you've done well for yourself without any help from him. But he's alive and kicking – although not kicking, as it happens . . .'

Ada listened in dazed confusion to Jem's attempts to break this harsh news the best way he knew how.

'Seems he's sick, Ada. He's in some . . .' Jem hesitated again, as if he did not want to say the word. 'Well, a dosshouse – round the back of New Street. And he's asking for you.'

Fifty

'Elsie!'

Ada went tearing upstairs the second Jem Atherton took off again. Elsie was cooking on the fire when she burst in and the room smelt of frying kidneys. Tom had just got in and was sitting, pulling off his boots.

'Elsie – leave that . . .' Ada stalled, in such a state she hardly knew how to break the news to her sister. 'It's . . . Oh, Elsie . . . It's . . .' Ada sank down on a chair, her head spinning. Nothing felt real.

'Who was that?' Elsie asked, pulling the pan off the fire with its sizzling contents.

Ada began to explain. Jem Atherton – did Elsie remember him? No, she did not. And . . . And . . .

'Our father?' Elsie looked blank. 'But . . . He passed away years ago, didn't he?'

Ada was shaking her head. 'He left. Disappeared one night. And . . . Well, I never thought he'd just leave us. Never believed it. I thought something had happened to him. But . . . He's alive, Elsie. Our pa. We have a father! And he needs us.'

'What about me – d'you want help, Ada?' Tom got up.

'No,' Ada said abruptly. No one who was not family, she found herself thinking. But she tried to soften her tone. 'Elsie and me'll go. You finish doing our tea.'

'What?' The last words the girls heard as they grabbed their thickest shawls and hurried downstairs were, 'How'm I s'posed to do that?'

They couldn't help laughing together as they left him to it.

The girls linked arms as they hurried along the freezing streets, their heads muffled in woollen shawls. The sleet was thickening to snow, a whirling veil which tickled against the parts of their faces still exposed to the air and danced in the pools of light as they made their way from lamp to lamp. With their spare hands they gripped their shawls under their chins, and clung together with the other. Shadowy figures around them walked heads bowed, all seeming in a rush to get under cover.

All the way there – a matter of almost a mile – the two of them barely spoke, each trying to take in the situation. The only words they exchanged were an occasional, 'I can't believe it,' and, 'Is it true? Can it be true?'

Seeing Jem Atherton again had been strange enough for Ada, a face from the past which she had almost forgotten. But the news he had brought was so extraordinary – so longed for, yet so unlikely – that she still felt she had slipped into a dream.

They turned down a narrow side road parallel to Navigation Street, an even darker place with a sordid feel to it, though Ada guessed the sheer misery of the cold was keeping a lot of the street's usual clamour inside. Close to one of the lamps she saw a woman's face, her cheeks unnaturally red, peering out as if she thought their approaching footsteps might mean business. Seeing two young women, she tutted and retreated back into the doorway.

'He said the Hive,' Elsie murmured, looking about her in the snowy gloom.

Ada was looking up at the signs advertising rooms. Fourpence a bed was the going rate, some for men only. They squinted, struggling to read them in the dark: 'The

Haven, Mrs Kemp', read one, its sign, hung from a bracket on the wall, squeaking as it swung in the wind. Another announced, 'Good Beds, 4d, Men Only'.

'There's quite a few of them along here,' Ada said, also speaking quietly. Both of them were afraid of this street, of what might emerge from the shadows.

'Oh – here,' Elsie exclaimed. 'The Hive. You're sure that's what he said?'

'Yes. Quite sure.' It was engraved on Ada's memory.

It was at the furthest end of the street and even under cover of darkness, the place felt more oppressively dingy and run-down than others they had seen. They stared up at it, the sort of establishment they had never been anywhere near before, and they had to find their courage to approach the black, scruffy-looking door.

'What's he doing in here?' Elsie said in a small voice. 'I thought our pa was a rich man – a clever man. When he was alive, that is . . .' She trailed off, defeated by the turmoil in her mind. They knew nothing – not about any of it.

'Come on.' Ada stepped up and knocked at the door, which was eventually answered by a scrawny girl who only looked about fourteen, holding a lantern. Ada felt Elsie's fingers digging into her arm.

They could hear the sound of voices from an inner room.

'Fourpence a bed,' the girl said without energy or interest. But then she managed to drag enough attention to the situation and say, 'You're girls. It's men only.'

'I had a message to say . . .' Suddenly Ada could not bring herself to admit that the person who had summoned her to this place was her father. To this dingy passage stretching before her already giving off the foulest, most fetid smell, and those rough voices from close by. 'There's a sick man here – needs to see us.'

As she spoke, Ada saw a woman looming into view

along the passage. She was so wide of girth and her skirts so voluminous that she almost had to walk sideways. The stuff of her dress seemed to be of a pale lilac colour which did not seem at all practical in such a place, and her bun-like countenance was topped by a mound of dark hair. It was impossible to guess how old she might be.

'They come for the corpse upstairs?' she demanded, with a certain lack of sensitivity.

Ada's heart nearly leapt out of her mouth. 'No!' she cried. 'He hasn't died?'

'Might as well've done,' the woman replied, folding her arms. 'And I'd thank you to get 'im out of 'ere before 'e does.'

''E's paid 'is fourpence,' the girl pointed out.

'I'd've charged 'im 'alf a crown if I'd known he was going to mither me this much,' her employer grumbled.

'Can we see him?' Ada asked.

'You can do what you like with 'im so long as you get 'im out of 'ere before 'e starts to pong – worse than they all do, that is.' With a jerk of her head, she ordered, 'Take 'em up, Tilly.'

'Yes, Mrs Daws,' Tilly said, scuttling forward.

Ma Daws disappeared through a nearby door into what, as Tilly beckoned Ada and Elsie inside, they saw to be the communal kitchen and sitting room. Even the quick glance they had inside of a range and of a huddle of people on benches nearby close to the warmth, gave an impression of filth and destitution. She and Elsie exchanged a glance. Ada had removed her shawl from her head but Elsie kept hers swaddled over as much of the scarred side of her face as possible.

Tilly did not spare them any more words. They followed her scrawny form and bare legs, her feet pushed into some flimsy little slippers, up a narrow wooden stair. The treads were broken in places and each of them creaked with its own discordant groan. Ada withdrew her hand from the banister rail at the first touch, it was so greasy.

The fetid stench grew stronger along the landing. An open door revealed to them a room lit by an oil lamp and so crammed full of low, cot-like beds that there was hardly space for even the frailest of legs to fit between them. Bodies lay on several of the cots and the air was a miasma of foul breath, decayed teeth and booze.

But this was not the room, apparently. Passing an even narrower staircase that led to the upper floor, Tilly pushed open another door at the end of the landing and stood back for the girls to go in.

The same pattern was repeated here: overcrowded, airless, stinking, only bare outlines visible in the flickering light of the lamp hanging from a hook. Ada's eyes scanned the room.

'Where is he?' she whispered to Tilly. The girl's blank eyes looked up at her and she shrugged.

'He can stay 'til morning, then 'e's got to go,' she said and took off back along the landing.

'Oh, Ada,' Elsie whispered. 'D'you think he's really here? Could this be a trick?'

Even though the idea that their father might have been returned to them was a wonder they could scarcely take in, the thought of him reduced to lying in this place was almost enough to have them both taking to their heels.

From the far side of the room they heard a man coughing and coughing, his lungs sounding like a soaked sponge. Something in the sound of that cough, long forgotten but familiar, told Ada that this was where they must look. Taking Elsie's hand again, she led the way slowly, squeezing between the cots.

'Eh, ladies,' a man's voice piped up as they passed him.

343

He was frenziedly scratching himself as he spoke, half-sitting up. 'Ladies in 'ere, eh? Come to give us a nice time, 'ave yer?'

The coughing stilled for a time. Reaching the bed, Ada leaned over it, making space for Elsie at her side. The light was very poor, but she saw the outline of a face in the gloom, a lined, leathery-looking face, the eyes closed, the lungs whistling as each breath was drawn in and out. She turned and looked into Elsie's appalled eyes and gave a slight nod. The shape of his face – it was him, surely it was? She dared to speak.

'Pa?' she said in a low, trembling voice. 'Is that you – Richard Fletcher? It's Ada and Elsie – your daughters.'

She saw his eyes open, peering at them, trying to make sense of these figures who he had not set eyes on since they were young girls. Ada felt herself freeze. What if he had no idea who they were? Could not remember his family at all? It would be worse than his not coming back at all.

He licked his lips, went to speak and was seized by a fit of coughing which made him strain to sit up. Ada went to help but somehow could not find it in herself to touch him. Not until she was sure. Once he was still, in a croaking voice, he managed to say, 'Ada?'

'It's me, Pa.' She could hardly speak, such was the wave of longing and pity that washed through her. That voice, even though croaking and pathetic – it was him! 'And Elsie.'

'Ada – my lad?' he said wonderingly. 'And little Elsie?'

All the thoughts that would come later – Where have you been all these years? How could you leave us and never come back? – were forgotten in those moments.

'Oh, Pa!' Ada's legs went weak and she sank suddenly on the next cot which was empty. 'You're here,' she breathed. 'I can't believe it. You're alive and you're here!'

Her father managed to push himself up, coughing

dreadfully, into a sitting position. Ada flung her arms around him and in that moment she was taken up in a heaven of feeling. Pa – her pa was really here and for now, nothing else mattered! Elsie sat beside her and took his hand.

He was so weak that it was only a moment before he had to lie down again, coughing and coughing. But as he calmed, his face wore a smile.

'My girls,' he said. 'I knew you'd come and find me.'

And what a place to find him: in this refuge of the destitute. As Ada came back to herself, she smelt again the foul stink of the room that made it hard to breathe, felt herself itching from bites of vermin that were already making their way into her and Elsie's clothes. Even before all the cots were full, the place seemed alive with bugs and with the nightmares of the desperate.

'We've got to get him out of here,' Ada murmured to Elsie. 'Tonight.'

Fifty-One

'Go and get Tom,' Ada instructed Elsie, as she paid the driver of the hansom cab they had found to bring them through the snow, to the end of Galton Passage. The three of them had squeezed inside and having completed the journey, the driver was now plainly keen to get shot of this disreputable passenger and hurry away.

'She won't be a moment,' Ada said sternly to him as she supported the bones of her groaning, barely conscious father. She held on to her money for the moment – she'd pay when she was good and ready.

Moments later, Elsie returned with Tom striding at her side, asking bewildered questions.

'Just help us get him out,' Ada snapped.

She hated this, seeing her father in this terrible state and having to answer Tom's questions. She just wanted to get to a place where they could be private, away from eyes which she thought must be watching even though nearly everyone was inside and the street shrouded in darkness.

Richie Fletcher's legs would not hold him. Once Ada had paid the cab driver, the three of them half-carried, half-dragged him into Galton Passage, Tom taking Richie's shoulders and the girls each a leg. For a scrawny bag of bones, he was surprisingly heavy. As the sound of the horse's hooves died away on the cobbles, they heard footsteps.

'Ada – Elsie? That you?'

Ada realized with a burn of shame that it was George

Drake. And now he was going to know about their father and see him like this!

George saw the problem immediately and rushed to help.

'Leave us be, George,' Ada snapped.

'Don't be silly,' Elsie panted as they started trying to squeeze along the entry. 'We'll never get him up the stairs by ourselves.'

The entry was so narrow that Ada and Elsie had to surrender and let Tom and George carry their father into the house and up the two flights of stairs to lay him on their bed. They walked into the room just as George was pulling the quilt over Richie. It was tender, the way he did it, helping this man who was a stranger to him but sensing he belonged to them.

'There you go,' George said as he turned to leave. 'All right now?'

'Thank you, ' Ada said stiffly, still prickling all over with discomfort at seeing her father put to bed like a baby.

'Thanks, George.' Elsie's voice was softer. 'We'd never have made it without you.'

As George tactfully took himself off down the stairs, Tom turned to them both.

'So, what the hell's going on?'

Ada lay beside her father that night and the next few nights while Elsie made up a bed on the floor.

For those first hours Ada barely slept, jerking awake every time her father stirred in the bed or coughed, alert for anything he might need.

Her emotions were so stirred up in any case, a circling mixture of wonder and pity, tenderness and anger, all mixed in with a milling crowd of questions. Where have you been all this time – these ten long years of silence? Why did you leave us – what about our mother? *What about us?*

And during those long hours lying in the dark, she spun

dreams of the future. They would nurse him back to health, to being their strong, all-powerful pa who knew how to do everything. He would live with them, help her in the business. At last she would have someone to turn to! And he would tell them the story of why he had to leave, that he had set off to find a way of making everything even better for Mom and all of them, something that would make them understand and forgive him. They would be a family again, support one another . . .

Her father's sleep was not peaceful. He coughed and murmured to himself, never seeming at rest in mind or body. Whatever he was dreaming seemed full of threat – 'No!' He thrashed his head from side to side. 'It's too late now – no – no!'

In the middle of the night she got up to give him a drink of water. As she crept round the bed Elsie stirred.

'He's disturbed in his mind, isn't he?' she whispered, seeming almost frightened. 'Maybe it's the fever.'

Ada lifted the cup to her father's lips and he sipped, then coughed so hard she thought it might be the death of him. As he finally lay back, limp and exhausted, he croaked, 'Don't let that varmint near me . . .!'

The next morning after almost no sleep, Ada was up early to open the workshop. It was hard to keep her mind on the job – Pa had come back to them, Pa! Lying upstairs in their bed!

All day she and Elsie took turns to run upstairs and attend to his needs. It was a shock to both of them at first, having to pot a man as you might a baby and coax him to eat broth. When work was over they steeled themselves and washed his body, taking his clothes to wash.

'This is a rag.' Ada held up his shirt to show Elsie, finding tears suddenly in her eyes. Her father watched – they could see the shine of his eyes in the lamplight.

'You're good wenches,' he whispered.

Suddenly, as Ada went to dry his chest, he grasped hold of her wrist. The strength of his hold startled her.

'If he comes here, don't let him near me. Not ever, d'you hear? For God's sake – keep him away from me.'

'Who, Pa?' Elsie said, leaning in.

He stared at her, his expression taking on a look of horror. 'What's wrong with your face?'

Elsie's hand went to her cheek as if she had been stung.

'A wicked woman threw vitriol on her,' Ada said.

Richie Fletcher stared at his daughter. 'All pretty, my wenches were,' he rasped. 'You don't look like one of mine.'

Elsie stepped backwards, these words like a cruel blow.

Ada was stunned. 'It wasn't Elsie's fault, Pa,' she said, not wanting him to be like this – like anything that he was now. She wanted Pa to be powerful and clever and kind. And humble, able to admit the wrong he had done them. 'It was terrible – a crime.'

'Not your fault,' he said to Elsie, as if grasping what had happened, his voice softening. 'Poor wench.'

The girls looked at each other across the bed. Ada had imagined their days of tender nursing, Pa sitting, recovered in a chair down by the fire, the conversations they would have when he explained everything to them. When he was better he would think of them, of their mother. For now he was sick and wrapped up in himself. He tensed up again and grasped her arm.

'If he comes – don't ever say I'm here . . .'

'Who, Pa?' Ada said.

'Eb, of course. Eb Mullin. Don't you ever let that filthy rat come in here . . .'

Ada could only dimly remember the name Eb Mullin, a far-distant echo from their childhood. Another worker at the foundry? She could not bring a face to mind and Elsie could not remember hearing of him at all.

Days passed as they did their best to nurse their father with loving devotion. All Ada's thought of giving Nancy help and company were lost in the reappearance of her father – the fulfilment of the dream she had nursed inside her ever since the day he left. Pa. Here.

As soon as the workshop closed in the evening, Ada would rush up to see him, make tea and sit beside him. The novelty of having him there was a wonderful thing. She would be working in the daytime and would suddenly remember, a smile creeping over her face. Pa had come back! Her young heart which had been so wounded by the loss of him was now full of hope and expectation. Pa had come to find her, called out for her. And with all her heart she wanted to save him and make him better.

But as the days passed, he did not get better. He was cleaner – they kept him spotless – dressed in a new nightshirt Ada had bought specially for him. They fed and nursed him, brought home medicines dispensed by the druggist, made health-giving teas from herbs. But nothing seemed to help: his strength was at a low ebb. He spent almost all the time drifting in and out of a feverish sleep.

One evening, as she sat with him, every cover they could muster on his bed to keep him warm, Ada saw that his eyes were open, staring up at the ceiling.

'Pa?' she said softly.

His gaze shifted towards her. He was so weak, she could see that, and she ached with frustration. Why could he not regain strength and get better?

'I was going . . .' He started to speak and she leaned closer.

'What, Pa – I can't here you?'

'I was going – to Australia,' he said. 'Make my fortune . . .' His voice sank even lower. 'Never made it . . .'

Her mind spun. Was that why he had left? To travel to the other side of the world? And if that had not happened why did he not just come home? Why, during these days of them looking after him had he still never said anything about them, about her and Elsie and their other siblings? About how he had forsaken them? And their mother?

Hurt and rage stormed up in her. Not once yet had he mentioned Mom, what he had done to them, plunging them all into poverty and leaving their mother expecting another of his children. He had not even asked what became of her, if she was still alive. For the first time in her life she had started to doubt him, this hero of hers. This dream of a father who would return, full of joy, to see them, giving the perfect reason why he had left.

'Where did you go?' Her tears flowed, even though she didn't want them to. 'Why did you leave us – just go like that? I thought you were dead . . .'

'I've had a rum life . . .' He sounded almost pleased with himself. 'Had my adventures – here and there. And . . .' Another contortion of fear went through him and he tried to lunge upright.

'Got to get out of here . . . He's coming . . . Help me – get me out of here . . .'

But he sank back on the bed again, eyes closing, too weak to move.

Elsie was coming back across from the lav, oil lamp held high, when George Drake came into the yard.

'Oh, Elsie,' he said, seeming flustered in his shy way. 'I was just coming to ask how your . . . relative is.'

Elsie felt a softening round her heart. The night they brought their father in with George's help, she had seen the gentle way he dealt with him, depositing Pa's wracked body so gently on the bed, this man he did not know. It had touched her, even though she tried not to admit it to herself. George, who had been so sweet to her all this time. And his voice was so tender.

He's just being kind, she told herself. It's not that he has any special feeling for me – how could he, the way I am now? A sting passed through her damaged eye at the thought of the acid burn, of what she had become. They're a kind family – nice to everyone. But now her own expectations for her life had sunk so low and kindness was a gift she would not refuse. She had come to realize it meant everything.

'Still quite unwell, thanks,' she said.

'Oh – sorry to hear that,' George said.

They both stood there a moment, neither of them sure what to say next. They'd find out about Pa in the end, Elsie thought. He might as well be told who he was, this broken wreck of a man they were sheltering upstairs. 'He's our father, George.'

'Oh!' She could tell he was really taken aback. 'But I thought . . .?'

'That he had passed away? Yes, so did we.' There was a brutal part of her that did not want to hide anything from George at all. Her ugly face: the ugly history of her family. Then she would really see how much he wanted to bring her flowers.

'He suddenly decided to turn up again,' she said, hearing the hardness in her voice. Because – and this came as a sudden surprise – she felt hard. Hard and angry, not like Ada who still wanted to believe in him. 'Suddenly decided to show his face now he can't get by ducking and diving or whatever he's been doing.'

She knew she was trying to push him away, this kind

man. This person whose family stuck so close together. There was no one in the Drake family like Richie Fletcher, their long-lost father. And it was as if she wanted him to see everything that was ugly about her – her face, her temperament that did not, at this moment, feel forgiveness for her long-lost father. Instead she felt bitterness and a sense of betrayal.

'Goodness me,' George said. But he sounded more sorry than shocked. 'That's a hard one, I must say.' He paused for a moment. 'Well – you're doing your best for him.'

'Yes,' Elsie said. 'I suppose we are.'

She kept expecting George to move away but he kept standing there.

'How's Nancy?' Elsie asked, keen to change the subject.

'Oh, well – going along,' he said sadly. 'It's good she's come back to work – can't stand being in the house without the little'un.' He looked very directly at her in the lamplight. ''Er'd be pleased to see you and Ada, when you have the time. That'd perk her up a bit.'

'We've been a bit taken up,' Elsie admitted. 'But I'll tell Ada. And say to Nancy to call into the works again if she feels like it.' Then: 'I'd best get on, George.'

'Course. Ta-ra, Elsie.'

Was she imagining the wistful tone in his voice? And she knew it was not her imagination that he stood watching her as she went back inside. It stirred her feelings, but she shook herself, pulling back her shoulders and telling herself not to be so silly. Though he was a kind lad, she had never given him reason to think she was interested in him. Damaged goods, she was. That was the truth – and that was what she was going to have to live with for the rest of her life.

Fifty-Two

'How is 'e, Miss Fletcher?'

Ada was startled, as she came into the workshop, to hear Biddy's question as the child looked anxiously up from her work counting buttons. What an old soul the little girl seemed! Word had quickly got round as to who it was lying so gravely sick on the floor above – there was no point in trying to hide it. And Ada had to ask herself sternly why she would want to hide the return of her pa from the people around her. Was she not proud to call him her father? But she was none too keen to face the true answer to that question.

And Biddy was only a child and her employee at that.

'He's doing all right, thank you, Biddy,' Ada said, turning away. But Biddy hadn't finished.

'I dunno what I'd do if anything happened to our da,' she said with feeling.

Ada felt tears spring into her eyes at this loving speech. At the love of this child whose father had not deeply betrayed her. She walked off and down the stairs to the sorting table, the beginnings of a row of snail shells carefully laid out. But she could not stand working there for long in the winter cold. After half an hour she climbed the two flights of stairs up to the workshop to oversee everyone working away and be near the stove. Towards dinner time she went up to the bedroom.

Pa was no good at talking, she thought, as she climbed. Had it always been this way? She put the kettle on the fire, her thoughts running down the painful paths that her father's return was forcing her to visit. She had only been a child before – she did not really know what this man, Richie Fletcher, was truly like, beyond her childish hero-worship. Was it shame that kept him from telling them about these lost years, or from asking after them and their mother? Maybe she would have to press him.

Going into the room at what was now mid-morning on this chill day, she found him asleep, his face still stubbly as they had not yet shaved him and pale from the white winter light seeping through the window.

She watched him sleep for some time, full of mixed feelings of longing and anger. Then she went next door and lifted the kettle off the fire, making him a drink of hot water and milk with a spoonful of sugar which she took back to him.

'Pa . . . Brought you a drink – keep you warm.'

He stirred as she approached and seeing her, gave a half-smile.

'Thanks, wench . . .'

She helped him sit up partially and on feeling how weak he was, her heart buckled. Was he ever going to come downstairs, see the business she had built, that she kept trying to tell him about, get him to take an interest? She sat on the edge of the bed, handing him the cup which he took with shaking hands.

'Pa . . . Can I ask you something?'

He gave a slight nod as he moved his lips to the rim of the cup.

'Where did you go, all this time?'

There was a pause. Eventually he came out with, 'Down London.'

Ada digested this. London. It was not so far away – they had travelled there in a few hours. Yet he had never once come back.

'What did you do?' She still had a gleam of hope. Something noble, or exciting – the things she thought her father was, that she needed him to be.

'This and that. You know. Getting by.'

Her bafflement deepened. Getting by? Surely he had been doing more than just 'getting by' even when he was still at home with them? So why did he bother to leave? What deluded dream had he followed all this time?

'You never ask about our mother. About Mom. Don't you want to know?'

She felt the rage and sorrow that she always tried to push down in herself forcing up at her. Yes, he was ill and weak – but was he not concerned about anyone except himself?

Richie kept sipping the sweet drink in silence.

'Well, I'll tell you then,' she went on, brutally. 'We all had to move on to a yard – Jem helped us, as he was here and you weren't. He was good to us, Jem was, as much as he could be. Mom and the rest of us – we all did what we could, scraped for every farthing, and then Elsie and me started work at the button factory. But Mom . . .'

She swallowed. She could not be sure if there was a glimmer of interest in her father's eyes, though she could just sense something.

'She had your latest child in her belly and she bled to death having it,' she said. 'The baby died. It was a boy.'

On saying this she barely knew how she had known this information but it had come from somewhere, emerging from the deepest recesses of her memory.

'And then all the others except me got taken away to the workhouse . . .'

It was like talking to a stone, she thought. No movement, no reaction.

'Have you got nothing to say?' she said, the pain crushing her heart as she looked at this empty shell of a man who she had once thought was the best person in the world, the hero she was going to live by.

'Can't . . .' He started coughing and thrust out the cup for her to take it away. He convulsed for some minutes then lay down, limp as a rag. 'Can't do anything about it now, can I?'

Ada stood up. She stared down at him. 'You could at least say sorry.'

But his eyes were closing as he slipped away from her again into sleep.

Ada left the room, shaking with anger and sorrow and grief. In the kitchen she sat down and sobs burst out of her. She doubled over on the chair, trying to muffle the howls of emotion which burst from her in her hands, her lap, anything to stifle the noise that no one else should hear.

All her life she had clung fast to the belief that her pa could never have betrayed them, that he had gone off for some reason that would be good for all of them. She had persuaded herself that he had departed on some heroic journey, that he missed them and cared for them. That either the journey had been the death of him by some twist of fate, or that one day – one glorious joyful day – he would come back and dazzle them all with his tales of adventure and the fortune he had made.

Now, all she could see was the remnant of a man who seemed to have only ever cared about himself.

'Oh God,' she whispered, bunching up her skirt to stifle the sound from her lips. 'Why did he have to come back? At least I could have carried on believing in him, loving him . . .'

As she sat letting out her grief, she was horrified to hear someone climbing the stairs. It was most likely Elsie, come to check on their father, but all the same Ada did not want anyone to see her crying. She was hastily trying to wipe her eyes when there was a tap at the door and it opened.

'Ada?'

'Nancy!' Ada could hear that her own voice sounded thick with tears.

'I came over to see how things are. George told me, about your dad coming back . . .' She crossed the room. 'Oh, Adie – what's wrong?'

Nancy's voice was so sweet and sympathetic. Her face was pale against her black mourning dress, her eyes ringed dark with evidence of sleepless nights of grief, and seeing this Ada could not control herself and she burst into tears all over again.

'What is it? Is he very poorly?'

Nancy knelt in front of her and took her hands. Ada, not able to speak for a moment, tried to nod and shake her head at the same time.

'I'm not getting you,' Nancy said earnestly. 'Is he still poorly or not?'

Ada looked into her eyes, this new friend. She had shared Nancy's pain and now, she who found it hard to share anything felt she must speak, must be a friend and be able to tell her the truth in return.

'He's bad,' she said, patting her sleeve for a slip of rag. 'But it's not that . . .' She looked at Nancy as she wiped her nose. 'He went off, left us – I was ten then. I thought he was dead, in the end. And then – I told you, our mom died having a baby and the others were taken away . . .'

Nancy squeezed her hand, her eyes full of sympathy.

'I always dreamt of Pa coming back, and now . . .' More tears ran down her cheeks. 'I just thought he might care about us. That he loved us – I thought he loved us . . .' She was sobbing.

'Oh, Ada.' Nancy was stroking her hands, not knowing what other comfort she could give.

'Like your pa does. A proper father. But he doesn't. He doesn't care. I don't know if he's even thought about us at all. He's . . .'

She hesitated, looking across at the window, her face wet. Then, dully, she said, 'He's not the man I thought he was, that's all.'

'Poor you.' Nancy sat back on her heels, her face appalled. 'And poor Elsie.'

'Yes, well.' Ada looked down, fiddling with the rag in her lap. She felt washed in shame. 'It doesn't feel like much to be proud of, none of it.'

She dared to look into Nancy's face.

'None of it's your fault, is it?' Nancy said.

Ada grasped her hands in return. 'Thanks, Nance. It means the world to be able to talk to you.'

They put their arms round each other and held one another close, true friends in their worst hours of sadness.

'Elsie?' Two nights later, Ada sat bolt upright in bed. 'Light the candle, can you?'

She knew her sister slept like a cat and would wake the moment she hissed her name in the pitch darkness.

'Hold on.' The rasp and flare of a match spread flickering light through the room. Elsie lit the candle and scrambled to her feet.

'Something's changed.' Ada's voice was small and shaky. 'I think he's . . . going.'

Elsie held the light over their father. Richie was lying on his back, his breathing, which had been loud and regular, suddenly shallow. Ada leaned close to hear him.

'I suddenly woke up . . .' She sounded shaky. 'Thought he'd gone for a moment.'

She looked up at Elsie who was staring at the bag of skin and bones which was now their long-lost father. Elsie had not said much about Pa since he had been back with them. Now, she said, 'He's never going to tell us anything, is he?'

She sounded resigned more than sad.

Her throat aching, Ada replied, 'I'm not sure there's much to tell.'

Elsie came round the bed, put the candlestick down on the wooden chair on Ada's side and got in at the other end of the bed, pressing her feet, chilled from standing out on the floor, against Ada's warmer calves. Ada flinched at Elsie's icy toes but in a way it was a comfort.

They both sensed it would not be long, that their father had now gone on to a place from which he was not coming back, however many questions they still had to ask him.

The end came an hour later, close to four in the morning when the night had sunk to its lowest ebb. His quiet, intermittent breathing carried on and on. Then stopped. The girls looked at each other, each checking to see if they were mistaken. But Richie Fletcher had breathed his last.

Ada and Elsie quietly shifted down on to Elsie's makeshift bed on the floor and curled up together, managing a short, fitful sleep before the morning light seeped into the room and confirmed what they already knew.

Their father lay lifeless on the bed, silent as a stone and now even more of a stranger in death than he had been in life, this man who they had never known and now, for certain, never would.

Fifty-Three

Elsie covered the mirror and made sure the curtains were kept closed. They had no clock to stop at the time of death.

They were to bury Richie Fletcher, this man they had to call their father, in Birmingham's General Cemetery in Hockley.

'Mom's buried there,' Ada remembered. Another of the things she usually tried not to dwell on.

'Well, there's no point in putting them together, is there?' Elsie said bitterly. She turned from the slow daily task of bringing the milk to the boil over the fire to make sure it was safe to drink. Her face was pale and sad. 'Don't s'pose there'll be anyone there except us.'

'I sent word to Jem,' Ada said. 'Nancy said she'd come. And maybe George as well.'

Elsie stared back at her and Ada could not read what she was thinking.

'They're ever so kind, aren't they?' Ada said.

Elsie gave a nod, as if she still found kindness suspicious. Suddenly she said, 'I wonder where the others are? They'll never know our father was still alive.'

Ada watched her sister's back as she stood waiting for the milk to heave and bubble. Maybe they're the lucky ones, she thought. Her own grief at having lost her father was made so much worse by the shattering of her dreams of him and discovering the kind of man he had become – and perhaps always was.

*

It was a freezing February day, once again threatening snow.

They only needed one mourning carriage to follow the hearse bearing their father's coffin to the cemetery. It was pulled by two gleaming black horses, each with a black feather fixed to the browband of its bridle and fluttering in the breeze. Ada and Elsie, accompanied by Tom, George Drake and Nancy, all squeezed in and the carriage rumbled through the streets to the gates of the cemetery, on the edge of the Jewellery Quarter. Jem Atherton had said he would meet them there.

The air was bitingly cold, the cemetery blanketed in white, the black of a twig poking through here and there, and the graves each wearing a snowy hat. Jem was already waiting when they got there, at the side of the path which had been brushed clear of snow, dirty mounds of it gathered on each side. Although they had seen next to nothing of Jem for years, Ada found the sight of his stocky figure and grizzled hair comfortingly familiar as they drew to a halt.

'Thanks for coming, Jem,' she said to him quietly as they followed Richie on his last journey to the grave. 'Not as if he's been much of a friend to you.'

Jem looked at her, his watery blue eyes full of emotion. 'Or a father to all of you. Wish I could've done more, but . . .' He stopped, shaking his head.

'Jem, it was his job, not yours. You had enough of your own problems.'

As she spoke, Jem turned to her with tears in his eyes and Ada was deeply moved to realize he had been holding on to his guilt about them all these years. She took his hand and squeezed it and he smiled sadly down at her.

'You've done well, wench, even after all of that.'

'I just wish . . .' She could hardly go on. There were so many things she wished about her father. 'I still don't know why he left or what he's been doing . . .' Her voice broke. 'He never told me, even after he came back.'

Jem looked sorrowfully at her. 'Maybe it's for the best, Ada. Some things are best left alone.'

She nodded, numbly. If Jem knew anything it didn't seem he was going to tell her either.

Tiny flakes of snow began to trickle down as they went to stand by the grave. Ada and Elsie stood on one side with Tom, George and Nancy on the other, and Jem at the foot. The flakes grew bigger and brushed their cheeks as they watched the men lower the coffin into the ground.

As the vicar intoned the solemn words, 'ashes to ashes, dust to dust', the snow thickened further and swirled round them. Ada, raising her eyes to look across the cemetery for a moment, saw it falling like a speckled veil of white across the graves and distant bushes. Dimly, she noticed someone moving towards them from far off, a little black beetle amid the snow. She gave it no thought. Her feet were already numb and she realized her feelings were much the same. This man, Richie Fletcher, had not given her the satisfaction she had craved for so many tender years – the love of a father which she thought she had had from him as a child, his support and approval, his just simply being there. And now he was gone – and still he remained a mystery, leaving them with bitter feelings of repeated loss and betrayal.

Well, she thought, staring down at the coffin as the final words of the prayer book dispersed into the flurrying snow all around them, I got on without you before, Pa, so now I can do it again.

'Oi!'

Ada's head jerked up as the rough cry echoed round the cemetery. The black beetle whom she had seen in the distance had turned into a tall, thin man in a black coat, the collar turned up, cap pulled down over his face, striding angrily, his arms flapping. 'Oi, you lot – Fletcher's kids!'

The voice was full of rage. Before Ada could work out anything of what was going on, Jem Atherton had leapt into action and dashed towards the man, grabbing him, holding him back. But he could not hold back the words that poured from him.

'Burying him, are yer? That filthy swindler! Wish I'd got a-hold of 'im while he still had life in 'im. 'He'd have been buried sooner I can tell yer – I'd've punched his lights out for 'im!'

Ada could only watch this bewildering scene as Tom and George leapt into action and rushed to help Jem who was barely able to hold the man back – he was wrestling him like a madman. Tom seized hold of one of his arms and George the other.

'You want to stop this,' George said. 'Calm yerself down, pal. This is a funeral not a bar room . . .'

'Yeah – and the bloke in that grave robbed me of all I had!' he raged, struggling, seeming to foam at the lips as he shouted. 'Ten year ago – took off with the lot.' One of his arms broke free and he pointed a bony finger towards Ada and Elsie.

'You – Fletchers' kids, are yer? Well 'e might be gone, the varmint, but you can pay me back – a small fortune 'e owes me, that thieving bastard!'

'Eb!' Jem was shouting at him. 'Stop it, you fool – they know nothing about this! Just get away from here. Forget it. You leave those wenches alone, or I'll have you picked up by the Peelers.'

'Come on, mate . . .' Tom was saying.

'Calm yourself down.' George and the others were pulling him away.

'Go on, Mullins.' Jem got close up in his face, his own

red with fury. 'It's too late. Give up on it and get yourself gone. And don't you go anywhere near his daughters . . . There'll be trouble if you do.'

The three of them pushed and dragged the man away into the distance. At last they persuaded him to go. He walked away backwards, still pointing a long, bony finger in their direction.

'You owe me! You give me what I'm owed!'

'They don't owe you nothing!' Jem yelled after him. 'Forget it.' As he, George and Tom stood making sure the man kept moving in the opposite direction, still raging and carrying on, Ada and Elsie looked at each other, Elsie's face full of bewilderment.

'Who on earth was that – what did he want?'

Ada stared grimly after him. 'I think I know who that is – but as for what he wants . . .' She shrugged, full of terrible, uneasy feelings.

Jem came back to the house. Ada and Elsie had laid out a modest feast of cold beef and bread and cheese and the crispy sponge fingers Nancy had baked and brought over. They all sat at the table close to the fire, warming up with tea which they turned into a hot toddy with the drop of brandy Jem added to each cup from a flask he produced from his pocket.

'There yer go,' he said. 'That'll warm yer cockles. We could do with it after all that carry-on.'

Ada, who did not usually drink spirits, sipped gratefully, feeling the warm burn of it down inside her. She let out a long sigh, beginning to feel the circulation return to her feet and a warm glow spread through her body.

'Ooh, that's better,' she said as everyone ate their fill. 'Very warming. No, Tom!' she admonished as he held his cup out for more of the liquor. 'You've had your share.'

Jem smiled, screwing the top on the little pewter flask. 'All gone anyway.'

'Just as well,' Nancy said, her cheeks pinker than they had looked in a long time. 'I feel quite squiffy and I've got to get back to work soon.'

Ada noticed that George, who was sitting next to Elsie, was giving her sidelong looks every so often as if he could not keep his eyes off her.

Jem slipped the flask into his pocket and turned to Ada, as if unsure whether to raise the subject. 'I suppose you know who that was . . .?'

'Eb Mullins,' she said. 'Pa was scared stiff he'd turn up. He went on and on about it. You know, don't you – what that was all about?'

Jem looked round the table uneasily. 'Yeah. I do. But I don't know if you want me to tell you in private, like?'

'We can go?' George said, on the point of pushing his chair back.

'No,' Ada said. She could feel Elsie watching her, completely baffled by what all this meant. 'I know Pa swindled some people – took their savings. Elsie and I don't know what other secrets Pa had but they certainly weren't of our making. And we're family here – almost, anyway.'

She saw George look immediately at Elsie again, who also glanced at him, blushing, then looked away.

'I don't want secrets,' Ada went on. 'Not from you people – you've all been so good to us. There's been more than enough of it – never knowing what's what. It's been like that nearly all our lives. Our father was not the man I always hoped he was—'

'Jonas has been more of a father to me than him,' Elsie interrupted.

Ada nodded. Even when Pa had been there and things

were better, somehow, looking back, she wondered if every-thing had not been designed only ever to suit him.

'We still don't know the half of it,' she said. 'Why don't you just tell us, Jem?'

Jem sat back, gathering his thoughts.

'Well,' he began. 'Your pa worked in the brass foundry—'

'Arkle and Lilley,' Ada remembered. 'You're still there, Jem?'

Jem nodded. 'Never saw a good reason to move on. I'd've only gone to another foundry so why not stay put? Thing is, you get to know the way of it – skills of it, work-ing with the alloy, moulding and stamping. And later they learned how to put a silver coating on them – electroplating they call it, like . . .'

Ada stared at him, her mind trying to keep up. 'You mean . . .?'

'Coins. Heaps of 'em, Ada. Poured them out, they did.'

'But where?' Elsie asked, bewildered.

'When?' Ada said, her voice hardening. Then she remem-bered. 'Pa was always out – evenings, late at night. Don't you remember?'

Elsie shook her head.

'Eb had a cellar – just along the street from you, not far. Any road, your father was a clever man. Very clever. Learned about all these coatings – he could make anything look like anything else by the end. They could do your brass – pennies, halfpennies, farthings . . . But with the plat-ing it wasn't just the brass – it was your silver threepenny, half-crown, florins even . . .'

'Oh!' Ada exclaimed, memory throwing up that night: 'Elsie, d'you remember – in London?' After the Great Exhibition, all of them walking through that tunnel under the river, the crowds and excitement and lights on the colourful stalls, the fury on the stallholder's face. 'That woman – she was so angry with him for giving her that dud coin!'

She gasped as more and more things fell into place. No wonder their mother had been so worried about money all the time. She would not have known how they could afford it all either. That week, the whole trip, the only one in her life out of Birmingham, the Great Exhibition everyone was talking about, the comfortable place they had stayed, the food and treats – it was all *stolen*? Based on cheating and forgery! She could see Elsie was starting to have the same thoughts, her face tight with shock.

'Any road,' Jem went on. 'Richie and Eb built up quite a pile. I was never involved,' he added anxiously. 'I never knew any of this at the time, by the way, and I'm quite sure your mother would've had no idea. So when Richie upped and left – well, seems he took the lot. Eb's share as well. And Eb wasn't as sharp as him at . . . at the job, I mean. Or at anything else for that matter. So once Richie had gone – and he went off with all Eb's share they'd been building up for months – Eb was beside himself.'

'He still is, so it seems,' Ada said.

'But where did Pa go?' Elsie asked.

'London, he told me,' Ada said.

'Well, he could've got work somewhere there, I s'pose. Kept his head down. Birmingham's the brass city but there'd be some work down there. Couldn't come back to Brum, could he? Not with Eb on the warpath. Eb's never been able to let it go. He's gunna have to now though.'

'Pa said something about wanting to go to Australia,' Ada said.

Jem snorted. 'He'd never've got to Australia. Even if he had he'd never've lasted out there. He was a dreamer – liked to tell the tale.'

'He never once wrote to us – never let us know he was alive,' Ada said slowly. 'Not even to our mother.'

'And he left us with nothing.' Elsie's voice was hard. 'Me and the younger ones ended up in the workhouse.'

'So that's how you came to live with us, Ada!' Tom said, only now piecing together what had happened. His face creased in pain, as if thinking of this brought back the memory of his mother and what had happened to her as well. He was another one who kept his thoughts at bay.

'Your poor mother,' Nancy said, laying her hand over Ada's, her blue eyes full of tears.

'Yes,' Ada nodded, tears springing into her own eyes. All that time she had still been worshipping her father and craving for his return. She had not valued her mother enough or realized all that she endured to try and keep her children together, until death had intervened and taken her from all of them.

She raised her eyes slowly, letting them see her sorrow. She was still full of a shame that did not belong to her. What must they think of her family? But as she looked round at Nancy, George and Tom who had sat listening, astonished and appalled by turns, all she could see in the faces turned towards her was a shocked, kind sympathy.

V

Fifty-Four

1862

In the weeks following their father's funeral, Ada and Elsie buried themselves in work, putting in long hours. The grip of winter finally began to loosen, the season inching its way into longer days, the biting cold fading to wet grey.

'I s'pose things have gone back to normal,' Ada said to Elsie one evening when they had closed up and were frying some herrings for their tea. When Elsie looked at her she knew she did not have to add, *even if they don't feel normal.*

Both of them were in mourning dresses, rustling black bombazine.

'I don't feel I ever knew Pa,' Elsie said, poking the boiling potatoes to see if they were cooked.

'Nor me,' Ada said sadly.

'No, but I mean – I really didn't know him. You were close to him when we were little. He was all over you – "my lad" and all that. Poor John never got a look-in. But I was closer to Mom really. Dad never took much notice of me.'

Tom came in then, hanging his cap on the peg behind the door.

'I thought the sun shone out of him,' Ada said. She shook her head. 'But he was only ever thinking of himself. I can see that now.'

'Who – your dad?' Tom said. His voice was kind, sympathetic. Tom had changed a lot over these few weeks. Getting him away from Sam Bligh had been a good start and young, sensible Dinah seemed to be having a very good influence on him. 'I s'pose mine weren't much better.'

From the day he left with Ada, Tom had never gone back to the yard in Summer Row. Ada thought about Seamus Connell. She had seen the worst of him for sure, and there were things for which she found it hard to forgive him. But she had seen him live through some terrible times and she knew there were others who remembered him more kindly.

'He wasn't all bad,' she said. 'He'd had a plateful.'

Tom's eyes met hers hungrily and she saw that this was something he needed to hear.

'You could go back,' she suggested gently. 'Just now and then. Wouldn't hurt, would it?'

Tom turned away, but she could see that her words had hit home.

As Ada worked the next day, supervising the workshop and sorting shells down in the store room, her mind kept returning to all that had happened. Although mourning the father she had lost – the one she had never had in the first place, she now realized – she also felt stronger.

For a moment she stopped work and went and stood leaning in the doorway, her shawl pulled tight round her, looking out on to the damp blue bricks of the yard. Sounds and smells, now familiar, came to her from the nearby yards and businesses and she felt a surge of fondness. It was a drab, dirty old place, but it was home.

And, she thought with a surge of pride, Fletchers' – my business. Our name over the door and very soon we'll be doing everything – all the way through to completed buttons. And we'll design our own as well!

She reached into her pocket and touched her good-luck trochus shell, feeling its smooth, ridged surface. She felt lighter and hopeful.

We've always got along somehow, Elsie and me, working together. She saw the future stretching ahead, their business growing. We can carry on as we are, her and me, whatever happens.

But things were not going to go quite as Ada predicted.

She and Nancy spent quite a bit of time together now, their friendship blossoming, and Ada tried to keep Nancy's mind off her grief over little Billy. Sometimes Nancy would pop over to see them all. She liked the other women at Fletchers' and from time to time she came over in the dinner break to eat with Ada and with Gert, and Jess, Margaret and Biddy.

But one afternoon in early March when Nancy slipped over with her dinner she found Ada down in the store room.

'Hello, Nance,' Ada said, her own spirits lifting on seeing her. Even in her sadness Nancy could still manage a smile and her face was so pretty it was a pleasure to look at her.

'Hello, Ada. I was hoping to talk to you for a second.'

Nancy gave Ada a look which seemed to have a special meaning in it and she raised her eyebrows.

'Oh, yes?' Ada laughed. She came out from behind the table and they both stood looking out. 'What about?'

'It's George,' Nancy said. She paused, her face growing more serious. 'You know how soft he is on Elsie, has been for ages?'

'Yes,' Ada said. 'And he's been so kind to her, sending flowers and everything . . .'

'He's mad about her,' Nancy said. 'But he thinks she doesn't like him and he's a bit on the shy side. He's frightened to ask her.'

Ada gave a wry smile. Thinking of some of the things Elsie had said to her about men, she was not terribly surprised. The only man she ever seemed to trust completely was Jonas Parry who was more like a father, or even grand-father, to her – to all of them, truth to tell.

'D'you think there's any hope?' Nancy asked. 'You know George – he means it. He's not playing around.'

'No – course he isn't,' Ada said, thinking how decent George was, a good, kind man through and through. One of the rare diamonds around the neighbourhood. 'She's a rum one, our Elsie. I can't tell you anything for sure – she's a bit of a mystery to me as well. She's had some rotten times with men, Nance – there's so many bad'uns around.' Ada touched her friend's arm. 'I know George is a good man and I know she likes him. I think he's just going to have to pluck up the courage to ask her himself.'

That very evening, as they were downing tools for the day, tidying and brushing the soft white powder off their lathes and the floor, George appeared in the doorway of the shop. He chatted generally with them for a few moments as the workers got ready and took themselves off.

While Ada was still in the workshop he turned to Elsie. Ada watched, seeing the lad was almost rigid with nerves.

'It was you I came to see, Elsie. I wondered if you'd come out for a little walk with me?'

'What – now?' Elsie said, her tone rather sharp at this unexpected turn of events. After all, it was nearly dark. 'I mean, we've got the tea to cook, and—'

'I'll do that,' Ada said quickly. 'Go on, you go. It's fine out at the moment – do you good.'

Elsie stood staring at George for a moment, her face hard. Ada could see she had suddenly filled with an uncer-tainty that made her next words even harsher.

'You ain't shamed to be seen out with me then?'

For a second George did not even seem to know what

she meant. Elsie went defiantly out on to the streets when necessary. But this invitation was something different.

'No,' he breathed. 'Course not. Proud, is what I'd be, Elsie, that I would.'

Ada watched her sister who seemed to be in a storm of confused emotions. Then she went and fetched her shawl from the hooks on the wall.

'All right then,' she said.

The two of them walked down Livery Street in the dusk, the noise and crowding of the street making it difficult to talk or even walk side by side. People were emerging from factories and from the myriad of small workshops in the area and hurrying home. The road was busy outside Snow Hill station which was congested with carriages and delivery wagons and carts so that the clattering and noise of hooves and voices drowned out almost everything else.

They headed for St Philip's, the old graveyard offering a green refuge at the heart of the town. By the time they got to the churchyard, George seemed to be in such a state of nerves that he could hardly speak. As they walked slowly along one side of the imposing church, Elsie felt her own hardness, the face she put on to protect herself, being pierced by the goodness of this man walking so stolidly at her side. She was moved by him, by his consideration in leaving her alone during this difficult time when she knew, deep down, that he felt so much for her. And she knew that above all, she felt safe with him. She felt her whole body begin to tremble before he had even said anything – at the thought of what he might say.

'Elsie – stop,' he managed at last. They were at the back of the church and faintly, from inside, she could hear the organ playing. The shadows were gathering and in the gloom, other people milled back and forth but somehow none of them seemed to matter as he turned her gently to face him.

Elsie hung her head at first. It was so hard, her face being the way it was, to look directly at anyone. She had got into the habit of trying to turn her good side to people, or of keeping her head down. But now George put his fingers under her chin and very gently made her look at him. She flinched, feeling his gaze on her face, her whole scarred, distorted side as well as the sweet-faced side of the old Elsie.

'I don't know what else to say to you, Elsie, and I'm no good at – you know, dressing things up. So I'll just come out with it. You're beautiful, you are—'

He raised a hand to stop her as she tried to argue, her face flushing, words rushing to her lips to deny this.

'You are – whatever that woman did to you. I love you, Elsie – I can't help myself. I fell for you the first day I saw you – when you and Ada first come here. And I got the feeling you didn't want me so I've held off. But my mom said, "George, no one can read your mind however much you wish they could. If you don't open your mouth and tell that young lady what you feel, how is she ever going to know?" So that's what I'm doing . . .'

He stopped gabbling then, though seeming afraid that when he did she would say something he didn't want to hear; and as he stood looking at her she could see how scared he was.

Elsie was so confused by her emotions that she suddenly burst into tears. All these years of loss, of not being able to trust anyone – and then her terrible misjudgement over Sam Bligh and the ruining of her face – had convinced her that there would never be anyone who could love her. Or give her what she most yearned for – a stable home, a family and children, all the things she herself had lost at such a young age. Someone who she could love and trust had seemed beyond any hope. Yet here he was, a good, kind man standing in front of her, pouring out all he felt for her as if it was the most important thing he would ever do.

'Oh, George,' she sobbed. 'I'm sorry – I dunno why I'm crying.' She put both hands over her face for a moment as she choked out the admission. 'I never thought anyone could love me – ever. Not with me looking like this. So I stopped myself from liking – or hoping. But I . . .'

She drew her hands down and looked up, searching him for any hint of falseness, but there was none to find. Only that lovely kind face, full of love.

'I never let myself think . . . But I do love you, George. I do!'

Moved, he stepped towards her and she allowed herself to be wrapped in his arms, sobbing out her emotion against his chest as he stroked her, making sweet, soothing noises.

'Oh, I love you, Elsie. There, there – don't cry, my sweet . . .'

And she felt safe and loved. Neither of them paid any heed to the other passers-by as George, lips close to her ear, said, 'I want to marry you – for us to spend our lives together. Elsie, my dearest, will you be my wife?'

Fifty-Five

Elsie and George's wedding was to be on the first Saturday in June. George had initially suggested May – a pretty month, he said.

But Elsie had chided him. 'We can't get wed in May, it's unlucky! You'll have to hold on a bit!'

The Sunday before the wedding, Ada and Elsie were at home with Nancy and Lizzie – George's sisters were both to be the bridesmaids, or matron of honour in Nancy's case – alongside Ada. They were all busy putting the finishing touches to their dresses.

A local seamstress had been commissioned to make them: soft white for Elsie with a close-fitting bodice and a full skirt of tulle and lace. The others were to wear little coronets with lace veils and dresses in a soft shade of crushed raspberry, also amply edged with lace. All of them would wear crinolines, Elsie's being the widest of them all.

'You'll have to keep well away from the fire in that,' Ada warned Elsie, looking at the steel hoops stretching the skirt so wide it hardly seemed possible to manage it.

None of them bothered with crinolines in the working week – they got in the way. Only Jess, who loved the fashions, sometimes wore one of a modest size under her work dress.

But the final decorations, Ada had insisted, they were going to do themselves. The wrists, collars and waistlines of the bridesmaids' dresses were to be studded with pearl buttons, as well as decorative clusters of tiny, jewel-like pearls on the skirts. And Elsie's lace bodice was richly patterned with them.

'It's a pity we couldn't have made these from start to finish,' Ada sighed, running her fingers through a little pile of buttons as they sat round the table, stitching away. She begrudged sending their blanks on to be finished at Beardsmore's now.

'Never mind, you'll be able to soon, knowing you,' Nancy smiled. 'And these are lovely.'

In the centre of the table were heaps of other glistening pearly buttons of several different sizes, all catching the light with the iridescent rainbows gifted by the shells. Fletchers' had made all of them up until the last processes of drilling and polishing.

'Yes.' Ada picked up one of the smallest and peered at it. They were beautiful, simple little wafer-thin buttons with a slightly raised edge and two stitch holes. 'They've made a good job of it,' she conceded.

Elsie laughed. 'Listen to her.'

'You'll have a big works one day,' Lizzie said, eyes glowing. 'Bigger than Beardsmore's.'

Ada winked at her. 'Just you try and stop me.'

Lizzie, who at twelve was a surprisingly neat needle-woman, looked over at Elsie's dress hanging on the back of the door and sighed.

'I'm gunna get married one day – find me a handsome man, like George.'

The others laughed. 'Spoken for, I'm afraid,' Ada said.

'You can't marry your own brother, Lizzie,' Nancy said, elbowing her.

'I *know*,' Lizzie protested. 'That's a *sin*. They told us at school. I just mean someone like George, who's nice and does all the right things, like buying you gobstoppers on Saturdays!'

Amid the laughter Nancy said, 'I bet Walt wishes I had the odd gobstopper in my mouth sometimes!' She stroked her hand over the soft stuff of the dress she was trying on. 'Ooh, this is lovely – can't wait to wear it. We'll all be like princesses going into St Philip's in these – specially you, Elsie.'

Elsie looked up, blushing. Ada was still taken aback by the change in her sister since she had become fully aware of how much George loved her – and since she had admitted to her own feelings. She could see that Elsie loved him back devotedly, though she was shy of saying so, and that she felt safe and secure for the first time in many years.

'Well, we ain't got much of a bottom drawer for you, Else,' she said softly. 'So you might as well at least have a nice dress.'

Ada and Elsie's funds for the wedding had been generously topped up by the Drakes.

'Do it once and do it well,' Edwin Drake had said gruffly when he handed Ada an envelope. Inside she found two gold sovereigns. Ada gasped, overwhelmed. 'I know you girls haven't much behind you,' he'd said, backing swiftly away as if retreating from his own kindness.

Later, once the Drake sisters had gone home for their dinner and the dresses, encrusted with buttons, were hanging in the bedroom out of harm's way, Ada and Elsie sat down to some cold beef and bread and butter. Tom was off out with Dinah as usual.

'Adie,' Elsie said hesitantly as she dabbed some mustard on to her plate.

Ada looked across at her. A pang of pain went through her, seeing Elsie's scars. She often felt this on looking at her little sister but never so much as now. The unscathed part of her face was so pretty and now she had to go into her wedding day with the results of that vixen Hetty Hinton's spite carved into her face. It made her feel very tender towards her sister.

'I was just thinking . . . Can we go to Pa's grave this afternoon?'

Ada stared at her, astonished. Her own sense of hurt by her father was still burning in her. But Elsie had not been so close to him and seemed to have got over her bitter feelings more quickly.

'If you want,' she said. 'And Mom's.'

Elsie could hear her hesitation and she looked sympathetically at Ada.

'It's just – that's all we've got,' she said.

It was a warm afternoon, blue skies and a breeze blowing clouds across the sun, patching the cemetery with shadow which soon shifted and moved on.

They had not managed to buy flowers, but they found some clusters of buttercups pushing up at the edge of the green space, bright and shiny as enamel, which they lay on Richard Fletcher's grave. That was how Ada thought of him now: Richard Fletcher, Richie, a man she had never really known. Pa – the god she had loved as a child – had died many years ago and using his full name helped put the pain of that at a distance. Richie Fletcher – forger, fugitive from justice, abandoner of his family, ducker and diver for years, at a distance from all of them by choice – and sometimes, a long time ago, her amusing, exciting father.

'I wish I could believe he did it all for us,' Ada said sadly, as they stood looking at the carved letters on the gravestone. 'But I don't think even that was true.'

'I know.' Elsie sighed. She looked at Ada. 'But he was clever, wasn't he?'

Ada stared at her, then started laughing. 'That's one way of looking at it, I s'pose! Yes, he was.'

'And so are we. Come on.' Elsie took her arm. It was as if she had grown up suddenly, was all of a piece. 'Let's go and find Mom's grave. Why should he get flowers and not her?'

'Look at her – she does look like a princess!' Lizzie said dreamily as Elsie stepped into one of the carriages they'd hired to take them to St Philip's.

With her veil over her face, Elsie, small and curvaceous, looked just as much of a princess as she walked up the aisle of the grand church at the heart of Birmingham.

'Can people like us get married at St Philip's?' Elsie had asked.

'I don't see why not,' George said. 'I think anyone can.'

Ada, Nancy and Lizzie, in their beautiful dresses ashine with pearl buttons, followed her along the aisle to the boom of the great organ as they all sang, '*Love Divine, all loves excelling*.' And supporting Elsie, straight as a ramrod and looking as proud as if he was her own blood kin, was Jonas Parry. Clad in a dusty old suit, well scrubbed, and with his hair and whiskers trimmed, Jonas was more respectable-looking than they had ever seen him. And Ada knew Elsie had found someone else to be a father to her and it helped her not to mind the betrayal by their flesh-and-blood father quite as much. As he delivered Elsie to George's side at the altar, their eyes met for a moment and Ada could see Jonas's fond, twinkling smile.

Ada glanced at Nancy, wanting to squeeze her hand as the three of them waited behind Elsie at the altar. But Nancy was staring ahead at her brother, his hair cut more neatly than Ada had ever seen it, standing straight and tall in his wedding suit. Even from the back, there beside Elsie,

Ada could see that George looked fit to burst with pride and happiness. Nancy, on the other hand, appeared pale and strained. Ada felt a pang of sadness for her. Maybe she was remembering her wedding day to Walt, and then having Billy . . .

Lizzie, on the other hand, her mousey hair prettily pinned up which made her look suddenly like a young woman, grinned up at Ada and she could only smile back, seeing such happiness.

Ada herself, holding her little bouquet of lilies and orange blossom as the two of them made their vows in front of her, shed tears of joy for her little sister. Images flashed through her mind: Elsie dragged away across the yard from their house by the workhouse officials, in the Dugdales' house, forced into those clothes, molested by that perverse man, Arthur Dugdale . . . Then Sam Bligh, her obsession with him, her need which blinded her to what a scoundrel he was – and Hetty Hinton . . . All the sad and terrible things which had happened to this little girl who just hungered to be loved. And now George – a good man and a blessing in all their lives, bringing their families together. Elsie and George were to live at the Drakes' in the attic room, so Elsie would be near at hand.

George gently lifted Elsie's veil once the vows were exchanged, the ring settled on Elsie's finger, and there was a collective sigh of happiness as George, as if looking at the most precious thing he could imagine in the world, reached down to kiss her. Ada saw the smile Elsie gave to him just before their lips met and it told everyone all they needed to know.

They processed out again to jubilant organ music and once again, while Lizzie was almost skipping, Nancy had an air of endurance about her that did not quite fit with the joy of the day.

'You all right, Nance?' Ada murmured, leaning close as they reached the back end of the church.

'Oh. Does it show?' Nancy's face suddenly broke into a smile so joyful it seemed to light the place up. 'I was just worried I might be sick while they were tying the knot,' she said, taking in a deep breath. 'That's how it's been for a few days now . . .'

Ada stared at her. Did this mean . . .?

'Yes, Ada.' Nancy gripped her hands, full of excitement. 'I think I'm expecting again!'

'Oh, Nance, that's the best news – on top of all this!' Ada beamed at her, then threw her arms around her, both of them crushing their big skirts against each other.

'We're sisters-in-law now!' Nancy said as they held each other.

'Yes,' Ada said, beaming into Nancy's face. 'I'm so glad.'

Nancy squeezed her arm and they stepped back from each other. 'Me too. And I'm glad I don't wear have to these flaming things every day,' she laughed as they separated and straightened out the crinolines. 'What a kerfuffle!'

They walked out of the church, arm in arm.

Elsie and George were outside, laughing and brushing rice off their clothes, thrown enthusiastically by Ernie and the women from the factory.

Afterwards they mingled with the guests. George came up to Ada, beaming.

'Well, sis,' he said, kissing her cheek. She could smell something sweet and delicious on him, a hair pomade perhaps. 'We're all family now, eh? And I'll look after her – you can be sure of that.'

'She couldn't have married into a nicer family,' Ada said, joyfully.

Because, she thought, watching George move on to greet Jonas, it was true. They were now joined to the Drakes, she and Elsie. Even Tom, in her strange gathering of a family. For a moment her heart ached, the usual pain of amputation from the rest of their siblings.

Where are you? she whispered into the breeze, amid the happy chatter. *Wherever you are, I hope you know we haven't forgotten you, my dears. We'll never forget you.*

And then she went to embrace Elsie, her sweet sister and the new Mrs Drake, whose face was alight with happiness.

Acknowledgements

Yesterday, as I write, I went for a ride on a big, beautiful carousel in Hyde Park in London (I couldn't persuade my four-year-old grandson to join me as a respectable excuse, so it was just me!). I was immediately transported back to a different time by all the colours and lights and hurdy-gurdy music as we went soaring round on painted wooden horses.

The Victorians seem tantalizingly close to us. There are so many objects of theirs about, like that carousel, many of which we still use or can dimly remember, so much architecture and history, and the memory of that atmosphere of coal dust and fireplaces that many of us grew up with. Yet at the same time they look strangely distant, those men with mutton chop whiskers and especially the women, with their bonnets and ringlets, the long dresses and hour-glass, corset-squeezed figures. The later Victorians lived close enough to our time to still be looking at us from photographs, or even remembered in person. My grandmother was a Victorian, born in 1882. This is all part of the fascination ...

So I decided to start a little further back than in my previous books, and explore the lives of the Children of Birmingham – those born there and those, like so many then and since, who have joined the city's life from outside – and to move forward with them.

Writing about Birmingham in the 1850s feels almost – though not quite – like learning about a new city altogether. As obviously no one is still around from that time to ask, it's a case of piecing it together from all sorts of sources, and I owe thanks to more than I can really mention here.

Maps of the city in the 1850s are a good start, as well as Chris Upton's excellent *A History of Birmingham* and Richard Vinen's *Second City*. A staggering amount of hard and very skilled work went on in Victorian Birmingham, which fills me with a sense of wonder every time I read about it – hence the 'Workshop of the World' 'poem' at the beginning of the book. Two books that are a goldmine of information about this are Samuel Timmins' *Birmingham and Midland Hardware District* and *The Morning Chronicle's Labour and the Poor, Volume IX, Birmingham*, compiled by Charles Mackay from reports written between 1849 and 1851. I also drew with gratitude on George Hook's history of his family business, *The Birmingham Pearlies*.

Broader histories of the time, such as *Life in Victorian Britain* by Michael Paterson and *Heyday* by Ben Wilson, have also been a help, as well as *Wayward Women* by Lucy Williams, *The Blackest Streets* by Sarah Wise and *The World for a Shilling* by Michael Leapman, about the Great Exhibition in 1851.

While factual histories set the scene, and in many ways bring it alive, the novel can be just as helpful – especially as the form really took off during the Victorian era with its popular magazines and ever-rising literacy rates. George Gissing's *The Nether World*, Elizabeth Gaskell's *North and South* and Wilkie Collins' *The Woman in White* are all fabulous reads of the period.

Apart from writing sources, I owe many thanks to my agent Darley Anderson, who has always been there with wise words, along with his staff in the office in Fulham. Also to the wonderful team at my publishers Pan Macmillan, who create the lovely books we end up with. A big thank you to the staff behind the scenes, who fight hard to get our books out there into shops and supermarkets – not an easy job in a country that produces an extraordinary number of books every year. To the art department for the creative work on our covers. And a big thank you to my recent editor, Gillian Green, and her assistant, Ellah Mwale, for all their help, and now to Katie Loughnane who I look forward to working with in the future.

Thank you to fellow writers who are always there for a chat and to help keep each other sane, especially Elizabeth Heery (Eliza Morton) and Joanna Toye – it's been great getting to know you both.

This is my thirtieth novel published by Pan Macmillan, and above all I want to say thank you to those of you who read my books and enjoy them and who often kindly let me know. In the end, of course, it's really all about you and I am so grateful for the loyalty and appreciation shown by so many of you over the years.